A Curious Eve

By E.J. Bertel

aka Henry Bartelsen

Publisher
BookIM, LLC
Centereach, NY 11720
Published 2018

ISBN 978-0-9822576-4-7

Version 1.a

'All religions were invented by the devil to conceal god from mankind.'
— Arthur C. Clarke

'All religions were invented by conniving old men to conceal god from Mankind.'
—Raphael

Dedication
Dedicated to my muse, Jessie, whose spirit went supernova. May you forever shine brightly in the night sky and in my memories. I will miss you!

Notes to the Reader

This novel is the companion novel to the *Curious Eve Musings*, which is the author's account of his trials and tribulations with his polyamorous muse during the writing of this sci-fi novel. You can read the two novels in any order you desire. They stand alone and together.

Gender-Neutral Aliens

The aliens, or Epicoids, in the novel are gender neutral. Lacking distinct sexual dimorphism, the use of traditional gender pronouns for the Epicoids would betray the reality being portrayed in the novel. Unfortunately, English doesn't have gender-neutral pronouns, which is also a source of consternation for many members of the LGBTQ community. Calling the aliens—or any human being, for that matter—an 'it' both objectifies and dehumanizes a sentient being. We apologize for the reading inconvenience, but for the purposes of this novel we have adopted the following conventions for genderless pronouns to describe the aliens:

He, she:	ze
Him, her:	zir
His, hers:	zirs
Himself, herself:	zirself

In later chapters some of the gender-neutral aliens may take on more traditional gender roles as they transform. You may note some of the characters using gender-specific pronouns to describe the aliens; however, they are confusing the Epicoids' semblance of sexual dimorphism with vanilla human gender roles. Being the horrors they are, the Sentinels are simply referred to as 'it's. ***Hint: if you see a 'z' in the pronoun, then the reference is to an alien!***

Notes on Psi

ψ – Psi or the wave function/waveform in a quantum state describes a probabilistic system versus a deterministic physical system and outlines a probability distribution for the value of each observable variable; i.e., all of the states of emotion between hate and love or 'hate ψ love.'

Crimson Echoes

The tall redheaded woman was frantic, her eyes crazed with fear. She shouted to her giant companion, "It's got to be here. Keep looking, right?"

Her hands furiously searched the surface of the bronze statue, touching, stroking, groping, but there was no change to the surface color. She was dressed in combat fatigues and boots; however, her long red hair seemed surprisingly out of character with her militaristic garb. She appeared to have once been a handsome woman until recent battles had left her battered and disfigured. An angry five-inch red scar across her left cheekbone appeared to have been hastily stitched up just a few days earlier.

"Shit. Are you sure it's located here, Thadir?" she said.

The giant nodded as they continued searching.

Surrounding them, a small group of protesters with placards marched and demanded President Bill Clinton be impeached. The tourist crowd paid scant attention to the protestors but instead gawked at the antics of the redheaded woman and her freakishly tall and pale companion. The onlookers took great care to keep out of their way as the pair continued their frenzied search about the statue. They were not sure what to make of the bizarre duo; however, many assumed they were avant-garde performance artists. After all, it was New York City.

A middle-aged Chinese man approached the redhead and tugged on her sleeve, trying to get her attention. She towered over the shorter man, forcing him to peer upward at her as he said, "This is good luck."

He tried to hand her a folded twenty-dollar bill but she slapped his hand away.

"What the hell? Get away from me, asshole!" she said.

"You don't understand. Throw this—" he protested.

"What you don't understand is that I don't have time for this bullshit," she snarled at the man as she shoved him aside.

She shouted to Thadir, "Can you believe this shit? I hate these damn tourists."

She glanced down at her hand and realized her fingers had turned a glowing reddish color.

"Got it. Come on, Thadir, we don't have much time left."

The giant lumbered over to her and touched zirs hand to the spot on the statue. They stepped back as a large mirrored sphere emerged, engulfing the pair within its reflective surface. The orb ascended into the sky, whisking them away from the cobblestoned park. The tourists became quiet and watched the sphere with a mixture of awe and delight. The sphere silently disappeared into the low clouds of the grey sky.

A few minutes later the tourists were still abuzz with the encounter. The perplexed crowd was at a loss to explain what had happened when murmuring sounds filled the air with a strange immediacy. They looked about and realized the sound was originating from the very same statue the sphere had emerged from.

The sounds coalesced into a voice and the crowd heard a woman yelling, "What the fuck is this thing?"

The sound of gunshots rang through the small plaza and echoed among the tall buildings, causing many among the crowd to scatter in fear. Nobody knew where the shots were coming from.

"Do something! God, my skin is burning," a terrorized woman screamed. Over time, the screams became cries and the cries shifted to infrequent sobs that seemed to fade away in the breeze.

Silence, save for the low murmuring of the crowd trying to understand where the sounds were emanating from.

A strange, tortured, childlike voice broke the stillness. They could all distinctly hear a small girl plaintively whimpering, her sobs rising in tone and reaching a fevered pitch in her death pain. Moments later the cries stopped altogether, followed by an ominous silence that hung in the crisp fall air. The remaining crowd stared at one another, trying to comprehend what they'd experienced, with many in tears or others shaking their heads in disbelief.

Soon the air filled with the peculiar sound of flesh being torn from long bones. It was followed by the intimate and hideous gurgling noises of a beast enthusiastically ingesting its meal. The few onlookers that remained to witness the horrors quickly fled the plaza. In the distance, police sirens rang out.

The Chinese tourist stood in place, his face contorted in pain. He sat down and held his head in his hands. He had so hoped that the encounter would be different. He fought hard to hold back tears of bitter disappointment. He was so disgusted and weary of watching foolish young women defiantly going to their slaughter.

Day 1 – Orange Miasma

Charlie opened her eyes and looked about her small Atlanta apartment. She felt her long red hair dangling from her shoulders onto her nightgown. She nervously twirled the ends of her hair with her fingers while seated in the kitchen chair in front of her laptop.

She glanced down at her pale arms and legs, noticing the telltale blue-black markings tinged with yellow from the raps she received during her quarrels with Bradley. He never deliberately hurt her but he often lost his cool when challenged, pushing and shoving her about their tiny apartment. Bradley called her bruises 'love taps,' badges of affection that showed how much he cared about what she thought of him.

That time had been different. She stared at her laptop, at the small horror displayed by the tiny white numbers on the screen. Their shared bank account was empty. Their credit cards were tapped out. They had no money for food or rent, and the landlord was less than sympathetic to her continuous excuses despite her considerable Southern charms. Her mother had warned her about Bradley, and now they were falling together into the abyss of his making.

She turned towards the window, noticing the grey skies as a light rain fell. Nobody in the building cared about her little personal hell, or even if she existed. She was empty, alone, and desperate. She debated confronting him, knowing he was in a foul mood, but she was done with him.

"Bradley, I went to pay the cable bill and there's no money in the checking account," she said to him as he watched sports on the TV.

Bradley said nothing, transfixed by the television. There was the smell of alcohol in the air and he was unusually quiet.

"Did you hear me? There's nothing in the savings account either. What did you do?"

More silence.

"Tell me you have some money somewhere. Or did you lose everything betting on the games last weekend?"

"Leave me alone," he said.

"I will not. You lost everything we owned gambling on baseball? Who in their right mind gambles everything on baseball?"

"It'll be all right. Isn't it always?" he asked.

"No, it isn't. What the hell are you talking about? Everything will be all right? Nothing is all right. This is no way to live. Answer me!" she said angrily.

Nothing from Bradley.

"I've had enough of your shit," she said as she stood before him and the big-screen TV.

Still no emotion as he waved her off.

"That's it; I'm done," she said as she went to pack her belongings. She packed her suitcase, changed her clothes, and readied herself to leave. Still Bradley barely moved from the couch.

She grabbed her bags and headed toward the door. Bradley got up and stood in her way.

"Okay, you made your point, woman, now sit down," Bradley said.

"I will not. Out of my way, Bradley, I'm done. I'm not enabling you anymore."

How many times had he heard her tired routine? "Where do think you're going?" he asked.

"Does it matter? I've asked you for years to get some help. Instead, you refused, and now we have nothing. I can have nothing on my own," she said as she grabbed her pocketbook.

"Come on, babe, don't be like that," he said as he tried to hold her.

She pushed away from him and said, "Don't touch me."

"We have each other," he said.

"You mean we had each other. You killed the 'we' in our relationship a long time ago," she said.

Bradley grabbed Charlie by her shoulders. She turned her head away and he said, "Look at me. I promise I'll make it up to you."

"You're always promising to make it up to me."

"This time will be different, I promise," he said as he peered deep into her eyes.

She could smell the repulsive odor of a Bradford pear tree blooming nearby through the open window.

Through drowsy eyes Charlotte surveyed the distant horizon. A miasma of angry orange and green clouds stretched across the ocean, making for a most curious eve. She scanned her surroundings and saw she was topside on the deck of the cruise ship, taking in the late afternoon sun. Only there was no sun, just the radiant heat filtering through those same ugly clouds. It was clearly her reality, but something seemed off. Why? She wasn't quite sure.

She glanced down at her legs and saw she was wearing her favorite white two-piece swimsuit. Her eyes moved to the deck; it appeared to be empty, save for a few couples gathered towards the stern.

As she ruminated, the constant drone of the engines ceased and the ship coasted to a slow stop. Why had they stopped? Had they arrived? Strangely, she couldn't recall the actual destination of her cruise. How she got on the ship was unclear to her; she just had some vague recollection that they were cruising towards the tropics. It was warm, so they had to be heading to the tropics, right?

What was the name of the ship? It was something peculiar. Man…Mandy something. The *Mandjet*; that was it. Strange name. Something about resurrected Egyptian gods and solar energy, she recalled. The itinerary just read 'tropical vacation' with no clearly defined island ports of call. For Charlie, life was motion; however, if you were going nowhere, all sense of purpose literally stopped. Just bizarre—like her life to that point.

Large, modern, and clean, the huge azure-tinted ship appeared to be brand new and on her maiden voyage. Everything was oversized and spaced out, quite unlike the other cruises she had taken in the past. The design of the ship was an eclectic mix of modern and old. The actual furnishings weren't old; everything was new, but styled in the manner of vintage Art Deco. The deck chairs seemed to have been plucked from the deck of the *Titanic*. The phones in the room were from the 1950s, and there were only some canned programs on the flat-panel televisions. The furniture was an eclectic mix of IKEA and Danish modern. It was both retro and new; quite unusual.

However, it was the vastness of the ship and the relatively small number of passengers that puzzled her even more. She could walk five minutes topside and not see another person. Who in their right mind operated a half-empty cruise ship?

The engines fired up again. She glanced up and saw the ship's three massive smoke stacks but not a single puff of darkness from the engines.

Charlie felt so alone. She realized her husband had abandoned her once again to play in the ship's casino. Bradley had a problem, but he would grow out of it, right? Soon the few visible passengers dissipated into the vast expanse of the ship.

She started to panic and wondered if she had her meds with her. A full-blown attack was just moments away, and she was alone with nary a Xanax or Valium in her possession. She pondered what to do next when she felt a change in her emotions. Like a morning fog dissolved by the rising sun, a sense of calm and ease fell upon her. Curious and better than her daily medications yet she wasn't sure why.

Several chairs down from her was a mature woman in a one-piece black swimsuit with long straight brown hair. She was very lean, with an attractive face that was perhaps a little too long. Charlie was getting desperate for human companionship and she said to the woman, "Strange-looking sky, huh?"

The older woman exclaimed, "Yeah, but at least it's warm out."

"Oh, my name is Charlotte. I'm on the cruise with my husband, Bradley. What's yours?" Charlie extended her hand for a shake. She knew she sounded a little needy; however, she desperately wanted to make some friends, fast.

"Hi Charlotte, I'm Rachel and my Hank is around here somewhere," she said.

The woman was tall, suntanned and nearing fifty. She shook Charlie's hand as she looked her over and said, "Why, you're a pretty little thing, aren't you?"

"Thanks, and you can call me Charlie, by the way. Hey, I know this sounds strange, but do you recall planning this cruise?"

"Funny you should mention that. It was a very spur-of-the-moment thing. Hank was going crazy dealing with the family business so we decided to get away for a few days—you know, to relieve the pressure," she said.

"I don't know why, but this whole cruise seems a bit off," Charlie said.

"Off? That doesn't begin to describe this curious cruise."

"What do you mean?" Charlie asked.

"So I guess you haven't seen them yet?" Rachel replied.

"Who is 'them'?"

"You'll know them when you see them. I'm talking about our hosts. They're so weird and so tall, and all of them have the same shaved heads. Their skin coloring is strange, too. Almost pure white—too white," Rachel said. "Someone said they may be Mormons; even so, I don't ever recall Mormons shaving their heads like that, do you?"

Charlotte shook her head. "No, I haven't had the pleasure of seeing them. Shaved heads sounds more like a Buddhist or a Hare Krishna thing. How many are there?"

"I have seen a dozen attractive young men and women. They mostly keep to themselves. They seem very nice and very polite," Rachel said.

"All pale and bald?"

"All of them albinos with not a single hair among the lot," Rachel said. "All taller than a basketball player."

"Maybe they're models doing some strange photo shoot?" Charlie asked. She had modeled a little in the past, mostly for department store clothing, and had seen all sorts of perverse shoots in her time.

"Maybe, but to shave all your hair including your eyebrows…that is a bit extreme, don't you think?" Rachel asked.

"Yeah, that is extreme. Did you talk to them?"

"Not yet. I'm trying to work up the courage," Rachel said.

"Hey, do you have a cellphone I could borrow to make a quick call?" Charlie asked.

Rachel laughed and said, "No, somebody took them all from the passengers. Believe me, I asked a hundred times. Some nonsense about getting away from it all."

"Are you shitting me?" Charlie said with disgust. "It's almost as if Bradley arranged this cruise so I couldn't keep tabs on him."

"Oh, I see Hank waving to me; I've got to go," Rachel said. "See you later?"

Charlie just nodded and Rachel got up from the chair and left.

Finding herself alone again, Charlotte's mind wandered. Sitting in the sun with the warm tropical breeze, she found herself getting horny, yet even though she was alone she wasn't about to touch herself. Raised as a strict Baptist, she believed that type of self-pollution was a sin. Instead, she'd learned to do secretive thigh rubs that sent small waves of pleasure through her being. As a young girl she had a beloved teddy bear her grandmother had given her. Crissy the Bear was her favorite; she loved that fuzzy warm pink teddy bear that was nearly as large as her. One day while lying in bed with the doll, she remembered the warmth she felt. It was pleasant as the bear rubbed against her private area.

Unfortunately for Crissy, Charlie's mother came into the bedroom unannounced and saw her daughter entangled with the amorous bear. She yelled at Charlie and Crissy the Bear, telling her she shouldn't do such shameful things to herself; it was a sin, as told in the Bible. If her father saw her, the punishment would be severe. No, Crissy had to go, and the lustful bear was banished forever despite Charlie's tears and pleas that Crissy would be good.

Touching oneself was the devil's playground; Charlie had learned that lesson years ago. She didn't want to be forever banished like Crissy.

Why the hell was she thinking about Crissy? She hadn't thought about her childhood bear for years. Being alone like that clearly wasn't good for her sanity.

She decided to return to her cabin in the hope of seeing her husband. She put her wrap around her hips as she got up from the deck chair. She passed the activities board and noted there were just two days posted, reading 'today' and 'tomorrow.' What about the rest of the week? The schedule listed the usual cruise ship activities: volleyball, crafts, wine tasting, movies, and other such nonsense. Disinterested, she moved on.

Deck 3, Blue Section, Room 32, Tour Group M.

Why she knew this information she wasn't sure, but she searched in her beach bag and found her cabin key. She even knew that her cabin was huge, more like a VIP suite. Bradley must have gotten some special off-season rate as part of his promise to apologize for his recent behavior. Just strange.

Surprisingly, she navigated the ship with little difficulty and found the cabin. It was as if she already knew where everything was. As she opened the door, there was Bradley, casually dressed in white shorts and a green knit shirt. Her heart soared at the sight of him.

Bradley was a good-looking man with clean, sharp features and dark hair. But it was his penetrating blue eyes that had won Charlie over when she first met him. He wasn't as muscular as when she first met him seven years earlier, but he was still in pretty good shape. If only she could see him naked once again.

Bradley saw his wife in the wrap and took a moment to look her over. Charlie's breasts strained against the bathing suit, showing a lot of cleavage. She watched his eyes and as they moved to her waist, she dropped the wrap. Her bright red hair made a sharp contrast against her pale white skin. She still had her figure, even after years of marriage; nonetheless, she wondered if

Bradley even noticed.

"Where are you going, honey?" she asked in her sweetest South Carolina accent.

"I had to make a pit stop and was headed back to the casino," Bradley said.

"Can't you spend a little time with me, maybe go to dinner with me? I'll make it worth your while," she said in a seductive manner.

Bradley ignored her invitation and kept packing. "I'm on a hot streak with the cards. Tell you what, when I cool off we'll do dinner, okay?" he said.

He left the cabin, avoiding eye contact with her.

Charlie could have been insulted but she was used to Bradley's gambling rituals. He always felt she was bad luck, a personal belief that put a considerable strain on their marriage. Worse, she knew that once he cooled off he would be miserable company.

On a chair a lone dirty polo shirt had been left behind. She picked it up and gave it several sniffs, in part to reconnect with Bradley and partly wondering if she could detect the scent of cheap perfume. Nothing—just the faint scent of that repugnant tree from outside her apartment.

Charlotte sighed at being left alone and turned towards the empty bed. On the bed was the usual towel animal display. She assumed it was a mouse, but upon closer inspection it resembled a rat. Whoever did those towel origamis was truly a master; however, their choice of animals bordered more on the bizarre than the whimsical. She assumed they had a peculiar sense of humor, one she didn't necessarily appreciate.

There was a card next to the towel art that read:

We hope you enjoy this special cruise. Every effort has been made to secure your privacy and comfort during this cruise, including isolation from your hectic everyday life.

She sat in a chair and surveyed the open ocean from the sliding glass door. Shit, she hated to be alone with her thoughts almost as much as she hated being alone with a shipload of strangers. Bradley's abandonment a few minutes earlier made it very clear she was totally on her own. Frankly, it was one matter to face a shipload of strangers as a couple but quite another to do so singularly. Moreover, knowing she had once been part of a loving couple wasn't exactly helping her sinking feeling either. Isolated and cut off from her friends as she was, the cruise was becoming a challenge instead of a welcome relief. She felt grey and heavy and went to bed early.

She awoke the following morning at six a.m. She knew breakfast began at seven every day and decided to arrive early, at a quarter to the hour. She sat in the dining room alone, waiting to be served but seeing no signs of life. Strange? There weren't very many crewmembers and when asked a question, they didn't speak English; maybe it was Italian. That wasn't entirely unusual for a cruise, yet the crewmembers often appeared to be as confused as the passengers as to what was going on. It was unclear who or what was managing the ship. Yet, managed the ship was.

Charlie decided to spy on the proceedings. Just how did that scrumptious food get prepared? Another passenger, an older woman, straggled in looking for coffee.

"They serving yet?" she asked.

Charlie shook her head. The woman walked away, leaving Charlie to her solitary watch.

Soon it was 6:55 and still no food. In fact, there were no signs of food preparation or setup at all. It was just bizarre. A kitchen door opened and Charlie saw a tall figure peer from the darkened room. After a moment, she watched the figure disappear back into the room, abruptly closing the door.

Thump!

Charlie heard a loud thud near the glass window. As she turned, she saw a large seagull on the deck, seemingly stunned by its collision with the glass. She wondered if it was hurt. The gull began walking about, then shook its head while giving a cry, and promptly flew off.

Charlie turned back to the buffet; there was the food, all laid out in its glory. How did they do that setup, without her hearing or seeing them, in the span of a few seconds?

The pungent odor of breakfast meats filled the air—pungent only because Charlie was a supposed vegetarian; the spirit was willing but the flesh was weak. She walked over to the food and grabbed a piece of the bacon. Fresh, hot, and crispy, it was cooked to perfection. *Stupid seagull,* she thought. But she wasn't going to be persuaded to quell her inquisitive nature! In actuality, most of the cruise was like that, with the passengers helping themselves to the bountiful amenities of the ship with little assistance from any crew.

Charlie wanted to know when they would make landfall, but as she scoured the activities board there still was no mention of an actual weekly itinerary. Frustrated in her efforts to learn more about the cruise, she made her way to the health spa for a workout. When she entered the room, the equipment appeared to be pre-war — Vietnam War. There was nobody else in the room; normally someone was in attendance at the exercise equipment, supervising to make sure no one got hurt. It was a ghost ship.

"Can we get some equipment from this decade?" she yelled to no one in particular.

"Just bizarre," Charlie said as she stepped onto the ancient treadmill. The machine was a noisy horror and she quickly got off.

She went topside and noticed that the ship was totally becalmed, somewhat like a sailing ship of yore in the equatorial doldrums. Charlie waited for announcements telling passengers what had happened to the ship, but there was no explanation offered by the crew or the captain. The strange skies marked their journey to an uncharted state of inertia.

Even with the ship dead in the water, Charlie observed that all other life support systems appeared to be functioning fine so there was nothing to cause concern. Electricity flowed, the toilets worked, and there was plenty of food and drink. Dining rooms functioned and people gathered poolside despite the lack of proper sun. The eve that surrounded them basically glowed, changing from a bright luminosity during the day to a much darker simmer at night. A light breeze blew, but with no cell phones and no Internet service there was nothing to indicate they were still part of the larger human community on Earth.

A light shower began on the upper deck and Charlie didn't feel like getting her hair wet, so she went below deck and down a long, empty corridor she wasn't familiar with. She felt very alone walking the darkened hall, but she trudged on. In the background she heard Muzak being played at a very low level. The tune was bright and bouncy but grew aggressively louder with each successive song. She noticed some fellow travelers with their families and luggage moving through the corridors.

Charlie debated asking them where they were headed but instead decided to walk faster to elude the sonic nightmare. As she hurried, the lights started to flicker on and off.

"You've got to be shitting me," she said aloud. The lights went off in the corridor, which became solely lit by the emergency exit signs.

She kept walking, and spotted somebody at the end of the corridor. They were far away, hundreds of yards off, tiny in the distance, too far away to be a serious threat but also too far away to be sure that they weren't.

She continued walking and, to her right, down a smaller darkened corridor, she saw four adolescent boys hanging out. The teens saw her too and started smirking among themselves as they scrutinized the attractive, shapely redhead. She suddenly felt vulnerable, attired only in her bikini and wrap. She was about to run back but she knew she couldn't move fast in the sandals she wore. She decided not to back down from those sixteen-year-old punks. As she walked, the teenage boys moved towards her. She felt a deep, queasy feeling that reached into her gut, a savage, primeval feeling of fear.

Charlie froze but gave them a look as if to stare the young punks down. Mustn't show fear to the predators. She tried to determine who the alpha was among the pack and glared at one boy who appeared taller and stronger than the rest. The teen had dark hair and began involuntarily licking his lips. She realized she had no weapon in the clutch she'd brought with her. She was caught totally off guard; how stupid! The smell of sulfur permeated the air.

She'd decided to run and yell when she noticed that the expression on their faces had suddenly changed. They quickly began walking away from her.

Good; her bluff had worked—but she heard loud shuffling footsteps behind her. She sensed a large presence looming at her back. As she turned, the shadowy image of a creature blocked all light. No wonder the boys had run!

As her eyes continued to adjust to the light, she realized how tall the apparition was. She was about to run when the lights in the corridor turned back on. The sudden brightness blinded her and she staggered away from the creature, her hand feeling along the wall of the corridor searching for an escape. The pale hairs on her arms stood on end and she felt the blood drain from her face.

Whatever it was, it suddenly stopped moving.

She blindly took two steps, stopped, and then waited. A few seconds later she heard several shuffling footsteps behind her. The Muzak began playing again. That was her signal to move. She decided to make a run for it but her legs felt too heavy. She doubted her ability to get away from that thing. She tried to yell but only a small, dry yelp escaped from her lips. With the teen boys, at least she'd known what she was facing: rape and humiliation. But this fear was very different; she felt like prey.

She turned to confront the creature. Unlike the confrontation with the teens, she didn't feel any fear at all as a palpable sense of calmness settled over her. The queasy feeling in her bowels dissipated. Why?

She held her ground again, knowing full well her stubbornness would cost her big-time one day. She looked up at the giant.

"Were the boys bothering you?" the giant asked. Ze wore a shiny blue suit with nothing about zirs waist, just a skintight suit that covered most of the creature's body and extended down to zirs feet.

She studied the giant. No hair anywhere, no eyebrows, and no fine hairs on zirs bare hands; just smooth, whitish-blue skin with nary a wrinkle, blemish, or pore. Damn, the creature was tall, towering almost two feet over Charlie's head. Ze had a large barrel chest, but zirs shoulders were relatively narrow.

The overall appearance was that of a masculine presence, but there was a certain softness to the giant's physique since zirs muscles lacked definition. For such a large, apparently male-being the giant seemed to be very effeminate. Zirs features were fairly normal, with a symmetrical face; in fact, it was too symmetrical. Humans spent their lives studying faces for minor variations, the tiniest of inflections and the look of the eyes. One glance told her that the giant mimicked a human, but wasn't quite human.

"Not yet, but thanks for coming by," she croaked.

"You're welcome." The giant's mouth barely moved. "Can I walk you to your cabin?" the colossus asked.

"I'll be just fine, Dad," Charlie said as she studied the giant's face.

The creature appeared confused as she continued to scrutinize it. Funny, the giant didn't seem to be Mormon. Even zirs azure eye color seemed off, too pure in its perfection.

"I'm not your father, in the spirit of the Quanteme," ze said.

"I know you're not my dad; it's just a little bit of humor."

"I understand, only I don't understand humor, little or big," the giant said while walking away.

"Hey, what's this 'quantum' business?" she shouted.

"Quanteme; it is the oneness of the universe."

"As in one god—you know, like Brigham Young?"

"No god; one isn't apart from the universe or any god. Not sure about Mr. Young."

With that response, Charlie knew there was no way ze could be Mormon. "So, who are you?" Charlie asked. There was no response from the lumbering giant and ze was soon gone from view.

She walked back and saw matches lying on the ground. The boys had probably been grabbing an illicit smoke when she came upon them. Back in her cabin, Charlie found her husband quickly changing his clothes once again as if they were on fire.

"Thank God, Bradley. I just had the fricking scare of my life," she said as she walked in.

Bradley barely glanced at her and gave her a perfunctory response. "Are you okay?"

"Now I am. Please, Bradley, can you spend some time with me? I feel so damn alone aboard this ship."

"Can't, I'm on a roll. I'll see you tonight, okay?"

Having lived with her husband's perpetual lying over the years made Charlie wise to his ways. Sensing his lies and knowing his tells had become almost second nature to her. Equally important was knowing when to call him out and knowing when to look the other way. On occasion she would let Bradley think he'd gotten away with his latest ruse, allowing him to be overconfident when executing the next big lie. This time, she decided to call him out.

"No, it's not okay. Jesus, Bradley, I nearly wet myself I was so scared and alone on this ship."

"Hey, it was your idea to take this cruise," he said.

"Was it? Because I really don't recall. Do you?"

Bradley said nothing as he brushed his hair.

"Tell you what. I'll come with you to the casino. I've never seen you win before," she said.

"Shit, no, you're not. I want to keep on winning. Stay away. I promise we'll grab dinner tonight."

"Have you seen them?"

"Who is them?" he asked.

"Never mind," Charlie said.

Bradley practically ran from the cabin, leaving Charlie by herself and confused. She sat alone for a few minutes before wandering into the bathroom.

She stripped off her bathing suit and examined her body in the full-length mirror. She was in her mid-twenties and her body was still tight with youth. Her white skin remained pale even though she liked sunning herself. Her figure was almost Rubenesque, with large breasts and pale nipples and a tiny waist with wide hips. She touched her pubic hair, noticing the slightly darker red that almost matched her shoulder-length hair.

Charlotte had been married for close to six years and clearly she was no longer catching the eye of her husband. Shared intimacy was a distant memory, which didn't make sense to her since most people considered her very attractive. She had small facial features and a big, genuine smile. It was bad enough they'd stopped talking, save for the occasional harangue from him about starting a family. Or the argument from her regarding seeking treatment for his gambling habit.

The provocative teddies she wore stirred no passion from him and Charlotte had begun to lose interest in igniting his flagging desires. Bradley was far more interested in eating, drinking, and fueling what appeared to be a reemergence of his nasty gambling habit.

She stopped touching herself, wondering when she would be intimate with a man again.

Day 2 – Steve

Later that afternoon Charlie put on a different bikini and a wrap and sat down by the pool in close proximity to a young African American man. He was energetically listening to some tunes with his headset. She watched as his head nodded in rhythm to some private beat. He peered up and caught her watching him. He smiled back at the shapely redhead but Charlotte ignored him as she moped over her wayward husband.

Damn you, Bradley, she thought to herself. Something had happened between the two, but what exactly transpired continued to escape her. The young black man kept staring at her. So rude. She was going to say something to him.

"Excuse me, but haven't we met before?" the man asked.

Charlie glanced up at him and took a long look. He was a dark, good-looking man. She shook her head no.

"Yes, we met at the docks in Cairns, Australia, a couple of days ago. Remember, I mistakenly thought you were part of that cult in the news? Funny though, your hair was shorter, but I'm sure it was you," he said. "You had a small scar on your cheek."

Charlie just shook her head at his puzzling line of inquiry.

"Strange since I've never been out of the country, never mind Australia. And see, this is my real, very long red hair that I grew out for this cruise in just a couple of days," she said as she dangled her red locks in front of him. "And no scar, see?" She turned her face toward him.

"It had to be you, or perhaps your doppelganger?" he said in earnest.

"Just what did this woman do to gain such notoriety?" Charlie asked.

"Ah, some gossip about, you know...her fooling around with her followers. Never mind. But she did strongly resemble you."

Charlie laughed and started to clap and said, "Folks, we have a winner for the most elaborate pickup line I have heard in years. Excellent work, but, sir, you are fishing in the wrong pond," she said as she showed off her wedding ring.

Before the man could react to her taunt there was a commotion poolside; one of the older male passengers appeared to be having a heart attack. He collapsed some thirty feet away and Charlie saw his face turning blue. People rushed to his side while someone called for a doctor.

Within minutes a giant that appeared similar to the one Charlie had encountered in the corridor diligently attended to him. Several other giants joined him; one was dressed in a red uniform, and the rest in the same blue outfits. They surrounded the stricken man and in unison touched his prostrate body as it lay on the ground. Their faces contorted as they administered a strange communal groan that they rhythmically repeated several times. The color returned to the stricken man's face. The heart attack was apparently over and somehow healed by the strange visitors. He went to thank them but they just shuffled away, not willing to acknowledge their miracle. Their departure created a crescendo of talk and gossip among the watching vacationers.

Charlotte watched the episode with rapt attention and said to no one in particular, "They are a peculiar lot, our new friends."

"Yes, they are; I can barely tell the males from the females. I hear they call themselves Epicoids," the young black man said.

Charlie scrutinized his face and noticed he had hazel eyes. It was unique for a man of his complexion, but very attractive on his masculine, square-jawed face. He had a broad nose and buzzed black hair with a touch of growth on his chin. Yes, he was a pleasant, good-looking man, almost handsome in appearance.

"Epicoids?"

"It's a riff on epicene, meaning having both sexes," he said.

"What are you talking about? Transvestites? Transsexuals?" Charlie asked.

"You don't know, do you?" he asked with a chuckle.

"What?"

"The buzz is that they are actually aliens."

Confused, she asked, "Aliens? Like illegal aliens from Mexico or South America?"

The man laughed and said, "Hell no, nothing that pedestrian. You know, extra-terrestrials, like E.T. Welcome to your own private close encounter."

Nothing from Charlie as she digested the words. She shot up from the lounge chair to face him and said, "Shut up, you're shitting me! No freaking way!"

"No shit, really, how did you think they would greet us? In flying saucers?"

"Radio message, Instagram, maybe a tweet, but on my cruise ship? Why here?" she asked.

"No doubt they gathered us here to study us. I mean, they got a nice sampling aboard this ship, a lot like the marine tanks I keep for the university aquarium. Besides, it's not your cruise ship—it's theirs!"

"You're a biologist?" Charlotte asked.

"You sound surprised," he said.

"Didn't mean it that way. I haven't met many biologists period, never mind an African-American one."

"Consider me your first. And I prefer being called black, by the way."

"Really?"

"Family is from the Caribbean. My name is Steve—Steve Monroe. What's yours?" he asked with a big smile.

"Charlotte MacDonnell. I'm here with my missing-in-action husband, Bradley. Everybody calls me Charlie," she said as she extended her hand for a shake. As he shook her hand she noticed he had a firm grip and a nice touch. She just had to know more.

Holding her hand, Steve moved into the empty lounge chair next to her and said, "Nice to meet you, Charlie."

Steve's dark hand firmly held hers as he drew closer and in a whisper asked, "Don't take this the wrong way, but you are a real person? I mean, from Earth?" His cheerful demeanor changed and he suddenly turned serious.

"I'm originally from South Carolina. That counts as Earth, right?" she asked.

"Close enough," he said as he released her hand.

"Why would you ask such a strange question?" she asked.

Charlie looked Steve over again and realized he had an athletic build with a body that was lean and muscular. He was about her age, but his face was etched with worry. That worry made him appear to be very human.

Steve leaned in closer and whispered, "Why? Because this is bullshit. Just look at who our hosts are. I don't assume anything about this cruise, including the other passengers."

Charlie was concerned but she didn't say anything.

"What was your reaction when I said they were aliens?" he asked.

Charlie thought for a moment as she pondered. She was surprised, interested, and curious about their hosts, but she wasn't scared or frightened. She wondered why. That didn't make sense.

"I guess surprise and curiosity," she said.

"But no panic or fear, right?" Steve asked. She nodded. "I just can't believe nobody else is freaking out over these creatures," he said.

"Who are you traveling with?" she asked.

"Strangely, no one. I mean who the fuck— Excuse me, who the hell goes on a cruise by themselves other than complete losers? But here I am in Tour Group M," he said. "Must be a loser, I guess, being a black nerd and all that."

"You don't have a girlfriend?" Charlie asked. "Am I being rude?"

"No, that's okay. I just broke up with her, if you count a year as being 'just,'" Steve said.

"Her loss. And that's your problem, being totally alone aboard this strangeness. I know what that's like, with my husband constantly disappearing and all that. So do they?" Charlie asked with a heightened sense of curiosity.

"Do they what?"

"You know, have both sexes," she asked in a whisper.

"Damned if I know. Not that I want to find out, either, but that's the rumor," he said with a big smile. Nice teeth, she noticed.

"Sounds kind of icky."

"Icky? I guess that's one way of describing their sexual orientation," Steve said.

She just smiled and said, "Ever talk to the crew? They sound like they speak Italian."

"They are Italian and *sì, parlo italiano ma solo un po' quanto*," Steve said.

"What? You speak Italian?"

"*Sì*, did some graduate research in Italy, of all places. So I started talking to them, maybe four crew members so far, and guess what? They're also on vacation; they're not working the ship, either," Steve said. "This is the strangest shit."

"What? So who's managing this ship and taking care of us?" Charlie asked.

"Come on, you know the answer to that. Our friends the Epicoids are running the entire show," Steve said. "Face it, this ship is to your normal cruise what Trump University is to higher education."

"What do you mean, besides the weird décor of the ship?" Charlie asked.

"Yeah, a bit eclectic for my tastes, too, but we have no phones, no Internet other than… never mind. I haven't seen another ship since we've been at sea. Just bizarre."

"Yeah, the whole thing is bizarre beyond words. Do you remember even planning a cruise?" Charlie asked.

Steve started to think back to the days prior to the cruise. As he did, he remembered diving off the coral reefs to take some samples. As he tried to visualize the events of that day a thunderous noise, almost a rumbling that shook the ground, suddenly overcame him, causing his head to pound. The events just prior to his arrival were shrouded in the grey mist of time.

"Shit, you're right. Like I said earlier, I was scuba diving off the coral reefs near Cairns, where I recall seeing your twin. I remember taking some samples. It wasn't that deep but I decided to go near a small cave for some new species. That's the last thing I can remember; that is, until I got aboard this alien booze cruise."

"I remember arguing with my husband at our apartment, so what else is new."

Silence for a moment and the two quietly reflected.

"I have these headaches now," Steve said.

Charlie just shook her head.

Steve whispered to her, "For some reason, I think we have all been collected and deposited aboard this ship by the Epicoids, possibly to study us."

"But how?"

"Obviously with science and technology far beyond our own," he said.

"Well, I wish they would release us sometime soon. They have my husband totally engrossed with that sad little casino. Have you talked to any of our hosts?" Charlie asked.

"Not yet, but I'm planning to. Have you?"

"Yes, a nice one came to my rescue after some teen boys tried to corner me."

"What? Were they going to assault you?"

"They were just being punks. I can handle myself."

"So what was the Epicoid like?"

"Tall, slow. He seemed very nice and very polite; definitely non-violent. I mean, I assume he was a 'he.'"

"Non-violent? I don't even see any weapons, but if they staged this entire ship I think it's safe to assume their weaponry is far beyond our own," Steve said.

"Where are we?" Charlie asked.

"Not sure; they have us physically isolated from the rest of our kind to observe us."

"Think we're ever going back home?" Charlie asked.

"Don't know until I talk to them," Steve said. "This is beyond weird to me. If I walk down a street in some white town, a hundred eyes are on the strange black guy, but these albino freaks walk by on this ship and nobody gives them a second look."

"White privilege," Charlie said.

Steve glanced at her and then did a double-take. Charlie started laughing and said, "Got you!"

Steve started to chuckle and said, "So that's how you play?"

"Yep, that's how I play. But you're right. In fact, I haven't been this calm in years. I mean, I should be planning to kill my husband, the way he's treating me, but no, he's alive and gambling away. It's almost as if the ship was a large Xanax for all of the passengers."

"They're playing us," Steve said with some concern, "and quite effectively, it would appear. Maybe drugs, something in the air or food, who the hell knows?"

As Charlie glanced up, a tall female-looking Epicoid strode by the pair of lounging strangers. Dressed in casual wear, the seemingly feminine Epicoid scrutinized the two. Zirs facial features were pretty and ze wore, upon closer examination, what appeared to be a tennis outfit. The creature was curvy and very buxom. Zirs skin was pale, so pale it was actually a porcelain white with a bluish tint. The giant's posture was perfect and zirs long legs quickly moved across the room. Yes, ze was a beautiful specimen but with no hair—not a single eyelash. The Epicoid walked by and gave them a strange smile, seemingly lingering over Steve.

Charlotte returned the smile but she quickly turned to Steve, somewhat embarrassed she'd been caught staring.

"Shit, what was that about?" Steve asked.

"She wants you," Charlie said.

"What?" Steve asked.

"Just busting. Creepy, the timing of that. But no kidding, she does want you," Charlie said with a laugh.

"Great, I got an alien admirer."

"You don't think they came here just to have sex with us, do you?" she asked in a lower tone.

"You women, pretty or otherwise, always think men want sex with you," Steve said.

Charlie appeared a little offended but Steve quickly said, "Got you with that one! See, two can play that game."

She gave a laugh and Steve said, "I know better than anyone that finding the right date can be rough, but isn't that a bit extreme? And no thank you, by the way. I'm not that kinky. Who would want sex with these weird androgynous creatures?"

She felt comfortable with him and asked, "You're a homophobe, aren't you?"

"No, I'm not. I'm cool if a brother or sister is gay. It's their androgyny that's so freaky. Like you even have a gay bone in your body, saying they were icky."

"That's nonsense; I've kissed a girl or two in my time," Charlie said.

"Now you're just messing with me. I can tell," Steve said.

"Fine, suit yourself," she said with a smile. Charlie was fidgeting with the strap on her bikini when she asked, "What's creepy is the idea that we are being held captive. Think about it—do you ever release the fish in your tanks back into the wild?"

"You already know the answer to that question. Hopefully they will value us a little more than I do my fish specimens. Kind of a kick in the head, huh?"

"For you, perhaps. The irony is lost on me since I don't collect specimens," Charlie said.

"You mentioned the casino and your husband. You think it's rigged?"

"Definitely; he keeps winning at blackjack. Back home he never wins at the casinos or online, at least not for long. He's a horrible gambler, the worst. Stupid, impulsive, no system. He does everything wrong; works against the math with every big opportunity. He's a pure hunch player. They're hooking him big-time."

"I hate gambling. I like to control my own future and not rely on luck. Better yet, make my own luck," Steve said.

"Control is an illusion as imagined by victims," Charlie said.

"What?"

"Everybody imagines some measure of control over their life but it's an illusion, like Bradley winning at the casino. They may just be toying with us," she said as she pulled the straps down on her bikini top and exposed the top of her breasts. She really missed flirting with handsome men.

"How are they toying with you? Like you're doing with me?" he asked.

She felt a small longing between her legs and just fluttered her eyes at Steve. "By taking Bradley away from me, that's how. We've been on this ship for two days now, right?"

Steve nodded.

"A solid two days of him being a ghost. Maybe they want to see what I do in his absence. And I don't toy, by the way—at least not right away."

"Good to know—that is, about the toying. Being a scientist and survivalist, you know, I'm searching for a way out of this mess. Maybe that's why I'm here, to observe how I handle this challenge," he said.

"Well, let me know if you figure anything out."

"Will do. Thanks for the company. And by the way, I am available if you want to do something stupid," he said with a smile that bordered on a leer.

She got up and brazenly bent over to retrieve her towel to give him a good eyeful of her butt.

"Damn, your man is crazy," he said, not caring to avert his eyes for a moment from her rounded bottom.

"Let me guess, you want me to help a brother out? Sorry, no offense, but now I'm steering clear of you," she said as she gathered her towel.

"Why? Because you're married?" Steve asked.

She smiled and said, "Why? Who knows what they have in store for you, my collector friend, knowing your proclivities? After all, these aliens may be an aquatic species."

Charlie sauntered away, putting on a show for Steve.

Too bad, she thought. Steve was actually a pretty good-looking guy. Strange that he wasn't attached already. Had to be something wrong with that dude. Maybe he wasn't manly enough for some of the ladies, being a nerd and all that.

Steve yelled to Charlie, "Your girlfriend, what color hair did she have?"

"Huh?" she asked.

"The one you kissed?" Steve asked.

"Blond. Dyed blond, with large boobs," Charlie said while turning away. Okay, Steve may have been a nerd, but clearly he was also a man.

Jawara

Charlie went down the following morning at six-thirty, but this time the doors to the dining room were closed. The cruise's hosts must have gotten wise to her curiosity. At seven on the dot the doors automatically swung open. She walked into the banquet room to the same glorious presentation of food. Beyond weird.

After breakfast, she went exploring and decided to check out the shops aboard the ship. While she was window shopping, a pair of seemingly male Epicoids strode by her looking very tall, pale, and particularly bland. It was as if they were designed not to provoke an emotional response from humans. They acknowledged her with a small quizzical nod and walked by. Curious about the pair, she decided to follow them. They walked into one of the small boutique stores and she hurriedly tailed them while trying to appear nonchalant. Inside the store they vanished, nowhere to be found.

Charlie left the store feeling confused as to how the slow-moving creatures could elude her so effectively when she spotted a shop with some nice designer dresses on display. She knew she needed a dress for the Captain's Dinner, but couldn't afford the dresses displayed in the window. Still, she just had to take a peek.

She saw several beautiful designer black dresses with a high front and a low back. She knew the style would look good against her pale skin, and she found one in her size. She took a quick glimpse at the price, bracing herself for the sticker shock.

Seventy-nine dollars? What in the world? She'd had the dress pegged as being north of five hundred dollars, easily.

A very human-looking woman working at the store came by and asked, "Can I help you?"

"Yes, is this priced right?" Charlie asked, and noticed the woman had a bluish hue to her skin.

The woman checked the sticker and said, "Yes, that's the correct price."

Charlie scrutinized the dress, wanting to make sure it wasn't a cheap counterfeit knockoff. But it seemed to be the real thing.

"Why don't you try it on? The changing rooms are over there," the clerk said and she pointed to a far wall.

Charlie nodded and practically ran back to the dressing room. She had the wrong type of bra for the dress but left it on anyway. She came out to check herself in the mirror while the store clerk waited. The dress was a perfect fit, showing off her curves.

"That dress was made for you," the effusive clerk said.

"It does look great, doesn't it?" she said. She couldn't believe her luck and she asked, "Why is it so cheap?"

"They have a new designer line coming in so they want to clear the store of the older inventory. So should I charge it to your room?"

Screw Bradley. Charlie emphatically nodded. She changed and found a perfect pair of black designer 'fuck me' platform pumps to go with her dress. She brought her treasures back to her room while wondering when the Captain's Dinner was going to be held.

Charlie was in such good spirits, looking forward to showing off. She decided to go topside for a walk; maybe she could find Bradley and tell him of her luck. As she walked she found the deck relatively empty. She stood at the rail watching over the calm waters when an Epicoid approached her. Normally she would have been afraid and begun a hasty retreat to safer grounds. If she was in the city, she would have run, but at that point in her life she was beyond the thrills of placating a vicarious fear. She was genuinely interested in finding out more so she held her ground at the railing, wondering what the alien would say to her.

The approaching Epicoid was tall, like the others, at over seven feet. Zirs stride was off somehow, resulting in an awkward shuffling walk. Likewise, the creature's arms were stiff, not quite in time with zirs stride. It was the same gentle giant that had come to her rescue the other day. Ze walked slowly — painfully so—and she felt the anticipation rising within her with each step.

"Beautiful night for a beautiful woman," the Epicoid said in a soothing but vaguely masculine voice.

Charlie nearly broke out in laughter at the quaint pickup line and said, "You're an alien, like an extra-terrestrial, right? I mean, you are not human?"

"That is correct, in the spirit of the Quanteme," the giant said.

"Well, I'm not sure who is coaching you on your human interactions, but why are you using a pickup line with me?" she asked.

"Pickup?" the giant asked, zirs voice conveying puzzlement.

"Pickup is a colloquialism—a line used by human males to bed a woman."

The Epicoid said, "I know. I was, as you say, messing with you."

"Wait, does that mean you don't think I'm beautiful?" she said, playing along.

The Epicoid stopped and reflected for a moment, no doubt not having grasped nor knowing how to navigate the complex minefield of the human female mind.

"In other words, for a human do you consider me beautiful, or was that a backhanded way of insulting me?" Charlie asked.

The Epicoid, feeling even more confused, became quiet.

Charlie decided to let the Epicoid off the hook. "Now, that's what we call messing. I'm not so stupid as to think your standard of beauty and attractiveness is the same as our own species. Let's start with something simple. My name is Charlotte, and my friends call me Charlie," she said, and extended her hand to shake. The Epicoid stared at her hand and extended zirs own. The alien's massive hand engulfed hers with the equivalent of a limp dead fish handshake, as her father used to call it. Despite the lack of strength in zirs handshake, the alien's touch was almost erotic, creating a tingle that extended deep into Charlie's loins. She quickly withdrew her hand.

Funny—ze was a giant, easily over two feet taller than her, but she didn't feel at all intimidated by zirs presence.

After the handshake there was another awkward pause. "So what's your name? You do have names, right?" she asked.

"We have something that is equivalent, but it's more of a labeling of our characteristics. I am called 'One who tastes great feelings before all of the others.'"

"Crap, calling you 'One who tastes great feelings'? Jeez, that's a long name. Okay if I just call you 'Feely'?"

"Please don't call me Feely!"

"Okay, how about Tasty? And how in the heck do you taste a feeling?"

"Taste is different in our species. My adopted human name, Jawara, will do. Our senses are somewhat different than yours. It was nice talking to you."

"That's it?" Charlie asked.

The lumbering giant didn't answer; instead, ze just walked away.

That afternoon Charlie was sunning herself once again. Even though there was no real sun, she appreciated the warmth and the fact that her freckles remained at bay. As she applied lotion she spotted Steve walking with his head down, seemingly engrossed in some task. He was dressed in a pair of walking shorts with a knit shirt and he appeared to be sweating quite a bit.

"Steve, what are you doing?" she asked.

No comment; he just kept walking, head down. He walked a few more paces and then he stopped.

"Hello?" Charlie said.

"Sorry, I was counting—didn't want to lose my count. How's it going, Red?" Steve asked.

"Good. Did you try the lunch buffet? Uh, oh!" Charlie said when she saw Jawara slowly approaching the pair.

"Crap. Let me do the talking, okay?" Steve said. "We have no clue as to what these creatures want from us. Better to be safe than sorry, don't you agree?"

Charlie just nodded and smiled at Steve.

Steve steeled himself for the confrontation and stood between Charlie and the approaching giant. As Jawara drew closer, Charlie yelled out, "How are you, Jawara?"

"I'm good, Charlie. Hello, Steve," the alien said. The giant stopped and looked down on the pair.

Steve mumbled a hello, both amazed and alarmed that Charlie actually personally knew the alien.

"So, Jawara, why are you here observing us?" she asked. Steve did a double-take and gave Charlie a stare. He wondered what the heck she was doing.

"You would call it knowledge. You have much to teach us," Jawara said.

"That's rich, we teach you? Teach you what?" she asked with a small snort.

"Charlie!" Steve said, hoping to stop her unartful encounter with the alien.

Jawara ignored the interruption and said, "About how you feel; your spirituality; our common place in the universe."

"Where are you from? What planet?" she asked.

"Actually, we live very far from your planet. It was a journey many light years in the making," ze said.

She was about to speak when Steve decided to jump in and cut her off by asking, "How does your technology manage to travel vast distances?"

Charlie rolled her eyes at his oafish behavior.

Jawara continued to ignore him and asked Charlie, "You were asking another question?"

She gave Steve a smug smile and asked, "So why didn't you go directly to our leaders and governments?"

"We know and anticipate the challenge our presence will pose to the normal order on your planet once we introduce ourselves."

"More like disorder on our planet, you mean," Charlie said in jest while looking at Steve. Steve shook his head.

"We need to understand you better before making contact with the whole of your planet. This cruise allows us to know you as a people." Jawara sounded like ze was telling the truth, but the creature's monotone voice and expressionless face made it difficult for Charlie to gauge zirs trustworthiness.

Charlotte decided to cut to the chase and asked, "Are you going to let us go and return us home?"

"Charlie, I thought I was going to ask the questions?" Steve said. Charlie shrugged.

"Yes, you will go to Stage Green when we are done with this sequester, in the spirit of the Quanteme," Jawara said.

"Sequester?" Steve asked, but Jawara ignored him once again.

"Does that mean that the man you cured is returned to his original health?" she asked.

The Epicoid didn't answer at first. "We do this so as to not make any value judgments and interfere with your species."

"Oh."

"Your hair is very red," Jawara said.

"That's a bit random. I hated my hair as a kid growing up, but as a woman I think it's quite distinctive. Do you like my hair?" Charlie asked.

The tone in the Epicoid's voice rose and the alien said, "No, I don't; it's very disturbing, in the spirit of the Quanteme. We don't like long hair at all.

Perhaps you can cut your hair like Steve's?"

Charlie glanced over at Steve's buzz cut and said, "Not happening; I'm not cutting my hair for you. So you don't like long hair, or is it all hair in general?"

"Charlie, just leave it alone. The man is clearly not a fan," Steve said, worried after hearing the change in the giant's tone of voice.

"Yes, we have issues with hair in general," Jawara said.

"But we are otherwise attractive except for the hair business, right?" she asked.

"Yes, as a species we find your people attractive," ze said with a strained voice.

"Stop it, Charlie, I think you're upsetting our alien friend," Steve said.

Charlie waved Steve off with her hand and said, "You're a chaetophobe. I get like that when I see a hairball at the bottom of the tub. When you say attractive, are you saying we are easy on the eyes? You know, are we horse-like or dolphin-like?"

"I'm not sure what you mean," the alien said.

"Humans love looking at horses for their musculature and power, while dolphins have a more sensuous appearance with their smooth skin."

"Dolphin-like, definitely," ze said.

"Okay, so we're dolphin-attractive," she said.

Jawara gave Steve a puzzled glance, as if ze wanted to be anywhere else.

"Hey man, you started this conversation with her," Steve said.

"So, Jawara, what do you want to learn from me or Steve? I mean, that's why you approached us, right?" Charlie asked as she left the rail to sit down on a deck chair. Her back was killing her. Jawara followed her and stood tall before the sitting woman.

"I have been tasked with understanding your relationships as couples, particularly your sexual relations. It's very different from our own."

Charlie let out a small laugh. "How are you going to do that?"

Steve looked up and said, "We're a couple?"

Jawara replied, "I haven't decided, but talking with you is very enlightening. I find you a very entertaining species. Like that strange noise you just made."

"Strange noise?" she asked.

"The rhythmic sounds you make when you exhale together in a group."

"Huh? Oh, you mean laughter?" she asked.

"Yes."

"We do that when we find something amusing or funny."

"But it wasn't funny," Jawara said.

"Great, now you're a critic. So do you care about me as a person or am I just an interesting specimen to you?" Charlie asked.

"No, we all see you as intelligent, feeling, sentient creatures, but...."

"With some rough, violent edges?" she asked. Some of her women friends were big into guns and shooting. It gave them a sense of power, but Charlie loathed them. She always feared Bradley having a gun.

"You sometimes act so primitively. You show your teeth a lot; it's very unflattering," ze said.

Funny that the Epicoid mentioned teeth, and Charlie realized the alien barely opened zirs mouth when ze spoke. She wondered if they even had teeth.

"Yeah, we do act like animals sometimes," Charlie admitted.

"Do you like your husband? You don't seem to spend much time with him," Jawara said.

Steve watched Charlie's face. That was kind of a personal question, but she answered anyway without flinching.

"I used to like him, but this cruise to nowhere is creating some serious doubts," she said. If the aliens were watching them, they could be observing everything: eating, bathroom habits, and lovemaking. Damn, they must have been disappointed with their output.

"Do you love your women?" she asked.

The Epicoid stared directly at her and said, "We don't have females."

"So you're all males? What are the ones that resemble me, then?" she asked.

"Functionally, we aren't male either. We're what you might call hermaphrodites; all of us have what you would describe as both sexes, but that's not quite right either. There's no sexual distinction between us, we. Externally we may appear a little different to socialize better with you and your species' apparent sexual dimorphism."

So Steve was right about them. Charlie was thrown by the explanation, not quite understanding. She asked, "So you're intersexual? You have both male and female sex organs?"

The Epicoid walked away from her and said, "Not quite. I have to go now."

Charlie didn't know what to make of the strange admission. She could ask more questions to get to the bottom of it, so to speak, but more importantly, why was she having that strange conversation with a bizarre, seemingly pansexual creature, anyway? Still, and for reasons quite beyond her understanding, she felt her face blush a little. Knowing that she was embarrassed caused Charlie to become even more flustered.

"It was good talking to you, Jawara. See you around," Charlie said.

She turned to Steve and said to him with a smile, "Well, that went well, don't you think?"

"I thought we agreed to let me do the talking," Steve said, sounding peevish.

"I'm sorry. It's just that I felt like I had a rapport going with Jawara, that's all," she said apologetically. She could tell Steve was pissed.

Charlie thought for a moment, her demeanor changing, and then added, "You know, screw that, I'm not sorry. I'm tired of being told by men what to say and think. I've got enough crap on my plate with my husband. I don't need to add your bullshit into that mix, mister."

Charlie stormed away. Steve shook his head at their strained exchange and returned to his walk toward the stern. He was annoyed and vexed by Charlie's childish question-and-answer session with the alien. No wonder she had so many problems with her husband, he thought; she just wouldn't shut up. At that moment, Jawara approached him again. Steve looked about and realized he was alone with the alien.

"I have been meaning to talk to you," Jawara said.

"Are you sure you don't want to talk to Charlie instead?" He couldn't believe he was giving the alien some attitude.

"No, only you can answer these questions for me."

"Really? Well, that's good, because I wanted to talk to you but Charlie kind of monopolized the conversation. So what are we doing here? Is this an experiment or a field observation in the wild?"

"The Greeting is for observation purposes only. You will all be returned. Your species intrigues us quite a bit and we have some questions."

"The Greeting, huh? And you consider yourself a scientist? Okay, I'll play along and answer your questions if you answer mine," Steve said. "So, is this a close encounter of the fourth and fifth kind?"

"It's interesting that your species has actual measures for such a Greeting."

"There's that word again. Well, let's just make sure your Greeting doesn't end in a close encounter of the sixth kind, okay?"

Jawara just stared at Steve.

Steve said, "I mean avoid having your Greeting end in a human death."

"Your safety is of paramount importance to us, I can assure you of that."

"Good to hear. So why aren't we panicking upon meeting you? Are you manipulating our minds?"

"Because there is no reason to panic, that's why," the Epicoid said.

"You didn't answer my question," Steve said.

"You are capable of sensing our good intentions; that's all. Our species has a calming effect upon your own. We call that state the Irenic."

"A calming effect, huh? Well, you do appear to be sentient creatures."

"Yes, we are, and very much like yourselves," Jawara said.

"I'm just shocked that being such advanced creatures you don't have more AI incorporated into your bodies. You know, like more cybernetics."

"Artificial intelligence is a misnomer on your part. Sentient existence, or what your people call consciousness and self-awareness, requires a centralized nervous system managing trillions of independent living cells in a prescribed density. The quantum entanglement of those cells creates what you call consciousness or what others call the quantum mind. Further refinement of those entanglements outside of the corpus with other living creatures creates what you call self-awareness."

Steve gave Jawara an incredulous look.

"Why are you looking at me like that?" ze asked.

"Dude, I'm just a marine biologist, and I'm not really buying this."

"This was even suggested by physicist Erwin Schrödinger in his book *What Is Life?* over seventy years ago. Bohm, Penrose and Hameroff have all made the case for the quantum mind. You must have heard of quantum tunneling in enzymes?" ze asked.

"Yes, I have."

"Then you know quantum physics being used to describe a biological function is not unheard of. A computer or robot could never become conscious, never mind self-aware, unless it somehow managed trillions of other independent entities and they became entangled together. As to cybernetics, we have chosen to augment our living bodies in other ways rather than through non-carbon implementations. To be frank with you, we have no desire to play God with self-awareness."

"Thanks for quantum physics lesson. So your genetics, is it similar to our own?"

"Yes, our genetics are DNA, RNA, and mitochondrial-based—different somewhat, but functionally very similar to your own," ze said.

"Number of chromosomes?"

"Ninety-two."

"Really? Exactly double our amount? That's very interesting. So do you have finite lives as well?" Steve asked.

"Yes, of course. What is born will also die; that is the way of the universe. We live much longer than you, but we all come to an end. Many times our spirit weakens."

"So you can get sick and be hurt?"

"Yes," Jawara said.

"Do your people tell lies?"

"A lie meaning a knowingly false statement?" ze asked.

"Yes, that's what we call a lie."

"That concept confuses us. How does a lie or a deception help the greater good? Why would an individual tell a falsehood? No, we don't lie, in the spirit of the Quanteme," Jawara said.

Steve studied Jawara's face. Zirs face was devoid of emotion, so there was no way of telling if ze was lying or not. "People lie to obtain an advantage over others. It's about putting the individual good above the greater good, perhaps to gain a genetic advantage. So no lies among your people?"

"No."

"So what is the most effective way to kill one of you?" Steve asked.

Jawara didn't blink at the comment and said, "I said we don't lie; that doesn't mean I have to provide a truth, particularly one that is potentially harmful to my kind. You keep searching for our weaknesses as if we were your enemy. I assure you we are your friends."

"Trust and friendship have to be earned."

"There will be time enough for us to earn your trust."

"Funny thing about trust—it can sometimes take a lifetime to earn, but you can lose it all in a single moment," Steve said.

"Perhaps. My turn. Your species—are you in communication with other species?" Jawara asked.

"Uh, I guess. I mean, we do try to communicate with other species—you know, chimps and dolphins."

"What about higher creatures?" ze asked.

"No, as far as I know, barring some great government cover-up. You're the first higher creature we have been in touch with that I know of."

"What of God, Jehovah, Jesus, and Allah?" the Epicoid asked.

"What the heck?" Steve asked.

"Some of your males talk to Jehovah and Allah on a regular basis, do they not? They are higher beings, correct?"

Steve was about to give a flippant response about delusional people claiming to be talking to God. Frankly, Steve's religious convictions were limited to his own internal debate as to whether or not he was an atheist or an agnostic, but the inquiry from the Epicoid gave him pause. Did they really believe humans were in touch with a higher being? Did they have the same concept of faith and, if not, how would they react to the human conception of faith? There was only one way to find out, but Steve decided to be deliberate regarding his inquiry rather than confrontational.

With Steve's hesitation the alien asked, "You do communicate with higher beings? Your priests, rabbis, and imams, the males of your species, are trained to talk to the higher beings?"

Steve exhaled and said, "Some specially trained people do claim to talk to God and say they receive guidance from God, yes."

"Why the males of your species?" Jawara asked.

"You would have to ask the male clergy that question, and learn their rules regarding engagement with the gods," Steve said. He started to sweat since this shit was getting tricky. He felt almost apologetic with his janky explanations as he commented, "Sometimes people are delusional. They're incapable of distinguishing a lie from the truth. It's almost a mental illness for some."

Steve wondered if that assessment carried any weight regarding religious leaders, but he didn't dare utter those thoughts to his Epicoid host.

"When you speak to other species, how does that work?" ze asked.

"Well, you mean when we talk to chimps and others?"

"When you speak to your gods."

"Oh, that's through prayer."

"Show me."

"Pass. I haven't prayed in years, so I would be a poor subject for your study. I thought you said you were being tasked with studying couples?"

"We are capable of multi-tasking. Your religious beliefs are very important to us, but we also find your monogamy interesting and more than a bit peculiar. We feel they are somehow connected and should likewise be studied together," ze said.

"You might be making the common mistake of confusing monogamy with morality."

"We'll sort that out later. You say you stopped praying?"

"I did."

"Why?" Jawara asked.

"My god never answered back. Let me ask you something: What happens, or what do you believe happens, when one of you die?"

"With death, the totality of the being is inherited by the collective."

"What about us? We have no collective. Each of us is separate and alone."

"Upon death your essence dissipates into the cosmos. We call it the Quanteme. Birth, death, you were always connected to the greater whole. All living things are connected in the universe through quantum entanglement. Others among you might call it heaven, or the afterlife. "

"Yeah, something like that."

"There's another matter that confuses us about your belief system," Jawara said.

"Just one thing gives you pause about our religious beliefs?" Steve asked with a smirk.

"We also noticed that your religious people have issues with *Unioeros,* in the spirit of the Quanteme."

"Unioeros?"

"What you call sexual relations, the union of two or more."

"Ah, yes. For some reason most religions don't like us doing the big nasty. You know, something about the big guy not approving of us enjoying ourselves."

"The big guy?" Jawara asked.

"You know, God disapproving of us having sex unless it's for procreation."

"So your god is similar to our Sentinels?"

"What's a Sentinel?"

"We will revisit this point sometime later, when you are more conversant with them."

"Sounds like your study is more about religious mores among human couples."

"Not exclusively; we have some other relationships in mind to research as well. I didn't want to share this with Charlie, but please explain this behavior," the alien asked.

"What behavior?"

A moment later, Steve saw what appeared to be a video from a world news story, only it wasn't a video. It appeared to be actually happening before him. Some unfortunate Afghan woman who was unhappy with her horrible arranged marriage attempted to run off with the man she loved. The Taliban caught up with her and her lover, giving the man a whipping, while forty men proceeded to stone the poor woman to death. She was only nineteen, and within several minutes she was reduced to a bloody mass.

"Why?" Jawara asked.

"I can't explain their behavior," the biologist said.

"Are you not the same species?"

"Yes, of course we are. We humans just have some serious issues getting along on this planet because of significant cultural differences."

"I thought the females were the weaker of the two sexes and that the males normally protect the females. Where is the male parental unit of the female?"

"Most likely he was the bastard throwing the first stone since his daughter disrupted his arranged marriage. Normally, yes, the males do protect the women, but to be honest, you're observing some powerless human troglodytes exerting what limited power they have over their women to maintain some kind of breeding advantage. They're a primitive Bronze Age culture, and if you ask me, mentally one step above the other primates on the planet."

"So you're different? Different groups may have superior cultural development?"

"I like to think so, particularly in regards to how we respect our women," Steve said with a sense of pride.

The Epicoids were normally devoid of any facial emotion but the biologist almost swore he saw a quizzical expression that bordered on incredulous from Jawara. The alien then said, "Strange, I didn't sense that with your hostility toward Charlie when we were talking earlier."

Steve didn't reply and the giant walked away from him without saying another word. Suddenly he realized he actually could have used Charlie for that conversation.

Pulling Your Leg

Dressed in her red bikini, Charlie decided to go to her favorite Jacuzzi on the ship, and when she arrived, there was Jawara sitting alone in the small pool. The alien's towering torso extended awkwardly above the water and ze appeared to be relaxing. Despite being in the hot tub, the Epicoid wore zirs usual full blue suit.

"Jeez, Jawara, you are quite the player."

"I'm not playing anything as of the moment," Jawara said.

"Well, this is just too bizarre for words," Charlie said, looking to see if anybody else was around to share in the spectacle.

"I find the experience with the hot water jets and bubbles somewhat exhilarating," the alien said.

"You just need a piña colada to complete your vacation motif. Were you waiting for me, by chance?"

"Yes, I was seeking your company."

"Great, now I have an alien stalker." Well, ze was still better than some of the guys she used to date.

"Join me?" Jawara asked.

"I guess so."

Charlotte slowly lowered herself into the Jacuzzi. The water felt particularly tingly on her skin for some reason. It had to be Jawara; the Epicoid always seemed to be giving off some curious sexual vibe.

"Hello, Charlie, I spoke to your boyfriend," Jawara said.

Charlie was confused and a little concerned. "What boyfriend? Shit, Jawara, I'm married, so that's not funny. You do realize that when we marry we have to remain monogamous, right?"

"Just pulling your arm."

"What? You mean pulling my leg, right?"

"Yes, leg, definitely leg. Why leg, by the way?" Jawara asked.

"It refers to a time when people tripped one another to rob them. But do me a favor, no more boyfriend jokes. Do you want me to get beaten by Bradley?"

"I promise, no more jokes, but your species does have a troubling tendency to be nasty to one another," the alien said.

"Guilty as charged. I have to ask, but are you normally seven feet tall as a people?" Charlie asked.

"We tried to approximate your physical condition but the intern we used for our research fell in love with your basketball."

"What?"

"Ha, ha, ha," ze said mechanically.

"Pulling my arm again?" Charlie asked.

"I don't get it," Jawara said.

She felt an involuntary contraction between her legs, which prompted her to ask, "You do have rules and boundaries for studying us?"

"We do—what your medical practitioners call 'do no harm.'"

"How about relations? You know, restrictions regarding sex?" she asked.

"Well, as a species you are all very tasty."

"Okay, I'm out of here. I feel like I'm part of a really bad vaudeville act," she said.

As she got out of the Jacuzzi, Jawara asked, "Please explain humor?"

Charlie turned around and said, "I don't know, but laughter is the absurdity of life shared between people. It's a social lubricant that breaks the tension and helps us bond. It's not unique to humans, by the way. Laughter, they say, is contagious. It gives us an opportunity to be one."

"What's actually funny?"

"I don't know. When somebody slips and falls in a comical manner, that's slapstick, for example. A play on words or saying something absurd, like saying I like the way you style your hair."

"But I have no hair."

"That's the joke."

Jawara gave a blank look and then said, "Oh, I see. Ha, ha, ha."

Jawara's laugh was a horrible forced affair that contorted zirs face into the most horrendous expression.

"Dear god, don't do that," Charlie said as she toweled off.

"Sorry, in the spirit of the Quanteme," Jawara said.

"I'll tell you what, I'll see you later, okay?"

"Goodbye, Charlie. Oh, why is your species monogamous?"

"Damned if I know," she said as she walked away.

Charlie walked down the main corridor. The lights went out and the Muzak began playing. A few seconds later the dim emergency lights turned on.

"Not this nonsense again," Charlie said as she felt her fear mounting. In the dark distance she heard heavy footsteps and realized it was Jawara.

She turned around and said in jest, "Now what do you want, Jawara?"

There was no response but instead a heavy, hideous breathing that sounded like the death rattle of some large creature. The smell of sepsis and burnt flesh lingered in the air. Jealousy. Hate. Loathing. She felt it all. No…she tasted it in the air. It was something palpable that settled deep in her gut.

She moved forward and it followed from behind, keeping pace with her.

The evil malfeasance that lingered in the air wasn't Jawara. She turned around slowly in fearful anticipation. Out of blind instinct she closed her eyes for the briefest instance and when she opened them a tall ominous creature with yellow eyes appeared before her. She smelled the creature's fetid breath. It had a series of tentacles about its entire head, except for the beak-like mouth and tusks extending from its lower jaw. Naked, its angular, humanoid shape was covered with a thick mat of wiry black hair that appeared to have spikes on the ends of the shafts. Entire chunks of flesh and muscle appeared to have been torn off from its arms and legs, leaving behind large, hideous scars. An oversized, mangled penis-like lump of flesh dangled rigidly between its legs. As it moved, a trail of slime seemed to follow and then dissipate into a cloud of arancia vapor that seemed to envelop the monster.

Charlie was frozen, unable to react. She wanted to run but her legs were locked and paralyzed. Visions of her pretty soft flesh being torn from her bones suddenly flooded her consciousness as she realized there was no escape from that thing.

She was about to yell out when she heard someone approaching from the other end of the corridor. It was Jawara. The giant walked towards her while staring down the creature and moving to Charlie's side. The Epicoid instinctively grabbed Charlie's hand in the same manner a protective parent grabs a small child's. The monstrosity walked by the pair and Charlie felt as if the creature was somehow dismissive, sneering at their sudden bond. In five minutes the creature was gone from view.

"What was that vile thing?" Charlie asked. The lights came back on in the corridor and the Muzak ceased playing.

"A Sentinel." Jawara released her hand. "Whatever you do, don't allow it to touch your skin. It's sheer madness to humans."

"Touch me? I don't even want to be on the same ship with that creature. Just why is that disgusting thing giving us dirty looks?" she asked.

"To keep us in line, and as a reminder to us not to become attached to humans."

"Why?" Charlie asked.

"Because you should never play with your food," Jawara said.

"What?" Charlie yelled.

"I pull your leg," the Epicoid said as ze began to laugh in an awkward mechanical manner.

She hated that horrific laugh of zirs, a hideous reminder the Epicoids were not human, and she said, "Don't laugh my fears off like that."

"Why? Your fears make no sense. I would think that a species capable of reaching out to you from light years away would also be very capable of feeding themselves."

"Not that funny, Jawara. We're kind of vulnerable here," Charlie said. "That type of humor borders more on the cruel, especially after meeting that horror. The Germans even have a word for it: Grausamen humor."

"We are all vulnerable. It's the nature of existence. All is ephemeral but nothing to fear," ze said.

"*Sic transit gloria mundi* is all you have to say? Real original. Jawara, don't take this the wrong way, but can you get lost?"

She heard the sound of the engines of the ship starting once again, with no apparent port of call. She wasn't enjoying the alien encounter one bit, and once out of the corridor, she went her separate way.

Day 3 – Indigenous Fauna

Charlie went to sleep early that night on her own, finally resigned to Bradley's absence. She hated sleeping alone, especially under these strange conditions, but she was tired and the thought of Jawara's antics during the Sentinel encounter continued to exhaust her. She just needed to sleep on the day's doings, so she completely darkened the room. The gentle roll of the ship was the perfect antidote for her weariness and she hoped for an engaging lucid dream to entertain her.

Charlie awoke early the following morning but there was still no sign of the gallivanting Bradley. She a note on the floor by the door. She picked it up and her heart soared, realizing that tonight was to be the Captain's Dinner! Finally, she had an event worthy enough for her black dress. She spent the morning frittering away her time.

In preparation for the night, she decided to treat herself to a mani-pedi. The ending foot rub was a small delight for her but in a moment she was on to more important matters. Charlie went in search of Bradley at the casino. She wandered among the throngs of people engaged in their gambling revelry. He wasn't to be found at any of his normal gaming tables. Towards the back of the casino there was a quiet space designated with a sign that read, "Private Reserved."

She walked back and was greeted by a tall, very human-looking female Epicoid.

Charlie asked, "What is this area reserved for?"

"Private high-stakes games, invitation only. You must be Charlie?"

"I am, but how do you know that?"

"Bradley told me about you and your red hair. He is in a private game with stakes for over a million dollars, no guests. He asked that you remain out here; he said you would understand. You know, his rituals and all that."

"Oh," Charlie responded. "How long is the game scheduled to last?"

"At least another day. I hear he is up almost a million dollars. You should be very proud of him."

"Yeah, I'm something, that's for sure."

Charlie walked away crestfallen. She realized Bradley wouldn't be coming to the dinner with her and that she had no date. She went topside and observed Steve from a distance, taking sun with a beautiful African-American lady. They were laughing and obviously enjoying each other's company. For some reason Charlie felt her heart sink at the sight of the loving pair. She must have stared too long because Steve saw her and waved her over.

"Hey, Red, I want you to meet Teresa."

Charlie smiled and shook the woman's hand. "Hi, I'm Charlie," she said.

"Red, you're going to the Captain's Dinner, right?" Steve asked, practically busting with excitement.

"Definitely. Just try to keep me away."

Teresa turned to her and asked, "I'm so torn. Are you wearing a formal gown to the dinner?"

"No, but I do have the perfect black dress. I'll see you both there."

"Great, I can finally meet Bradley," Steve said.

"Yes, that would be a nice treat," she muttered as she walked away.

Sad and defeated, Charlie retired to her cabin. She was almost in tears when she noticed another one of those stupid flyers on the bed. She looked it over and observed scores of headshots for a series of handsome young men. Too bizarre. As she scrutinized the page she slowly realized that the flyer was for an escort service. She wasn't sure if it was tacky or just crazy effective marketing, timing the flyer with the Captain's Dinner.

She turned over the sheet and saw a dark-haired young man named Derrick who caught her eye. She studied his statistics and bio; he seemed to be quite the catch, even it was a paid date. If she ordered him up it could be quite the fairy-tale match-up. No doubt as a gigolo he would be expecting another boring night with a moneyed dowager, not a young redhead.

Hell, why not line up a date for the dinner? she thought to herself.

She called the number and asked, "Is Derrick available for this evening?"

A woman responded yes and Charlie ordered her date.

She languished in her bed most of the day and leisurely got dressed that evening. She scrutinized herself in the mirror, observing how the tight black dress clung to her curves. She turned sideways and admired the profile of her jutting breasts and flat tummy. She knew she still had her figure.

No Bradley, but there was a knock at her door: Her escort for the evening had arrived.

Charlie opened the door and to her surprise, there was Jawara, but appearing totally different. The alien appeared human and greatly resembled Derrick! Even better, Jawara was decked out in a tuxedo.

"I heard through the grapevine you might be minus a date for the Captain's Dinner."

To her shock, Jawara gave her a look-over, as if ze was taking inventory of her assets in a very male manner.

"Would be a shame for a beautiful creature in such a spectacular dress to miss out on this dinner."

"You set this all up for me?"

Jawara shook zirs head yes and took her by the hand. Charlie walked into the dinner with the large alien at her side, knowing all eyes feasted upon her. She felt like a princess, and she was seated at the table with the captain. Jawara held her chair for her and was the epitome of suave maleness, not the awkward alien she'd once known. They talked and laughed at the table, with Charlie particularly enjoying the spotlight as the *'it'* couple. Their merriment ended when Bradley burst into the banquet room and ran to her table.

"You stupid whore, you're with this freak. You're not leaving me—you're staying with me forever!" he yelled. Bradley waved a handgun menacingly in the air.

Seeing the gun, Charlie said, "Please don't. Let me go, Bradley, if I ever meant anything to you."

Bradley stared her in the eye and said, "Nah, I'm calling your bluff."

The small-caliber gun went off twice.

POP! POP!

The gun sounded as the bullets hit Charlie twice in the chest.

Startled by the dream, Charlie woke up in the dark. She wearily turned her head in the direction of the alarm clock. The bright red numbers indicated it was just two thirty-two in the morning.

Something else had woken her besides her crazy lucid dream. Was Bradley back? She raised her sleepy head and looked about the dark room. Nothing; just the hum of the ship's engines and the room's AC fan. The bed was empty next to her. Bradley was still AWOL.

She returned her head to the pillow just as she heard something different, something resembling a scratching noise. She was getting creeped out.

"Who's there?"

Something small scurried across the room. Charlie felt herself panic. What on Earth was that? Some alien creature? After meeting the Sentinel, she imagined all kinds of extraterrestrial horrors. On her own in the dark, the enormity of her desperate situation finally hit her: She was alone on a cruise ship with aliens! She began to panic.

She fumbled at the headboard in search of the overhead lights but in her panic she couldn't find the switch. She jumped and ran to the small hallway by the bathroom and turned on the room lights. She hit the switch with her palm and the room was lit.

As her eyes adjusted, she turned around and on the table directly adjacent to the bed was something small and grey. With beady eyes and a twitchy nose, it peered back at her in an inquisitive manner just as she let out a shriek. A Norwegian rat at least six inches long sat on the table innocently staring at her while it fastidiously cleaned itself. She screamed a second time and ran into the corridor outside her cabin dressed only in her T-shirt and panties. The rat seemed unperturbed by her antics.

As she ran down the corridor, Jawara was there to greet her.

"What's wrong?" the alien asked while grabbing her by the arm in an effort to calm her.

"There's a fricking rat in my room!" she screamed.

Jawara's normally impassive face somehow showed concern. "Of course there is. There should be one rat to each cabin, to match the conditions in your natural environment.'

"What did you just say?" Charlie asked.

"There's an assigned rat to every cabin."

Half-expecting Jawara to begin zirs horrendous laughter she said, "Are you kidding me? What the hell for?"

"We estimated that there is one rat per human on your planet. We wanted to simulate your home environment as closely as possible by including some of your indigenous fauna. To make you feel comfortable—or, as you say, so you can *feel at home*."

She stared at the giant.

"Is something wrong?" Jawara asked.

She stood before him with her mouth open and then said, "What, no cockroaches?"

"We did briefly consider—"

Charlie hit the giant on the arm while screaming, "Rats aren't fauna, you stupid jerk! They're vermin, pestilence that spread disease. We exterminate them; we kill them. If all the fricking rats went extinct on the planet, nobody would give a rat's ass. Hence the phrase, you big moron."

"No, we took great care to make sure they didn't carry disease. We did debate what their relationship was with you as a species, but—"

She started hitting Jawara and yelled, "I don't care if each of them comes with pedigree papers from a breeder. Get that fucking vermin out of my cabin, now!"

Jawara and Charlie headed into her cabin. With a wave of zirs hand, Jawara conjured a small blue sphere no more than a foot in diameter. The sphere slowly glided towards the rat, engulfing it. The dazed rat suddenly appeared floating before the pair, trapped within the sphere. Through the sphere the rat stared back at Charlie, its nose nervously twitching as it squeaked incessantly. As Charlie stared back she noticed the bottom of the sphere was wet from the rat urinating in fear. The sphere began shrinking in size, disappearing altogether with the doomed rat.

"Is he dead?"

"She is gone, in the spirit of the Quanteme," Jawara said.

"Get rid of all of them, now," she demanded. There was a small of crowd of people around her doorway, having heard the commotion, and they were clearly siding with Charlie.

Jawara nodded in agreement and said, "We will make an adjustment."

"What was that sphere?" she asked.

"We call the sphere an *orbis;* it's our technology."

"Cool. Now what about roaches? Are you sure you didn't add those as fauna, too?"

"We may have to make another adjustment," the alien said.

Charlie guided Jawara out of the cabin by the arm. There was that electric touch of zirs, and she quickly closed the door behind her, not wanting to invite the Epicoid in.

Charlie was still shaking, but then she wondered how Jawara had arrived so quickly. Was the giant actively monitoring her? Worse, what else did the Epicoids get wrong about humans?

She went back to her room, feeling trapped, and left the lights on. She couldn't sleep, and for some reason she felt bad for the doomed rat. Next to her bed was a paperback science-fiction anthology. She randomly turned to a story with plentiful sexual imagery. Reading on, she realized that the encounter in the story was with a randy alien. *How convenient,* she thought, but she continued reading anyway.

After a few pages she put the book down and felt herself calm down and become more peaceful. She felt warm and took her T-shirt off, lying face-down in her bed. The silk sheet felt good against her nipples and those waves of desire started to ride over her. She felt like a teenager again with her horniness as she thought about Steve.

Why now?

Where the hell was Bradley? She liked it when her husband would suck on her excited nipples. Her hands began pinching one nipple and then the other. She began her thigh squeezes and a familiar warmth spread across her groin. Tonight would be different. Her hand went down to her panties and she rubbed herself. It felt good and she took her panties off. She grabbed one of the pillows and positioned it between her legs and began moving slowly against it. The waves grew in intensity.

Screw sin, she wanted an orgasm. No, she actually needed an orgasm. Her hand went between her legs and she rubbed her moistened lips. Soon she inserted a finger into herself and then followed it with another. She thrust her fingers back and forth with increasing ferocity. Within minutes she had a massive shattering orgasm that left her legs trembling against the bed. A few minutes later she collected herself while thinking self-pollution was actually pretty good stuff.

Charlie fell asleep with the lights on and when she awoke in the morning she realized she wasn't alone. As her eyes focused, she saw that someone was in the chair by her balcony. She was about to yell for help but a sense of well-being overwhelmed her. It was Jawara.

"How long have you been here?" Charlie asked. She felt herself flush, knowing that she was naked.

"When I realized you were having trouble sleeping. We feel bad for scaring you in that manner."

"Staying in my room uninvited is not exactly cool either, Jawara," she said.

"I'm sorry. I'll leave now," the Epicoid said.

"Stay—the damage is done," she said. "You don't sleep?"

"No, we don't. We find your sleep curious, and especially the way your consciousness takes a hiatus. It is very peculiar to us, like trying to understand your indigenous flora and fauna."

"What do you mean?"

"You carry almost thirty-five trillion cells of bacteria and other creatures living within you. Should we consider them pests?"

"No, the bacteria in my gut is in what we call…what's that word again? A symbiotic relationship with us. Yeah, that's what we call it. The viruses you can do away with."

"There is no way for us to know that necessarily."

"It's in our science books," she said.

"Your texts are often in error."

"Well, it takes time to understand other people and cultures. I mean, you should know this from studying other beings, right?" Charlie asked.

Jawara said nothing.

"Shit, we're your first?" she asked.

"Yes, you are the first intelligent species we have contacted outside our own species, in the spirit of the Quanteme."

"Oh, dear god, this is going to be an epic cluster…. Yeah, a true cluster fornication. Do me a favor and toss me my robe," Charlie said as she got up to put on the robe.

"What is a cluster fornication?"

"Never mind, you'll know soon enough. And please turn your back when you see me changing. You should go now," she said.

Jawara left her cabin.

Charlie decided she needed fresh air and went to the top deck for a walk. She saw Steve in the corridor and with a big smile asked, "So, how big?"

"Gigantic," Steve said. "You do mean the ship, right?"

Charlie nodded yes.

"This ship is enormous. I walked it from bow to stern, almost 800 paces or close to 2400 feet. My stride is a bit longer than the average man, at close to thirty-five inches, so I'm just off a few feet."

"What else did you think I meant? Oh, for Christ's sake, forget it. You have too much time on your hands," Charlie said.

"Hey, I'm a scientist. I observe and I measure things. The longest ship on earth is 1500 feet and the newest cruise ships are near 1200 feet. This sucker is twice that." In a whisper he said, "I seriously doubt this was built on Earth."

Charlie turned away. She noticed a small throng of people walking with two Epicoids, talking and chatting away with the aliens. Several men and women were aggressively shaking hands with the giants. The passengers appeared to be assimilating quite well with their hosts.

Steve drew closer and said, "Charlie, I really don't like this cruise and how we are isolated here. I've got a bad gut feeling about this."

"You got issues with Jawara?"

"You mean our alien friend with a bad case of the tall-white-guy syndrome? If you ask me, they're all off a bit," he said.

"Who isn't a bit off on this cruise?" Charlie said while walking away.

The Phantasmagorical Magic Show

Under every cabin door and posted on all of the community bulletin boards was a flyer announcing a new cruise event for the day. There was to be a magic show that afternoon in the main theater.

Charlie couldn't find Bradley so she decided to go alone. The crowd gathered and milled outside the theater. It was the first time she'd observed the gathering of such a sizable crowd aboard the ship. Up to that point, the sheer size of the ship made it appear sparsely occupied. The heads of a few Epicoids poked above the swirling mass of humanity. They casually stood in line with the humans but a few people made it a point to introduce themselves and vigorously shake hands with the tall creatures.

Charlie caught a glimpse of Steve and waved to him. He quickly made his way over to her with a big grin.

"Wow, I didn't expect to see you here," she said.

"I'm so bored, and as long as it isn't an alien mime, I'm all in. Seen one mime trapped in an invisible box, you've seen them all," Steve said as the two sat together. There were several hundred others in attendance inside the expansive theater. The seating was more akin to a sports arena, with the steep stadium seats circling a small center stage.

The stage darkened. A solo spotlight shone down and Jawara appeared alone onstage, wearing what appeared to be a tux. The spotlight made zirs pale complexion appear a ghostly white.

"Isn't that your boy?" Steve whispered.

"Yes, it is. This is just too strange for words," Charlie said with a small smile.

Jawara said, "I want to thank you all for coming to today's show. We have many strange sights and delights to share with you this afternoon. Each of you will be given your own private experience. Some of the visions may be startling at first, but I can assure you that you are all very safe. This is an illusion, after all, in the spirit of the Quanteme."

Jawara disappeared and the theatre became totally dark. The ceiling of the theater appeared to vanish, opening into a vast, dark evening sky complete with twinkling stars. The tranquil sky was interrupted by the shadows of several large creatures that flew overhead. They were clearly larger than the entire theater and danced in the sky with one another to the accompaniment of a loud rumbling noise. They began to couple in mid-air and their insect-like abdomens filled the space above the auditorium. Many people were terrorized by the mating apparitions and they sought to run from the creatures only to find themselves paralyzed in their seats. After the mating they could only watch as a massive shaft resembling a giant ovipositor began releasing large clear eggs that transformed into hundreds of orbises that floated upon the air. Within each floating sphere were strange chimerical creatures that grew from small seeds to large creatures. Seconds later the creatures morphed into fantastic landscapes. The spheres moved silently among the audience, driven by an unknown force.

Two of the floating orbises stopped by Steve and Charlie as Jawara's voice announced, "Everybody choose one of the spheres for your own private experience."

Charlie saw several strange alien landscapes inside the orbises; one caught her eye that she wanted to explore. She gently touched the orb and watched its surface shimmer and transform. The alien landscape was a dusky azure punctuated by numerous Dragon's Blood trees with their strange umbrella canopy. A giant succulent tree stood alone, and sheltered many small, strange, chimerical floating creatures that moved within its branches. The creatures had a curious mix of bird and monkey features and they noisily went about the business of living their lives. Water flowed in the distance through a series of small waterfalls and tranquil pools, leaving Charlie in a serene, peaceful mood.

Steve also had several spheres floating before him. He touched one tropical scene but another came aggressively forward and immersed him within the orbis. Trapped inside, he saw the Earth and the orbis descended to the surface. Steve wasn't sure where he was; however, he could make out a man and a woman walking alone in a very arid climate.

Deep in Iraq a young woman and her father struggled to walk on the rocky slope as they approached a cave. The woman was crying while clutching and holding on to her newborn baby. The father was practically dragging her and her illegitimate son. Without a word exchanged they abandoned the baby in a cave. They committed W'ad, leaving the baby to Allah and the elements, a mortal sin. However, the mother was free to remarry.

The following day a mineworker was out looking for some new prospective digging sites. As he approached the cave he heard a crying baby. He found the baby, gave it a little water, and brought the child home to his wife. The child was adopted by the family. They named him and a happy ending was in the offing for the abandoned child.

The young boy was loved and he readily accepted his adoptive parents, unaware of his rough start in the world. For several years all was well, until the Shiite Revolt against Saddam Hussein. The countryside was in turmoil as the war raged on, but the child continued to prosper.

One day, when the child was four years old, he was in the backyard removing the wings from a captive beetle. His mother watched the child playing from their kitchen window. A jet screamed overhead, shaking the ground and causing the little boy to turn his head upwards. A bomb landed on the house before him, creating a massive explosion that killed his parents and buried the boy under a layer of dirt.

A victim of the war, the boy was relocated to the United States, his case managed by several relief agencies. He was adopted by another family, prospered once again, studied hard and did well in college. He became a programmer and immersed himself in his work. Still, the undercurrents of his life seemed to pull him away from his comfortable existence into the tumultuous world of jihad.

Over the years he returned to the Middle East and he slowly became immersed in the jihadist movement. During his travels he returned to the village where his adoptive parents had died. While there he learned of a rumor about his birth mother. He searched for his birth mother and from a distance observed her comfortable existence with an older man.

He knocked on her door while she was alone at home. She opened the door to the handsome young man and he introduced himself, mentioning his adoptive parents in the States.

"Do you speak English?" he asked.

She nodded and said, "A little."

"Good. Do you remember me?"

She shook her head no.

"You know, infanticide is a grave sin. So why did you let that old man do that to your child?"

The woman was at first confused and then her eyes lit up.

"My baby boy?" she asked. She started to cry and turned away from him. He followed her and tried to comfort her by taking her in his arms.

"All is forgiven, Mother; everything turned out for the better," he said and her tears stopped as she smiled. They embraced and he separated from her.

"Remember I forgave you," he said as he gave her a strange look. His hands moved to her neck and slowly tightened about her soft flesh. He peered into her bulging eyes as he slowly strangled her, listening to his mother's gurgling sounds.

Steve shook his head, wanting release from the tortured world of the orbis. His gaze changed and he focused on the stage, leaving the other world behind.

The sky closed above the audience and a spotlight shone and focused on the center of the stage. A small flower could be seen in the exact spot where Jawara had been standing. From the flower a large creature grew, towering over the audience and morphing into a dragon-like beast. It hissed at the human audience; they could almost smell its rancid breath. Before they could be fearful, a shower of twenty-dollar bills from the sky transformed the dragon into a large flower that gently swayed in a breeze. The flower vaporized and there was Jawara standing back on the stage.

Jawara peered up from the stage at the audience and said, "Reality is an illusion, albeit a very persistent one." As the lights dimmed there was a smattering of applause and disgruntled murmuring from the crowd as they exited.

Steve walked out with Charlie, shaking his head. Charlie said, "That was amazing; mine was a trip to a beautiful alien world. What was your experience about?"

He shook his head and said, "Sheer evil. My experience was about infanticide, death, and matricide. Shit, all it was missing was a little suicide. Just horrific. What the fuck was that about?"

He sounded angry. She just shrugged, not quite understanding what he had experienced.

The Beautiful One

Steve heard a Muslim call to prayer and was interested in seeing who was answering the call. He was a secular Muslim raised by his Jamaican parents, but he was curious about the selection of passengers, particularly after Jawara's comments.

Upon reaching the dimly lit prayer room he saw several older men hurriedly leave the room designated as a mosque. In the darkness there was a lone figure in a wheelchair.

"Who's there?" the figure called out in a murmur.

"Steve. Who are you?" he answered.

"Ahmed," said the broken voice.

Steve had problems understanding the man in the wheelchair; his speech was basically a mumble. He decided to approach him. His eyes took some time to adjust to the darkness but he was shocked at the sight of the broken figure.

The man was less than human. Maimed—no arms, one leg, mangled face with one eye, and a mouth so severely contorted that the remains of his face were hardly recognizable as a human visage. He was in a wheelchair with a remote throttle that he operated with his good leg and bare foot.

"What happened to you?" Steve asked, unable to hide his shock at the man's appearance and disability.

"A bomb."

"Shit, where? In the States?"

The man seemed to nod his head and muttered some words about prayer.

"That's just sick. I'm sorry. You can't even kneel to Mecca. What direction do you pray to?"

In a more distinct voice the man said, "I don't know; even a compass doesn't work here. But you can kneel for me."

"Oh, I haven't prayed in years. Sorry, I'm more a secular Muslim."

"Yet the apostate came to the prayer chant."

"More out of curiosity; my mother was a devout Muslim. I'm a scientist," Steve said.

"You can be a scientist and still be a devout Muslim."

"Not really—not if you are free to think it all through."

"Still, you could earn some credit with Allah. So will you kneel, brother, one more time with me? For me and your mother?"

Steve didn't believe in Pascal's Wager about praying to a god even if you didn't believe. It was a cynic's way to cover his ass for the possible afterlife. There were just too many variants in the world's religions and it was far too easy to believe in the wrong god for the wager to make any sense. He felt torn; he was a strong agnostic and had forsaken his mother's chosen religion while she was still alive. It broke her heart but he had to be true to his calling as a scientist. His choices in life were the source of much rancor during his teen years. Guilt tore him up, but looking at the twisted remains of the man in the chair pulled at his very soul.

"Sure," Steve said and he prostrated himself to the supposed direction of Mecca. The cripple muttered some prayers and Steve felt ill at ease to be suddenly bowing to Allah.

The disabled man went through a litany of evening prayers, and when he was done, Steve stood up. He knew he should feel good doing such a beneficent deed, but instead felt like had betrayed his own principles.

"Do you need help returning to your room?" he asked.

"I am in my room," Ahmed said, and he closed his one eye in meditation.

Steve left, feeling bad for the man. He felt worse for himself.

"Fucking terrorists," Steve muttered to himself.

The following day, Ahmed saw Steve with Charlie and made his way over to the pair in his wheelchair. He was still severely maimed, but Steve realized that portions of Ahmed's limbs appeared to be growing back. Small, embryonic hands grew from the end of his lengthening arm stumps.

"Ahmed, you seem to be better. How can that be?" Steve asked, trying to be civil.

"Better, praise be to Allah, and thanks for asking. All of the other infidels aboard this ship avoid me like the plague. Even the Epicoids hide from me. But the Sentinels are healing my broken body."

Ahmed's voice sounded American with a slight accent. Steve said, "Not sure what a Sentinel is, but let me introduce you to Charlotte."

Charlie smiled at Ahmed and was about to say something but he contorted his disfigured face and pulled away, clearly showing his disdain for her.

"May I speak to Steve alone?" Ahmed asked in a cold tone.

Charlie nodded and walked away, happy not to have to confront the rude, bizarre-looking creature.

When Charlie was gone he said, "I'm glad she is gone and I can speak frankly. You could do better, brother, than being with that white demon. She is another man's wife, after all."

"No disrespect, but what I do with my life is my business alone, not yours or your god's."

"That's where you are mistaken. You should return to the faith and marry one of your own."

"Again, feel free to keep your opinions to yourself. It's not like your god has been that kind to you," Steve said.

"There is so much hate in the world that it's not surprising what happened to me. I must put my faith in almighty Allah."

"I'm sorry, it's just crazy to have so much hate," Steve said.

"They do hate so much, the non-believers," Ahmed said.

"I'm talking about the bomber, the hater who did this to you. Violence is the lowest form of human expression."

"But sometimes hate can be so pure, almost like my love for Allah. I can assure you he is forgiven," Ahmed said.

"Your last moments before the cruise—do you recall them, by chance?" Steve asked.

"Yes, very distinctly. It was a sunny day but I was inside working. I am always working. It was my most intricate assignment and I was adjusting the timers."

Steve stared at Ahmed.

"I just connected the wires to begin soldering to the charge, and then I awoke in the hospital with just one eye and three limbs missing."

"I don't understand."

"I know you don't, but I was channeling all of my hate into my bomb-making."

"What? Weren't you the victim?" Steve asked.

"A victim of cheaply made timers, perhaps, but no. I was the bomb-maker, building a bomb for use against the crusaders. You know, for a scientist you are not too fast on the uptake. I'm telling you this since I sense you are also searching for a better answer."

"Fuck, this is not a better answer, killing and maiming innocent people."

"The crusaders do this every day in our homeland. When one is powerless, you must use the weapons on hand. Give us planes and tanks and we will use them in our holy war. For years I worked as a coder, working on assembly compilers, quietly going about my business. At night I was a gamer while the whole time the crusaders kept killing my fellow Muslims. I was wrong. I have a better vision now."

"Dude, you're an American; drop the crusader bullshit. You're just a fucking coder with no soft skills."

"And you, of your own free will, joined the crusaders' army, did you not?"

"How did you know that? Yes, I was in the Marines, but there's a big difference when one side is struggling to minimize civilian casualties and the other's sole goal is to inflict as many as possible."

"As I said before, you fight with what you have."

"So just how are you healing so quickly?"

"The Sentinels have taken a liking to me, though some may consider them to be monsters."

"Monsters? Interesting that you prefer the company of non-Muslim monsters now."

"You sure there aren't other monsters aboard the ship? Maybe that little redheaded whore?"

"You're a fucking asshole. You know, maybe the reason you don't have planes and tanks for your holy army is because most sane Muslims don't share your twisted vision of the world," Steve said.

"That is understood, my friend. Don't you know why we continue to provoke the crusaders? So that they do declare all-out war on all Muslims and force our more timid brothers to join in the fight. We don't care about the U.S., but we do want moderate Muslims worldwide to join in the fight against the oppressors. Praise be to Allah."

"I'm done with you, asshole. You were fucked up the day you were born. Your adoptive parents should have left you to die in that cave."

Ahmed just stared at Steve.

"Yeah, now I recognize who you are, asshole. A little alien clued me in." Steve walked away.

Day 4 – Gambler's Fallacy

Bradley was on the run of a lifetime. He could literally feel the cards and taste what was hidden in the shoe. It was unprecedented for him. Being on a run, he particularly liked going heads-up alone against the dealer. He felt he could play faster and not worry about the sloppy play or the distracting comments of the rabbits. Sticking to his routine was how he'd managed to go up nearly seven figures. Besides, if he wanted distractions, he had his eye-candy at his side.

Most of all, Bradley's winning streak needed nurturing, protection from those negative forces and vibes that conspired against him in his life. Nonsensical interruptions were to be avoided—and that meant staying away from Charlie.

Bradley had always felt there was something off with his wife. She was too needy, too demanding of his time with her chronic panic attacks and meds. Her lack of faith in him was also telling. He tried to bring her into his world but it was always one prolonged losing streak after another with her. Way too much negative energy!

Sure, she was attractive, in a redheaded sort of way, but that mattered little when a woman didn't have your back. Face it: she wasn't a classic beauty. Her skin was too pale and those damn freckles distracted from her looks. She was a passive lover as well; she never seemed to be engaged with him in bed. Her insistence on calling him Bradley was another irritation, a sad reminder of her whole Southern attitude and disposition. What he once thought was sweet and charming was now just simple to him.

Charlie didn't mind when he showered her with gifts during their courtship, but her constant nagging after getting married was taking a toll on him. It caused him to doubt his own abilities. Before marriage he'd made a nice living off his gambling, but lately it was like pulling teeth with her. That is, until this cruise.

Yes there were down times before; every player had those days. But you needed to get back in there, invest, and play towards that big winning streak. And even when you lost it all, when you faced complete ruin, you realized one very important fact: You were still standing and very much alive! Charlie never understood the sheer exhilaration of facing and surviving total ruin.

Suzy, the cute blond in the tight black dress, was back at the table and asked, "More?"

"What? You burnt through the five hundred I gave you already?" Bradley asked.

"I just don't have your skill, Brad," she said with a coy smile. Bradley handed her a small stack of chips. He figured the whore wasn't playing the chips but instead stashing them. That was fine; he would make her work for them later. He slapped her on the ass and sent her on her way.

While Bradley was entrenched in the casino, Charlie did a brisk walk on the top deck as a group of French tourists approached her. They appeared seriously lost and confused.

"Do you know way to casino?" asked one older brunette woman in heavily accented English.

Charlotte did and she knew it well. "Deck 3, towards the stern. You can't miss it." As she pointed, a long line of Frenchies walked past her.

She continued her walk but it was too humid on the top. She sought out the air conditioning of the lower decks. As she walked in the corridors, she neared the dark area where the three boys had tried to stop her. She felt a malfeasance permeating the space. It was as if evil had decided to pervade a small section of the ship, hoping to trap the unwary. As she quickened her pace a muffled voice called out.

"Hello, Charlotte!" said a mumbled male voice.

She turned, not sure where the voice came from. She saw an apparition in the shadows and turned towards the mysterious figure.

"Yes?" she said as a small nervous smile came to her face. As she did a gnarled, deformed human foot touched her arm. The foot was darkened, missing several toes, and the skin appeared burned and fused together. The touch was so dark and full of hate. The look of horror was etched upon her face as she jumped away from the deformed Ahmed.

"What the hell! Why are you touching me? What do you want from me?" she asked as she touched her skin to see if it had been harmed in some sinister manner.

"Trying to understand what Steve sees in the redheaded demon woman. Nothing I see."

"You touched me with your foot. Why?"

"Just remember, you fight with the weapons on hand."

She was preparing to lash out at him when the small broken figure retreated into the darkness to the sound of an electric motor. She had no desire to pursue the twisted creature.

As she hurried away, she felt sad and depressed. She wanted her impasse with Bradley to come to an end. He'd stopped sleeping in the cabin altogether, only occasionally stopping by for a change in clothes or to take a shower. When she did see him she couldn't help but notice the scent of cheap perfume on his clothes. Charlie wasn't going to wait for a chance encounter at the cabin to confront him, so she had little recourse but to go to the casino herself.

She dressed casually, so as not to draw attention to herself. After entering the casino she watched from a distance, pretending to be playing the slot machines. She walked to the back by one of the low-stakes poker tables; there was a woman dealer at the five-dollar table. Attractive and middle-aged, the brunette was actively recruiting customers.

"How are you doing?" Charlie asked while searching for her husband. She half-expected to see Jawara dealing cards but there didn't appear to be any Epicoids in sight within the casino.

"Good, do you want to play?" the dealer asked, hoping for a little action. "I could get another player, if you'd like?"

"No, I'm just looking for my husband. It seems a bit empty tonight," she said.

"Yeah, it's early in the cruise, but it will pick up once people become familiar with the layout of the ship," the woman said.

"Tips must suck," Charlie said.

"Yeah, but the pay is good, so who's complaining?" she said. "Have a good night."

"Thanks, you too!" Charlie continued to scan the casino for the wayward Bradley. It was such a large gaming space, but it was sparsely attended. She looked towards the high-stakes blackjack tables and there he was, in the company of two women: a striking, tall brunette and a shorter, pretty blond girl. Both appeared to be in their early twenties and they were basically fawning over him.

Bradley was playing blackjack against the house. It was the perfect setup for an alien experiment in winning and losing, Charlie surmised. He had a sizable stack of chips in front of him and appeared to be winning. The dealer was an older mature blond.

Charlie suddenly felt desperate, almost as if she had been cornered. She could barely breathe and she thought back to the deformed foot that had touched her.

Bradley was on a roll and he decided to make the maximum bet of five thousand dollars. He drew a king and an eight of hearts, bringing a smile to his face. The house showed a deuce, what some called the dealer's ace. Bradley decided to stand pat at eighteen. The house turned over a second deuce, drew a three, a seven, another deuce and, still needing another card, drew a four of hearts, winning the hand for the house.

Bradley turned away from the table. He stood up and appeared to be nervous. Suddenly his luck had changed with, of all fucking hands, an improbable *Six-Card Charlie* by the dealer. Bradley felt as if he was being watched and looked around the casino.

Charlie saw Bradley scanning the casino and she took cover. In her haste, she ran into an older lady, inadvertently knocking her bucket over and spilling the woman's winnings.

"Oh, I'm sorry," she said as she tried to help, but Bradley spotted the commotion and the wailing by the elder lady.

"Ladies, watch my winnings; there's exactly 173 G's here," he said, and he ran after Charlie.

He grabbed her by the casino entrance and yelled, "What the fuck are you doing here?"

Red-faced, she said, "I'm sorry, I just wanted to see you."

"You know you're bad luck, I've told you that a hundred times," he said as he pushed her toward the door. "Get out of here before you queer my run, you stupid bitch."

Bradley's face was red and his anger so fierce that she feared he was about to strike her. He yelled so loud the other casino players stopped to watch the pair. She was paralyzed with fear and anger.

"Just go! You're not wanted here!" he yelled.

"I'm not leaving. Not until you tell me what happened between the two of us."

"I'll tell you what happened: It's over between the two of us! It's been over for years," he said.

"I saw you in my dreams. What did you do to me? You bastard, I know you did something horrible to me!" She stood her ground, infuriating Bradley.

"What the fuck are you talking about? Go, you freaking psycho!"

"No, not until you tell me what you did!"

The brazen defiance was too much for Bradley and he slapped her in the face. Several men stepped forward to come to her defense, but she waved them off. Bradley's two paramours slowly retreated to the safety of the crowd.

"Stupid bitch, I have won close to a million dollars over the past couple of days. You never had my back. Get the fuck out of here."

"Call me stupid? Do you think for a moment you're leaving the ship with that money? You've always been a freaking loser. Can't you see they're playing you, letting you win?" she said.

Bradley didn't react and Charlie cried, "Why are you treating me like this?"

At that point, most of the people in the small casino stopped playing to watch the warring pair.

Charlie was crying and distraught, ashamed that she was the center of a domestic drama. She stared at the small group of people gathered and began yelling. "You're all stupid, wasting your time here. Do you think these things are going to allow you to leave this ghost ship? We're all doomed!"

Bradley just shook his head at her.

"They're watching us now. The Epicoids are watching us, taking notes as we fight our private wars. Can't you see that?" she said.

"Go, you're not wanted anymore. Get some help, will you? You were a depressed mess long before you met me," Bradley yelled.

Several security guards approached the fractious couple and Charlie left the casino of her own accord. She wandered about the ship in a daze. All she had now were her dark musings of the past and the knowledge that she had no future.

Brain Bleach

It was a beautiful South Carolina summer day, not one of the harsh, hot, humid days but one where the crisp, cool air of the morning was just being touched by the sun.

A young girl was about to have her first kiss with a boy of her age. He was a nice-looking, light-skinned black boy with short-cropped hair, a big smile, and a good sense of humor. She had pale skin, green eyes, and flaming red hair. She felt awkward, but she was a pretty girl. She was just developing into a woman, a child trying to adjust to the strange transformations occurring in her body, but the kiss foretold pleasures to come. Her breasts were just starting to swell and she hoped she could convince her mother that it was time for a bra. Really, just several months earlier she'd started her cycle.

They were fishing and talking by the local pond and nobody was around. They had gotten in the habit of fishing together over the past year, though they had relatively little luck with any significant catch during that time. One moment he just stopped talking and kissed her on the lips. Nothing big, a chaste kiss that lasted just a second. Curiously, he then touched her small breast as he kissed her a second time. The kisses were pleasant enough, but his touch of her breast left her more than curious. For some reason she felt a small tingle in her nipple. It was nice and they held hands for a few minutes afterwards. She was about to ask him if they were going steady, but from the distance they could hear his mother calling. He turned, red-faced, and quickly got up and left her by the pond.

One of the neighbors must have complained to Charlie's mother about her and the black boy being alone at the pond. That night her mother betrayed her and told her father when he came home from work. She guessed her mother feared what would happen if a neighbor had approached her father first. And she had good cause. She regularly heard the beatings her father gave her mother at night. Her father was a large, powerful man and a strict Baptist when he wasn't drinking. As to his drinking, well, his behavior turned even more violent, almost sadistic.

She heard her mother crying one day and went upstairs to investigate. She saw her mother clothed, but with her skirt hitched high and held in place with her hands, bent over the arm of the couch with her white panty-clad buttocks protruding high in the air. Her shirtless father was holding that damn belt of his. That belt was a two-foot-long stretch of black leather at least two inches wide. He was about to strike her mother again when the young child interrupted them. The reddened welts across her mother's legs were clearly visible as Charlie stared at the two adults. Her mother was crying, red-faced and filled with shame that her daughter was seeing her exposed and being treated like this. The look on her father's face was a bemused mix of anger and something else that she never quite understood. The two adults yelled at the young girl to leave the room and close the door. As she walked away, her father continued meting out the punishment. She heard the snap of the belt dancing on her mother's skin.

Just as she feared, her father had learned that she was seen alone with the black boy.

"Take your jeans down," he instructed. When Charlie hesitated, he yelled, "Now!"

She pulled her jeans down and adjusted her panties, taking care to cover her buttocks with the flimsy material.

"Now bend over the arm of the couch like you saw your mother do the other day."

She bent over the sofa arm and waited. She could feel the soft material of the cover against her bare skin. Why was he taking so long? She wasn't sure. And without warning, her father struck the first blow across her buttocks. She thought her heart had jumped into her throat with the searing pain. There was a large wall mirror across the room; she saw herself struggling on the couch and she watched intently so she could time the belt. She saw her hips grind their way into the arm of the sofa in a belated effort to retreat from the stinging force of the belt. Fifteen blows of the belt she endured, and the snapping sounds filled the air with her cries.

"I will not show my love to her children, because they are the children of adultery," he said. "God is punishing you, remember that. So I will cast her on a bed of suffering, and I will make those who commit adultery with her suffer intensely, unless they repent of her ways."

When he was done she pulled her jeans up and ran to her room crying, without glancing at her father or her mother in the kitchen.

When she was fourteen her father caught her smoking a cigarette. He wanted to beat her again, ordering her to the room. Charlie was very womanly then, the childish, androgynous body transformed into sensuous adolescence. Her mother protested and her father chose to beat her mother instead. Again, Charlie heard her mother's cries fill the small house. Her father possessed a powerful weapon to control Charlie because her transgressions would cause her mother to suffer, more so than usual. And then there was the awful time she broke curfew and he beat Charlie once again despite her mother's protests.

Over the years Charlie found that there wasn't enough brain bleach to chase away those childhood feelings and images from her soul. Later, during her relationships with men, she thought back to the days of her father and the episodic beatings. She fell into a serious depression and found it hard to trust the men she dated. Only when she was eighteen did she finally feel the cloud lift with medications, and that was when she allowed Bradley into her life.

She hated her father and was glad when he left her mother for his next victim. She married Bradley shortly after that. Three years later, her broken mother died of breast cancer and her father reappeared at the wake. He pulled her aside at one point and said softly, "Charlotte, you are not alone, baby girl."

She stared at him, carefully studying his face. He was much older and frailer now and didn't hold anywhere near the terror she had felt as a child. He just seemed like a tired, grey old man worried about Judgment Day and making things right with his only daughter.

"No, you are wrong, Daddy. I have never been more alone in my life, and frankly, I'm going to keep it that way," she said and walked away from him.

Charlie had fallen in love with Bradley for his blue eyes and the desperately sought escape from her family he represented. She married him at age twenty, but she somehow managed to go to college and earn a degree in psychology. The woman she was becoming slowly began to understand what had happened to the child. Yes, understanding and meds helped her cope with her past.

In time she realized she'd married her father in the guise of Bradley. Her virginity and chaste behavior signaled to Bradley that she was the perfect subservient for him. And like so many subs, she confused Bradley's controlling behavior for love and caring. Bradley never hurt her when they dated, but once married, he jealously guarded his property. Love taps during their arguments became the norm, but they were never the full beatings she had to endure as a child and as a young woman from her father. So Bradley was tolerable—that is, until the gambling bug hit full-time. Still, she made her bed, and now she would have to lie in it. Others had it worse, right? With her sad rationalization, she realized she never felt safe with the men in her life, sleeping with one eye open always in fear that the dragon would raise its ugly head.

All of these repressed memories hit her at once. They seemed so vivid, their pain as intense as when she first experienced them. Why she suddenly recounted those traumatic events in her life was unclear to her, but a sadness settled upon her that she couldn't shake. She hated being alone to relive all of her childhood misery, and blamed her wayward husband for her black musings.

As she walked, a stranger approached. He was an older white man and was talking to himself. The words made no sense but when the crazed man saw her, his eyes lit up as he stared intently at her.

"You, you are that redheaded avatar, the evil one! Adulterer! Scarlet whore! You will bring death to all!" he shouted.

Charlie tried to sidestep him but he grabbed her by the arm while yelling, "But the sexually immoral, those who practice magic arts, the idolaters and all liars—their place will be in the fiery lake of burning sulfur. Do not allow a sorceress to live!" he said.

Charlie was about to say something to the crazed fool, but instead she broke free and walked away. No, there was no need to confront the lunatic that reminded her way too much of her father.

An older woman watched the strange encounter and said, "You'll want to keep away from that one."

"Who is that freak?" an exasperated Charlie asked.

"Reverend Bannan. He's one of those fire-and-brimstone preachers. He's here with the other lunatics in his flock. They call themselves the *GodNauts*."

"God knots?"

"No, it's *nauts,* like in astronauts, but just call them what everyone else does: *godnuts.*"

"What are they doing here?" Charlie asked.

"Why they are on this pleasure cruise is beyond me. They've got their noses in everywhere and move like one big pack throughout the ship, all wearing those white outfits with their stupid dark Nikes. I hate it when they take over the restaurant. No manners at all. Did he say anything to you?"

"Yeah, that he really wasn't into my red hair," Charlie said as she walked by the woman.

Off on a Boat

After an hour of distraught wandering Charlie saw Jawara in the distance. She called out to the alien and the giant slowly lumbered towards her.

"Are you okay?" ze asked.

"You heard about my meltdown at the casino?" she asked.

Jawara nodded.

She turned away while saying, "Something changed between us and it's not just what Bradley did in the casino, but before our arrival on the ship. We have moved apart; a chasm has opened between the two of us. We arrived as a couple on this ship dead on arrival."

Nothing from the giant.

Charlie watched Jawara's expressionless eyes and asked, "What happened? Do you know the circumstances in my life prior to our arrival on this ship?"

"I wasn't part of the selection team. They share nothing with us regarding the events that led up to your arrival on this cruise. I can neither confirm your suspicions nor disprove them."

"I just feel so lost with no purpose. Jawara, why should I bother?"

Jawara was silent.

"You've got nothing to say, nothing to help me?"

Jawara's impassive face just blankly stared at her. The Epicoid was about to touch her when she bolted away. Shit, she might as well be talking to the wall.

"Thanks for nothing! You've been a big help," she said as she hurried away from the alien.

Charlie walked with the realization that she had lost Bradley forever. The thought of being alone on a meaningless cruise ship without anyone to accompany her was too much. The thought that she relied on a hopeless gambler to save her was even more depressing.

She returned to her cabin, showered, and then meticulously applied her makeup. Charlie then put on her best bra and panties. She went to her closet and reviewed her clothes. She took out the black dress she bought for the Captain's Dinner. The very special dinner with her husband that would never happen. She put the dress on but the bra still didn't work so she tossed it aside.

Charlie began tearing up and within minutes was bawling like a small girl. She couldn't escape the horrible sinking feeling of falling into despair.

Still weepy, she left the cabin and went in search of alcohol to calm her nerves. She found a bar, unattended, and the liquor was basically a self-serve setup. She saw a bottle of Scotch. Shit, it was eighteen-year-old Glenlivet. She took the bottle and a glass, grabbed some ice, and headed to her cabin to drown her sorrows.

She knew she was a lightweight when it came to alcohol. After three drinks she was out of her head. Every mistake she'd made in her life percolated up through the alcoholic haze to torment her. Marrying Bradley was the most egregious mistake, but there were plenty of others in her life. She was always worried about the future and her fate. Now she knew she had none. She blasted the music on her room stereo. Stupid pop music. She danced barefoot with no one in the spacious cabin, sometimes frenetically, sometimes with just a gentle sway of her body.

She wanted to be free and not in the confines of the cabin, so she walked out to the balcony. It loomed a hundred feet above the ocean. She watched as the water rushed below her feet while the ship surged through the calm sea. So vast, so free, so welcoming to her.

She didn't want to ruin her dress so she took it off and kicked it back towards the room. Braless and attired only in her panties, she climbed up on the railing of the balcony, her bare feet precariously perched on the railing while bracing herself with her hands on the balcony above her. Her red manicured toes curled on the wooden railing. No sun, just the radiant heat hit her face as a tepid breeze moved her hair. What she would give to see or feel the real sun again.

She looked down at her feet and the carefully polished toenails nobody noticed. Waste of time, much like most of her life. She gazed up at the wispy clouds, closed her eyes, and removed her hands from the balcony above and stretched them up towards the sky. No thoughts ran through her mind as the sense of dread and foreboding finally lifted. For a few seconds she seemed to maintain her balance and was in a state between caring and not caring. In essence, a perfect quantum balance between all of the states—ψ—of existence *and* non-existence. At first there was Charlotte, Bradley, life with all of its pain, and then there was no Charlotte, no Bradley, no life and no pain, only pure emptiness. She wished that she could hold on to that moment for eternity.

It was a gentle swell, more a nudge, and her body was in motion. Forwards, she fell towards the ocean with her arms stretched out. Her descent seemed to start slowly and then pick up speed as she opened her eyes to accept her fate. Yes, acceptance; for a brief second she was happy that she was finally assured of her just fate. Her body twisted as she fell and the retreating sky had never appeared so inviting to her. Her sole moment of freedom was followed by a heavy thud, as if she'd hit a wall. Instant darkness swallowed her universe whole.

Day 5 – Echoes

The small redheaded girl was seated at a table with her father waiting for dinner to be served. Her mother had baked her favorite, candied sweet potatoes, for the Thanksgiving dinner, and she just had to have a small taste. As her fork touched the top of the steamy orange glaze she felt a heavy blow to her arm. Her father smashed his forearm into her young arm.

"Wretched creature with no manners…and before grace, mind you!" he yelled to no one in particular.

The crying girl's sobs quieted as she transformed into the adult Charlie. She rose from her chair like a vengeful specter and grabbed the carving knife from the turkey. Her wizened father shrunk before the demon with long red hair. Charlie advanced, cutting off his retreat, and his eyes bugged out.

"Please, don't, baby girl," her father said as he aged and became more shrunken.

She smiled at him while plunging the carving knife into her frightened father's chest. Blood spurted at first, then flowed and decorated his shirt with a red abstract pattern of a dragon that faded into blackness.

At about forty miles per hour, Charlotte's small body hit the water head-first with such force that her neck snapped back. The bones in her spinal column fractured instantly while nearly severing her spinal cord. She was paralyzed and unconscious. Worse, the damage to her spinal cord was near her fifth cervical bone so she could no longer breathe. With no control of the limbs, her immobile body began to rapidly sink below the waves. She was drowning as the air left her mouth and saltwater flooded her lungs.

Steve saw the crowd milling around by the railing on the top deck and overheard a husband and wife excitedly talking. The woman said, "It was that cute little redhead. I heard she just threw herself over the railing from her cabin."

Before the other passenger could comment, Steve frantically asked, "Just now she jumped into the water?"

"Yes," she said.

"You said redhead? Here?" Steve asked.

"Yes, off the port side. Do you know her?" the man asked. He received no answer from Steve and the man continued talking to his wife.

Without hesitation Steve kicked his shoes off and went to the railing. He perched himself at the edge and searched for Charlie's body in the water.

One of his shoes shifted from the ledge and fell towards the water below. As he watched its descent, he realized the distance to the ocean was at least twice as long as the cliff he regularly dove off as a kid. "Red, you better be worth it!"

Steve jumped away from the ship, diving legs-first into the water while gritting his teeth for the impact. The jolt from the water was like a kick from a mule and he felt a molar crack in the process.

"Where did that young man go?" said the woman.

"Jesus Christ, he jumped in after her," the man said as he peered over the rail.

"She must've had some real issues. Come on, who does something like that on such a nice cruise? Do you see them yet?" the woman asked as she joined the others watching the rescue effort.

"Probably drunk off her ass," the husband said. "They lose a few people that way on these cruises. I don't see either of them."

Fortunately, the ship wasn't moving, but Steve needed a few moments to find her. Once he spotted Charlie, he swam to her immobile body. She was face-down in the water with her red hair splayed across the surface. She was slowly sinking below the gentle waves. Before her body could completely sink into the abyss, he grabbed her hand and pulled her up. He lifted her head from the water and with one arm around her checked to see if she was breathing.

"Red, what did you do?" he yelled. "Breathe, goddamn you!"

As he checked her eyes, her head flopped to one side and he immediately began CPR. A small bluish orb appeared and danced in the breeze above Charlie's head and drew itself closer to the water surface. It grew larger in diameter, descending, and engulfed her broken body while lifting her from Steve's embrace. The orbis left with Charlie's body, leaving Steve to paddle alone in the vast ocean.

Charlie watched her bloodied father fade away at the dinner table with her mother. She felt an infinite sadness, one that wouldn't let go.

She didn't know where she was or what had happened. Seemingly moments later, her eyes opened and the filtered light stirred her consciousness. Convinced she was alone, she raised herself from the covers and looked around the room. She glanced down at her body and realized she was naked.

She also realized she wasn't alone. Embarrassed, the little girl within her tried to hide her shame under the covers. Jawara stared at her, zirs impassive facing showing no emotion but the eyes told a different story. She felt the Epicoid's sadness.

She had been returned to her cabin, only now there was no door to the balcony, just a lone porthole. Jawara continued to watch her. She felt fine, despite her ordeal, and didn't bother to conceal her nudity from Jawara when she sat up.

"I remember falling. Did you save me?" she asked.

"There was an alert and Steve jumped into the water to rescue you. You did some considerable damage to yourself with the fall."

"Really?" she asked.

"Yes, a minute later and you would have been gone forever."

Charlie moved her arms and limbs; she seemed to be whole.

"I'm okay, no lasting damage from my fall?" she asked.

"No, we have restored you to your original health, in the spirit of the Quanteme."

"And Steve, is he safe too?"

"A little battered and bruised, but he is quite fine. Now it's my turn to ask a question: why?"

"Sad, just very sad. I lost Bradley and I was alone with no purpose. I drank heavily and I just fell to my destiny," she said. She studied his face, but couldn't see any signs of outward concern.

"So, it wasn't an accident?" Jawara asked.

"No, yes, I just didn't care anymore," she said. "Really, why do you care about me? We must seem so primitive and pathetic to you, the way we behave."

"There are those who embrace variety and differences, but there are others who want conformity and solidarity at any cost. I see your technology as primitive, not your existence. Your life is as valid an expression of existence as my own," Jawara said.

"If my life was so valid, why did I try to commit suicide?" she said as a lone tear slowly descended down her cheek.

"I cannot explain or even understand your mental state. No Epicoid willingly commits suicide. How do you feel now?"

"I still feel so alone," she said. "And then that evil cloud followed me, the one of total despair and no purpose."

"When you tried to talk to me earlier today I realized afterwards that I had failed you," the Epicoid said. "I will not make that mistake again. This time I will help you, in the spirit of the Quanteme."

With a small gesture of Jawara's hand a light-tinged, transparent blue orbis appeared before them. On its surface she could see her reflection and Jawara's. It gently bounced in the air, the two reflections merging as the sphere became smaller in size until it disappeared into her chest between the top of her bare breasts. For a moment both Charlie and Jawara were frozen while they looked at each other.

"Now, for better or worse, we are connected. You will never be truly alone," Jawara said.

Charlie gazed down at the top of her breasts. Where the orb had disappeared, her skin was glowing blue. The blue glow subsided and she felt an immediate change in her disposition, almost as if she had taken several Valiums. But this was better. She felt connected to someone; she felt almost happy at not being so alone in the cosmos. She felt loved.

"Better?" ze asked.

"Yes, much better, but why?"

"That was a Unity Orbis. For lack of better explanation, we are now entwined together with what your physicists call quantum entanglement. You won't be needing your medication anymore."

"Connected for how long?" she asked.

"For as long as we both draw breath. You and I will never be alone; we will have each other for comfort, even from a distance. From now we will both play the cards that are dealt to us together and to the bitter end."

Could an alien technology remedy her seemingly deficient soul and chronic melancholia? Did she really want a lifelong connection to this strange creature? And then there was that curious allusion to gambling…but before she could press Jawara on the subject there was a wild pounding on the door.

Jarawa opened it and Steve burst in yelling, "Is she okay?"

Jawara nodded. Steve saw Charlie in her bed and went to her side. Charlie just looked at him, confused by the attention, and noticed he was totally soaked.

"Charlie, what the hell? Why?" he asked as he held her hand. Charlie tried to cover herself and she felt embarrassed once again, almost flushing.

"Sorry, Steve, I made a big mistake. I'm so sorry, thank you!" she said as she started to tear up.

He grabbed her by the shoulders, and said, "Big mistake? What do you mean? How could your life be that bad?"

She started to softly sob and said, "I'm sorry. I was in a terrible place."

"Believe me when I say I know what it's like to be alone. You can always talk to me, girl."

"I know, I know, and I acted like such a shit toward you the other day," she said as the tears flowed.

"You're worried about a little attitude after you tried to kill yourself? I don't get your priorities," he said while he held her tight.

"I was confused—confused about my life, my marriage, and you. Hell, this alien encounter isn't helping. I actually feel fine now; I can't explain it," she said while choking back the tears.

"Forget about the attitude; I've heard far worse from my girlfriends. My bad for being such a patronizing ass. Just as long as you're okay," he said as he gazed into her eyes. Charlie liked his hazel eyes; they seemed sincere to her, not like Bradley's cold steel blue eyes that just looked past her. She gave him a small smile.

"Please, I'm here if you need to talk. No more jumping, okay? Shit, I think I lost my good shoes," Steve said. Charlie just nodded and continued smiling at him.

Seeing she was all right, Steve pulled Jawara aside and said, "Jawara, thank you for saving Charlie."

"It would have been very upsetting to lose her, and I want to thank you as well. Very heroic," the alien said.

"You said you would be upset to lose her but you barely know her," Steve said.

"She's a very commendable being."

"Why Charlie? I'm not insulting her, but what she just did was beyond stupid. I expected your people would, above all, prize rationality and intellect."

"No, it's the union of two or more sentient creatures that are in love that is the most important to us. Charlie is capable of great love, even when she is totally despondent. She just hasn't found her place in the universe, as they say."

"I don't understand," he said.

"And perhaps you never will. For Epicoids, it's about love and empathy for other sentient creatures. Charlie knows this too," Jawara said. "I can taste this in her."

Charlie was becoming more coherent and she asked, "Did you tell Bradley about what happened to me?"

Jawara turned to her. "No, should I?"

"No, let's not bother Bradley," she said. She didn't care to hear his feigned efforts of concern regarding her well-being. "Steve, I'm going to change, and you should, too."

Steve nodded in agreement and left. He retired to his room, showered, and changed his clothes. He was exhausted, drained from the experience, yet he was still worried about Charlie. It was near dusk when he decided to check in on her and headed back to her cabin. As he walked he heard a commotion in one of the meeting areas.

Charlie's attempted suicide had created an air of discontent among the passengers. As if wrested from a dream, the passengers in unison began questioning their tranquil but strange existence aboard the cruise ship. Most knew who she was, if only for her bright red hair and her screaming confrontation with her husband at the casino. Many blamed her husband, while others found it troubling that one so young and seemingly so alive would become that despondent. Not that many of them had even bothered to speak to her. Clearly, as seemed to be the current train of thought among the passengers that a young suicide never happened in the real world. Accusations started to emerge that perhaps the Epicoids were responsible for her sudden depression.

Consequently, Charlie's plunge into the abyss reverberated among the many passengers, fueling their own personal doubts and concerns regarding the true nature of the cruise. On Deck 23 Blue there was a meeting of several hundred passengers. Steve reluctantly attended, feeling uncomfortable with the mostly white crowd. They started asking questions about the cruise and why they were been held aboard the ship. Some of the passengers asked for patience, others became very agitated, and the more extreme passengers advocated for violence against the Epicoids.

Steve recognized Pastor Jones from the lunch crowd and pulled him aside. The pastor was a balding, middle-aged man who was a little overweight and easy to talk to.

"How's it going, pastor?"

"Fine; I'm finally getting a chance to relax, thanks to our alien friends. I heard about your heroic efforts earlier today and I just want to thank you for saving that young lady. Did you know her?"

"She's a friend, and thanks."

"Is she okay?"

"Yeah, she's recovering nicely thanks to the Epicoids. So what do you make of our friends?" Steve asked.

"They seem very nice and very polite. Unfortunately, others may not see them that way, but hopefully we can head people off before they act too rashly," Pastor Jones said.

"Nice and polite? Funny how I've heard that before," Steve said, but he was interrupted by the arrival of the other clerics, including Deacon Gordon, Rabbi Myer, and another strange holy man named Reverend Bannan. He was a white man in his forties, of average height and weight, with slicked-back dark hair that straggled down to his shoulders. His skin had the deathly pallor of a committed alcoholic but he was otherwise fairly innocuous-looking…except for the extravagant brown suit and orange shirt that he wore with his mirrored sunglasses.

He looked like he could sell cars. At least, until he took his sunglasses off. Then you had to deal with his crazy eyes. Plus, he chain-smoked.

The rabbi asked the reverend, "What do you make of our Epicoid friends?"

The reverend flicked his cigarette ash to the ground and said, "They may be God's angels acting as his messengers, but they're a bunch of cunts to me."

Disgusted with the reverend's comments, Pastor Jones said, "You're not allowed to smoke in here."

"Funny, I don't see a sign. Do you see a sign anywhere? What in Hades are you talking about?" he said as he dangled the lit cigarette from his lips.

"Have a little consideration for other people, will you?"

"I don't have time for these lost sinners!" Reverend Bannan said. He then began yelling, "You are not listening to God. Listen to me, you sinners! These creatures are the devil's agents!"

Everyone stopped talking and turned towards the demented man with the burning cigarette. The room was quiet as they tried to understand the commotion.

"You are all dead; the Lord has told me so," Reverend Bannan said.

He closed his eyes, his body assumed a rigid pose, and he uttered, *"Tere zera kik sed ohm rasidgif zera tyo kik raeilim fask cridf sed ba rasid."*

"What the heck? Did he have a stroke?" Steve asked.

Pastor Jones knew better and said, "Glossolalia. He is talking in tongues."

"What?" Steve asked.

"Supposedly a sacred language from the Bible."

"Ah, this is bullshit. I think he's just another crazy mother that's off his meds," said another man.

"Wegs zera tyo sed raeilim ohm crid ba," the reverend said, his body rigid and the whites of his eyes showing. He collapsed to the floor and writhed as the torrent of words streamed from his mouth. People watched the spectacle for a few minutes and then lost interest after a while.

"Get that babbling idiot out of here," one man yelled. Several men picked the spasming reverend up off the floor and deposited him out of the room as he continued talking in tongues.

"Now can we decide what do? Time to be proactive," one man said.

"We should round up those creatures and take them hostage," another passenger yelled.

Steve couldn't believe the stupidity he was hearing. Looking at all of the white men in the meeting, he hesitated to say anything about Charlie. They might not be that receptive to his interracial friendship with a married white woman, or what they could construe as something much more. No need to add fuel to that small fire.

"Let's kill one of the pale freaks and show them we mean business," one man bellowed with pure hate.

Now wasn't the time to remain quiet and Steve shouted, "No disrespect, people, but that borders on the fucking moronic. You know they're listening, right? And you know their technology can stop any half-assed scheme you put together? You've got to figure out how to neutralize their technology before doing something rash."

"So what do we do, just sit here and take this crap?" another man said.

"Yes, take it for now and learn about them first. Until you can think of a way to neutralize their technology, I suggest that you sit tight and enjoy the cruise."

"Why should we listen to you?" a younger man yelled.

"No reason, really, but I am trained as a scientist and we're dealing with a race with very advanced technology," Steve said.

"No shit, Sherlock," an older grey-haired man said.

"I'm also an ex-Marine who knows better than to take on a superior enemy until you have a coherent plan."

"Who the hell is this jerk?" an anonymous face yelled from the crowd.

"Shut up, asshole, listen to what the kid has to say!" another man yelled.

As the argument went on, they were disrupted by the return of Reverend

Bannan and the members of his flock; men and women alike invaded the room. The reverend referred to his followers as his "lambs of God," to be sacrificed as he saw fit.

"Lambs, make the sinners repent!" he yelled.

Steve shook his head as the reverend and his congregation began pushing people around. The reverend incoherently yelled about sin and repenting as he threw punches. Some of the other passengers stood up and began pushing back at the cult members. Steve watched as some of the older passengers started grappling with one another.

One older, middle-aged white man moved toward him menacingly and Steve smiled while saying, "You don't want to do this, buddy."

"Yeah, I want to do this," the other man said as he took a swing. Steve easily moved away from the punch and shoved the man into the swirling maelstrom of the fighting mob.

As the brawl ensued, a series of red-tinted orbises measuring a foot in diameter appeared in the air and moved toward the crowd. As the spheres touched the men and women, the fighters slowly collapsed to the floor, seemingly having lost consciousness. Within seconds there was a tangled pile of prone bodies. They didn't appear to be dead, but Steve wasn't about to stay around to make sure.

The remaining conscious people who'd been involved in the brawl began panicking and running. Steve sprinted from the room with several other men, including the reverend. He turned back to check and the tangle of bodies was gone, but a red orb appeared to be following him. He was close to Charlie's cabin and decided to seek refuge with her. Once at her room he furiously banged on her door.

Charlie called out, "Who's there?"

"Quick, open up, it's Steve."

"Steve it's late," she said.

"Just open up, will you? It's an emergency."

Dressed only in her nightgown, she opened the door and a frantic Steve ran in. He quickly slammed the door behind him.

"Quick, hide somewhere," Steve said as he ducked into the bathroom.

"Where?" she asked.

"Anywhere, dammit."

The red orb passed through the door. Frozen, Charlie stared at the orb that seemed to have nonchalantly wandered into her room.

"Charlie, get away from that thing," Steve yelled.

The sphere began to pass through Charlie. A sense of evil gripped her but then the sphere turned a bluish color and disappeared altogether behind her. It reappeared in the room with its original red color and headed towards Steve.

"Oh, no you don't, you little bastard," she said. She swatted the sphere with her hand and hit it across the room. It bobbled a bit in the air and left the cabin to continue its journey through the ship.

"What the fuck?" he asked. "Are you okay?"

"I'm fine."

"How did you manage to do that?"

"Not sure. But after my...." she said. "After my incident, Jawara shared a blue orb with me; he said we were now connected. He called it a Unity Orb."

"I watched that sphere subdue several dozen other passengers during a fight, and yet it had no effect on you. You seem to be very special, Charlie."

"Don't feel very special. Are they dead?" she asked.

"I don't know. I don't think so; maybe it was just crowd control. Hey, can I hang out here for a little while until I can figure this mess out? I really don't want to be caught out there."

She nodded.

He finally calmed down and then he stared at her. His eyes moved to her erect nipples, which were protruding against the flimsy nightgown. Involuntarily he licked his lips. She knew what he was leering at and turned away to put on her robe. She really needed someone to talk to, but Steve didn't appear to be the talking kind of man tonight.

Close Encounters of the Epicene Kind

Steve hid in Charlie's cabin until the next morning. He barely slept, and seeing that Charlie was still asleep, he got up from where he lay on the couch and ventured out to check on the other passengers. The meeting room was empty and Steve began to seek out people he knew had been at the meeting. He had to know their fate.

He knocked on the cabin door of Pastor Jones. There was no answer and he began to panic. What if he was wrong and they were all dead?

He pounded the door with his fist one last time and it slowly opened. Pastor Jones was at the door attired in his pajamas.

"Are you okay?" Steve asked.

Pastor Jones blinked and shook his head as if he was groggy and said, "Yes, everything is fine. I had a good night's sleep—that is, until you woke me. So why are you waking me so early?"

"You remember the meeting?"

"No, what meeting?" Pastor Jones asked.

"The passenger meeting last night. You know, the one that culminated in the fight with Reverend Crazy?"

Pastor Jones just blankly stared at him.

"The red spheres?"

"Nope, I went to bed early. What happened?"

"What do you mean, what happened? For god's sake, you were there talking to all of the idiots that wanted to take alien hostages. You don't recall last night at all?" Steve asked.

"No, what happened?"

"Forget it. I'm sorry to have troubled you."

"No problem, son. I'll see you at breakfast—or maybe you should get some sleep first. You look beat," Pastor Jones said.

Steve could hear the pastor's wife stirring. He nodded and walked away.

Steve went topside. He was exhausted from the previous night and the lack of sleep. He sat on one of the deck chairs and laid back for a few minutes. Within moments he had fallen asleep. A red orbis materialized before him and descended upon him.

When Charlie awoke, she saw that Steve had left and felt relieved that he was gone. It was near noon.

"Crap, I missed breakfast," she said aloud to herself.

After her depression and deprivation, she felt hungry and decided to go to the lunch buffet. She headed to the dining room named 'Marina' and saw fresh, hot food laid out at the serving tables, but strangely, she was alone. She didn't care; she was growing accustomed to dining alone during the cruise and decided to help herself. No vegetables for her—the supposed vegetarian was feeling carnivorous. Nothing said you were alive like devouring the flesh of another. She smelled lamb chops in the air. As a vegetarian, that smell would have normally repulsed her, but at the moment it seemed like a nice treat. It was then that Jawara showed up.

"Are those lamb chops?" she asked.

The Epicoid said, "Yes, do you want some?"

She nodded yes and to her surprise, Jawara started plating several chops for her.

"So, Jawara, working a new day job now?" she asked, amused at the thought of having a seven-foot alien serving as her waiter. As ze handed her the plate, Charlie swore she almost saw a smile on zirs impassive face.

"You seem to have a good sense of humor, Charlie. How is your day so far?"

"It's good. I'm going to sit down and eat this," she said. "But where's the mint sauce?"

She saw that look of concern the Epicoid had shown previously with the rats.

"Select a seat and I will bring it over to you."

She walked over to a small table; she had her pick since no one else had arrived yet. As she sat, she could see Jawara making zirs way over with the mint sauce.

She took her sunglasses off and motioned to the Epicoid to join her. The alien grabbed a chair and sat rigidly across from her.

She decided to play up the barbarian. "Ah, baby lambs. So cute, so defenseless." As she chewed on the rib, she added, "And so damn tasty!"

She dipped the meat into the mint sauce and then placed the morsel into her mouth. As she ate, she noticed what appeared to be a sign of repulsion on the Epicoid's usually calm face and she returned to her eating with even more relish.

"So, do you eat food?" she asked.

"We obtain our nutrition differently."

The alien watched her eat. She made a point of tearing the small rib apart with her fingers; she wasn't about to be apologetic for her sudden carnivorous ways.

"Do you eat other animals?" she asked.

"Eating any live creature is not an option in our culture. We manufacture all we need, in the spirit of the Quanteme."

"So this has to be sickening for you, watching me tearing apart the flesh of another with my teeth?"

"Somewhat, but I also find it fascinating," the alien said.

"Fascinating, like watching a car accident fascinating?" she asked.

"No, just very different."

"Speaking of different, I've got some questions for you. You do have sex, right? Your whole sexual apparatus, whatever you call it, how does it work?"

"It works very well, thank you," Jawara said with a deadpan delivery.

Charlie laughed. This guy, or whatever the hell Jawara was, was a real jokester. "Now that's funny," she said as she grabbed zirs large hand. "Really, you have sex, don't you? Make love?"

"Absolutely; it's one of our great pleasures in life, the one similarity between our two species."

"Details, please? I mean, you know how we do it, right?" she asked, enjoying the erotic tingle of his touch.

"Yes, your plentiful Internet porn from the past decade made research a lot simpler for us."

"Ah. I would be careful about using porn as a guidebook to understanding human sexuality. We're really not that frenzied in our mating."

"Oh, that's somewhat disappointing."

"Enough with the porn. So how do you do it?" she asked.

"We have one organ that functions in different ways. It can be receptive or probing, male or female, sometimes all at the same time. Superficially, you might think of it as a penis, but it's not."

"How big?"

"Significantly larger as compared to your males. It's just different."

"Got any Epicoid porn you care to share with me?" she asked.

"We're not as visually directed as your species. Much more tactile and *vibrational*."

Vibrational? She wondered what in the world that meant.

"Too bad," Charlie said, and she returned to nibbling and tearing the meat from the small ribs.

Feeling churlish she asked, "So who goes on top?"

Jawara matter-of-factly responded, "Being sexually fluid, we don't have clearly defined genders; consequently, we find your gender roles very intriguing and tasty. Unioeros with your kind assigns a gender role to us based on what you could euphemistically call a quantum coupling. Being a female, you would assign a male role to me. Likewise for your males; we then assume a more female posture. It's very liberating to have someone else define your sexuality."

"Really? How about someone, eh, let's say more alternative?"

"I don't understand."

"You know…gay."

"Oh, you mean homosexual. That's fine too; we adjust and accommodate accordingly to our partner, as sexuality in humans varies considerably. Your own Kinsey Scale states that sexuality is a spectrum over three poles."

"Three? I distinctly recall two from college."

"Yes, three. All humans are a blend of heterosexual, homosexual, and asexual in varying degrees. We don't have that spectrum, so we enjoy your tastiness. Sex among my own kind is more like what your species calls masturbation; it is still very good, but is missing the excitement of a new and different partner."

Once again she felt very comfortable hanging around Jawara and asked, "Hey, are you, like, assigned to me?"

"No, I just like your company; it's very refreshing."

With all of this attentiveness, she started to feel guilty and wondered if she had to leave a tip for the alien. Nah, she decided—where would ze spend it?

Heading back to her cabin after her feast, Charlie observed a young man slumped in a lounge chair. He was attired in a brightly colored red floral Hawaiian shirt. A hypodermic needle dangled carelessly from his forearm. A small trickle of blood ran from the prick of the skin. She couldn't see him breathing and debated what to do. Fearing that the man was dead, she tapped him on his shoulder to see if he was still alive.

Nothing, no movement. She tapped him again. He jumped up and the man slowly opened the heavy lids of his eyes to peer out at her. "Hey Linda, I'm glad you're here."

"I'm not Linda. Are you okay? Did you overdose?"

"Never better, this is great shit," he said and closed his eyes again.

"You need help?"

"Never better. This ship has everything," the drugged man said as his eyes rolled back.

Charlie had seen enough and kept walking. A brown-haired, middle-aged woman held a large tray of soft drinks and was struggling to get through the door. Charlie held the door open for her and the woman smiled at her while walking through. The older woman was in her forties and was a little heavy with an attractive face. Charlie noticed the woman's white outfit and Nike shoes.

The woman said, "Thank you, you're a sweetheart."

"Are you with the reverend's group, one of those GodNauts?" Charlie asked.

"Yes, I am a member of the flock. I'm Claire, and isn't this a glorious day?" the woman said as she continued walking with her tray of drinks. Some of the drinks were spilling.

"Well, the days are all kind of the same aboard this ship," Charlie said.

"Doesn't matter now that we have finally made it," she said.

Made it? Charlie asked, "Where do you think you are?"

"In heaven, of course. Where do you think you are, child?" Claire asked.

"I don't know, the world's strangest boat cruise? I mean, you have seen some of the antics that go on aboard this ship, right? And those aliens aren't exactly angels. They're actually a bit strange."

"Oh no, child, you are in heaven. The reverend said so, and those creatures are God's angels. We just have to do a little cleanup. Seems like a few sinners made the transformation with us. Unfortunate, but never you mind; we'll rid ourselves of those sinners soon enough. Have a blessed day!"

Claire kept walking and Charlie retired to her cabin. As she entered, she found Jawara sitting there waiting for her. She kicked off her shoes.

"You forgot these." The alien handed her the sunglasses she had left behind.

"Thanks, Jawara. Come on in and sit for a moment. I've got to change."

She put the radio on and heard a dance tune. She started dancing and Jawara stared at her. She moved her hips and arms in rhythm to the pop music.

"Come on, join me," she said.

The alien gave her a confused look. Charlie grabbed the giant's two hands and urged the creature to stand up. Jawara stood up and began shuffling zirs large feet around. The alien's upper body was perfectly stiff, with neither arm moving.

"You can do better than that," she said as she held Jawara's large hands up and over the giant's shoulders.

"Push the ceiling, big guy."

Jawara was tall enough to touch the ceiling and began pushing against the tiles.

"Not literally, silly," she said as she swayed to the music.

"Are you okay, Charlie?" Jawara asked.

"Not really, but I will be. Just lately, I have been dealt some shitty cards. Let's see if I can salvage this hand," she said.

"Why dance?"

"I think it's the most expressive art form of the human condition. You can almost feel the energy of the music; it's almost tactile, as you say," she said. "I always loved to dance, even as a kid, though I had to hide it from my father."

Jawara nodded politely, not understanding.

"Come on, let your hair down, big guy. More dancing always makes me feel better."

"I'm not sure I understand," Jawara said while lumbering along. Charlie didn't care; she felt free as her bare feet moved to the music, even if it was for the briefest moment.

Day 6 – Raving

It was early evening and Charlie was settling in for the night when she looked across the empty side of the bed next to her. Her eyes then moved to the black dress that rested forlornly on a chair.

Screw you, Bradley. I'm tired of playing the victim to the broken men in my life.

Charlie got up and put her black dress and makeup on. She debated putting her hair up to give herself a more elegant appearance but went with it down, liking the way her long red locks dangled against the black dress. She went directly to Steve's cabin and loudly knocked on his door.

Steve groggily opened the door attired only in his boxers and a T-shirt. He seemed to be very uptight and was more than a little embarrassed by her presence.

"You said to look you up if I wanted to do something stupid," she said.

He did a double-take at her attire. "Damn girl, you look fine. That dress with those shoes. Where's the hubby, by the way?" Steve asked.

"Where is he always? Winning money, then losing it all. Really, who cares? Let's do something stupid. So are you game?"

"I'm all in. What a fool. I wouldn't leave you alone for a moment, especially in that dress," he said. "Come on in and give me a moment to change so we can get the hell out of here."

"So, what happened to the other passengers last night after that fight? Everybody seemed to be fine today," Charlie asked.

"What are you talking about?" Steve asked.

"Last night, you came to my room in a panic and then that freaky red orbis followed you into my cabin. You said the passengers were attacked or something. You were being very paranoid and agitated."

"No idea. I had a good sleep last night," he said as he gathered his clothes.

"Really, Steve, are you losing it?"

He turned her way and said, "No way. Just what do you think happened?"

Charlie was puzzled and worried but then the moment of concern escaped her consciousness.

"No clue. Hey, I have an idea, let's go dancing!" she said.

"Really?"

"Please, please, please, it's been ages since I've gone dancing—well, not counting Jawara. And now I have a handsome dance partner to step out with."

"Jawara dances?" he asked.

"No, not really; it wasn't pretty. It was more of a pity dance. Come on, please, is it a date?"

"Ah, all right. I'm game, but none of that twerking nonsense, okay?"

"Don't think I have it in me?"

"Really, those curves in that tight dress? Trying to give me a heart attack, girl?"

"Yeah, you're right. Okay, I promise, no twerking!"

Walking towards the club, the two could hear the thumping beat of the dance music. Charlie was positively giddy, knowing she was going dancing while wearing the black dress. Inside, a crowd of men and women watched others energetically dancing to the club music served up by a pair of comely blond DJs. Their collective eyes moved in unison to admire the handsome newly arriving couple. Charlie grabbed Steve's hand and immediately led him to the dance floor. They were accompanied by a few couples and a number of women pairing up to dance.

"No jokes about white people dancing?" she asked as she began dancing and twirling away. She felt free, as if the grey clouds were finally lifting away from her.

"Despite popular rumors to the contrary, I've got my own challenges with dancing to deal with," Steve said. "But I see you are really into it. You're actually damn good!"

She nodded and kept dancing to the club music. The music changed to electro-house and he marveled at her moves. Cleary, she had been to a rave or two. He watched her intently as she became immersed in the music, her body and long red hair swaying in rhythm to the sounds. But it was her shapely hips that were truly mesmerizing. Every so often she would return to him with a warm smile and her welcoming eyes. She was both bewitching and guileless, all at the same time.

After twenty minutes an energized Charlie was seriously cutting shapes, but a sweaty Steve raised his hands up to motion for a break. She appeared a little exasperated but they sat down together at a table.

"Red, you are quite the freak the way you dance, and I mean that in a good way," Steve said as he wiped the sweat from his brow. "Did you just give me a few dubsteps near the end of that song?"

"More a shuffle I've been working on—no easy feat with heels, by the way," she said with a coy smile as her body still moved to the music. "I told you I like to dance."

"Damn, no way I can keep up with that."

"No need to; just accompany me."

He surveyed the crowd and said, "Rome is burning and here we are dancing the night away."

"I always did prefer dancing to Nero's fiddling."

"What?"

"You heard me. You know you don't have to be on all the time with me, always thinking. I get it, you're a bright guy and I like that about you, but you could just compliment me on my dress and my red hair. You know, small talk."

"You're right, I do suck at small talk, but I do love your red hair; it gives you an exotic appearance. What I like is that you're kind of special and you don't even know it," he said as he gazed into her eyes.

"Special, huh? You mean special in a good way, right?" she asked.

"Absolutely. That red hair and black dress makes you look hot and very different."

"Did you know redheads require more anesthesia?" she asked.

"Actually, I do. It's part of a recessive gene mutation redheads possess."

"Of course you do, you're a biologist…right," she said. "So why marine biology?"

"I know it seems a bit random, but both my parents were professors. They were born in Jamaica and when I visited family back home I loved swimming and diving in the ocean. I was hooked, so after the Marines I got my bio degree. Why are you giving me that look?" he asked.

"No, it's just that my parents barely got out of high school. However, I made sure I got my college degree."

"I like that there's a brain under all that beautiful red hair. Parents from South Carolina, too?"

"Yes."

"So is your old man old-school? I mean, what would he say if he saw the two of us together?"

"He can go fuck himself for all I care. That bastard never wanted me dancing either. He has no control over me, and the same goes for my asshole husband," Charlie said.

"Wow, the mouth on you," he said. She was now fuming. "Okay, verboten topic to talk about. Let's chill and take some of the excess energy back onto the dance floor," he said as he took her by the hand. They danced to a pop tune and Charlie's disposition noticeably brightened once again.

The music slowed and they began a slow dance, with Steve's arms hanging over her bare back. Charlie didn't pull back. He pushed his hips into hers and they remained intertwined. She rested her head on his shoulder. Later the music picked up but the two remained locked in their embrace. Steve nestled his nose in her red hair, enjoying the scent of this beautiful creature. He glanced up at the other dancers.

"What the…? This is so bizarre," he said. "Are you seeing this, Charlie?"

She watched the crowd; everybody seemed very preoccupied with one another, touching, holding, and groping in some manner. She said, "I thought we were going to give our brains a rest?"

"Who else can I talk to about this?

"Okay, but what's the big deal? They all seem pretty horny to me."

"No, not only that, but not one dirty look from the white folk in our direction, not even one from the seniors. What the hell is wrong with these people? Am I really that non-threatening?" he asked.

"You seem like a nice guy," she said. "I don't understand."

"You have never been hassled by police for driving while black so I'll give you a pass. But the lack of reaction here is causing me to ask: Am I black enough, or is something else going on here? Can't believe I'm having this conversation with the little white princess."

Charlie gave him a stern look and said, "Jeez, can you stop bullshitting yourself? Face it, you're soft and practically Obama's younger brother. Shit, it's not like someone is going to confuse you with being a member of the Wu-Tang Clan, right?"

"What?" He stepped away from her in disbelief.

"You heard me," she said.

"Say that again?" Steve asked.

"Word," she said while desperately struggling to keep a straight face.

Steve started to laugh and drew her closer. "Stop that and stop that now, you silly little snowflake. Do you even know who the Wu-Tang Clan is?"

Charlie burst out laughing and said, "No fricking clue, do you?"

"Some old-school rappers, I think. I'm more a Jay-Z guy. All right, you got me, but does anybody say 'word' anymore?"

"Well, if you don't know, I certainly don't," she said as more of her laughter filled the air. Her giggles were like musical chimes to his ears; she was so damn cute.

"You're a ridiculous woman. You know, it's not like there are a lot of brothers aboard this cruise. And if this is how white people normally behave, why the hell did they all just vote for Donald Trump?" he asked.

Charlie wondered why Steve was mentioning voting for Trump, but she left it alone. "Made you laugh, didn't I?"

"I do love the sound of your laughter," he said as he drew her closer.

Once again the tone was just a little too serious for Charlie and she decided to change the topic. "You know, come to think of it, I haven't seen any other African-Americans—I mean, black people. In fact, have you seen any real redheads other than moi?"

"Real, no. There's a young teen girl with different-colored hair, most of it red."

"She's a poser."

"So there's one real redhead and one real black man on board. Why the hell am I the only black person aboard this ship? Did these fricking aliens really have to be so pale white?"

"Look, I feel it too, being alone and apart from everyone."

"There's that, but there's something else going on. Think about it: we're basically being held hostage by aliens and yet I'm more worried about what you think of me. Why? This makes absolutely no sense to me!"

"You worry what I think about you?"

"Of course; it's not like anyone else notices me, but you're missing the point. We're living in a weird bubble of the Epicoids' own making. This whole cruise is bullshit."

Steve realized he was turning Charlie off and said, "Hey, sorry for mouthing off like that."

Before Charlie could reply, a large party of people suddenly arrived at the club and headed to the dance floor. They were dressed in all manner of costumes with the prevailing theme being science fiction. Princess Leias danced with Vulcans. Green aliens danced with Stormtroopers and Luke Skywalkers. All of their costumes were very ornate and intricate while revealing lots of flesh. Bare arms and legs were the norm, with many women going topless. Men wore jockstraps and codpieces. They were all dancing while lasciviously grinding and rubbing against each other.

"Did you see an invite for a masquerade party go out?" Charlie asked.

"No, but they're really getting into this, aren't they? Sure this isn't more of a swinger's soiree?" he said with his head on a swivel.

As Steve watched, a small party of seemingly male and female Epicoids walked into the club. They intermingled with the humans and began stiffly dancing among the crowd. People grabbed the giants and tried to show them how to move. The Epicoids were shuffling and picking up their feet as if they were at a hoedown rather than a dance club.

"Shit, you're right, Charlie, the Epicoids can't dance. Jesus, they are pathetic," Steve said.

"This has become quite the freak show," she said.

Despite their horrendous dancing, everybody wanted to dance and touch hands with the Epicoids. As they watched, many of the people shed their clothes and started engaging in all manner of erotic activities. Many were kissing or groping one another. Clothes littered the dance floor and bare white flesh flashed under the strobe lights. Men and women danced as well as same sex partners, all excitedly cavorting, fondling, and rubbing against one another. All pulsated to the music. The crowd was a throbbing orgasm seeking release.

"This is so bizarre," Steve said as a woman with bare breasts started dancing with him and Charlie.

"What's with all of these horny people?" Charlie asked.

"I don't know, but let's go before they pull us into their mosh pit," Steve said as he smiled at the woman with the bare breasts.

"Yeah, you look really worried," Charlie said with a grin.

Before they could leave they were surrounded by a wall of half-naked revelers. The dance floor had transformed into an impromptu orgy with the strobe lights and industrial music creating a heavy, thick beat that resonated deep into the pelvis.

"Get a load of this," Steve said as he pointed to an attractive, topless cigarette girl. She was walking around with cigarettes and pills, including Molly, Special K, acid tabs, ED pills and poppers. The partiers descended upon the hapless woman, eager to sample her inventory.

Dancers now sported fluorescent dildos and panties that glowed with darker openings to reveal their sex. Condoms that glowed crazy colors were being worn by the men while glow sticks were soon attached to any sexual organ.

Charlie's provocative dancing made the pair very popular with the partiers. Women were grabbing Steve and forming a sandwich around him. Another naked man asked Charlie, "Is your hair real?" He played with a lock of her hair but his large erection indicated that he had other interests in mind. Those who weren't dancing were feverishly engaging in coitus on the dance floor.

Charlie grabbed Steve's hand and pulled him from the frenzied crowd. They sat down at a small table off to the side and surveyed the curious display of human behavior.

"Wow, what the fuck got into these people?" he said.

She turned away, not knowing what to say. He was right, none of this made sense, but she just didn't want to be reminded tonight about this strange cruise.

Steve overheard another man in a panicked voice yell, "Shit, Pessimus has arrived, let's get the fuck out of here." It was then that a strange apparition caught Steve's eye.

"Holy shit, Charlie, this close encounter is about to get weirder. Look at this fucking dude's costume. Don't stare," he said.

They turned in unison to watch a shadowy large bipedal apparition walk into the room. Between the different-colored strobe lights a creature with massive arms, a wiry torso, and hooved legs moved methodically towards the dance floor. On its head, strange tentacles that resembled mangled dreadlocks dangled into its large, bulging black eyes. Below its eyes the creature's mouth was beaked, with a lower jaw that unhinged to reveal a pair of small tusks. Its darkened skin appeared to have numerous deeply etched scars, and festering open sores lined its hunched back.

The beast had clawed hands with dry, scaly, mottled skin of different colors and spiked porcupine-like hair of different lengths on its back. The creature snarled and drooled as it walked across the room sneering at the sexual antics of the humans and Epicoids. A murmur went through the crowd and all of the revelers began dispersing upon sight of the creature. The Epicoids were among the many leaving the dance floor.

Charlie took a quick glance at the horror and whispered to Steve, "That, my friend, is not a costume."

"You've got to be shitting me."

"Remember your friend Ahmed talking about the Sentinels? I met one of those horrible creatures alone in one of the corridors. Jawara told me they're the Epicoid version of emotionally constipated fascists."

"Beyond repulsive, and Ahmed is no friend of mine," Steve said.

"This one is much larger than the one I encountered."

The Sentinel gave the pair a look and stopped at their table to deliberately stare at Charlie. Charlie was engrossed by the creature. She stared back at the tentacles on its head and realized they were actually yellowish tubercles that grew from its skin. As she watched, a loud rumbling noise began to resonate through their bodies. Charlie was startled by the creature's sonic roar and jumped backwards as she gave a small guttural cry. Steve stood up and got between the creature and Charlie while he glared. The creature towered over Steve and continued to walk by them.

In a deep, resonating voice the creature said, "Sit down, little man. If I wanted to hurt you and the scarlet one, you would both have been dead a long time ago."

"Just keep moving, you ugly motherfucker," Steve said.

"Stupid animals," the Sentinel said and it slowly walked by the pair, a trail of mucousy slime marking its trail.

The joyous party mood evaporated with the arrival of the Sentinel. The humans and the Epicoids quickly disappeared into the night air, knowing their rave was over.

Alien Voyeurs

The couple watched the creature leave the club and Steve said, "Shit, let's go. I need some fresh air."

Charlie meekly nodded and got up with him. They took the elevator topside and walked the upper deck as they gazed up at the stars.

"I don't care what you call that thing, but that Pessimus is one fugly-looking creature."

"Fugly?"

"Fucking ugly, if you excuse my language. You okay?" Steve asked.

"Yeah, I'm fine, and those things certainly look like they were beat with an ugly stick. Did you see the way it stared at me?"

"Yeah, what a freak."

"Thanks, by the way," she said.

"For what?"

"Coming to my defense. It's been a while since a man stood up for me," she said.

"My father always said you are not much of a man if you can't defend your woman. Not that you're my woman, but you know what I mean, right?"

"Like the way you got all gangsta with that thing," she said with a smile.

"Gangsta? Busting on me again?"

Charlie just nodded and giggled a little. He replied, "Cute!"

He did like the way her face lit up with a joke. He scanned the sky and shook his head.

"On the positive side, that thing at least put an end to that horrendous dancing from the Epicoids," he said as he peered skyward.

"Come on, they were kind of endearing with all of their shuffling. Just what are you staring at in the sky?" she asked.

"I'm so fucked—I mean, screwed. Even the layout of the stars seems strange to me tonight. Not like on Earth. I mean, never mind the constellations, but even the Milky Way seems changed. Really?" he asked.

"Have you seen the moon since we've been on this cruise?" she asked.

"No, I'm not sure we should."

"Where are we then?" she asked.

"Definitely not in Kansas, Dorothy. Damned if I know. Not like I have some star charts, and if I had access to the Internet maybe I could hazard a guess. But I got nothing aboard this ship. Funny, I can get Internet porn, however."

Charlie just turned away and said, "I can't say I've watched."

Steve was about to comment when Charlie blurted out, "It's over between me and Bradley. He doesn't love me anymore, hasn't for a long time. Now I'm sure I don't love him anymore."

"Wow, that seems somewhat random."

"What you did with that creature for me, I couldn't imagine Bradley doing the same. It just hit home that a relative stranger was treating me better than my husband does."

"Sorry, I can only imagine the pain you're going through. I mean, I was with my girlfriend for five years and it was hell when we split up. Are you getting divorced?" he asked.

"I guess so. I mean, that's what you do when your love goes sideways. It's not like I need Bradley to support me. And this is not out of the blue. This storm has been brewing for years. I made a big mistake marrying that jerk."

"Why are you telling me this?" Steve asked.

"Who else cares about me on this ship besides you and Jawara?"

"Who wouldn't care?" Steve said. He gently grabbed her hand and held it. "You're beautiful."

Charlie felt a little uneasy with his quaint comment but didn't say anything to him. She did like the touch of his skin.

"All of this just seems to pale in comparison to our captivity on this ship to nowhere," she said.

"Funny that no one is panicking after meeting that freaking walking nightmare. They are managing us very well so far," Steve said. "In fact, save for the Sentinels, we might readily accept our gilded cages."

"Haven't we already?" she asked.

The pair approached the Tranquility Area but saw it was roped off. The Tranquility Area was the quiet section of the ship for 'adults only' that allowed the passengers some calm time away from the normal hubbub.

'No Children Allowed!' the sign boldly proclaimed. They felt a strange vibration to the air. It was not at all unpleasant, and was accompanied by a discernible, visceral hum that seemed to reach deep inside. It clearly wasn't emanating from some forgotten machinery aboard the ship.

"Let's be bad and sneak in?" she said.

"Yeah, I really want to see where that sound is coming from," he said and lifted the rope for Charlie. They moved forward and saw that the swim area was darkened with low blue ambient floodlights. The strange humming noise came directly from the pool area.

"What's that?" she asked.

"Not sure if that's our friends or not. It's coming from over there," he said as he pointed to the pool area. As they descended the steps they saw a large illuminated pool and heard a group of people approaching. The mist parted and it wasn't a party of humans but a dozen or so Epicoids walking to the pool.

"We're going to get caught," Charlie said.

Steve pointed to an empty chair container. "Hide in here," he whispered as he grabbed her hand. The two crouched down and he closed the large swinging doors behind them. Through an opening in the top they had a full view of the pool.

Charlie whispered, "This reminds me of when I was a kid and we used to play hide-and-seek at dusk. I always got found first because I never strayed too far, you know, in fear of the unseen monsters in the shadows."

"Seems some things never change, huh? Shush, little one, they're here," he said.

They watched a mixed group of seemingly male and female Epicoids walk to the pool accompanied by the humming noise. The Epicoids were becoming more human-looking over time as they assimilated among humans. They still lacked hair, teeth, or fingernails, but their faces were becoming more distinct. Darker pigment above their eyes simulated eyebrows, and there was color to their irises. Pores, wrinkles, and color had been added to their smooth porcelain skin. They still resembled a work in progress, as if someone was building a human and got interrupted or just wasn't paying attention to the details.

The Epicoids removed their clothes, revealing androgynous bodies that resembled a child's doll, an incomplete imitation of the human form. Some had a female form, complete with breasts but no nipples. Boys and girls alike had a genital fold that resembled a woman's anatomy. Steve shook his head.

"So they're all girls?" she whispered.

"Beats me what is going on with their sexes," he said, hoping to catch a better look.

While walking they paired off, some boy-girl, some seemingly same sex, some in threesomes. Holding hands they waded into the pool and together they swam out to the deeper end. They were all waist deep in the water.

The Epicoids started touching one another, culminating in deep erotic stroking of each other's skin, and within minutes their genital fold turned a blue hue and began to swell. When fully aroused, a massive red-tinged sex organ slowly emerged from their pudenda.

"What the fuck?" Steve asked.

The engorged organ became erect, stalk-like, but the end featured a swelling tip that had lip-like folds. The stalk changed shape at the bulbous tip, sometimes appearing penile and other times blooming like a flower for a female appearance. All was dependent on the desire of the intertwined lovers.

"What the heck is that? Have you ever seen anything like that?" Charlie whispered.

"No, maybe on female hyenas. It would appear that our friends possess a large, prehensile pseudo-penis. It's called a 'pseudo' because these kinky bastards can receive as well as give with that thing...," he said as his voice trailed off, enthralled with the sexual antics of the Epicoids.

Their organs continued to swell and extend from the fold. Free, the prehensile reddish organs intertwined with the stalks of others. The humming sounds grew louder with each successive coupling and the vibrations could be intimately felt by the two humans. The Epicoids began a series of strange vocalizations that coincided with the descent of an azure-colored fog upon the pool.

Charlie watched the rising rhythm of their aroused flesh and observed one Epicoid that appeared to be surrounded by the others. Their prehensile organs wrapped about each other in a corkscrew manner, swelling and pulsing against each other. Their collective organs touched the body of the Epicoid in the middle, exploring and probing zirs orifices. The giant's body writhed in unison with them in a strange but sensuous ballet.

Charlie felt herself aroused, not because of the erotic visuals but from some deeper personal longing. Somehow, she was connected to the mating Epicoids. She wasn't sure why; however, she suddenly wanted to be the epicenter of their ardor and the eager recipient of their probing touches. And then she recognized the Epicoid in the middle of the pool, even though she couldn't clearly see the individual. She knew it was Jawara.

Realizing it was Jawara, Charlie felt personally connected to the sensual bodies in the pool. She found herself in the middle of the writhing masses, sharing Jawara's experience. She was having a physical, sexual response to the mating Epicoids. Her body became tumescent as she reacted to their touching and probing of Jawara.

A sweet, liquid sensation emanated from deep within her pelvis, foretelling her of delights to come. The feeling was almost taboo in its longing and intensity. In fact, her first reaction was to suppress the feelings and acknowledge to herself that she knew better than to indulge in even thinking about such base instincts.

But forbidden fruit was always the strongest, particularly in the form of a handsome black man. Her rationalizations about abstinence didn't matter anymore; there was no way she could ignore her desire. Charlie's normally reticent behavior was being supplanted by something much more primal and demanding. She wanted a lover, one who could match her intensity, and she wanted him deep inside her.

Unashamed, she squeezed her breasts through the dress while pinching her nipples. Her other hand made its way below and she hiked her dress up considerably. She knew Steve was there next to her in the darkness but she didn't care. She was deep in desire, actually wet with it, and she wanted release.

She heard the vibrations. They repeatedly said, "We are the Quanteme." There was something else in their primal, tribal chant but it was obscured, just a warm vibration that rhythmically swept over her like the waves of an orgasm.

In the darkness Charlie's hand slipped under her panties. She felt herself becoming liquid and her fingers found their way to her lips. Her fingers delicately danced on her womanhood, the moisture building. Soon she was furiously rubbing her engorged clitoris as a confused Steve tried to look on in the shadows. He began rubbing himself as he concentrated on watching his partner satisfy herself.

Charlie wanted to be in the middle of that alien orgy, imagining the overwhelming pleasure that seemed to combine sex with the seductiveness of liquid opium. The humming reached a musical crescendo; their bodies and organs twitched and spasmed together while their collective bodies acquired a strange blue hue. She heard— No, she actually felt their chant about the Quanteme.

Belonging to the whole, Charlie continued to pleasure herself, moving ever closer to a massive orgasm. Her muffled cries of desire joined the rapture of the other Epicoids, her voice lost in the mass orgasm. A loud noise, almost a final primal grunt, signaled their collective release and orgasm. With her climax Charlie began sobbing.

After the Epicoids departed, Charlie and Steve found themselves alone, aroused, and still somewhat breathless. They left their hiding place, with Charlie straightening her clothes and drying her tears while Steve tried to hide the lingering erection within his pants.

Charlie glanced over at Steve as he fiddled with his pants and wondered what his manhood looked like. Strange, she'd never felt that way before about a man's anatomy, but now she wanted to know his cock.

"What was that about?" he asked as he finished adjusting himself.

Charlie was quiet, still overwhelmed with that liquid sensation of heat within her pussy. Funny, she'd never called her womanhood a pussy before.

"Shit, it's almost as if their collective horniness was lingering in the air. You certainly got into it," he said with a big smile.

Charlie realized something had changed for her. No longer consumed with guilt or worrying about her husband, she was free to desire once again in her life. No, make that lust—to feel pure, unadulterated lust once again. She wanted sex, she wanted orgasms, and Steve appeared to be a suitable and readily available lover. Charlie reached over to Steve and kissed him passionately on the mouth.

He eagerly returned her kiss. Her touch and kiss was practically intoxicating and far more sensual compared to his experiences with other women.

When they finally separated, he said, "What about your…?"

"To hell with him. I want you—I want you now," she said and continued kissing him.

"You don't have to ask me twice," he said as he returned her kisses and began caressing her breasts.

She broke away from him and went to her knees. She forcibly pulled his pants and underwear down. His large, dark erection stood out to greet her. It was beautiful to her. She wrapped her lips around the warmth and tasted the saltiness of the paler wet pink tip. She began moving back and forth and within minutes he moved his hips in unison as he groaned lightly. While she sucked him she began massaging his large balls, enjoying the warmth radiating from his skin into the cool night air. While pleasuring him with her mouth and lips she became lightheaded in sweet anticipation.

When he started to moan she got up and said, "Now, fuck me, lover." She was in no need of foreplay; she just wanted fucking.

"Here?" he asked.

"Yes, here," she said.

Without hesitation, she dropped her dress and stood before him in nothing but her panties, stockings, and heels. Her bared nipples hardened, reacting to the cool air.

Steve hurriedly began removing his clothes and soon stood before her naked. He took her by pushing her back onto one of the deck chairs. He grabbed her red silk panties and roughly pulled them down her legs and tossed them aside.

He began sucking on her pale breasts as he spread her legs apart. Her erect nipples were hard and excited as his lips pulled on them, teasing each with his teeth. His hands boldly explored her body, stroking and toying with her soft skin. She spread her legs further, wanting him to explore her womanhood with his strong fingers. As he did, her body shuddered with delight; it had been years since someone paid such lavish attention to her flesh.

She was ready to receive him. She reclined back as he climbed on top of her. She felt his warmth, that beautiful sensation of being skin-to-skin with another being. He looked her in the eyes as he entered her and her wetness eagerly greeted him. No condom, no safe sex, just the passion and wetness of two beings finding each other receptive to their love. She wrapped her arms around his powerful back and pushed him closer to her. Her legs were raised in the air, showing her willing surrender to her lover.

Her breathing became halting and labored with each stroke. He pumped and she received, then she would push back at him. For several minutes the two writhed back and forth, their small cries of passion urging the other lover on.

"Harder, fuck me, Steve," she cried. Her small grunts and moans filled the air.

He gave her several strong pushes of his hips and she cried out. He felt like he was even deeper into her.

"Don't stop, please, more!" she yelled as she grabbed his buttocks and pushed him deeper into her pleasure.

His breathing was faster and heavier with his exertions as he quickened his pace. He couldn't hold back anymore and exploded deep inside her, filling her moistness with his own. Charlie heard his groan and made sure to continue to milk his penis and then felt her own orgasm rise within her. Even after he was done Steve continued to pump her, as if to prolong their shared pleasure. For several minutes he enjoyed her soft whimpers of delight until he finally wilted.

In the distance a glowering entity watched the amorous lovers. Bitter and full of hate, he watched the twosome, one dark, one light, couple together and rhythmically rise and fall, their hushed cries filling the air. Neither capable of love nor sex, his solitary anger grew in the darkness.

"I told you, Ahmed, your kind has neither loyalty nor shame. They are basically animals," Pessimus said.

When Ahmed could take no more, the sound of an electric motor whirred and transported him away.

The amorous couple lay together for a few minutes on the chair holding one another. Charlie loved the contrast of Steve's dark skin against her pale white skin in the dim light of the evening sky. Steve kissed her on the lips and toyed with her erect nipples.

He noticed the scent of their sex in the air. Charlie's smell of arousal was somehow different from his past girlfriends. Perhaps a little stronger but still sweet, an erection-producing event on its own.

Charlie felt no remorse and no shame. She knew what she wanted from life; she wanted the passion that had been missing for so long. Steve was a stranger, yet she trusted him more than her own husband. She debated staying the night with him, but she did not want to appear needy. Instead, she got dressed and kissed him goodnight to retire to her room.

"Can I stay with you tonight?" Steve asked.

Charlie shook her head and said, "I need a little time alone to sort through this. I've never done anything like this before. I'm beyond feeling conflicted. I hope you understand." She kissed him lightly on the lips and walked away.

She turned back to him and said, "Thank you, lover."

Steve gave a heavy sigh but left her on her way.

She retired to her cabin to confront her mixed feelings about her infidelity. Anger that Bradley had pushed her to the arms of another man, sadness that her marriage was over, and joy at the sexual rush she felt with a man who genuinely cared about her. But there was something else: the realization that her marriage had died long before her infidelity. She wasn't sure if she was finding comfort in that rationalization.

As she undressed in the bathroom she surveyed her body in the mirror. Her nipples were erect and as she took her panties off, her dark red pubic hair was still damp from their shared love's nectar and her wet, puffy lips could be seen. Her engorged clitoris was visible and she touched herself. So wet, it felt so good, and she started rubbing herself thinking about Steve's dark cock. The skin on her chest was red and flushed. She inserted two fingers deep into her wetness and slowly continued in a leisurely rhythm. Within a couple of minutes she felt herself starting to orgasm. She thrust more rapidly while watching herself in the mirror as she climaxed.

When Charlie caught her breath she just stared at her reflection, not recognizing the wanton woman in the mirror. Her normally porcelain white skin by her pussy was now flushed, moist, and reddened as if in a constant state of arousal.

Who was this lustful stranger that seemed so insistent about taking over her life? As a young girl she remembered an attractive woman who lived next door. She was a brazen blond who wore her sensuality like a suit of armor. Charlie would stare and watch her from the bedroom windows whenever she had the chance. In her repressed household this stranger became the embodiment of sensuality to the pubescent girl, and now the stranger was back visiting the woman. Part of her wanted to refuse this stranger, and yet another wanted to embrace this newfound sexuality. She realized that sensuality, once found, could no longer be easily ignored, especially given future temptation. Surprisingly, rather than troubling her, the thought actually delighted her, teasing her with the possibilities of even more forbidden pleasures to come in the days ahead. Reconciled to her fate, she showered and went to bed alone. Contented, and without Bradley, she fell into a dreamless sleep.

Day 7 – Girl Talk

The following morning she went topside and, seeing Rachel, joined her to take in some artificial sun. Rachel rubbed lotion all over her skin, making Charlie feel horny. Charlie began doing the same but she decided to do something she would never have done before: She asked Rachel to rub the lotion onto her back. Rachel obliged her and she marveled once again at the touch of another person.

They began to have their drinks when Rachel asked, "I heard some gossip about a ginger who tried to hurt herself. Know anything about that, Red? You didn't do anything stupid, did you?"

"Rather not talk about that," Charlie said.

"Are you okay?"

"I'm in a better place, yes," Charlie said, but it wasn't a very warm response.

"Fine, let's change the topic, but if you need to talk I'm here. I saw you again with that young black man, the handsome one," Rachel said.

Charlie just stared at her.

"Are you two an item? Tell me you're fucking that delightful licorice stick," Rachel asked.

Clearly Rachel was feeling no pain and Charlie said, "Did I just hear you right? Don't tell me that you just called Steve a licorice stick?"

Rachel laughed. "Oh, the stick has a name?"

"Steve is a good friend and the man is a scientist, by the way. And before you spread any more rumors, he is about my age," she said with a blush.

Time to change the topic. Charlie asked, "You know that our tall Mormon friends are aliens, right?"

"I found out shortly after I spoke to you that first day," Rachel said. "Damnedest thing. You could have knocked me over with a feather."

"Yeah, damnedest. Does everyone aboard the ship know now the truth?"

"Are you kidding? For the first couple of days, that's all anyone talked about, but that buzz soon changed."

"And nobody is worried?"

"Frankly no. I guess que será, será. That is kind of strange, don't you think?"

"Duh, of course it's strange. Speaking of strange, I saw them by the pool; a whole group of them were having sex last night. It was most the erotic thing I have ever seen, or should I say felt."

"Really? Group sex among our alien friends?" Rachel asked.

"Yes, the air was so charged. I mean, it made me so horny," Charlie said. It felt weird; she'd never talked about sex so openly before with another person, not even her husband.

"I bet it was. After all, they are excellent lovers."

"How would you know?" Charlie asked.

"Some of the passengers have had sex with them already. That became the new buzz among the passengers, by the way."

"What? Really? With the Epicoids? How could they? I mean, they are so freaky-looking," Charlie protested, yet she felt a deliciousness at the thought of having that large penis enter her.

"Don't knock it, honey, until you try it," Rachel said. Her large beaming smile told of pleasures already shared.

"What? Wait, you didn't?" Charlie asked with a laugh.

Rachel was practically radiant when she said, "I didn't get this blue tan by staying home with my magic wand, honey. I have been dying to tell someone."

"Blue tan?"

"You haven't noticed the blue cast to some of the passengers' skin?"

Rachel's skin did appear a little blue but it wasn't anything extreme. "No, I didn't notice. Really, you had sex with one of them? How, or should I ask, why?"

"The alien named Freyr came to my room when I was showering. Hank shook hands with the alien and let him in. I heard Freyr in the room talking to Hank and I greeted them dressed only in a bathrobe. Freyr stared at me, gently touched my hand and then it hit me—this wild, crazy feeling of lust. I mean, I've been on autopilot for years, and then this horniness just took hold of my body. My girl was so wet you would have thought I was a thirteen-year-old on my first date with a boy in the backseat of a car. I just had to drop the robe. So there I stood, totally naked before Freyr and Hank, wanting someone, anyone, to fuck me."

"What about your husband?"

"Oh, poor Hank hasn't seen his dick in five years and neither have I. He was just glad somebody was servicing me. And service me my little alien friend did. Freyr took that red uniform off and then had his way with me. That organ was spectacular, reaching spots I didn't even know existed. They are very perceptive in sensing what you like and don't like. There were many things I thought I didn't like before that it performed on me that I found just amazing. I can't begin to tell you how many orgasms I had."

"And Hank?"

"Shit, he watched on while playing with his tiny pecker. It actually got hard for the first time in five years as he watched us. I never saw him so happy as he was busily stroking himself. You know what it's like for a man when they can't get hard?"

Charlie shook her head.

"Don't look at me that way," Rachel said as she lit and puffed on a cigarette. The pair was quiet for a moment.

"Was it like a cock?" she asked.

"Sort of. It's way beyond that, though, with the shapeshifting. I mean, he had his way with every orifice on my body. And it's huge! Orgasm doesn't begin to describe the sex with them. Even anal is sublime."

"Sex with the aliens? That's just crazy."

"Perhaps. Some call it 'Satan's penis' but I call it heavenly. I'm shocked you haven't been fucked yet since you're so gorgeous. It's not like your hubby is around doting on you. You must have done it with that black stud, right? I mean, I would do him in a minute."

"Jeez, you won't let it go, will you? And the black stud has a name. It's Steve." Charlie felt a wetness beginning between her legs, thinking about sex with Steve. And then she wondered about Jawara.

"So, is he a stud?" Rachel said. "Be honest—did you?"

Charlie was busting. She couldn't keep her affair to herself; she had to tell someone.

"Yes, and he was fantastic," Charlie said, only she didn't know how much of that was because of Steve or a hangover from the alien's orgy. "I never had such orgasms."

Rachel smiled at her and said, "So he gets to keep his man card?"

"Hell yes," Charlie said, almost beaming.

"Have you ever cheated before?" Rachel asked.

"No, I'm really having mixed emotions about the affair. You?"

"Me neither. I've been on the shelf for years because of Hank. I guess this cruise was my coming-out party. To think, with all things, a randy alien."

The pair grew quiet when a young couple stopped walking and starting kissing in front of them. They were an attractive white couple, both in their mid-twenties, beautiful physical specimens. Their mouths were locked in a serious kiss and the man's erection poked through his trunks. The young blond went to her knees and began pulling down his trunks.

Rachel shook her head at the pair and yelled, "Hey, take that shit to the Sin Decks. There are kids playing around here."

The young blond giggled, helped pull her boyfriend's trunks up, and they blithely walked away.

"I may be a slut but I'm a respectful slut," Rachel said to Charlie.

"Sin Decks?"

"Yeah, towards the back of the boat—you know, where the casino and all the bars are located," Rachel said. "It's a regular Sodom and Gomorrah back there. Thank goodness the passengers are at least policing themselves. Not like there is a crew to manage anyone."

"Yeah, the crew is missing in action," Charlie nodded.

"Is this really adultery? I mean, sex with an alien? I'm pretty sure the Bible talks only about sleeping with a man or woman. I mean, is it a sin?" Rachel asked.

"Is it a sin? Only if the sex was good," Charlie said.

Quiet for a moment and then Rachel said, "I'm going straight to hell, right?"

"Oh yeah. Which is fine—I'll need the company, because I know for a fact that what I did last night was a sin!" Charlie said with a bemused smile on her face.

Rachel toasted Charlie with her drink. "See you on the other side, my friend!"

Later in the day Charlie spied on the other passengers and noticed many of them did have a blue tinge to their skin, including some of the men. She'd had enough of their sexual antics and went back to her cabin. She was showering when she heard the insistent banging on her cabin door. Had Bradley locked himself out? The pounding grew louder.

"Damn," she said as she grabbed a towel and wrapped it around her wet body.

She opened the door and yelled, "Bradley, you are such an ass."

It was a startled Jawara.

"I came by to make sure you had no more unwanted visitors," Jawara said. "Why are you wet? Were you having Unioeros?"

"No, I was taking a shower and you interrupted me. What's Unioeros?"

"It's sexual union and the subsequent oneness afterwards, in the spirit of the Quanteme."

"No sex. Are we done here?" a peevish Charlie asked.

"It's more than just sex. It is a deeply spiritual ritual among my people. I actually don't understand the ritual of showering by your kind."

"It's not a ritual. It's what we do to stay clean. You know, to remove the dirt and smelly bacteria from your skin."

"Symbiotic, right? Can I watch?" Jawara asked.

"What?" Charlie asked.

"Can I watch how you do it, how you shower?" Jawara repeated.

"Of course not. Next you'll be wanting to watch me tinkle."

"Why not? I have seen you naked before," Jawara said.

"And aren't you the lucky little alien? Now get the hell out of here," she said and she pushed zir towards the door with her hands. Strangely, the touch of zirs skin somehow excited her. She felt a familiar longing reaching deep within her pelvis.

As she watched zir she realized Jawara actually appeared disappointed. That was strange; the alien was somehow displaying human emotion.

"You are looking more human every day; in fact, much more so than the other Epicoids. Why?" she asked. She now wanted zir to stay.

"Unioeros, for a lack of a better description, also passes genetic information between my people and others. It's not unknown among different species of your own; it's called horizontal gene transfer."

"Is that why my friend Rachel has this blue tint to her skin?"

"There is some transformative change in the other direction. It's not permanent; that is not without continued Unioeros."

"Good to know. So that's why your people are having Unioeros with us—to acquire more of our human characteristics, so you can better interact with us?"

"I want Unioeros with your kind because I like you and it is pleasurable; there's no other motive. This transformation is just the nature of our kind."

"So union feels good with humans?"

"It just feels right," Jawara said.

"What about the Sentinels? Do you ever have Unioeros with them?"

Jawara made a face of disgust and began jumping around while yelling, "Ugh! Never, that's a horrible thought!"

"Settle down, big guy, what did I say?" she asked.

"They are the one in a thousand in our species that hate being a gateway species. It has always been a source of friction between our clans. They think we are committing apostasy to our kind when we *species-shift*. We find their appearance abhorrent and their thinking even more vile and anathema to our own values of oneness in the universe."

"Why do you stay in contact with them, then?"

"They are our warrior race and protected us during the dark years when a civil war threatened us with extinction. Those days are long gone, but our promise to have an alliance with them is not."

"A deal made with the devil, huh?" she asked.

"Back to your original question. When we originally observed your species we thought your teeth were just for feeding and they could be omitted; that's why we added nails later."

She grabbed Jarawa's hands; so tingly. She looked at his nails. They were long and uneven. "Your nails are a bit long. So how do you taste if you have no mouth?"

"We can taste you with our skin."

"Really?"

"Yes."

Curious creatures, but she didn't want him to leave. She said, "Let's do something with those nails of yours. You're not going to get many dates resembling a homeless alien."

"Dates?"

"Never mind," Charlie said and she retrieved a nail file. She grabbed zirs hand and felt a slight erotic twinge. Curious, the way touch worked with the Epicoids.

She began filing zirs nails but to her horror the nails crumbled under the pressure of the nail file. The skin underneath was exposed and she expected a torrent of blood to flow. But there was nothing—no blood or expression of pain from Jawara.

"Oh my god," Charlie said. "Did I hurt you?"

"No, you didn't. What's wrong?" Jawara asked.

"They should grind down evenly, not crumble like dust."

"What should I do?"

"Well, first of all, you're not going to tip me. I guess more Unioeros is in order," she said with a laugh.

"Should we start now?" Jawara asked.

"I was kidding. Jeez, you still don't understand humor or laughter, do you?"

"No. I do try to understand, but it's very strange."

"How so?"

"Like this," ze said and suddenly the pair was seated at a showing of a popular comedy movie. Like on any good cruise ship, entertainment was always available. Even though it was near midday, about fifty people were sitting and enjoying the movie.

"Jeez, Jawara, I've just got this towel."

"They can't see us," ze said. Ze grabbed two folding chairs and set them up at the end of the small theater facing the wall. "Now just sit and listen."

It was strange, Charlie thought. "I don't understand."

Jawara waved zirs hand and they couldn't hear the movie. With their back to the screen the two were reduced to listening to the peals of laughter that rose among the audience like waves.

"Hear that?" Jawara asked.

It was curious to hear laughter rise and fall independent of a cause. In the vacuum, human laughter was basically a very common animal call. In a moment they were back in her cabin. Clearly some human traits weren't universal.

"When we first observed you, we didn't know what to make of that behavior."

"How did you even know we were here on Earth?" Charlie asked.

"We felt an intelligence. I should say, our Council did."

"You felt us? How is that even possible?"

"No, not your species; the cetaceans in your oceans, of course," Jawara said.

"What?"

"Just kidding. Consider that there are over seven billion of you. Your quantum minds are so entangled with the cosmos that your species is almost impossible to miss."

"Okay, well, this has all been very illuminating, but I have to finish my shower."

"It would also be illuminating if I could watch you shower."

Charlie was about to say no but that prehensile thing, whatever it was, seemed like a pretty nice organ to explore. She was feeling so horny.

"I don't know, I guess you can watch."

The two walked into the bathroom and Charlie dropped her towel, put the water on, and stepped into the shower. She felt a delightful tingle at being so exposed in front of the alien.

"Can I join you?" ze asked.

"What? Really?"

The alien gave her an almost plaintive look and Charlie said, "Sure, why the hell not?"

Jawara undressed and got into the shower. Charlie started to soap zir up, starting with zirs shoulders. As she looked Jawara over, she noticed zirs body had changed since she first met ze. It was more muscular, more male-looking rather than resembling pure androgyny. Despite zirs recent changes the alien's body still appeared almost featureless.

As she rubbed the soap into zirs skin, Jawara began hopping up and down while unleashing an unholy scream. The howling caused Charlie to jump out of the shower as she yelled," Oh my god, oh my god, what's wrong?"

Jawara gave a strange chortle. "Nothing, I'm just having fun with you."

"You're a fricking prankster? Get the hell out of my shower," she yelled.

"Did I do something wrong? I thought you like humor."

"I like your humor as much as I like that damn rat."

Jawara stood there trying to comprehend.

"What's wrong with you? Out now!" she yelled.

Jawara fell over zirself as the alien grabbed zirs suit and started to leave.

"Don't go," she said.

"Why?"

"It was my turn to mess with you. Yours was funnier, however," she said. "Is this considered foreplay?" Jawara asked.

"No, not in anybody's book."

"No Unioeros?" Jawara asked.

"No, we are not having sex."

"Too many nos."

"Now you are sounding like a man," Charlie said.

As they dried off, Jawara asked, "How do you manage to live so apart from one another?"

"Not sure; being alone is all I have ever known. It also forces you to communicate better. Besides, not sharing means sometimes you have an opportunity to hide. Try doing that being connected all the time. Here, help me dry my hair," she said as she handed the alien a towel.

She turned her back to zir and lifted her long red hair for Jawara to dry. Jawara hesitated and stepped back from her.

"Something wrong? Not that hair phobia again?"

"Your hair, it's very disturbing. For humans it's a sign of sensuality;

however, for us it resembles the diseased among us."

"The diseased among you? You mean the Sentinels, don't you?"

"I'm sorry, that's the way we are. It would be so much better if you were hairless."

"Including this?" she said, pointing to her somewhat hairy red bush.

"Especially there."

"We are what we are. Wait here, then, while I dry my own hair. I wouldn't want to upset your delicate alien sensibilities."

Unioeros

Bradley came into the cabin and appeared surprised to find the giant Jawara sitting in a chair.

"Where's Charlie?" he asked.

Jawara pointed to the bathroom and said, "We just had a nice shower together."

Charlie heard Bradley's voice and came out in her bra and panties. "Look what the cat dragged in."

"I'm not staying. I'm taking all of my clothes and leaving," he said as he stared at the alien.

"So go," Charlie said.

"You had a shower with this thing?" Bradley asked, sounding peeved.

Charlie walked over to Bradley and whispered, "It's a bit of a simpleton, if you know what I mean."

"I heard some gossip that a redhead tried to hurt herself. Know anything about that?" Bradley asked.

She put a sundress on and said, "No, you know how people love to talk. Do I look okay?"

"You look good. I've also been hearing that you have some new friends."

"Really?"

"Yeah, some shit that you're going black and have been hanging around this freak. Looks like this might be true."

"They're friends, and like I said, people like to talk," she said.

"Yeah, friends. So what are you now? An old lady for the aliens? And you know better than to hang out with some black thug," he said. "I don't need you embarrassing me."

"Please, Bradley, what do you care? You haven't touched me in months," Charlie said as she slipped her sandals on.

"You're still married to me, that's why; just remember that. You can at least act like a lady," he said with some intensity.

"But yet you get to sleep with the lollipop of your choice, huh? That doesn't embarrass me somehow?"

"We'll put this all to bed after the cruise. In the meantime, you've been warned to keep away from the Oreo-colored freaks."

Charlie felt vengeful.

"You know, it's funny, but in either case, you can always tell your lollipops you lost your wife to a superior race," Charlie said with a small smile.

Bradley walked over to Charlie with a strange smile on his face. He looked her in the eyes and slapped her across the face, sending her reeling. It was a hard hit and she tasted blood from a cut inside her cheek. It was so forceful and the hate on his face seared into her soul.

"Consider yourself touched, you fucking bitch. Next time you won't be so quick to mouth off, will you?" he said as he raised his hand again.

Charlie flinched but stood her ground as if to defy him.

"Just remember, keep away from the freak and that spade."

Jawara stood up and intervened by standing between the fractious pair. Ze towered over the shorter Bradley, who hesitated for a moment as he sized up the massive giant. His anger won out and he sucker-punched Jawara. The giant groaned and slowly collapsed to the floor with a heavy thud.

"You'll think twice about your next shower with someone's wife, freak," he said.

The large alien rolled onto zirs side in apparent agony while howling in pain. After a couple of minutes ze stopped moving.

"Shit, they're not so tough are they?" Bradley said.

Charlie went to Jawara's side and, after examining zirs lifeless body, said, "Shit, Jawara's not breathing, Bradley."

"They breathe? I didn't hit him that hard, come on," he said. "Sure he's dead?"

She searched for a pulse but there was none; the alien wasn't breathing or moving. She shook the large creature by the shoulders, saying, "Jawara, are you okay? Come out of it."

No signs of life.

"Jesus Christ, Bradley, you killed him," she said.

"No, this is wrong," Bradley said with a look of bewilderment. He pushed the listless body with his foot. There was no reaction and Bradley left the cabin with his clothes while saying, "Say nothing to them about me if you know what's good for you."

Charlie stayed at Jawara's side, hoping somehow to revive the alien. "Someone, please help!" she yelled but she was alone with the stricken alien.

"Come on, Jawara, snap out of it," she said as she shook zirs torso and she felt her eyes start to well up. "I can't believe this shit."

She surveyed the room trying to decide what to do next. Would CPR work?

"Is he gone?"

Jawara was talking without opening zirs eyes.

"What in the world? Yes, he's gone. Are you okay?"

The giant opened zirs eyes and gave her the most human of responses: a smile!

"I played dead, as you say."

"And you're damn good at it. Let me help you up." She helped the alien up by an arm. "Why didn't you defend yourself?"

"We're not violent and I believe he was stronger than me. I thought I could scare him," Jawara said as the alien stumbled a little. "He really hit me good." Jawara glanced at Charlie and noticed she was bleeding from the corner of her mouth.

"Are you okay?" the alien asked.

"I'm fine. I've had worse from that bastard."

"He really is a torch head."

"A torch head? Oh, you mean a hothead. No, Bradley is a total asshole, the complete package. Let's get you back to your cabin—or, come to think of it, just where do you stay?"

"Help me to Deck D, Hall E."

The giant wrapped an arm around her and they slowly walked to the elevator. After arriving at Deck D they made their way to Hall E. When they came to the end of the corridor Jawara told her to keep walking.

"There's a wall here my friend," she said as she banged her fist on the wall but Jawara kept walking. The two walked through the wall as if it was air.

"How did you do that?" Holy shit, this is your room?" she asked.

"No, my space in the universe. I call it Area 51."

"Area 51? That's funny," she said, but she became quiet upon looking at zirs room. Jawara's space was totally open without any boundaries, only a dark blue sky visible in the distance. A number of twinkling stars could be seen, but below their feet a large ringed planet could be observed. There was no floor. Instead, Charlie just moved through the space surrounded by floating translucent spheres of varying sizes. Jawara led the way and they both entered a massive translucent sphere with a large, thick gold sheet suspended in mid-air. Jawara climbed onto the levitating sheet and laid down with zirs large feet hanging off the edge.

"What are these spheres? More machines?"

"No, not the actual machines, but think of the orbises as an interface to our technology. They represent minor distortions in the space-time continuum—tiny black holes, if you will,—where we are able to manipulate matter and time."

"Are you okay?" she asked.

"There is some pain. Can you check my stomach to see if there is a wound?"

"Sure. You know, Bradley just hit you with his fist, not a baseball bat. There should only be some bruising."

"Please check."

Charlie cautiously put her hand on the sheet, checking to see if it would support her weight. It didn't budge and she hopped up onto the sheet, making her way to zirs side.

"Is this your bed?" she asked as her hand ran along the silky cloth.

"We don't have need of a bed; I devised this for you. Please check."

"How do you take this suit off?" Charlie asked.

Jawara's finger ran along the material and a seam appeared, splitting the fabric. The alien pulled the material to the side and asked, "How does it look?"

The bluish-white, featureless skin sported a massive ugly red mark resembling a horrific bruise.

"You'll live. Can't you see this bruise?" Charlie asked.

"Not that well; your eyesight is much better than ours in this spectrum. Here, take this orbis and run it along what you called the bruise."

Run what? Charlie thought. A strange mirrored metal sphere materialized from the air. "Let the orbis touch the affected skin," Jawara said. As the device floated near her, she grabbed it and ran it along the alien's bruised skin. There was no humming, no temperature change, but a slight vibration to indicate it was actually doing something. Within a minute the bruising was gone.

Jawara appeared better. "Now run it along the side of your mouth."

Charlie ran the orbis along her cheek and within seconds the pain was gone. In fact, her entire body felt better, as if she'd had the most refreshing sleep.

"Wow, that device is amazing," she said. "Feeling better?"

Jawara nodded and asked, "You think I'm a simpleton?"

"No, of course not. I would have said anything to Bradley to protect you."

"Can I share something with you?"

"Is it something sexual? Not that Unisex or whatever you call it business, right?"

"No, it's a journey I would like to take with you."

"Sure, you mean we can leave this ship?"

"With me you can," the Epicoid said.

Charlie laid back with Jawara on the flying sheet and gazed into the sky. There was nothing around them, just a fresh breeze and a starlit sky. Only she didn't recognize the constellations; clearly there was no Big Dipper. Were they in the Southern Hemisphere, and if so, where was the Southern Cross?

Jawara sat up and began undressing.

"Hello, what the heck are you doing, Jawara?" Charlie asked.

"It's uncomfortable with this suit on. Besides, this journey is better naked; nothing to hide behind," Jawara said, staring at the celestial sky. The Epicoid turned to her and said, "Trust me."

"Funny, I do trust you, but you really are quite the player."

"No, we're just very good about sharing our intentions and emotions. I think you can sense I mean you no harm," Jawara replied while touching her.

The touch was enough and Charlie didn't need more prompting. She kicked off her shoes and began undressing. She undid the front of her dress and shimmied it down beyond her wide hips. For some reason, she felt aroused taking her clothes off for the alien. **Soon the bra was gone and Charlie made a point of stroking her bare pale breasts and subtlety tweaking her large pink nipples.** Jawara watched her exhibitionism and seemed to taking interest in her pale white body. Without hesitation or remorse she dropped her panties. Knowing Jawara was watching, she allowed her fingers to dance along the red hair of her pussy.

"So you never told me what you think of my body," she said.

"Interesting."

"I guess that's good," she said but she didn't see any other changes in the alien's body. "I showed you mine, where's yours?"

Charlie still couldn't see anything but the alien's bare skin. It was almost featureless. No nipples, no breasts, no hair, nothing. As she stared down at zirs pelvis there was that hairless slit she saw at the pool, a crevice resembling a puffy pudenda. Expecting some great revelation, Jawara's nudity was very anticlimactic to Charlie.

"In time," Jawara said.

The two naked creatures laid back on the gold sheet as the alien grabbed her small hand. For a moment she thought Jawara was going to place it on zirs pelvis but instead the alien just held it. Hand in hand, they stared up at the changing celestial sky.

"Jeez, this is beyond cool. Where are we? Are we still in our galaxy?"

Jawara nodded and said, "Just enjoy what no other human has ever seen before."

"Is this a show or am I really traveling through space?" she asked.

Jawara shook zirs head. "No show, but to be exact, more a series of space-time jumps. It's the real thing."

She was actually traveling through space? The enormity of the moment overwhelmed her as a wave of emotion rose within. She became very quiet.

The sky began to move and stars and planets passed by them at a dizzying pace. Great clouds of dust swirled above them, creating gas giants, and they watched as stars lit up, coming to life, while others were in the throes of an agonizing death. As they approached a star, the space lit up in a blinding array of colors and energies. They visited planets, traveling to the surface and observing all manner of strange creatures rising from the dirt with the energy of their nearby star.

"To think when I was younger I used to say outer space was so fucking boring, but oh my God, this is incredible! Aren't you blown away seeing this?" she asked.

"Always."

They laid there for what seemed an eternity, watching the visions moving faster than light, moving beyond time. Mysteries appeared and revealed themselves and then disappeared over the horizon.

The journey finally came to an end and only one mystery in the universe remained for her. Jawara still held her hand but ze began guiding Charlie's small hand along zirs torso.

What is he doing with my hand? she wondered and the alien put it on top of zirs lower fold. The skin was soft, super smooth to the touch. She rubbed it lightly, enjoying the touch of the Epicoid's skin against her fingertips. The skin turned warm and as Charlie watched she saw the skin blushing, turning darker blue in color. She felt it tremble and swell. From between the folds it arose and emerged, a dark reddish, penis-like organ. Initially it protruded only slightly from the fold, vaguely resembling a large clitoris, but its engorgement continued unabated. Charlie jerked her hand away, shocked by its emergence while watching in fascination and trepidation as it continued to grow from the slit.

At first it was just six inches long, then a foot, and fully erect it was a two-foot-long red penis-like shaft extending from zirs body. She had never seen anything like it, but she did recall seeing a similar show once when she went riding at a stable. Christ, Jawara was bigger than a freaking horse! Charlie retreated from Jawara to the edge of the sheet that was still floating free in space.

Shit, this was too much. She should have insisted on sexting before having a sexual encounter with an alien!

It was red and pulsating. Stranger and unlike a human penis, the tip was narrower with a large slit at the end and the final twelve inches appeared almost prehensile, as the tip moved and changed direction from the erect rod. Sometimes it moved almost like a monkey tail. She was both attracted and repulsed at the sight and she sat there frozen by the tapered twitching spectacle.

Jawara asked, "Is my appearance upsetting you?"

She nodded. "What the hell is that thing? It's like a giant penis."

"We call our sex organ a culmus and we believe its morphology more closely resembles an enlarged clitoris. Strange, your reaction; the female of your species has been selecting males for their larger penis size since the dawn of your kind. Why doesn't this please you?"

"You know what they say about too much of a good thing."

"What do they say?" Jawara asked.

"Too much! Interesting, but way too much."

"Strange. You trust me to travel the galaxy but your personal space you jealously defend. Such contradictory emotions. It's a wonder your species has sex at all."

"Every day you sound more like a man."

"You are a curious species. I will grant you that."

"Sorry, that type of trust you have to earn."

"Let me earn it. Lie on your side and close your eyes."

"Really? With that tentacle?" she asked, almost fearful.

"Do you trust me?" Jawara asked as ze touched her arm.

She did and Charlie moved onto her side while closing her eyes. She felt the warm tip move along her buttocks. As it moved, it became softer and wetter. A warm, pleasant mist played on her skin and seemed to envelop the two beings.

It lightly traced her cheeks and then moved to her vaginal lips. The tip opened up, revealing a moist flap that covered her entire vagina. It felt warm and slightly electric as it began rubbing against her excited pussy. She felt almost as if a large tongue was both probing and tasting her at the same time. She'd never experienced a sensation quite like that before.

So wet!

Very intense, and the pleasure radiated from her pussy into her limbs.

The organ explored her body, creating the same delicious vibrations she'd felt when spying on the Epicoids at the pool. The vibration reached deep into her pelvis and she felt herself starting to contract and writhe. She suddenly felt very aroused, the wave building and growing within her. She let out a small yell as she orgasmed. She laid there with her legs apart, still twitching while watching the tip change back to its original penile shape.

The tip began entering her and she cried, "No, too much."

The tip didn't care; it penetrated her lovingly and slowly while filling her completely. What was forbidden was now allowed, almost desired. She became aroused again, noticing that she'd never recovered from an orgasm that quickly before. And then Jawara stopped.

"Wow, I just met a woman's best friend, a prehensile penis," Charlie said as she rested.

"We call this Unioeros, in the spirit of the Quanteme. It's a very powerful bond among my people. Are you okay with this?"

"Guess I'm exploring another side of my sexuality. I won't stop you."

"Are you sure? Because it will become more intense."

"In for a penny, in for a pound."

Jawara just stared at her, not understanding what she had said.

"Dammit, just go ahead, I just have to know what it's like to be fucked by that thing," Charlie said.

She watched, both repulsed but fascinated by the twitching organ. As if sensing her trepidation the organ slowly penetrated her vagina and filled her completely. With the strange but somewhat familiar sensations, Charlie was once again a teenage girl filled with the fear and excitement of a strange organ entering her body and pleasuring her. Then it left her vagina and moved towards her mouth, dancing before her and then darting between her lips.

She could taste herself on the peculiar alien's penile skin. The alien had no taste other than a delightful, almost electrical excitation when she ran her lips or tongue along the skin of the culmus.

The culmus returned to her vagina, gently inserting itself. Deep within, the stalk pressed against her G-spot while simultaneously rubbing against her clitoris. She felt almost lightheaded as another orgasm began to build up. The hum grew and so did the feeling deep in her pelvis. She moved to her back, spreading her legs even wider, wanting more of her body to be explored.

Instead, Jawara laid backwards and lifted the small woman on top of him. She writhed against the organ and began to shudder as she rode Jawara. The gentle blue mist that had played about the pair was now a roaring river that she rode with amazing ease.

She experienced her first body-gasm: her entire body, every tissue and every cell, was somehow being pleasured. Narrower and smaller, Charlie felt her orgasm building within her. This was Unioeros: the epiphany of one. Charlie wrapped her legs around zirs lower torso and kept stroking the massive shaft with her pussy. Her arms embraced zirs upper body and she rode up and down the massive shaft. She felt her vagina flood with a strange liquid, unsure if it was hers or from her alien lover. With her orgasm her surrender was complete and her body writhed for several minutes after her climax.

When they were done she glanced down and observed a pool of wetness that matted her red pubic hair. She was completely relaxed while Jawara watched over her.

"I'm not sure what on Earth this thing is but I do like it," she said as her hand stroked zirs silky stalk. "I guess it's a little late for me to be worrying about whether or not you can get me pregnant, right?"

"That makes no sense, and besides, our genetics are very different from yours. No strange alien diseases, either, to worry about. This is very safe sex, as you say."

"So how do you reproduce?"

"Reproduction? What does Unioeros have to do with reproduction? It's an expression of love unto itself, critical for bonding among my kind."

"Regarding that bonding, I observed you and a group of Epicoids having sex the other day. I see you try to keep that activity on the sly."

"The sly?"

"You know, keeping your gathering a secret, that is."

"Yes, sometimes we like to have Unioeros as a collective. We call that the Sacour Feast. A group consensus determines if and when we have such a feast. We do these at night so as not to upset the more sensitive among your kind. Do you approve of our feast?"

"It was very erotic, but to be honest with you it seemed more like your basic orgy."

"No, no, it's much more spiritual than your orgies, but your orgies do look promising. Are you having one soon?"

"I'll check my calendar for you. The thing I don't understand is that you said your genetics are very different from us and yet you appear very much like us. Well, at least a reasonable facsimile to us."

"I mentioned this before, but my kind was created and designed for this mission alone. Being a gateway species, we were created to be ambassadors to your people during the Greeting. Our bodies were designed specifically to meet the parameters of your species and the physical environment of your planet."

"Just what is a gateway species?"

"A variant from our own kind existing for the purposes of the Greeting with your people. We were genetically transformed over many generations and educated about your culture to the best of our capability. Consequently, we know little of our own culture and don't even resemble those of our kind, to be quite frank with you," ze said.

"What do the others of your kind look like?"

"You mean the non-humanoid Epicoids? Hmmm, I have no idea actually."

"Really? Do you miss your home and being with your kind?"

"Sometimes I miss home but I am very much in touch with my kind."

"What about your parents?" she asked.

"We don't have parents."

"You lost me. You mean you don't even know your own parents?"

"We don't have parents and were all raised and educated in a collective. Our creation and design was based on the best science and technology we had at the time regarding your species. Everything about us was based on the programming we found on your radio spectrum."

"Wow, that's some sacrifice," she said.

"We made many sacrifices, but it was a great honor to be part of the Greeting."

"With all that sacrificing, how come you didn't adjust your sex organs, you know, to be more in proportion with our own?"

"There are some sacrifices for science even an Epicoid won't make."

"Got it. Too small, right? But you must have known we had hair?" Charlie asked.

"Your hair, as I explained before, is a bit problematic for us."

"Seems like a sad existence, being separated from your planet and your kind."

"Do I appear sad? We are always connected, even when we are apart."

No, ze didn't seem sad, and Charlotte wondered if the Epicoids were on to something.

Back in her cabin Charlie scanned her birth control pills in the bathroom. It was strange; what if Jawara was wrong? Did she have to worry about spawning an alien child after Unioeros? What if she caught something, like a nasty alien rash? Too late for regrets, her concerns seemed a bit silly considering her captivity aboard the cruise ship. She heard someone talking in the room give her a start but there was no one present.

She turned towards her bed and a strange towel design sticking a foot and a half straight into the air was prominently displayed. She touched the design just as Bradley came into the cabin.

"What are you doing here?" she asked. The rise in her voice betrayed her fear. She had to get her emotions under control.

Bradley avoided her and went to the closet.

"I forgot my shoes. Sorry about getting rough with you earlier, but you know better than to mock me like that. You know I got some anger issues, so why yank my chain like that?"

"So somehow your issues continue to be my fault?"

"I'm not here to fight. So how's the freak?"

"Still dead," Charlie said in a monotone. *Keep your shit together and just get him out of the cabin,* she thought to herself.

"Sorry to hear that," he said, as if he was referring to the death of someone's pet. "Anybody come around searching for him?"

"Not to my knowledge."

Bradley looked about and said, "So where the hell is his body? Did you get Kanye to move him?"

"I don't know."

"Great, that means the freak is still alive."

"Don't worry, I'll cover for you. Like I did when John and his thugs went hunting for you on every payday."

"John? You mean that wop Giovanni? Yeah, sure you had my back. I saw him staring at your tits. Admit it, you fucked that dago prick, didn't you?"

"Always the idiot, I covered for you just like I'm doing now, but this time I need you to do something for me."

"Yeah, what?"

"Leave your key behind," Charlie said firmly. She was now resolute in wanting him out of her life altogether. She stared directly into his blue eyes but they remained cold and distant.

Bradley gathered his shoes together and tossed them into a bag. He threw the key on the bed and noticed the towel art while commenting, "What's this shit?"

"A culmus."

"What's that?"

"Your basic alien cock," Charlie said.

"Yeah sure, whatever, like I give a shit. Remember, just keep your fucking mouth shut if you know what's good for you," Bradley said and he left the cabin with his belongings. The door slammed behind him.

With his departure Charlie could breathe once again.

Day 8 – Shark and Pearl Fishing

Steve heard from Pastor Jones that a fishing contest was being held during the morning aboard the ship—not exactly a normal activity on a cruise ship. Steve couldn't help but wonder what species they would be hooking. He went to find Charlie and knocked at her door.

"Charlie, you've got to see this. They're going to have a fishing contest aboard the ship," Steve said aloud.

She was naked and about to go into the shower. She opened the cabin door, taking care to hide behind it, and said, "That's nice. You go ahead and tell me all about it. I've got to take a shower. I'll join you later for lunch, okay?"

"I guess," he said disappointedly and headed towards what was called the fishing balcony.

Steve had never seen anything like it aboard a cruise ship, but there was a massive opening in the stern some twenty feet above the water line and just above the quiescent propulsion units. The design of the ship made no sense. With one violent storm the rough seas would overtake the ship and it would be taking on tons of water, possibly sinking. Clearly the aliens were not great seamen.

As he surveyed the space he saw five chairs with dozens of men and women already hanging out the back with large sport fishing rods. They were enthusiastically casting away, fishing for god knew what. One of the men was adding chum to the water.

Pastor Jones was there with his wife.

"Going to try your luck?" Steve asked.

"Sounds like fun, to be honest with you. Better yet, it doesn't cost anything and maybe we can have fresh fish for dinner," he said. "I hear they'll cook up anything you catch."

"You know, this makes no sense. Nobody fishes off a cruise ship," Steve said.

Another man heard Steve and said, "Not true; I was on an Alaskan cruise and we did some fishing off the stern."

"First time for everything, right? Why don't you join us, Steve?" Pastor Jones asked.

"No thanks, I think I'll just sit back and watch the spectacle."

Not much happened for the first ten minutes and Steve was getting bored. One person caught a small snorkel fish that measured a couple of feet, to great cheers from the crowd. Steve studied the fish and it appeared real enough.

Then one of the big reels had a bite, creating even more excitement and buzz among the crowd. The fish ran with the hook and then the man began reeling it in. Steve just wished Charlie was there to watch the excitement with him.

Charlie was relieved Steve had taken no for an answer. The way she felt, the last thing she wanted to do was to watch people fishing. Beyond trivial! After her shower she was in bed thinking about her Unioeros with Jawara. She was naked and touching her body. She was still tingling from her orgasm with the alien. It was so complete and satisfying, yet she wanted more. After years of being on the shelf, her body yearned for a regular lover.

She went to her dresser and in her underwear drawer she found a vibrating dildo. That was strange because she'd never regularly used one before. Her sexual repression up until this cruise had been very complete, particularly regarding self-gratification. She turned the dildo on and listened to the vibration, but she was really yearning to be touched again.

As she began to search for some tissues, she saw something that caught her eye. On the night table was a flyer for a serene massage at the Tranquility Lounge. That sounded like a great idea, but she wondered if they were booked already. She called the number and learned they had an opening at that very moment.

Charlie arrived at the massage area and was greeted by a small, plain, almost handsome-looking Hispanic woman with light brown skin and a very lean figure. She noticed that her skin had a bluish hue to it.

"I booked a massage for eleven?" she said.

The woman pointed to Room B.

Charlie asked, "Do I have a choice between a man or woman masseuse?"

"He or she, it doesn't matter," she said wearily.

"What?" Charlie asked.

The woman smirked at Charlie and said, "You'll see. Just sit in the room and wait for the masseuse."

Charlie did as she was told and sat patiently in Room B. It had a large picture window and a table. While she was scrutinizing the room a tall Epicoid with a female semblance came in, giving her a start. Ze towered above Charlie. It was the same Epicoid that had given Steve the look-over.

The Epicoid asked in a flat voice, "What's your name?"

"Charlotte, and yours?"

"Janet."

Not every exotic. You come from light years away and you chose Janet as your name? Charlie thought to herself.

Still, Janet the Epicoid had a tall womanly shape and moved gracefully as compared to Jawara's lumbering gait. The alien's skin was beyond pale and there wasn't a single hair to be found on zirs body. Zirs face was very attractive, albeit in a neutral manner. Charlie debated whether or not she wanted a massage from an Epicoid female. It was one thing to kiss a girl, but a seemingly female Epicoid? Did Janet have the same large culmus as Jawara?

Of course ze did, right? That seemed a bit freaky, but she did enjoy Jawara's touch.

Charlie watched as Janet expertly set up the table with towels and put out for display a variety of oils. Ze nodded at her and said, "Please remove your clothes."

"All?"

"Yes, your panties too," ze said and turned away as ze handed Charlie a towel. "Wrap this clean towel around you and lie face-down on the table."

There was no place to change so she undressed in front of the Epicoid. She tied her red hair back and took her clothes off, placing them on the chair, and when she was totally naked, she wrapped the towel around her waist. The towel was small and would only wrap her bottom. Her boobs were exposed, and her nipples started to harden in the cool air. She lay on the table face-down with her boobs flattened but covered.

The Epicoid went over to a stereo and played some quiet new-age music. While watching her masseuse, Charlie had to suppress a giggle. Did aliens also listen to the same crappy mood music? Could explain the dreadful Muzak.

"This scent?" the alien said as ze held a bottle of oil under Charlie's nose. She took a sniff and noticed a very light coconut fragrance; she nodded her approval.

"Do you want a bite massage?" Janet asked.

"What?"

"Do you want me to bite your skin like your celebrities enjoy? I will be gentle," the Epicoid asked.

"Oh, I think I'll pass."

Charlie shook her head at the bizarre offer and blamed the Internet. Ze began rubbing her legs and the small redhead felt that same electric touch she received from Jawara. Very pleasant, but not quite as intense. The masseuse worked her calves, then moved to her feet. The Epicoid held Charlie's leg out and proceeded to rub her foot, and then ze stretched her toes. She was ticklish, and had to suppress a giggle or two. After she got accustomed to the touch and the kneading, Charlie sighed and relaxed to enjoy the sensation.

"Jawara is right, you are very tasty," Janet said in a monotone voice.

It appeared that Jawara was one to kiss and tell, and with that comment the vulnerable human instinctively clenched her legs tighter together. Ze didn't talk much after that comment other than the occasional instruction to Charlie to adjust her body. It was fairly quiet in the Tranquility Area, and she started to enjoy the massage. After doing both of Charlie's feet, ze returned to massaging her legs, zirs hands moving up to her thighs, kneading the flesh as ze moved along.

Then the Epicoid's hand darted under the towel and started to rub as ze explored Charlie's covered body. Fingertips made their way up her buttocks. Soon the hands were kneading her flesh, spreading her cheeks apart, and the small redhead began to feel uncomfortable. All she could think was, *What a pushy alien!*

Along the far wall was a mirror, and Charlie watched the ministrations of the masseuse. She could see the lower half of her bare buttocks and Janet's hands working her glutes. Jeez, her masseuse had some very long and strong fingers. She felt some strange sensations caused by another taking liberties with her body. Somewhat conflicted, she debated whether to tell Janet to stop or to just enjoy the massage. And then she felt the heat radiating over her pubic area that she'd enjoyed when watching the Epicoids mate.

As the masseuse grabbed her buttocks, she felt a quick tightening in her pelvis and realized she was becoming aroused. That wasn't good. Or was it? The feeling spread, and Charlie knew she was getting wet, which added to her consternation. Still, Janet's hands felt good, and there wasn't anything overtly sexual about the aggressive massage.

The Epicoid said, "Turn over."

She hesitated for a second, knowing her breasts would be exposed, but really, did she care if this Epicoid saw them? After all, Janet had just had her way with her ass. She obediently turned over and put her arms at her sides as the Epicoid readjusted the towel over her hips. Janet worked Charlie's shoulders, and it felt good. Ze grabbed some oil and dribbled a small amount on her chest. Zirs hands moved into the oil and began rubbing Charlie's chest, moving down to her breasts. She was now surprised as ze started to vigorously rub her bare breasts.

During the one massage Charlie had had a year ago, the woman masseuse had been careful to maintain her modesty and incessantly asked before touching her in certain areas to make sure she was comfortable. Frankly, the woman hadn't been close to being so provocative, and the whole massage was relatively chaste. In contrast, Janet was having zirs way with Charlie's body, and ze wasn't stopping to ask for permission. Ze rubbed and squeezed the human's breasts as zir fingers darted around her nipples. Charlie noticed that her nipples were bullet hard. Confused, she closed her eyes and decided to enjoy the sensations despite her reservations.

Janet poured some oil onto Charlie's stomach and began rubbing the oil into her skin. As ze rubbed, a hand made its way under the towel and in successive motions, slowly but assuredly, found her mound. Charlie felt her anxiety rise with the rubbing; she knew where the hand was heading. She tried to put her legs together to halt the advancing hand; however, ze wasn't having any of that as ze grabbed Charlie's legs and forced them flat, repositioning them and then pulling them slightly apart. Clearly, Janet wasn't going to take no for an answer. Zirs hands returned to massaging Charlie's stomach and sides as she waited for the inevitable plunge into her womanhood.

She waited, and then she waited some more, growing wetter with each passing second. Janet really knew how to drag out the suspense as zirs fingers danced about her pelvis and between her legs. And then nothing. Janet moved to the other end of the table and started rubbing Charlie's calves and legs while applying more oil. Ze bent her legs and massaged her feet again. This time zirs hands moved up Charlie's legs. Ze spread her legs apart, rubbing her inner thighs and then down and under her buttocks. The sure hands moved down from her buttocks to her inner thighs while lightly touching her lips. Charlie's breathing had become significantly heavier with the touch, and she hoped ze would begin a deeper massage. She waited. But nothing. Janet started to clean up.

"Is the massage over?" Charlie asked.

Janet nodded and said to her, "Yes, do you need anything else?"

Silence for a moment.

"Yes, a release, please!" she blurted out.

The Epicoid appeared confused.

Charlie's body screamed for release, and she had to act—even if it was with the androgynous masseuse.

"Orgasm, Unioeros, masturbation, whatever the hell you call it! I want it now!" Charlie threw the towel off her hips—it really wasn't covering much anyway—and grabbed the masseuse's hand. She placed it on her groin and began rubbing against the hand as she peered into the Epicoid's eyes. She studied Janet's face, but there was no reaction until ze saw her oily red pubic hair. It was an expression of pure revulsion. Charlie covered herself with the towel, leaving Janet's hand in place.

With the towel back in place. Janet's demeanor changed. Zirs fingers gently stroked Charlie's moist slit before a long finger assertively made its way into her tight vagina. Janet's other hand rubbed her mound and then moved to her swollen clit, which now extended above the fleshy hood. The Epicoid looked her in the eyes as she groaned with delight and spread her legs wide for zirs assured hands. Janet then inserted a second finger and moved in and upward into her moist tunnel. Charlie's legs proceeded to flex from the pleasure as the Epicoid picked up the pace, continuing to rub and stroke the small woman with zirs strong hands. And then it came—first that curious tingle, followed by a shockwave that seized her body.

Normally Charlie could tell if she was having a clitoral or vaginal orgasm, but this one just seemed to be erupting everywhere. The overwhelming pleasure forced her to close her thighs, as if she could somehow manage the orgasm. Only Janet was not stopping when ze forced the redhead's legs apart and continued the stroking. She surrendered and arched her back as she cried out a shrill, "Yes!" Her orgasm seemed to last forever and when she turned to the mirror, she could see ze was still gently rubbing her, albeit at a much slower and lighter pace.

Charlie examined her own face in the mirror; her eyes seemed heavy, almost glazed over, and she had a small, bemused smile. Her limbs were useless, limp actually, and exhausted from the orgasm. She was so wet, and it was then that she noticed a different, strange odor in the air. She could actually smell her sex mixed with the coconut scent. Fortunately, it wasn't an unpleasant smell. Janet left Charlie's side to clean up and wipe zirs hands. Charlie just lingered on the table, naked and with her legs spread apart, taking the moment in.

"Charlotte, time to go. Please grab a clean towel and take your shower," the alien said.

She nodded but she could barely move.

Steve watched as more people appeared to be joining the party. As he turned around he saw the Reverend Bannan with his flock approaching. Each of them appeared to be carrying a chum bucket. In unison they silently went to the rails and threw the contents overboard. When each of them was done, they headed back away from the other fishermen to rejoin the reverend.

Steve thought that was strange, but before he could reflect on their actions a heavy-set white man decked out in a Hawaiian shirt yelled, "Feels big! Strap me into a chair, boys."

As they struggled to strap the big man to the chair, more reels were getting hits and the deck was ablaze with activity. Soon the men, along with one woman, were working some sizable fish. One man got help with his catch and as the fish drew closer they could see a Mako shark breach the water. Thirty yards from the Mako another shark breached.

One of the men yelled, "Holy crap, they're literally jumping out of the water."

"You've got to be shitting me," Steve said. "Why are they breaching? This makes no sense."

As Steve watched, the size of the fish being hooked was even more troubling. He turned towards the reverend and his flock and saw strange bemused smiles on all of their faces as they were leaving the deck.

"Shit, cut the lines before someone gets hurt," he yelled.

Nobody paid attention to Steve's plea. One man reeled his catch in and hauled in a ten-foot shark that fell loudly on the deck. The fish floundered about, snapping and biting at the feet of the fishermen. People started to yell and scream. One man hooked the fish as another used a machete to hack at its head. Several men hauled in an even bigger catch; the shark was fifteen feet long as it dangled off the side of the ship. The large fisherman started yelling to have someone cut the line and help remove him from the chair.

"Cut that fucking line!" Steve yelled. Pastor Jones stared at him. "Sorry, pastor."

Another man cut the line but the large fish arched back and started jumping around the deck. The shark lunged towards the pastor and his wife. Before the thrashing shark could reach the couple Steve grabbed a large fillet knife and began violently stabbing the animal repeatedly in the head. Within minutes he was covered with blood, but the shark was lifeless.

"Holy shit," Pastor Jones said. "Nature does some strange things."

"No, not like this it doesn't. This shit isn't nature; this is a freak show. Our friends got it all wrong," Steve said as he looked about the deck for some Epicoid assistance.

From the back of the stern Steve scanned the ocean. As he watched he saw a dozen sharks breaching at any given time. The water appeared to be roiling with sharks, seemingly excited at the chum in the water.

"This is very wrong. Everybody off the deck, now!" Steve yelled.

Before Pastor Jones could say a word, a large great white shark, almost twenty feet in length, jumped from the water onto the balcony and began thrashing and snapping away at the retreating people. People screamed and went running for the exits. Some were cut by the slashing jaws of the beast. Steve clubbed the shark with a chair as it made its way after the people. He gave the beast a good hit before closing the door behind him.

Just as Charlie was about to stand up she heard a loud commotion in the hall.

"What's going on out there?" she asked.

The Epicoid gave her a blank expression. Charlie grabbed one of the white robes and headed out to the hallway. A number of people raced past her in a panic.

She saw Steve, his shirt covered in blood, and stopped him. "What the heck is going on?"

He didn't reply but instead stared at her in the robe, admiring her oily cleavage.

She tightened up her robe and replied, "Spa treatment."

Steve broke his trance and asked, "Where is Jawara? We need him desperately at the fishing balcony. There was a shark attack."

"What do you mean, a shark attack? Are you hurt?" The two of them stepped into the massage room to retreat from the frenzied passengers.

"A dozen sharks began attacking the fishing party. I'm fine, but there are a lot of people hurt," he said. Steve leered at Charlie, naked under the robe, and Janet's hands covered in oil and said, "Sorry, but did I interrupt something?"

Charlie just stared at Steve, noticing his dark arms were caked with drying blood and some stray drops were on his cheek. She said, "Does it matter now if you did?"

"Sorry, but take a look out your window if you don't believe me," Steve said.

Charlie walked to the window. She spotted dozens of sharks jumping and breaching alongside the ship.

Jawara entered the room.

"Jeez, let's invite the rest of the ship into the massage room while we're at it," she said. She pointed to Jawara and said, "Come over and take a look out the window. Tell me what you see."

Jawara slowly made zirs way to the window and said, "Looks like we provided a good selection of game for your fish hunt."

Charlie turned to Jawara. "First, it's called fishing, and it appears to me your intern screwed up on your species research again! The sharks are practically in a feeding frenzy."

"We thought you would enjoy a vigorous hunt. But why are they jumping from the water like that?" Jawara asked.

Steve shook his head and said, "It's called breaching and it started after the reverend and his flock of assholes added their special chum to the water. That's not normal behavior by most sharks, and I'm wondering what was in the chum."

Jawara began walking to the door and said, "Clearly we need to make some adjustments."

Charlie threw up her hands and said, "You know, Jawara, you always seem to be the surprise guy when something goes down aboard this ship. Just what exactly is your job title?"

"I am an Interspecies Event Facilitator."

Charlie said, "So basically you are Julie…. Julie from the *Love Boat*?"

Steve rolled his eyes at her comment. She glared at him and said, "So sue me, it's a guilty pleasure."

Steve began sniffing the air, noticing that intermingled with the coconut fragrance was a familiar smell of sex. He quickly recognized the second aroma as Charlie's aroused scent. He just stared at her, feeling himself twitch.

"I really did enjoy their lighthearted romantic comedy adventures aboard the *Princess*," Jawara said. "Did you have a good massage?"

Charlie sat down, the glow of her massage and orgasm long gone. She saw Steve distracted, talking with another passenger, and said, "As close as I will get to a happy ending on this damn cruise."

A Very Bad Year

Charlie was exasperated at having her peaceful massage afterglow interrupted by the antics of Jawara and Steve. She returned to her cabin, showered, and changed into her bathing suit. Seeking solitude, she went to sit in a lounge chair in the Tranquility Area to get some sun and to listen to music. Within minutes she fell asleep with her sunglasses and hat on.

A noise nearby woke her. A couple had joined her just a few chairs down. That irked her to no end; she wanted to be alone and didn't necessarily want company.

"Come on, babe," the young man said to the older woman.

"What? Are you crazy? There's somebody right there," she replied.

"She hasn't moved; probably drunk or stoned like everyone else on this party boat."

In unison the pair turned Charlie's way. She pretended to be still sleeping.

"See, I told you she was out cold," the man said.

Her sunglasses were extremely dark and from the corner of her eye she watched the couple. The woman was a beautiful mature blond attired in a black bathing suit with a matching wide-brimmed hat. She was extremely pretty, maybe some would consider her even beautiful, with a very nice shape. Funny, she bore more than a passing resemblance to the woman next door Charlie used to spy on as a young girl. A young, dark-haired man was paying lavish attention to her, holding her and kissing her. Damn, he was handsome and cut.

They started to kiss and Charlie could almost sense their sexual tension. That was when the woman's hand clutched the back of her lover's neck while displaying a sizable diamond wedding ring. Charlie doubted the young man was her husband; there was far too much passion for a married couple.

The young man boldly put his hand between the woman's legs and she jumped with his touch. The man's strong fingers searched under her bathing suit and Charlie saw the woman twitch and spread her legs wider to assist with his probing. As his fingers grew bolder the woman began to passionately kiss him in return.

The man withdrew his hand and pulled down her bathing suit by the shoulder straps, completely exposing her shapely breasts. Holy shit, they were going to have sex next to her! Charlie debated whether to get up or to just continue to feign sleep. She didn't want to disturb them and she had to admit to herself that she was rather enjoying her voyeurism.

With the woman's breasts exposed, the man began to roughly fondle them while tweaking and pulling her dark, turgid nipples. He bent his head down and began nibbling on each of her peaks. The woman's eyes closed and opened with each touch and kiss. Within moments he pulled her bathing suit down all the way, leaving her completely naked on the chair. She spread her legs wide, acquiescing to her younger lover.

He stole a quick glance in Charlie's direction but she didn't move or flinch, frozen in place like a frightened rabbit. For all intents and purposes she was still asleep to the amorous couple. No doubt they were getting off on their very public sexual hijinks.

The man pushed the small blond back and his head went between her legs. He began licking and kissing the woman's pussy. Her sighs and squeals of pleasure hung heavy in the humid air. Charlie could feel herself becoming liquid just listening to the amorous pair.

The man dropped his trunks and went on top of his partner. He roughly entered his mate with a very sizable erection. While receiving her lover, the blond extended her hand towards Charlie. Knowing her lover was preoccupied the blond stared directly at Charlie and smiled, basically acknowledging that she knew Charlie was awake. She dangled her fingers by Charlie as if to entice her to hold her hand. Charlie hesitated at first and then extended her own hand across the empty lounge chair. She lightly held the woman's hand, noticing her immaculate French manicure.

The blond woman's lover was pumping her hard and fast, his buttocks moving at a furious pace. He appeared to be an inexperienced lover but his intensity more than compensated for his lack of skill. The blond woman groaned and shuddered with every thrust. Charlie smelled their sex, a very pleasant aroma that played nicely in the salt air. She instinctively began squeezing her thighs together as she felt her own ardor building.

How long could that young man keep that pace up? He began to work up a considerable sweat. The woman's hand tightened her grip on Charlie's and she knew the woman was deep in the throes of her orgasm; she could almost taste it. Her squeeze and touch was so intense. The woman's legs and calves flexed and for a moment Charlie thought the woman would crush her hand. She looked over to Charlie, her eyes glassy, unfocused, and she finally relaxed her grip. Charlie's fingers continued to stroke the other woman's hand long after her orgasm dissipated.

A few minutes later the young man let out an audible grunt and he gave one last push of his hips towards his partner's. With no condom, he shot his love deep within his paramour.

Charlie closed her eyes as if to savor their moment. Her free hand darted between her legs and she began to slowly rub herself. She was still holding the woman's hand when she heard a commotion coming from the stern. A group of people dressed in white and dark Nike sneakers ran into the Tranquility Area. The GodNauts were carrying leather flogger belts and paddles. Behind them was Reverend Bannan yelling, "Rid heaven of the sinners. Send them all to hell!"

Charlie jumped up and yelled to the couple, "Run! Get away!"

Seeing the naked couple, the GodNauts ran towards them yelling and screaming in a crazed religious frenzy.

"Whores, harlots, cover yourself!" one woman yelled.

"The mouth of an adulteress is a deep pit; he who is cursed of the Lord will fall into it," the reverend shouted.

The angry reverend brandished a paddle and menacingly approached the woman. She tried to stand when he smacked her bottom. She yelped in pain. Charlie could see the woman's buttocks move and redden from the blow. Another man hit her across her breasts, forcing her backwards onto the deck.

Charlie stood up and began running away. The naked blond woman rose and ran through a gauntlet of GodNauts. The followers took turns, alternating between striking and smacking the woman's bare flesh. She yelled and cried with each blow as several other male members of the flock held back her naked lover.

Seeking escape, Charlie wanted no part of the angry mob but found herself confronted by one of the GodNauts. Belt in hand, the middle-aged bald man took a close look at the bikini-clad woman and took a swipe at her. The blow struck Charlie firmly in the buttocks but she kept moving. Seeing she was about to escape, the man grabbed her by her bikini top, threatening to rip it from her. She blocked his hands with her own and held onto the flimsy garment. With her hands on his arms she pushed, sending him flying backwards with considerable force. The startled man landed on his butt some ten feet away and sheepishly peered up at her. The fight was gone from him and he retreated to find easier prey.

Pandemonium spread throughout the entire Tranquility Area as a small riot ensued. Within moments the red spheres appeared. One by one they coalesced around and subdued the reverend's followers. Charlie was about to escape when one of the remaining GodNauts blocked her way.

It was Claire with a belt in her hand. Claire just glanced at her, smiled, and let Charlie go on her way.

Two of the followers, along with the reverend, saw Charlie escaping and began to run after her. She panicked and, in her haste, ran directly into two of the red spheres. The spheres passed through her and continued towards the reverend's followers. One by one, the spheres touched the GodNauts and caused them to collapse and fall to the deck unconscious.

Reverend Bannan observed Charlie's escape and shouted, "Who is protecting you, scarlet whore? I won't let you ruin my end days with your corrupt ways, polluting and ruining our reunion with God."

Charlie had had enough of running so she turned and faced the reverend. He stopped in his tracks, hesitating to move forward without his followers. She stared directly into his crazed, reddened eyes and she then slowly raised her hand. He stared, seemingly transfixed by her when she fully extended her middle finger. The reverend muttered to himself and quickly turned his attention to rallying the few GodNauts that remained standing. Charlie walked back to her cabin and hid out until lunchtime.

Steve felt particularly horny after seeing Charlie in her robe. After having made love his libido was in full swing and he couldn't stop thinking about her soft, pale skin. He made a point to catch up with her during the lunch buffet. Charlie smiled at him but busied herself with lunch. She seemed preoccupied.

"Everything okay, Charlie? You're not your usual talkative self."

"Sorry, but I had an early morning run-in with Reverend Crazy and his gang of godnuts."

"Yeah, Reverend Crazy seems to be messing up a lot of our mornings lately. Hey, sorry about interrupting yesterday but that shark fishing was insane, thanks to the reverend. Just what was I interrupting, anyway?" Steve asked.

"Learning more about our friends," she said.

"Through a massage? So how was it?" he asked. He wanted some prurient details.

"Very relaxing; your friend Janet has a nice touch. You should try a massage with your alien friend, perhaps take the edge off."

"My friend Janet?"

"The Epicoid that was ogling you the first day we talked."

"Really? I'm sure it can give quite the massage, but I'll stick with a human touch," he said with a grin. "So are they friends or captors?"

"Friends, I can assure you of that, but they are a bit confused."

"Shit, you think? I'm sorry, but do we really know what their motives are?" he asked.

"Jawara doesn't even know. His kind are what he calls a gateway species; they continue to evolve and change. But like you said, we should continue to investigate our friends."

"Well, that explains the common DNA and RNA. Don't let them fool you, Charlie, we really can't trust them," he said.

"Steve, who can we trust on this ship of strangers? Even the ones we think we know turn out to be complete strangers. So do me a big favor and let me eat my food in peace, will you?"

"Hey, I wasn't trying to upset you."

"Well you did, dammit! I've had it with this boat, the religious nut jobs, and Bradley. This has got to be the shittiest year of my life. First Bradley loses his job, and then this shit. I can't wait for this alien freak cruise to be over and for 2016 to come around for a fresh start."

Steve stopped eating and just stared at her. He appeared somewhat dumbfounded.

"What?" she asked, uncomfortable with his continuing stare.

"What did you just say?" he asked.

"I've had enough with this shitty year."

"No, no, the year?" he asked.

"I've had enough of 2015. What did you think I said?"

"Hey, baby girl, I think you're losing it. I know you've been on vacation for over a week but it's 2016 already."

"Do me a favor and don't ever call me baby girl again. And you're fricking nuts; I've kept track since my arrival. It should be Tuesday, April 21, 2015," she said.

"Hate to burst your bubble, but it's Monday, December 12, 2016. You know the Trump-Hillary presidential campaign? President-elect Trump?"

"Donald Trump? That billionaire TV clown? What are you smoking? Because you really need to share with the rest of us."

"I'm not kidding," he said.

Charlie didn't know what to make of his claim, since he seemed serious. She saw Rachel walking by in her bathing suit and said, "I can settle this nonsense real fast."

She hesitated, knowing she'd be calling attention to herself with Steve, but did she really care what others thought of her at that point? She called out, "Hey Rachel, whatcha up to?"

"Hello, Charlie, going for a swim," Rachel said as she scrutinized the pair. "Did you hear about the crazies this morning? Some poor woman got attacked by them."

"I did; I was in the middle of that fracas. Christ, I was lucky to get away from those idiots."

"So, are you going to introduce me to your new friend?" Rachel asked.

"Rachel, meet Steve. Steve, this is Rachel."

Steve got up, smiled, and shook Rachel's hand. "Very nice to meet you."

The attractive older woman made a point of overtly checking out the young black man and his physique. "Handsome and manners," she said as she looked him in the eye. "No wonder Charlie likes you."

"Rachel, if I can tear you away from eye-fucking Steve, we were debating what day of the week it was—you know, since we kind of lost track of time being aboard this ship. Is it Monday or Tuesday?

"Well, no wonder; it's not like there is a calendar to be found anywhere on this damn ship. I believe it's Wednesday, actually," Rachel said.

"Right, what month is?" Charlie asked.

"July. July 11, of course? What's this about?" Rachel asked, giving the pair a puzzled expression.

Charlie felt the blood drain from her face and she turned to Steve.

"The year?" Steve asked.

"Really, Charlie, I'm nearly twice your age and I'm the one who should be having memory issues, not you kids. It's 2012, of course."

There was silence from the pair. Rachel studied their faces and observed the couple's obvious concern. "Why do you ask? What year do you think it is?"

"2015," Charlie said as she fell back in her chair.

Rachel looked at Steve who said, "December 2016. Donald Trump is the President-elect."

"Holy shit. Trump?" Rachel said. "Steve, you're too funny. You almost had me with that one." There was an awkward silence in the air and she said, "You're not fucking with me, are you?" Her joviality turned to confusion and concern.

Steve shook his head.

"Yeah, holy shit," Charlie said. "How can this be?" She turned to Steve for some explanation.

He shook his head and then rubbed his face and eyes for a moment, as if hesitating to speak. He said in a soft tone, "Damn, I'm so stupid. I didn't see this coming. First, I'm not an astrophysicist, so take what I say with a shaker of salt, but I'm not exactly going out on a limb here either if I say that our friends appear to have mastery over both time and space. Makes sense in terms of the space-time continuum model. You can't effectively travel great distances without manipulating time. They can select the right assortment of human passengers from different times for observation at this particular space-time and...."

"What? Why are you pausing?" Charlie asked.

"And, by controlling the temporal reality for their guests on this ship, this gives them more options if we should somehow manage to escape. I've got to assume that all the passengers have been torn from their respective timelines and thrown into this parallel world of the Epicoids' making," he said.

"I'm not sure what this means," Charlie asked.

"It's simple. We can't possibly go home without their help. Not only do we not know where we are, but to make matters worse, we have no clue as to when we are."

Rachel sat down next to Charlie and asked, "So when are we being returned? To what time?"

Steve stared at her and said, "You mean *if* we are being returned. I'm guessing again, but if they do return us they may be able to return us to our individual timelines. Just wish I spent more time studying astrophysics."

Rachel got up and said, "Shit, I think I need a drink. I wish you'd never said anything to me about this." As she walked away she said, "President Trump? Really, that reality TV clown with the bad hair?"

"Can't make this shit up," he said.

"How is he?"

"Your basic racist clown best describes him, but then again, I maybe a bit prejudiced, being a black man."

"Just out of curiosity, who did he run against?" Rachel asked.

"Hillary," Steve said.

"Well, there's your problem," she muttered as she walked away.

Steve just nodded. Charlie appeared pale and she staggered a little while getting up to leave.

"Leaving?" Steve asked.

"I don't feel so hungry now."

"So do you want to do something a little later this afternoon?"

"Thanks, but no, I need some alone time to work this out. I'll see you at dinner, okay?" she said with a warm smile.

"Is this about the other night?"

"No."

"I get it, you're just not feeling it," he said.

"It's not like that. I just need a little alone time to myself. This isn't about you, Steve. You're fine, we're good, really," she said as she walked away.

After a moment Charlie turned back to him and said, "Holy shit, I just realized you're from the future."

"I guess you can look at it that way," Steve replied.

"Is it any better?"

"Did I mention that Trump is the President-elect? Same old bullshit; you'll hardly smell the difference. I'll see ya at dinner, fellow time-traveler," he said as he gave her a smile.

Steve walked alone on the top deck mulling his fate. As he turned, Ahmed moved towards him. Steve wanted to stay clear of him but it was too late. Ahmed walked on crutches; it seemed his legs had substantially recovered from his trauma.

"Steve, how are you doing, my brother?" he said with a strange grin on his face. Both eyes were now fully functional.

"I am not your bro, but I see you're recovering quite nicely."

"Yes, my friends the Sentinels have taken good care of me. Your friends, I'm not so sure of. Where is that white demon of a woman you regularly hang out with?"

"Racist asshole, it's none of your business who I hang with," Steve said as he walked away. Ahmed moved the crutches furiously to keep pace with Steve.

"Now I see. She gave up on you, brother, right? White women just want to play with you. They will take you to their bed, but they won't stay with you. Be honest, did the whore go back to her husband?"

"Say one more word and I'll rip you in two, crutches or no crutches," Steve said as he turned to face Ahmed. "Go ahead. I would love to shove those crutches up your ass."

"Just trying to talk sense to you."

"Talk sense? How is this for talking sense: you fucking fundamentalists are so far up your women's asshole, controlling everything, managing your property until there is no one home. Then at night, when she is lying there like a zombie, you're thinking about fucking Western women. Fuck your sexual apartheid and don't tell me who I can go to bed with."

Ahmed backed off and said, "Just trying to show solidarity with a brother."

"Again, I'm not your brother. Next time you see me, just keep walking by. Don't speak to me and don't even look at me."

Ahmed grabbed him by the hand.

"Don't touch me, asshole," Steve said as he swatted Ahmed's hand away.

"You will think differently very soon," Ahmed said. "It has always been about us versus them since the beginning of dawn. You better start understanding that and decide whose side you want to be on."

"Clearly, you have made your choices, Ahmed. Like I said, just keep walking the next time you see me."

Steve walked away, leaving Ahmed to himself. Feeling angry after the confrontation with Steve, Ahmed walked up to a group of teenage boys who were hanging out enjoying a cigarette. They wanted to move away from the strange creature on crutches; he just had a nasty air about him.

"What are you up to? Causing trouble?" Ahmed asked.

The boys backed away, sensing something was very wrong with the strange man.

Jim, the boldest boy, said, "Look, just leave us alone, freak."

Ahmed moved quickly and grabbed Jim's bare arm.

"We'll see what you think in a little while," Ahmed said, and turned him loose. He hobbled away from the boys, leaving them to mull over the strange encounter.

"Can you believe that freak?" Jim said to the other boys.

The boys continued to joke about the freak and share their cigarette. The hallway got dark again as a young teen girl made her way to them. They decided to have some fun with the emo girl as they blocked her way.

"What are you doing?" she asked.

"Not much, why don't you hang with us?" Jim said. She reluctantly joined them and shared their cigarette. Within minutes the other boys began to grope her. When she protested and tried to move away, another boy would block her escape.

Steve continued to walk and retraced his steps, hoping to shake the wave of anger and depression settling over him. The time-travel paradox and how Charlie treated him was leaving him in a bad way. In the distance he saw the boys harassing the girl.

Steve yelled, "What are you doing with her?" There was no reply. "Let her go, assholes."

The boys turned from the girl and stared Steve's way.

"Let's mess him up!" Jim yelled.

Steve boldly walked over to the boys and laughed. "You're not messing anybody up, assholes.”

"Yeah, why not?" Jim said.

Jim moved forward and Steve stared him down. Before Jim could move Steve fired a punch into the teen's stomach. The boy folded and collapsed to the ground while the other boys watched and then ran away.

The emo girl peered up at her savior and gave him a big smile. Steve smiled back at the small girl and noticed that she had a nice shape. Too bad about those stupid piercings and crazy tattoos. He walked forward and practically pinned her up against the wall.

Jim was getting up from the ground and Steve said, "Just had the wind knocked out of you, no biggie. Now get the fuck out of here, punk, before I do some real damage to you."

Jim slowly got up, staggered, and then ran away. Steve returned to the girl and looked her over with hungry eyes.

"You're a cute little thing. Now I know why they wanted you," he said. The smile evaporated from her face and she felt threatened once again. Steve's dark finger moved to the girl's neck and traced a lazy line to her pale cleavage. *Really nice tits for a little girl,* he thought. Steve was getting hard and he considered taking her. For some reason he wanted to take out his hatred of the world by abusing and degrading this young innocent.

Steve studied her eyes and saw they were wide open with terror. She was visibly shaking and he suddenly realized she was petrified of him. Steve had become the monster his own mother had feared.

"What the fuck is wrong with me?" he said aloud. "How old are you?"

"Sixteen," she said in a low, muffled voice. The girl was barely able to stand as she swayed to some unknown tempest.

"What's your name?"

"Denise."

"All right, Denise, let's be clear about this. I don't want to see you in these corridors again, understood? Just go and get the hell out of here before someone gets seriously hurt."

The girl hesitated and he yelled, "What the hell is wrong with you? Are you stupid? Go now!"

The girl nodded at him and at first walked away. When there was a little distance she began running. Left alone in the corridor with his own dark thoughts, Steve wondered what the fuck was troubling him. He decided to return to his cabin before he could do some real damage to someone. As he waited by the elevator he saw Rachel walking towards him. She was still in her bikini and wrap. Damn, that woman had some seriously long legs.

"Hi there. So we meet up again," Rachel said.

"Hey, so we do," Steve said as the elevator arrived. They entered the elevator together.

"Don't mean to pry, but are you, like, steady with Charlie?" she asked. "I mean, you did hook up with her, right?"

"Let me guess, girl talk?"

"Nothing girly about it, I can assure you of that," she said with a smile. Rachel had a long, lean, tanned body without an ounce of fat. She was kind of hot for a woman old enough to be his mother.

"I do like her but she's still pretty hung up about her husband. Kind of a non-starter." He noticed Rachel swaying in the elevator. "Shit, are you drunk?"

"After our little talk about time travel I did have a few."

"Define a few?"

"Three, four, maybe five screwdrivers. I can hold my liquor," she said as she licked her lips. "Hey, can I put you out for a few minutes? I need a man's hand to fix something in the bathroom. It's not like there's any crew around to fix stuff. Arc you handy?"

"Yeah, I sometimes work as a marine mechanic. What's broken?" he asked with a smile. He knew this sexy old slut wanted him and his cock twitched in anticipation.

She grabbed him by the hand and remarked, "You do have big hands. It's by the sink; I can show you. Oh, could you be a sweetheart and wait outside a moment while I clean up first?"

"Sure, no problem," he said while she went inside.

Several minutes later she opened the door to her darkened cabin and led him directly into the bathroom. She flipped the light on. He searched about but didn't notice anything out of place and said with a grin, "So what's broke?"

Rachel grabbed his large hand again and placed it on her pussy. "You see, it's here. I need a strong hand, you know, to fix my leak."

Steve just smirked at her but didn't move his hand. Instead, he reflectively began to stroke her.

"So what's wrong with it?" he asked, smelling the liquor on her breath.

"A very slow drip. It's very wet. Can you take a look and fix it for me?" she asked with a smile as she led him from the bathroom into main room.

"You're right, it does seem very wet," he said while moving his fingers under her bikini bottom and stroking her. "I'm not sure I can fix it."

"Dammit, just try," she said, and she went to her knees and pulled down his shorts and underwear. Steve's cock was starting to harden and she grabbed his member with her hand. Her tongue swirled along the tip, feeling it grow hard as she said, "Dear god, I love this big cock. I'm going to take very good care of you, young man."

She eagerly took more in her mouth and with her other hand she began to massage his balls. Steve enjoyed the sensation and involuntarily he felt his hips moving back and forth. He grabbed the long, dark hair of her head with one hand and began to aggressively pump her mouth with his hard cock.

Rachel didn't pull back but eagerly moved her soft mouth in unison with his thrusts. This wasn't making love but a serious animal fuck, one he desperately needed.

After a couple of minutes she pulled away from him while gasping, "Oh yeah, I love it rough, give me more of that cock." Once again he grabbed her hair with one hand and thrust his cock into her mouth. His cock pumped her mouth for several minutes and when he'd had enough he pushed her back to the bed.

She fell on her back and Steve roughly grabbed her bikini bottom and pulled it off. Rachel spread her tan legs wide for him, revealing her tan line and shaved pussy. Steve's finger went into her wetness.

"You seem to be getting wetter," he said.

Rachel pulled Steve's head between her legs and he began to lick from her bottom to her clit. It was Rachel's turn to roughly grab his head and hold it while grinding her pussy against his mouth. Her gasps of joy filled the air.

"Holy shit, this is good," she yelped.

He pulled away, pushed her legs apart, and roughly entered her. She gasped with the way his cock began filling her pussy. Her hands moved to his hips to slow him down but he didn't care and he kept fucking her anyway. Hard, quickly, he began a bed-shaking fuck. Damn, she was tight.

He started to groan, losing himself between her legs, but stopped when he heard a sound in the room. He jumped up from her and scanned about, knowing there was someone else in the room with them.

"Who the fuck is there?" Steve yelled as he bolted from the bed.

Rachel grabbed his hand and said, "It's nobody, just my Hank. He likes to watch."

In the darkest corner Steve caught a shadowy glimpse of a naked overweight man watching the pair.

"What the fuck? Watch what?"

"Watch me fuck, of course. Come on, lover, I need more of that black cock."

"Get the fuck out of here! I'm not putting a show on for that perv," Steve said as he pulled his shorts up and left the room. In the distance he heard Rachel's lament, "Please don't go; I didn't come yet. You know, I wouldn't have voted for Trump either!"

The Bitter Tasting

Charlie felt a curious vibration to the air that was somewhat similar to the poolside Sacour Feast. This time the vibration was less charged and erotic; it seemed almost mournful. Common sense told her to leave well enough alone, but common sense didn't necessarily apply to this alien cruise. Instead, she followed the vibrations to the unused convention center of the ship. She walked the massive, empty hallways and moved from room to room trying to locate the epicenter of the vibrations. The dimmed lighting made it difficult for her to peer inside each room, and finding a light switch was nearly impossible.

When she neared the end of the corridor a humming could be heard originating from a smaller room. She went inside and again struggled to see in the room that was only lit by the reddish light of the exit signs. She saw a party of Epicoids, totally naked and surrounding a prostrate body lying on the floor. Unlike the high energy of the Epicoids' sexual encounter at the pool, this was a slower, almost melancholy affair.

Charlie quietly crept forward to get a better view, taking care to hide behind the many chairs in the room. She focused on the body and noticed that it seemed shrouded in darkness. The other Epicoids were fondling the unmoving body, but unlike the sex in the pool the recipient appeared to be unresponsive. Horrified, Charlie wondered if this was an unwilling human victim.

She had to get a better look but the door to the room opened again. Someone was entering the room and the light from the hallway lit the scene before her. The pale white Epicoids were focused on the figure they surrounded and Charlie got her first glimpse at the body: It was an Epicoid, but zirs body had completely turned a blackish-purple color. A strange mist wafted from the body. The surrounding Epicoids were methodically probing the dead body with their culmuses from every possible angle.

The sight was horrific and she had to escape. She bolted from the room and ran past the startled Epicoid that had just entered. It was Jawara. Jawara saw the horror and revulsion on her face but ze didn't stop her. She quickly fled the convention center, hoping to return to the relative safety of her cabin.

She reached the elevators and entered the car. A hand stopped the closing elevator door: Somehow the lumbering Jawara had caught up to her.

"What was that? Was he dead?" Charlie breathlessly asked, with the horror clearly evident in her eyes.

"Yes, Freyr is dead," Jawara impassively replied.

"Did you kill him?

"Of course not. Freyr was a much loved elder, the leader of our team. Freyr's death came as a great surprise to us."

"Why was the body that horrific black-red color?"

"The lack of oxygen causes the cells in our bodies to die very quickly and we turn that color within ten minutes of our death. It's very natural."

"Natural? What the hell was that with the sex? Are you necrophiliacs?"

"No, that ritual you observed we call the Bitter Tasting. When an Epicoid dies we try to taste and savor as much as possible from the deceased. A final tasting will often be held so that the dead can be returned to the Quanteme. Think of it as a funeral. It's one of our holiest rituals," Jawara said as ze continued to hold the elevator door.

"A group of you have a naked orgy with a dead body and you call that a holy ritual? Your people are too fricking weird."

"It wasn't sex and we're just different," Jawara said in a flat monotone.

"How did Freyr die?"

"We found Freyr in zirs space that way. Freyr had been dead for hours but nobody tasted zirs demise. We all lost a true friend."

"I recall that Freyr was with my friend Rachel. Is there any possible connection?"

"No, why would there be? Are you okay?"

"Just fine. You can let go of the elevator now," she said.

Jawara released the door and she breathed a sigh of relief as the car ascended.

She was soon topside, pacing and upset, when Steve stormed past her.

"Steve, what's wrong?" she asked, wanting to talk to someone normal.

Steve was about to tell her to fuck off but he just couldn't utter the words. He was still horny and he decided it was time to move on Charlie.

"I'm good, you doing anything?" he asked.

"No, I just had the most—" Charlie said when he closed the distance between the two and decided to kiss her. She pulled away from his aggressive move.

"Come on, let's do it, girl!" Steve said.

She looked into his eyes and they appeared almost crazed. "Let me go! What is wrong with you? Are you high or something?"

"Don't be that way!" he said.

"Just stay away from me, will you?"

Steve walked away from her. Charlie was shaken and confused by his actions. After ten minutes of debate she decided to confront him and find out what was wrong with him.

Bradley couldn't understand his change in fortune. After four straight days of winning he was going through a prolonged losing streak. The girls he'd accumulated on his arm over the past three days grew disgruntled and disinterested; after all, he was a sore loser. Worse, he had no winnings to share. After another six-hour stint in the casino he was back in the red. He tried changing games but to no avail; his losses appeared to be a return to his usual form. It was getting late; he drank a lot and decided a walk was in order to get some fresh air and perhaps reverse his fortunes.

Bradley walked along the deck, aimlessly pondering his fate and his failed marriage. After this cruise was over he'd hoped to take his winnings to Vegas and bankroll a prolonged play while divorcing Charlie. Those plans were on hold. He ventured into an area he wasn't familiar with and noticed a fog had descended upon the ship. Strange, as it was still warm out.

As he walked he saw Steve arguing with Charlie. After Charlie stepped away Bradley saw his opportunity to confront Steve.

"There's the asshole who thinks he can sleep with someone's wife without any repercussions," he shouted.

"Fuck off, you're drunk," Steve said. Bradley grabbed him by the arm. "Don't touch me, asshole. Talk to your wife if you two are having trouble."

Steve pulled away.

"Hey, I'm talking to you, Kanye. Just gotta have those white women, don't you?" Bradley said.

Steve turned around to face Bradley, fearing the drunken idiot might sucker-punch him.

"Shit, it's the fucking degenerate gambler. Maybe you should spend some time with your old lady and she wouldn't be looking elsewhere to get laid. You fucking white people kill me." He watched Bradley's face turning redder and said, "Frankly, you should be more worried about that creepy alien she's hanging around with all the time. God knows what that freak is doing to your wife."

Bradley lost it and took a swing at Steve that glanced off the side of Steve's head. Shaking the blow off, Steve said, "Shit, you're the third white person to take a swing at me on this cruise. Sure you want to do this? Because you're really pissing me off."

"Sure I do," Bradley said as he squared up for a fight.

Steve frowned and said, "Oh, for fuck's sake. Go ahead, it's your funeral." He feinted with an overhand left to Bradley's head and then caught him with a rabbit punch to the kidney. The blow knocked the fight out of Bradley and he started to crumble to his knees. Steve hit him flush on the side of the head and he fell on his back. He was nearly out and Steve jumped on top of him to continue his attack. He threw a right that caught Bradley on the nose, crackling and breaking the cartilage. Blood began to gush from his nose, making Bradley choke.

Charlie heard the commotion and ran towards the two fighting men. She saw that Bradley was down. As Steve went to throw another punch Charlie ran and grabbed his arm. Steve nearly threw her to the ground as he tried to throw his fist. He stopped fighting upon seeing Charlie sprawled out on the ground.

"What are you gonna do? Take a swing at me, too?" she yelled.

Steve stopped and turned away, embarrassed. Her touch reminded him how much he wanted her.

"What is wrong with you lately? You are acting like a…." She got up.

"Go ahead, finish what you were going to say," he said as he turned to her with his eyes angry.

"Like a punk. You're acting like a common punk. You're better than this, Steve. I know Bradley is a piece of shit, but he's practically unconscious. You want to kill him?"

"His sorry ass deserves it," he said. "You know, that's why I hate hanging around white girls: You never know if they got your back when something goes down."

"Steve, this is not like you. What is eating you?" Charlie asked.

"Just getting smarter, that's all. You damn white folks stick together no matter what."

"Now I know that's not you talking," she said.

"You don't know me."

"Don't say that. I do know the man who saved me."

"Better figure out for the future, Charlie, who you are going to back. I doubt that I'm the last fool you fuck."

Steve gave Bradley a quick kick in the ribs and left the two.

Bradley tried to stand up and Charlie reached down to help him. As he got up on one knee he said to Charlie, "See what happens when you hang around a spade?"

"He's right. I shouldn't have stopped him from kicking your sorry ass. How do you like getting the shit beat out of you, asshole?" she asked.

"See, who says we have nothing in common?" Bradley said as he laughed and spit up a little blood.

"Son of a bitch, you deserved a beating, not me," she said as she let go of his arm and let him fall down. "Go fuck yourself."

She left in tears and went in search of Jawara. She found him topside, as she often did, zirs impassive face staring out to the horizon. Jawara barely acknowledged her presence.

"I need your help."

"With?" ze asked.

"Jawara, what I went through—that darkness, that depression—I know Steve is going through that very same darkness. For me the darkness became my depression, and my anger turned inward. Steve is reacting differently and intent on taking his anger out on the world. He is all twisted now, turning violent. He is in a dark, angry place not of his doing. He's not like that; I know that," she said.

"What do you want from me?"

"You have to help him out like you did me. I wasn't the same after being touched by that freak in the wheelchair."

"Ahmed? How did he touch you?" Jawara asked.

"With his disgusting foot of all things, skin to skin. Steve needs help like you helped me."

"I can't; our quantum pairing was a once-in-a-lifetime sharing," Jawara said. "I have been watching Ahmed. The Sentinels found a kindred spirit in him. They are transforming him into a Sentinel. That's not just a touch but a tasting, a deep exchange of chemical and genetic information between two beings. For the Epicoids it's bliss, and for the Sentinels it's a shared horror they enjoy perpetuating on others."

"The man saved my life. You have to do something."

"What little I could do Steve will not readily accept. He appears to be very tasty but I can sense he is strongly heterosexual and reacts to me as if I am a male of your species. He will not willingly join in Unioeros with me, in the spirit of the Quanteme. I'm sorry, but a simple touch is not going to turn Steve around."

"He's going to hurt someone or himself. You have to do something—force him if you must."

"I will take your request under advisement, but this is complicated. Forcing him will neither be easy nor well-received."

"Hey, you wanted to hang with humans, so welcome to our world," she said as she walked away. "But you also have to ask: Has Ahmed touched any other humans? You may have an epidemic on your hands."

Epi-Curious

Steve was horny and angry—not a good combination for any man. Exercise would help knock that shit right out, knowing that he burned his bridge with Charlie.

He took a swim in the pool and after a number of vigorous laps went to shower. He was alone at the facility with not a soul in sight. There was a large open shower area and he took his trunks off and rinsed his body. He was naked and washing himself, thinking about Charlie. He felt horny and avoided washing his penis too strenuously. Still, he could feel himself getting erect and turned on the cold water. Perfect; it was just what he needed. He jumped around in the cold water hoping to chase his erection away.

He felt better and decided a sauna would be good. Again there was no one around and he went into the sauna. He didn't bother to cover himself. Why would he, being alone? Besides, the mores of the passengers aboard the ship were quickly approaching baccalaurean proportions.

As he sat in the sauna for a few minutes, the heat had its tonic effect upon him. Once again, as he drifted off, he had a large erection. Damn thing wouldn't go away and he gave it a quick tug. It felt good; he could do with a quick release.

Steve glanced up and nearly jumped out of his skin when he saw Jawara watching him. Shit, he was busted!

Steve composed himself and coolly asked, "What the hell? Were you spying on me?" Jawara was easily a foot taller, unclothed, and staring intently at him.

"In the spirit of the Quanteme, do you want Unioeros?" Jawara asked. Yes, Jawara was totally naked, but nothing was showing on zirs featureless body other than the slightly raised ridge slit along zirs lower abdomen. Ze was about as exciting to look at as a store mannequin.

"What? You mean have sex? You and me?" Steve asked, a bit flustered by the alien proposition.

"Yes, we could do it here; it's important for me to taste you," Jawara said as ze looked Steve over and stopped to stare at his erection.

The dude wants to taste me? Fucking disgusting.

"Hell no! No disrespect, but get the fuck out of here before I smack you one!"

Shit, now Steve knew what it was like to feel like a piece of meat.

"Hey, asshole, my eyes are up here. I just don't swing that way," he said to Jawara as he got up and wrapped his towel quickly around his waist.

"I don't understand. You seem excited," Jawara said.

"I don't do sex with dudes," Steve said as his erection collapsed in revulsion.

"I'm not a dude. I told you we don't have individual sexes like male and female," Jawara said.

Steve was about to say something about having seen the Epicoids have sex and that he knew Jawara was pretty darn close to being the size of a horse. But he decided it was best not to mention his voyeurism with Charlie that night, not knowing how the alien might react to being spied on.

Steve had heard the aliens were regularly having sex with the other passengers, so he wasn't shocked at the sight of the naked Epicoid. Plus, the biologist in him couldn't help but wonder about the mechanics of sex with an alien creature. That said, there was no way he was going to take one for the team. Jawara, regardless, of zirs sex or lack of a sex, just didn't do it for him.

Steve shook his head. "Sorry, but you're pretty darn close to being a dude."

"Are you sure?"

Hell yes, he was sure. What a bizarre conversation. Steve peered at him dumbfounded and said, "Jawara, we have a saying in my country: *No* means *no* when it comes to sex."

No reaction.

"Fuck, I'll give you a pass since you are new to this planet. But if you persist, I am going to have to beat the shit out of you."

Jawara appeared confused at Steve's comment and that began to feed into Steve's greatest fear.

"Shit, this isn't happening. We're not on Earth, are we?" he asked.

Jawara shook zirs head.

Steve thought to himself just how fucked he was, stranded God-knows-where in the universe and, worse, with a horny gay alien.

"Come on, man, are you fucking kidding me? Shit, you just confirmed my worst fear! What do you got to say?"

Jawara said nothing.

"You're a lot of help. What brought this gay shit on, by the way, and why me?" Steve just hoped Jawara's alien gaydar was seriously broken and that he wasn't personally giving off some gay vibe to the hapless alien.

"I know Charlie likes you a lot and I'm trying to understand your attraction to one another. You also seem sad," Jawara said.

"Your hitting on me is not helping with my sadness. Just out of curiosity, did you fuck Charlie?"

"Yes, we had Unioeros, in the spirit of the Quanteme," Jawara said.

"Oh."

"And so did you with Charlie," Jawara continued.

Steve guessed nobody had told Jawara that kissing and telling was just poor etiquette. More importantly, how did Jawara know about Charlie and him doing the big nasty?

He studied Jawara's face but it was impassive. He felt his own stomach churning. Charlie was now having sex with the fucking albino aliens instead of him. Damn, it was lonely being rejected on this love boat.

"Ah, I see, checking out the competition, huh? Well, I'm going to have to say pass, but if I ever do go bi you'll be the first to know. Yeah, right, like that is going to happen," Steve said in a feigned air of nonchalance.

Jawara just stared at him.

"Shit! Tell you what, have a talk with Charlie and maybe we could arrange a threesome," Steve said in jest.

The Epicoid's face changed slightly, gaining almost a quizzical expression, and ze said, "That would be nice. Should I go see if she is available for Unioeros now or this afternoon?"

"Shit, that's sarcasm, you fricking moron. Don't go telling Charlie that I asked for a threesome, got it?" Steve said. "You know what, on second thought, I don't give a fuck what you tell her."

"But it's important for me to have a taste of you. I tasted Charlie and I tasted you in Charlie," Jawara said.

Taste? There's that word again, Steve thought. Now this was getting interesting. Just what was Jawara tasting?

"You tasted me how?" Steve asked.

"Through my skin during Unioeros with Charlie," Jawara said as ze touched Steve's dark arm with zirs large white hand.

Steve immediately withdrew his arm but Jawara's touch was electric. Within seconds his penis became erect again. What the fuck? The touch itself was nothing; frankly, it was more like contact with the skin of a warm white salamander, but signals were sent directly to his pelvis that penetrated deep within his organs.

Steve stared down at his lap. The towel barely covered the largest and hardest erection of his life. It was almost painful in its intensity. The damn thing had a life of its own, as if he'd just viewed two teen girls making out. He realized these were the vibes he and Charlie had both picked up on the other night by the pool. No wonder they'd screwed like two feral cats in heat that night after watching the sexual escapades of the aliens.

As large as his penis was, Steve knew his paled in comparison with the alien organs. God, why was he even thinking like that? Steve had to give the aliens credit; they did have some crazy sexual empath skills. Yeah, he wanted release, but not enough to have Unioeros or sex with the bi-curious androgynous giant.

Funny, he actually felt better after the touch, as if a burden had been lifted from his shoulders. Shit, maybe it was the giant-sized erection that had done it, but he suddenly didn't hate the awkward giant.

"Sorry, Jawara, go collect some other specimens," he said as he quickly got up. "And do me a favor, don't mention the threesome to Charlie, okay?"

It was all too weird for Steve. He tried to dress in the locker room but it took a while for his erection to settle enough for him to put his pants on.

Steve met Charlie that night at the dinner buffet. She appeared radiant, almost as if she was in love. As twilight dawned the two went topside. While they were walking along the deck, they saw two older mature white women who were naked and pleasuring each other on a large deck chair. They were locked in a sixty-nine position and didn't seem to care that they were being watched. Steve wanted to linger but Charlie moved on.

After putting some distance between themselves and the amorous dowagers, Steve said, "Hey, I'm sorry about fighting with Bradley and mouthing off on you. I haven't been myself lately."

"Steve, believe me, I understand what you are going through," she said. Her eyes were soft and seemed full of concern.

Steve vigorously took her into his arms to give her a kiss. Charlie pursed her lips together and withdrew.

"Steve, what happened the other night was nice, but on reflection it may have been a mistake on my part. I'm sorry. I care, but I'm not in love with you," she said.

"What was all the stuff you shared with me about your husband? About wanting a divorce?"

"I just needed someone to talk to, that's all. I'm sorry. This cruise has been very confusing. I owe you so much; you've been a great friend to me."

Ah shit, he thought; she'd just given him the 'great friend but why don't you fuck off' speech.

"Why? What's wrong with me? It's not about me being black, is it?"

"Hell no, not at all," she said, hesitating. "I know this sounds strange, but you saved my life."

"For fuck's sake, you're punishing me for saving you?" he asked incredulously.

"Sometimes you can owe someone too much. Sometimes they become a painful reminder about a debt that can never be repaid or a mistake made."

"I never said you owe me. That's it? Because I care about you?" Steve said.

"Why did your girlfriend leave?" Charlie asked. "Be honest."

"She said I wasn't fun anymore."

"She has a point. Sometimes you're too intense for me. And I really don't need that now in my life—not another possessive lover who will abandon me when he gets bored after toying with me."

Steve's face flushed red with anger.

He was about to confront Charlie about her alien encounters with Jawara but thought better of it. He realized acting the jealous lover just wouldn't be cool, especially after her possessive lover comment. No, he would bite his tongue and keep his anger in check. He would bide his time.

"Sorry you feel that way, Charlie. I get it, girl: you've been hurt. I'll give you your space," he said in a curt manner.

Charlie felt awful but before she could say another word Steve stormed off. She went in search of Jawara and found the alien on the upper deck.

"You didn't do it, did you," Charlie accused.

"No, I told you he would reject me."

"You've got to do something; he's getting worse. Can't you persuade Janet to sleep with him?"

"Despite rumors to the contrary, we're not sex workers," Jawara replied.

"Jawara, I don't care how you do it, but just fuck Steve, will you? And sooner rather than later."

Jawara nodded in agreement.

Defeated, Steve went back to his cabin alone. He had a beer, took his clothes off, and fell asleep in his boxers, wishing Charlie had joined him.

As he slept he dreamt of her warm pale body, her flowing red hair. He had an erection he rubbed against the silk bed sheets. He felt the presence of someone else in the room. His heart rose, hoping Charlie had changed her mind. Deep in sleep, he couldn't move but he felt a warm body moving against him in the bed. 'She' felt good against his skin; it was Charlie.

She wasn't shy and her hands went between his legs for his erect penis. Back and forth she rubbed against his hardness as she forced him onto his back.

Steve wanted to reciprocate but he was the receiver of pleasure, not the giver. His erection felt solid and hard as the heat radiated from his member. Locked together, Charlie and Steve disappeared beneath the roiling seas, riding up and down on the massive waves. They were joined by porpoises that seemed to delight in the coupling humans in their midst.

He felt his body narrowing, became smaller as the pleasure appeared to be more concentrated. His entire body felt energized; his nipples, his anus, and even his toes tingled with delight. Every part of his body felt wet with sweet desire, even though he didn't feel entirely comfortable with Charlie's newfound aggressiveness.

From this singular feeling came the explosion as his body joined the collective and the universe. It was no longer his orgasm but a shared event with the universe, a geyser unlike any other in his lifetime. From his penis copious amounts of ejaculate flew with a velocity he'd never before known. He clutched her body and trembled against her silky soft skin. After his release she was gone from him.

The Sacour Feast

Earlier that evening Charlie was alone in her cabin attending to her clothes. She wasn't feeling any emotion in particular; basically she was neutral, just existing. She was upset about Steve's belligerent behavior and she felt alone again. She felt even more isolated knowing they were trapped in some bizarre parallel world that existed who knew where or when.

As she folded a pair of her shorts she felt her body quiver. A wave of passion overrode her, seemingly emanating from deep within her pelvis. The liquid ardor was so strong she almost fell over, catching herself on the edge of the dresser. As the emotion rode in waves she felt her nipples tingling and hardening.

She was so connected to Jawara that she knew the collective would be having Unioeros tonight, or what Jawara called the Sacour Feast. The mass Unioeros was not a regularly scheduled event but rather a consensus of their groupthink. So many bodies, so tasty.

She gathered her composure and walked into the large bathroom. Charlie undressed and stood before the mirror naked, studying her body. Her pale skin had a bluish tint that didn't play well with her long curly red hair. She touched her hair, examining the ends. Her hand moved below, noticing the darker red hair between her legs. The curly hair wasn't very trim and partially obscured her femininity.

She envisioned scores of Epicoids having Unioeros with their intertwining culmuses binding them together as one and she shuddered with delight. She suddenly felt compelled to join them. Actually, it was beyond a compulsion; it was a need she couldn't rationally explain to herself. She had to be one with them among the masses.

Looking before the mirror, Charlie assumed the vantage of an Epicoid and realized her red hair just wouldn't do. She recalled the look of repulsion on Janet's face when touching her hairy mound. Jawara and the other Epicoids wouldn't feel comfortable with her parading about with so much red hair.

She grabbed a pair of scissors, pulled the hair from her mound, and began trimming her pubic hair. When she was done she applied some shaving cream and took her razor for shaving her legs and began shaving her mound. Within a few minutes she was completely hairless and she touched her naked womanhood. To be on the safe side she shaved her legs too.

Done, she ran her finger along the exposed lips, enjoying her own salacious touch.

Better, but she knew it still wasn't enough as she gazed at her long red hair. It didn't make sense—not for Unioeros with chaetophobic aliens, that is. Charlie began cutting her hair with the scissors, removing long handfuls at a time. Strangely, she felt as if she was receiving the approval of all of the Epicoids aboard the ship.

Encouraged by her unseen audience, she kept cutting her hair and placed the red strands in the wastebasket. When she was done the hair on her head was still a good half-inch long. Fortunately Bradley had left his electric razor behind and she began trimming the rest. When she was done only a short stubble remained on her head. She applied shaving cream and used her razor to remove the stubble. She then removed the few fine hairs she had on her arms with the razor. She ran her hand over her scalp, marveling at its exquisite smoothness.

When she was done she stared in the mirror at her nearly hairless body. The only part that seemed out of place was her eyebrows. She took the razor and shaved those off, too. Then, she stared at her naked body with nary a red hair in sight. Now the bluish tint of her pale skin didn't seem so out of place. Even her pale, unresponsive nipples fit the look; she resembled one of the Epicoids. She took an enema, purged, showered, and meticulously cleaned her body repeatedly as if undergoing a purification rite.

She stood before the full-length mirror in her room and touched her breast. Her hand moved down from her breast to her stomach, envisioning her large culmus tucked below.

She was ready to greet Jawara and the Epicoids on their own terms: Unioeros. There was no need for nutrition; she knew how she wanted to be satiated. Instead, she put a pair of shorts on with no underwear and a blouse. There was no urgency, but instead this intensely carnal creature patiently sat in a chair waiting for them to gather. She felt the moistness between her legs, the sweet anticipation of sex. She wanted to be tasted, over and over again, not by one lover but in chorus by a multitude of lovers.

When the time was right—somehow she just knew—she put a large sun hat on and walked to the pool by the Tranquility Area. The twilight skies were ablaze in color but she barely noticed; her heightened senses were decidedly more tactile. Instead, she felt their vibrations and knew all of the Epicoids were gathered for Unioeros. Once by the pool she walked toward the assembled Epicoids. Two naked Epicoids with a female semblance joined her at her side; one of them was Janet. They towered over the diminutive human as they slowly walked together. Charlotte stopped walking and Janet smiled at her and removed her hat. The other female Epicoid went to her knees and gently pulled down her shorts. Janet began to unbutton Charlie's blouse and free it from her shoulders, allowing it to fall to the deck. Charlie felt the cool air against her bare breasts, causing her nipples to tingle with delight. Totally naked, she walked a little farther and kicked off her sandals while entering a dark tunnel with the two Epicoids.

While walking, her senses changed. Light was less important as the vibrations took hold of her body. She kept walking, seemingly alone, but with each step she slowly melded with the churning mass of Epicoids. She came to the realization that they had accepted her and she would be the first human to join them in such a feast.

Her sight left her and she found herself dependent on and guided by her new lovers to the pool. She waded into the cool water, eager to join the awaiting Epicoids. Charlie's body was no longer her own but rather had become an element in a much larger entity. The hum grew in intensity and became a visceral vibration within her body, her orifices sensitized in sweet anticipation of allowing the multitude of Epicoid culmuses unfettered access to her erogenous zones. They stroked and probed, sensing what was pleasurable to her and then reciprocating in kind. Her orifices belonged to the group; her pleasure belonged to the group.

One culmus moved to her mouth and Charlie eagerly took the organ, swallowing in its entirety. Rather than choking her, the organ became one with her throat. Her normally languid nipples were erect while Epicoid fingers aggressively pinched and tugged. A culmus gently entered her pussy, exploring, extending, and probing. She concentrated on a part of her body and the Epicoids responded accordingly. Her thoughts moved to her buttocks and a single slender tendril inserted itself into her rosebud, slowly expanding and contracting within the orifice. It felt so good, so filling as the tendril danced within and with the other cumulus in her vagina.

Charlie closed her eyes as the cool water rushed over her body when the Epicoids slowly lowered her beneath the surface. There was no panic or fear that she might drown, but rather an acceptance of her erotic fate among the loving Epicoids.

Floating in darkness, her body writhed against all of the organs entering, sharing her pleasure with her many lovers, a communion of the highest magnitude. She felt her body vibrating, as if preparing for a spawning. The hum was overwhelming and started at one cell, then as a collective within her organs, and moving to her brain. All joined the Epicoids; all belonged to the shared climax.

Hands seemed to pin her down while they stroked her fingertips, darting between her toes, her anus, and her vagina, and finally she erupted with a heaving, convulsive orgasm that emanated within every cell of her body. This was beyond sex; her body was announcing to the universe that the thirty trillion cells within the entity known as Charlie was alive, growing, and dividing while making itself available to all! She was willingly offering her body to all of the Epicoids, not just her companions in the pool. She felt Jawara among her lovers, loving zir the dearest.

She was held captive by her ecstasy, only her captivity didn't end with a single orgasm. Instead, her body rode the waves of ecstasy from one peak to the next valley, only to rise again with little will of her own. Her legs constricted about one of the Epicoids as if her very existence depended on it. She opened her eyes underwater to watch the rhythmic swaying of joined bodies in the pool. All was a swirling mass of flesh; individuals disappeared into a vortex of arousal pulsating to an unknown metronome, one that was in harmony with the universe. Around the floating, writhing bodies the water was turning blue as the Epicoid culmuses released clouds of azure fluid, warm and bittersweet to the taste.

And she closed her eyes again. Disappearing into the shared tunnel of flesh blocking out all, she no longer existed as Charlie. A series of body orgasms took hold, one after the other, shared with each respective Epicoid. The series of climaxes culminated into a rolling orgasm and a shared massive release among the conjoined lovers. All of their communal ecstasy was experienced to the recurring chant, "We are all one, we are the Quanteme."

Her sense of self disappeared; she was no longer Charlie, no longer existing as a human. But it really wasn't a loss: it was the becoming of one; the self was now one with the universe. The epiphany of many together had her writhing in joy as she became one with them and the cosmos. She was one with the endless cycle of birth and death—the incarnation of self with birth, and with death the reunion with the singularity.

Her orgasm was no longer a singular event but rather one of many shared community orgasms combined and prolonged into a state of being that stood in defiance of those who would disapprove of their love.

Charlie woke up in the early morning hours, finding herself alone in her bed. She was naked under the covers, her skin feeling a strange excitation that seemed to actually tingle. It wasn't unpleasant but the prickly excited feeling wouldn't allow her to fall back to sleep.

Awake, she had to go to the bathroom. She turned the light on and sat on the toilet for a couple of minutes. While waiting for her stream to start, she glanced across at the opposing wall mirror and stared intently at her reflection for a minute. Shocked, she stood up and turned her body accordingly to inspect her front and back. Her hairless skin was a bold shade of blue. Not a light blue hue that added a little needed color to her pale white skin, but a distinctive deep blue coloring. Only her nipples retained some of their former pinkish color.

Charlie realized suddenly that not sharing meant that sometimes she could hide. But fully sharing with Epicoids meant not hiding from Bradley or any of the other passengers aboard the ship anymore. With a simple glance, everyone would now know she'd had coitus with the Epicoids. A lot of coitus!

It was light years beyond the simple wearing of a scarlet A. She couldn't recall seeing another passenger with such a deep blue coloring. That, combined with her shaved head, meant she would be outed as an alien collaborator, as being somewhat less than human ... or was it more?

She heard a noise that stopped her musings. No, it wasn't a noise, but human voices. She searched about the room. They sounded human, but there was no one present. She went to the radio to make sure it was off. It was off, and she remained puzzled about the source of the plaintive voices.

While moving around the room in search of the source of the voices, she realized how exhausted her entire body had become. She was too tired to care or even feign concern about her predicament. She went back to sleep and her deep bold coloring faded with the approach of the morning hours.

Bradley spent the rest of the day recovering from the beating he'd received from Steve. It was night and he looked in the mirror. His face was battered and he needed a drink to kill the pain. He went topside and heard a strange humming sound, almost like a hushed chanting, coming from the pool. He saw the pool area was dimly lit and populated with numerous aliens. They were totally naked and he noticed the large slits between their legs.

What, they all have pussies? he thought. *Shit, what a batch of freaks.* Still, the sight was somewhat engrossing. He watched as they touched one another and for some strange reason he felt himself become erect. *What the fuck?* It wasn't like they were all that attractive.

Bradley sat down far enough away so as not to be easily seen, but close enough to the pool to have a good view of their antics. As he settled in he noticed another person approaching the pool, a clothed Epicoid. No, the creature was too small, but a mist seemed to shroud the being. As he watched more closely the creature removed its hat. He realized it was a human with a shaved head, a woman, only he couldn't quite make out her face. The woman casually walked to the edge of the pool and then hesitated. The hum grew louder and two female Epicoids joined her and began removing her clothes. First her shorts, and he realized she was totally shaved. Now this was getting better for Bradley. The bald girl's top was then removed and tossed aside by the Epicoid and Bradley felt his balls tighten. She was completely naked and he instantly recognized the woman's considerable breasts even from this distance. They were Charlie's!

She slowly made her way into the pool. The Epicoids approached her and began touching her with their hands. Soon she was surrounded. To his horror Bradley watched as a penis-like appendage emerged from their bodies, male and female alike. The sex was visual and tactile, and followed with a vibrational hum as the bodies joined in coitus. As he watched their large penises become swollen he felt a loosening in his bowels. The penises swelled and twisted in different directions as they poked and probed Charlie's willing body. She spread her legs wider, seemingly sharing her body willingly with her new lovers. No orifice was safe from their inquisitive nature. She appeared to be eagerly offering herself as they carried her deeper into the pool.

The continual hum and the constant debauchery of his wife being used by those disgusting creatures caused his anger to rise. Bradley lost it and began to yell as he charged the pool. A large red orbis appeared before him and he found himself engulfed within the shimmering bubble. The sphere shrunk in size and floated him over the pool as if to coerce him into watching his wife be ravished by the Epicoids.

Bradley watched the orgy unfold, with his wife at the center of the Epicoids' attention. His resultant anger was only matched by his raging hard-on. He glanced down at his pants and noticed they were soaked. He was leaking copious amounts of pre-cum like a teen boy with a wet dream, and with just as much composure. He didn't want it—not with his wife—and he pounded on the sphere seeking escape from that sexual hell. The seemingly peaceful bubble danced upon the wind, belying the vengeful fury of the occupant within. From the vibrations the word '*sacour*' could be heard.

Steve woke in the morning light with a substantial morning glory. As he went to rub himself he noticed his underwear was a sticky mess and was immediately troubled by memories of his sex dream. As Steve peered down at his body, he saw from his matted pubic hair that he'd had a wet dream. As he touched his parts and the sheet, he noticed it had been a particularly wet one. What the fuck, was he thirteen again?

As he gathered himself together, Steve breathed a sigh of relief that it was only a nocturnal emission and not some weird alien encounter. That sauna scene with Jawara was just too bizarre for words. He got up to shower. Steve felt dirty about the wet dream and blamed the whole night on Jawara's erotic vibes. Or was it homoerotic? He just wasn't sure what you would label sex with an androgynous giant.

"Shit, I gotta find myself a regular girlfriend," he said aloud.

He checked the clock and realized he'd overslept. Funny, he no longer felt anger towards Charlie but instead found himself still wanting to be with her. Heck, he knew she was in a bad place with that idiot husband.

There was no reason not to join her so he could make amends. He hurriedly dressed and left the cabin. Like clockwork he met up with her for the breakfast buffet, mostly out of habit.

Each of them gathered a tray with a considerable amount of food. They grunted a hello to each other but then Steve did a double-take when he saw that under Charlie's hat she was completely bald with not a trace of her signature red hair. Even more damning, her skin had a blue hue. He turned to her and asked, "Charlie, what happened to your hair?"

"Don't ask," she said tiredly.

From that point, they spoke little as they sat and ate together. Emotionally, each was alone.

Steve was torn by Jawara's comment about being with Charlie. He couldn't help but notice the blue tint her pale skin had taken on. Was the shaved head also part of the Epicoid mating ritual?

Steve felt a rising tide of jealousy and he couldn't hold his tongue. "You're looking a little blue today, Charlie. A little bit of the alien flu?"

Charlie examined her skin and just nodded.

"You just couldn't leave them alone after watching their antics in the pool, could you?" he asked.

She gave him a dirty look but followed that with her own double-take and stare. She returned to eating her scrambled eggs without saying a word.

Steve was confused by her stare and asked, "What?"

"Nothing."

"Oh, it's something. What was that look about?" he asked.

"Check yourself in the mirror," she replied.

"That's pretty lame, trying to punk me like that," he said as he stopped buttering his toast.

Then, Steve stared in the mirror across from their table to call Charlie's bluff, half-expecting her to childishly call out, 'Made you look!' But upon examining himself, he felt the blood drain from his face.

As Steve scrutinized his visage in the mirror he realized his dark skin was actually lighter. Worse, there was a definite blue cast to his complexion. Clearly, Jawara hadn't gotten his message about *no* really meaning *no*.

"Fuck me," he said in disgust.

"I think someone did," Charlie said.

Steve stormed off to find Jawara.

Day 9 – Duo in Carne Una

"Time to smack that metrosexual look off Jawara's fucking face," Steve said.

"Steve, don't hurt him. It wasn't Jawara," Charlie said as he stormed away.

Charlie ran after him, realizing she alone was to blame for Steve's anger. She caught up and grabbed his arm. "Don't do it! Don't hurt him."

"What, are you crazy? I feel like so many damaged goods," he said.

"Are you forgetting that you're talking to a woman? I don't care how you deal with it, but leave him alone."

"So you're telling me women just take this shit?"

"No, not anymore."

"So why should I take this shit? I have a score to settle with the big guy."

"You can't. It's not his fault; it's mine. Jawara didn't want to do it, so take your anger out on me," she said.

"What are you talking about?"

"Are you in a better place, Steve?" she asked.

"Yes, for someone reason I do feel better, save being sexually violated."

"Walk with me to my cabin and I'll explain," she said. "I don't want others to overhear what I have to say."

Steve nodded and they walked quietly together. When they got to Charlie's cabin she motioned for him to take a seat.

"The reason you feel better was Jawara. I knew you were in a bad way, the same way I was," she said. "I was there myself, reliving every wicked and evil thing I've ever experienced or felt, including those horrible thoughts that race through your brain."

Steve just gave her a blank expression.

"Look at me. I shared that very same pain you felt; that's why I was on that balcony. I just wanted the pain to end. That's why I jumped. You know who started the pain?"

"No."

"Ahmed, with his vile touch. He is becoming more Sentinel than human. Their touch on the bare skin is sheer madness to a human. Did Ahmed touch you at some point?"

"Yeah, the freak did grab my hand. After that I was lost. God, Charlie, I never felt so alone in my life. But what's this got to do with Jawara?"

"You saved my life, but Jawara got me my sanity back. It was his touch that made me whole again. I was worried so much about you that I asked him to intervene. So if you're going to lash out at anyone, it should be me, not him. He was just doing my bidding by sending Janet to visit you." It was a lie, but a very necessary lie to keep Steve from going off on a rampage.

"Janet?"

"Yes, Janet, my masseuse from the other day. You met her. Unioeros with an Epicoid can reverse the evil effects of the Sentinels."

Steve was quiet. She knew of the dark place he had been; she had been there too. And she knew that with her love, Steve would forget all about his vengeance on Jawara.

Charlie grabbed his hand and said, "I just didn't want to lose you. How did you manage that pain? I knew I couldn't."

"I was barely hanging on. I tried to manage, but then I just couldn't handle your rejection."

"You don't understand; I wasn't rejecting you. Bradley was my first and only lover. You were my second. I don't take my lovers lightly. There has been a lot for me to wrap my head around the past couple of days. When Jaw— I mean, Janet visited you last night, what did you dream of?"

"I dreamt of making love to you again."

"I had the same dream," she said. It was another sweet lie, but Steve was hooked with the touch of her hands. Charlie cast the same crazy sexual hypnotic spell on him the Epicoids possessed. Charlie noticed it too, that tingling she felt as she held his strong, dark hand. She felt a tremble between her legs and knew she had to act the woman. No, she didn't want to fuck him; she had to fuck him.

"Why send Janet to visit me?" he said.

"I was personally very aware of some of her crazy skills, as they say. That other day, I saw you looking at me with Janet, wondering what had transpired between the two of us."

Steve's eyes brightened and he said, "I do remember your comment about kissing a girl back in the day. I could smell your sex in the air."

Charlie felt herself blush slightly with the comment and said, "I assure you this was no mere kiss between two girls. This was something very dirty and very wet."

"Oh."

"That got you horny, seeing me like that with Janet?" she asked as she rubbed up and down his arms with both of her hands.

"Wearing only that white robe with your skin oily? Hell, yeah. So what did she do to you? You seemed so satisfied," he asked with a small grin.

"I don't think I could adequately put into words what transpired," she said somewhat sultrily. "But if you'd like, I can show you."

Steve nodded.

"I thought so," Charlie said as she grabbed her suntan oil from her beach bag and said, "Strip everything off."

Steve just stared at her.

"What are you waiting for? Don't you have a lick of sense? I'm talking nudity and oil. What's to think about?" she asked.

In a whirlwind Steve removed his clothes and stood naked before Charlie. She admired his hard body as her hand traced the top of his powerful thighs.

His cock was starting to harden and his balls appeared so large and full. She had to hold herself back from touching his manliness as she lightly traced her lips with her tongue for him.

"Lie face-down on the bed, hands at your side," she instructed.

Steve did as he was told. Charlie took the bottle of oil and dribbled some onto his dark skin. He flinched from the coolness and her hands moved to his back to begin rubbing the oil in. God, he was so muscular, much more so than Bradley. Her hands moved to his dark butt and she added a little more oil that dribbled between his buttocks. With the Epicoids there were no visual sexual cues and their bodies were soft and anything but hard. This was such a treat to touch a real man, one that clearly appreciated her touch.

"This is what she did to me. This got me into the mood," Charlie said.

She grabbed his foot and began rubbing, taking care to touch and pull his toes. She then grabbed the other foot, giving it a vigorous massage as he squirmed. Her hands moved to his calves, rubbing the oil into the skin while riding up his thighs to his buttocks. She allowed her fingers to touch and then begin massaging his muscular butt. His muscles were so clenched at first but soon she felt him relax and tighten at the same time. Her hand went between his legs; his legs spread apart and she touched his dangling manhood. She delighted in squeezing the base of his rigid erection. She sought more of his manhood and touched his testicles while drizzling and spreading the oil onto his dark sack. He sighed again and her hands moved to his buttocks and dived between them, fingering and toying with him. Steve jumped with her touch and she enjoyed feeling his muscles tighten and become taut, followed by their relaxation.

"As she massaged me I could feel my pussy getting wet. Do you like that, lover? Do you like me touching you there?" she said as her fingers probed him.

She loved talking dirty, knowing her words alone excited him, never mind what her hands were doing to his exquisite masculinity.

"She was so much stronger than me. I knew what she was doing to me was wrong but I was helpless to stop her from toying with my body," she said breathily as she rubbed the oil into his glistening skin. "Only, to my everlasting shame, I didn't want her to stop."

He softly groaned and squirmed as his erection grew trapped between the bed and his body.

"Now I am toying with you. Feel good, lover?" she whispered into his ear. Nothing but soft groans from Steve while her fingers kept searching, exciting and penetrating him as if to let him know that she owned him.

"Then Janet turned me over. I was wet and open, really nasty-looking. Turn over for me. Show me how hard you are for me!" Charlie commanded.

Steve turned over and laid on his back, his massive erection sticking straight into the air. The tip was wet in anticipation.

"She spread my legs and played with me, spreading apart the pink lips of my wet pussy."

Charlie's skin tingled once again. She sucked Steve's nipples while her hands massaged his powerful pecs but she wanted more, to run her hands along his throbbing hardness. She grabbed the oil and allowed a few drops on top of the paler mushroom head of his cock. Her hands began rubbing along the length and Steve began groaning much louder.

"You know what I want now? I want that big cock of yours in my mouth. Does that sound good to you?" she asked.

She had to taste him, but before she did, she drizzled a few drops of oil on her shaven head and rubbed it into the skin. Steve watched and gave a puzzled look at her curious action. She just smiled at him and her mouth engulfed his cock, taking as much as she could. She did that for a few minutes and tasted his throbbing excitement as she moved up and down his erection. His hands involuntarily grabbed her slick, smooth head, guiding her mouth back and forth on his hard cock. The sensation of her slick head and her mouth drove him to near climax.

She sensed he was getting near and backed off.

"Now I just have to fuck you to show you the release I got from that dirty alien."

She poured a little more oil on his already slick erection. Satisfied his big dick was wet enough, Charlie stepped away from the bed and removed her blouse and then her bra. As Steve watched, she dropped her shorts and panties, smiled, and climbed on top of him. She was wet already and she positioned her slippery pussy on top of his erection. She pushed back, taking his fullness, and let out a small cry, almost a whimper. She began to ride him, enjoying the touch of his oily skin as her hands braced against his muscular chest.

Charlie wanted to inhale him, to possess him, to fuck him like an animal, so her pace increased, the intensity showing on both of their faces. She rode him hard, grinding her hips into him, taking his entire hard cock deep within her.

Steve struggled to hang on and not erupt. He grabbed her arms and roughly picked her up and threw her to the bed. She giggled as he jumped on top of her and kissed her on the lips. His tongue probed and she eagerly received him. Her pale blue breasts and their rosy tips were erect. His lips moved to her nipples, sucking, toying, and playing with them. Charlie reclined back and relaxed with his touch. Her legs spread apart, eager to receive him once again.

Steve repeatedly thrust deep within her and she began to come, her breath shortening and her sweet cries filling the air. After she came, he wanted more. Her chest was red and flushed, her breathing extra heavy. He wanted to pleasure and own her. She tried to move away and kept her legs together as if to forestall him. He forced them apart and dove between her thighs, his tongue licking her clit, adding to her wetness. He sucked and nibbled on her womanhood, forcing it out in the open as he gave her a series of multiple orgasms. Her hips and pelvis bucked as her legs flexed with the liquid pleasure.

"Too much, too much," she protested even as her feet dug into the bed, lifting her pelvis deeper into his mouth.

Steve stopped after a few minutes but he went on top of her again and rudely grabbed each of her ankles as he spread her legs apart. He rested her legs on top of his shoulders, pointing her feet to the ceiling. He peered into her eyes and kissed her with a deep, probing tongue as he pinned her legs to her chest and began fucking her hard and deep. The orgasm rose deep within her body; she outwardly flexed her pale legs and curled her toes. He owned her and she couldn't escape the thrusts of Steve's hard cock.

"Jesus Christ, don't stop, lover, fuck me harder," she cried.

She started to rise, not just her body but her entire being. With her urging he quickened his pace. As her orgasm spread, her soft moans became yells as she began to grab and scratch her lover's arms, urging him deeper.

She refused to journey alone. She took him with her, rising and falling together to some unseen cosmic metronome of life. With each of his thrusts they became more, her sweet surrender a shared gift of oneness, not just with each other but with the universe. Her touch was a sensuous jolt unto his body. She was imposing a total submission upon the conjoined lovers, only they weren't alone in their lovemaking. Unseen others shared their joy and pleasure while delighting in their rapturous pairing. Impermanence became permanent for the pair.

"We are all one, we are the Quanteme," resonated deep within her being and she was one with the universe.

The lovers disappeared and exploded together. Steve erupted within her with a flood of his love as she grabbed his buttocks. He kept pumping even after his orgasm, wanting to extend their pleasure for as long as he could.

The two finally collapsed onto the bed, panting and shaken. After they rested Steve lovingly gazed at her hairless, pale blue body. For ten minutes they remained quiet just looking into each other's eyes.

Catching her breath, she smiled at him and said, "Holy shit!"

"Yeah, holy shit. I mean, I never wanted a woman so much."

"A sexual epiphany," she replied, fluttering her green eyes at him.

"Damn."

"Just consider it a gift from our friends."

"Really, do all white girls fuck like that? Because I think I may have been missing out on something," he asked with a smirk.

Charlie saw a small drop of blood trickling down Steve's arm where in her excitement she'd cut his skin with her nails. She dipped her index finger into the blood and then licked her finger as she smiled and said, "Nah, it's just the redheads who are the freaks."

"Do you have a single hair remaining on your body?" Steve asked as his long fingers caressed her hairless pussy.

She spread her legs slightly to receive his hand and said, "All gone, so much the better to be accepted by our friends. Admit you were jealous when you realized I was with them."

"Yeah, more than a little; I just wanted you even more. But why them?"

"I just had to; I'm not even sure why."

"You know, I noticed as I made love to you, I sensed you were becoming part of something bigger. It was like you left me and then you came back to take me with you," he said.

"Very true, my love," she replied.

"Well, explain, girl, because I've never experienced anything like that before. You're like a force of nature. Even your touch was totally different, more like our friends," Steve said.

"The Epicoids shared something with me and you're with a fully realized woman now. When making love with you, I was part of something bigger. My passion consumed me and became larger than me, larger than you and me in this room," she said. "I like the way sex initially makes me smaller and smaller, as if nothing in the cosmos exists, including me. Everything dissolves away. All my cares, worries, and fears disappear. I am gone forever, only to be reborn."

His fingers glided from between Charlie's shoulders down to her rounded pale blue buttocks.

With her excited green eyes she looked at Steve and said, "And then, with perfect clarity: boom! My body surrenders and my orgasm is bigger, bigger than anything else in the universe, my own private Big Bang. Now only I matter, me and my orgasm, but there's more. Now I know I am sharing my pleasure with you and a multitude of others. Only it's not for a few seconds, but it's multiple pleasures riding like waves through my body for eternity."

Steve smiled and hid his concern that he could never match that ecstasy she felt.

"Just now when we were making love I had the same feeling, that very same connection—not just with you, my love, but with the entire universe. Thank you for igniting my love; this felt very real to me," Charlie said. Steve kissed her hand.

"You know, the very first boy I kissed was also black," she said.

"Really? What happened to him?"

"Not sure. We were twelve at the time and I got us both into trouble. Poor boy was probably told to keep away from that crazy redheaded bitch. Sometimes when you look at me I get the sense that you wished I was black."

"Nah, you being different is part of your appeal to me."

"It's just that sometimes you seem like you are fighting me."

"Wish life was simpler, that's all. Honestly," he said.

They were both quiet for a few minutes, each seemingly deep in their own thoughts. She interrupted the quiet by asking, "So how high was it when you jumped?"

"What?" he aside.

"When you dived into the ocean after me," she clarified.

"Oh, I don't know, maybe eighty feet or so, maybe more—enough to reconsider my sanity."

"You jumped into the ocean to save me without hesitation and then you give me this fantastic fuck? If you ask me, I think I got myself a keeper," she said as she grabbed his arm.

"Glad you approve. Gotta ask, but where did that slick-head business come from? I mean, that was kinky as all hell."

"It just came to me. I figured, when would I have an opportunity to do something like that again?" Charlie said.

"So you'll grow back your beautiful red hair for me?" he asked.

"I promise," she said while hugging him. She finally felt as one with a man for the first time in her life, and she wasn't about to let him go from her bed.

Jamais Vu

Jawara was confused when he was abruptly summoned from the *Mandjet* to appear before the Council. The Council consisted of the elder Epicoids responsible for the Greeting; however, Jawara sensed the presence of others that were not so welcoming. Fortunately, it was the Epicoids that were communicating to him.

As he faced them, the Council said, "In the spirit of the Quanteme, the *Mandjet* experiment and all subsequent Unioeros with the humans will now come to an end by order of the Council. Thank you for your inspired work in the Greeting. Your interaction with the humans has proven invaluable and we now believe we have enough data points to make our determination regarding our final Greeting to the humans. We are asking you to observe and report back to the Council regarding this new initiative."

"Thank you for this honor. What of the humans aboard the cruise ship?" Jawara asked.

"They will be taken care of accordingly. You have become attached to the human with the red-colored hair, correct?"

"Yes, I believe she is an exceptional human being."

"She is, and she will be rejoined with her kind on Earth to be part of the official Greeting. That will include all of the humans aboard the *Mandjet*. We noticed that your form now resembles that of a human male. Is that her influence as well?"

"Yes, with a greater influence from the male human named Steve," Jawara said.

"Of course it is. Very informative. You should go now."

Jawara hesitated and asked, "How will I know the Greeting is underway?"

"It will be readily apparent to you. Remember, you are only an observer present to measure the effectiveness of the Greeting with the humans."

"What am I actually measuring?" Jawara asked.

"Again, that will become readily apparent to you as the Greeting unfolds. You will then understand your instructions."

Jawara nodded and turned around, walking away. He entered the orbis at the end of the hall and arrived at Earth. He waited, wondering how the Greeting would actually transpire. His sphere danced above the atmosphere and he waited for the show to begin.

As he watched, a large translucent red orbis began to circle the Earth, lowering itself into the atmosphere. Over a mile across, the orbis became opaque and visible enough to be sighted by anyone on Earth. The atmosphere of the Earth took on a strange reddish coloring as the entire planet descended into a strange twilight. As he watched, the horrors began to unfold.

With Steve in the bed next to her, Charlie found herself too excited and restless for sleep. She left Steve snoring in her cabin, hoping that an early morning walk on the deck would tire her out. It was there that she observed Jawara sprawled across a deck chair thrashing about. His eyes were closed and he appeared to be asleep. With some trepidation, she decided to risk waking him and grabbed him by the shoulders.

"Come on, Jawara, snap out of it!" she said.

He awoke startled and yelled, "Who's there?" As he focused in the darkness he saw Charlie.

"It's Charlie. Did you get wasted tonight?" she asked. He shook his head no. "Let me help you up," she said as she extended a hand. As she touched his arm and hand, Charlie noticed how sweaty he was.

"Steve is searching for you and he's not happy with you. If he presses you, just tell him it was Janet having Unioeros with him last night."

"Lie?"

"Yes, lie if you have a lick of common sense. Jawara, why are you sweating? Since when do you even have pores? Even your skin is darker. What the heck is going on with your body and these changes?"

Jawara stood up somewhat shakily and mumbled, "I don't know."

"What happened to you?" Charlie asked.

"I was unconscious at first and then I had these vivid experiences, but I know they weren't real. So violent, with so many deaths."

"Were you sleeping?"

"Not sure. Maybe?"

"Since when? What's going on with you physically? From what I saw, you appeared to be asleep and having what we call a dream."

"I find this sleep condition very curious. No wonder your kind is so mystical."

"Dreams are part of our subconscious telling us things that may be masked by our conscious mind," Charlie explained.

"But they seemed so real and so terribly awful," Jawara said.

"Well, those dreams we call nightmares, and, yeah, they can scare the hell out of you. But a lot of the time it's your subconscious talking to you, warning you about things that you should be worried about. Some dreams can be very pleasant, by the way."

"What's a subconscious?" Jawara asked.

"It's the part of your brain that is on autopilot. Your conscious self usually keeps it under wraps; however, at night your subconscious can come out and play. I know this because I practice lucid dreaming and I try to make my dreams actionable, as they say."

"Actionable?"

"Assert some control over them," Charlie said.

"Now I'm afraid to close my eyes, but I'm so tired," Jawara said sadly.

"Tell you what, come to my room and sleep in my bed this morning. I won't leave you and you won't have to go through your dreams alone."

"How?" he asked.

"I'll explain in my cabin. Let's move because I see a Sentinel approaching. Oh, stay dressed, and no Unioeros, understood? I'll lie to Steve for you."

Jawara nodded in agreement and they made their way to Charlie's cabin. When she entered the room, Steve was nowhere to be found. As they lay in the bed, Charlie said, "You said we were connected, right? So you are going to practice lucid dreaming this morning. Before you dream, reach out to me and I'll guide you through your subconscious journey. I'll teach how to manage your dreams."

Jawara seemed confused and she asked, "So what are you going to do before you fall asleep?"

"Reach out to Charlie," he replied.

"Good. To lucid dream, you need to lie fairly still; don't move your muscles and drift off, but don't go to sleep. Got that?" she asked.

Jawara frowned but he nodded. He soon fell asleep, comforted by her proximity. Within minutes, he awoke to find himself on his back looking upward in a sterile white office. He was in a special metal chair, and a strange little man appeared to be attending to him. As his eyes focused, the white man with a mask held a strange instrument. "You'll feel a little vibration; remember to keep your mouth open," he said as the drill came to life. The whirring sound frightened Jawara and soon the dentist was drilling away, the smell of burning bone filling the air.

"What is this hell?" a frightened Jawara asked Charlie from his dream.

"Sorry, I fell asleep and went directly into a lucid dream state. That's my root canal from a few months ago. Just relax, I'll think of something else. But this is good; by reaching out to me you took charge of your dreams."

Charlie started to dream of a day at the beach. She and Jawara walked together on soft white coral sands. A blue ocean with a warm sun and blue skies welcomed the pair as a lone gull circled them and cried.

"Isn't this a beautiful day? Just gorgeous, with a real sun, don't you agree?" she said.

"It is beautiful."

"Feel that sun on your skin? Feel the warmth?" she asked. "And the air feels so soft."

"Yes, this is very pleasant. Thank you for sharing this memory, Charlie. Where is this?"

"Maui. I went there on my honeymoon."

The look on Jawara's face changed.

"Oh no, I am being summoned again by the Council. I have to go."

From his vantage point in the orbis, Jawara surveyed the seemingly tranquil blue world.

A commanding voice coldly said, "We have found your recent interactions with the humans to be troubling. Jawara, for your insolence and affiliation with the Red Avatar you are to personally monitor the Greeting."

As he approached, dark grey clouds shrouded much of Earth. The sphere descended below the clouds and swept through the desolated landscape. Most cities were in smoldering ruins, and those that were not were in the process of being systematically razed. On terra firma, Sentinel parties raced through the streets hunting and killing the remaining humans that had the temerity to survive the initial onslaught. Earth became a hunting preserve for the Sentinels as they took glee in the task of killing humans. Knowing some humans would fight back only added to the thrill.

"Jawara, what is this nightmare?" Charlie asked.

"Second Phase of the Greeting."

"Why is this happening?"

"I do not know. The Council is not acting alone; they are being influenced by outside agencies," Jawara said.

Jawara was back before the Council. He sensed the others but couldn't make them out.

"Why?" he asked.

There was no comment.

"Jawara, I can't see them, can you?" Charlie asked.

"No, I can't either. This exercise is futile."

"You have to push beyond that veil to see who is behind this attack on my people."

"I ask again, why?" Jawara said, hoping to see beyond the mist.

No reply. Jawara yelled, "Talk to me!" and he charged the Council. When he reached the Council he descended into a dark pit. He heard a low rumbling noise, almost an animal growl, but couldn't see or feel anything. His skin began to burn and he could see the skin of his fingers beginning to melt, exposing the bone. He began to scream but no sound emerged as a ferocious creature with tentacles rose from the emptiness to seize him by his head. It began systematically ripping his limbs apart and ingesting him.

Jawara woke trembling with fear in the bed. Charlie was awake with him and she comforted the giant.

"Who was there, and what was that creature? Was it a Sentinel?" Charlie asked.

"No, but it was one of the Sentinels' playthings," he said.

"They keep these horrors around?" she asked.

"Yes, they actually cultivate and breed these things as weapons of terror and for amusement," he said. "I believe you call it bloodsport."

"What do you think your subconscious was trying to tell you? Don't think about it; first impressions only."

"Not to trust the Greeting because of the Sentinels."

"It's just a dream, not reality; that's what you have to remember," she said.

"It may be more complicated than that," Jawara said. "My connection to the whole and the Quanteme means there may be much more to my nightmares than just a simple fright."

She was quiet, mulling over what it meant. "What else? They called me something, didn't they?"

"They described you as the Red Avatar," Jawara said.

"What does that mean? You know, don't you?" She stared at him, hoping for an answer. "Why won't you tell me? What else did you see? There was more, wasn't there?"

Jawara turned away, confused by his nightmarish visions.

Purgatory and Synesthesia

Steve sat in the dark of the ship's theatre watching a scrawny, strange man in white body paint dancing alone on the stage. The strange atonal music was a perfect accompaniment to his spastic, sinewy body. The spotlights, along with the eyes of several clerics and a small gathering of Epicoids, followed his every awkward move across the barren stage.

Steve grimaced as he watched the near-naked man make bizarre, exaggerated motions with his body. The man was Reverend Bannan. It wasn't exactly how Steve wanted to spend his time, an apostate among the true believers. Still, his mother had taught him to be polite, even when expressing his own opinions.

"What is this crazy shit?" Steve asked in a whisper.

"It's called Butoh," replied Pastor Jones, who was seated next to him.

"Just why am I here again?" he asked.

"You know we have lost moral authority and, to some degree, control over the passengers. They are so lustful. We need the assistance of the Epicoids to manage them somewhat. The Epicoids asked all of the clerics to make their case for their individual religions, but we also know you are good friends with the Interspecies Event Facilitator named Jawara. We need you to put in a good word with him for us," Pastor Jones said.

Actually, Steve had been in search of Jawara since the early morning hours to have his own, very private conversation with the bi-curious alien. To Steve's right, a party of Epicoids, along with Jawara, were attentively watching the bizarre dance.

Steve knew the holy men aboard the cruise were upset by the rampant displays of lust and hedonism among the passengers. With no strife and no fight for survival, the passengers did what all humans do during times of plenty, health, and relative peace: They fucked and partied to their heart's content. The passengers appeared to be indulging themselves in all manner of deviant sex with little consideration for morality, Steve included.

The clerics had tried talking and giving sermons to the passengers but the bond they enjoyed back home was missing. Most of the passengers were polite but would return to the very same behavior once the clerics went their separate ways. A number of people were less polite and in so many words told the holy men to fuck off. It didn't help that the presence of the aliens was a constant reminder that perhaps the Bible wasn't all that authoritative about the universe after all.

"Why the hell dance?" Steve said. "Eh, excuse me, pastor, for my language, but this is beyond bizarre."

"Shhhh," said someone watching in the audience.

Pastor Jones said in a lower voice, "They were quite taken with the people dancing at the club the past few nights; they just don't understand and want to learn more. We were going to put on a play for the Epicoids to instruct them about our individual faiths and perhaps enlist their aid in reigning in some of the more salacious passengers."

"Sounds like a plan. So why is the dancing lunatic here?" Steve asked.

"The Epicoids insisted on the reverend's presence. In fact, they don't want to see the play and we need you to intercede." The other clerics were listening and nodding in agreement. "We chose to ignore some of the more scurrilous gossip we have heard about you, particularly in light of your commendable actions during the shark-fishing fiasco."

Steve shook his head, knowing the gossip was about a black man having an affair with a white married woman. Again, he held his tongue.

As the dance progressed the reverend began talking in tongues. As he babbled, several male members of his flock joined in the dance, each almost nude except for a loincloth. For the finale the reverend yelled out, "But the cowardly, the unbelieving, the vile, the murderers, the sexually immoral, those who practice magic arts, the idolaters, and all the liars—they will be consigned to the fiery lake of burning sulfur. This is the second death!"

With the dance over, the reverend and his followers left the stage.

"Thank God," Steve said. He walked over to Jawara and asked, "Can I talk to you for a moment?"

"No problem, Steve, you seem agitated. How can I help you?" Jawara replied.

"I have a personal bone to pick with you that we will discuss a little later, but first, why the love for that lunatic Reverend Bannan?" Steve asked.

"He shows signs of communicating to other species. That is, to your god specifically."

"He shows signs because Reverend Crazy is schizophrenic. He's sick and needs to be medicated. Any voices he hears come from within his damaged brain, not outside from the universe," Steve said.

"Schizophrenia would be a misdiagnosis on your part. The reverend does hear voices, but those voices are emanating from within the Quanteme. We have long suspected that some of your religious people have been directly accessing the Quanteme. His kind has a genetic mutation that makes their brain much more sensitive and allows them to directly tap into the Quanteme. What you call the crazier ones are actually channeling some particularly dark voices within the Quanteme. We want to know more about who they are actually contacting," Jawara explained.

"Yeah, he is channeling something … some kind of crazy, if you ask me. As to you and me, we will have that talk about your late-night encounters a little later."

"I look forward to it," Jawara agreed.

"You shouldn't. Epicoids do have life insurance, right?"

"Humor?"

"We'll see," Steve said, but their attention was soon diverted to the clerics, who were now squabbling among themselves and with the Epicoids. The argument hit a fever pitch when the half-naked reverend decided to join them.

"This man doesn't represent my faith," said Pastor Jones.

"I agree he doesn't," the deacon said. "But sometimes I have my doubts about this God who treats His children so poorly."

The others stared at him in horror.

"I'm sorry; I have to tell the truth about how I feel to the Epicoids. I don't feel lies help us here."

A verbal shouting match erupted between the holy men and the reverend, with the Epicoids stuck firmly in the middle as ineffective moderators. One of the female-looking Epicoids turned to Steve and asked, "What do you make of your clergy and their gods?"

Steve felt conflicted and he hesitated to join the fray. Before he could talk, Ahmed marched in with a pair of Sentinels at his side. Ahmed saw Steve and walked over as if to confront him.

Steve stood where he was. "Wow, look at you embracing your evil side—not that it was much of a leap in faith for you."

"You're wasting your time with these fools. Seriously, my brother, you don't see the beauty in one thought?" asked Ahmed.

"Fuck no, especially when that thought is so twisted."

"Beauty in conformity and acquiescence to another superior being. But most importantly, there is beauty and godliness in controlling the thinking of others. You control how a man thinks, then he is your slave to do God's bidding. All you have to promise them is eternal life."

"What happened to Allah?" Steve asked.

"I see a bigger god nowadays," Ahmed said. "Now I must put an end to this nonsense."

"Knock your socks off, Ahmed," said Steve, and he left the meeting with Jawara. When there were no other Epicoids in sight, Steve pulled the alien aside.

"Where are you going?" Steve angrily asked. Some of the other passengers stopped to watch the exchange between the two.

"Oh, there was more to discuss?" Jawara asked.

Steve grabbed the alien by the shoulders and threw the startled giant against the wall.

"Remember you asked me what was bothering me? What you did last night was not cool, asshole," he said with some considerable anger. The passengers watching began to scatter.

The giant didn't react and calmly said, "What is it you think I did?"

"Are you fucking kidding me? Dude, you convinced that thing Janet to have her way with me last night. Unioeros, I believe you call it. Now before I kill you, why did you do that, knowing I said no in the sauna?"

"I had to taste you," Jawara said as he grabbed one of Steve's hands.

"What the fuck?" Steve felt his anger dissipate with the touch of the giant. "You were there with her?"

Jawara nodded and said, "I needed to share your experiences and memories. You were important to Charlie, so I had to know why."

"It was a fucking threesome?" he asked. Jawara said nothing. "I don't understand. How?" Steve asked. "You did this knowing I was going to kill you?"

"By tasting you. We are now one."

"What does that even mean?" Steve asked as he shook his head.

"Tasting allows us to share chemical and genetic information with a partner by skin-to-skin contact."

"Cut that shit out! I am not your partner."

"Okay, but that's how it works," Jawara said.

"Wait a second. Is your tasting like synesthesia, combining multiple senses like taste and sight into one?" he asked.

"Yes, but it entails senses you are not even aware of, and is a two-way exchange of information between partners."

"Now I get it. But why through tasting and Unioeros?" he asked.

"In the spirit of the Quanteme, it's a quirk of our evolution that Unioeros is the means to the collective and ultimately to the singularity. Unioeros is one of our main sensory pleasures and coming together as one is the highest pleasure we can partake of in our species. Unioeros with you has connected us."

"Still not cool," Steve said dejectedly. "Is that why you appear different?"

"Yes. From your tone of voice, does this mean you are not going to kill me now?" Jawara asked.

"Just an expression, big guy."

"You can punch me if that will help you feel better," Jawara offered.

"I'll pass on the violence, but if you pull that shit again with me we will have a serious talk about your future viability."

"Will you be punching Janet? If so, I need to warn my friend. All of this will come as a big surprise to Janet."

"I'm not punching anyone, save that idiot Bradley," Steve said.

"I never thought you would kill me. Guy talk, right?"

"Yeah, something like that."

"I thought so. I always knew you were one of the good ones," Jawara said.

"What the fuck?" Steve said. He turned to Jawara and almost saw a smile. "Let me guess, more humor?" Steve asked.

The Epicoid nodded and said, "One of the good humans."

"Almost funny. What exactly is this Quanteme business?" he asked.

"Eureka!" Jawara yelled.

"What's that shouting about?" Steve said, confused.

"Did you ever have what you humans call a eureka moment?" Jawara asked.

"Yeah … shit, yes, when I was working out the population dynamics of some of the fish species. It suddenly dawned on me that there was a symbiotic relationship between a number of different species that was driving their population numbers together. It wasn't just traditional predator-and-prey dynamics, but there were also a number of key symbiotic relationships driving their population growth," Steve said.

"You said it dawned on you, right?" Jawara said.

"Yeah."

"Sometimes your brain channels and connects to the Quanteme, a far larger neural network than your own. It works in a similar manner with the reverend, though he seems to be messaging something quite dark within the Quanteme."

"Holy shit. But how does that work?" Steve asked.

"Your species is part of the Quanteme. It's the quantum entanglement of minds, but not just our own; it includes other species as well. Think of it as a heightened consciousness of the universe. We Epicoids are connected as one, but we sensed your brains as well, prompting our visit. Your brain, being a quantum mind, uses quantum entanglement and superposition to create your consciousness and thoughts. As I told you before, this theory is not new to your people. You should know this, being a biologist."

"Yes, but it's just a wild-assed theory with literally no proof and a major issue with decoherence to address."

"We are here because it is not a theory. It is, in fact, true. We are not in close proximity to your planet. There is no reasonable way we could have detected your presence using what you call traditional physics. You now have your proof," Jawara said.

"So all this time we were thinking it was our radio signals that would give our presence away in the universe. Shit, we couldn't hide if we wanted to, right?"

"Yes, once your population hit the critical mass of a billion human beings, your quantum minds got the attention of my people and the Sentinels."

"Wait, we're over seven billion, so reaching a billion people was some time ago. Do you know when exactly you became aware of us as a species?" Steve asked.

"It was 4480."

"Give me a break, Jawara. I don't mean using your calendar."

"Sorry, that was the Chinese calendar. It was your year 1789 AD."

"You have been planning this visit for over two hundred years?" Steve asked, somewhat incredulously.

"Not exactly; our timeline is different than yours."

"Funny that you mention different timelines. We noticed the passengers on this cruise are not all from the same time period, are we?"

"No, that would have made it impossible to get a representative sample, but we have kept it as close as possible so there wouldn't be any culture clashes among your people aboard this ship."

"Why just one black person and one redheaded person among your sample?" he asked.

"Unsure as to the selection criteria for our human subjects within the Greeting. That's above my pay grade," Jawara replied.

Steve smirked at the comment and said, "Good answer. Interesting. So there is a criteria, right?"

"Yes, the Council decided on the selection of subjects."

"Why haven't we detected your civilization with our SETI radio telescopes?" Steve asked.

"Our technology works at different energy frequencies than those you are scanning for, and your assumption is that we are from the same time lens."

"What did you just say?"

"That we are not from the same time as you," Jawara repeated.

"Forward or backwards?" Steve asked.

"Neither, besides manipulating space through what you call wormholes we can manipulate time through time holes, creating minor temporal distortions. We can change individual timelines to a degree."

"How come you're telling me all of this now?" Steve asked. "Is this because you're suddenly afraid of me?"

"Quite the contrary. We are now connected, so I felt it was important to share with a friend. I now sense your implicit good. Am I free to go, Steve?" Jawara asked.

"You're free to go, big guy, but no more of this tasting shit, all right?"

"Understood. I warned Charlie that even though I am not a guy, you were very homophobic," Jawara said as he turned away.

Steve walked a few steps, stopped, and then turned towards Jawara and said, "I'm not homophobic!"

The Big House

Charlie had nothing to do and she couldn't find Steve. Attired in her black bikini, she sunned herself on the top deck as she looked out at the vast ocean. A Sentinel walked by, sending a frisson through her. The Sentinel gave her a malfeasant glance, as if to scare her. She stared back at him in defiance. The creature moved on and she returned to her preoccupation with spacing out.

As she surveyed the horizon there wasn't a trace of land—nothing other than a few frigate birds trailing behind the ship. Jawara approached and joined her in gazing out at the landscape. They didn't talk for a few minutes, an awkward silence serving as a temporary buffer between the two friends.

"Did Steve catch up with you?" Charlie finally asked.

"Yes, he did. We had a very enlightening talk."

"I'm glad you worked it out. Why a cruise ship, by the way?" she asked, breaking the stillness.

"You and Steve seem very inquisitive lately. A cruise ship scenario offers a number of advantages. The setting allows us to effectively manage the Greeting, and your people are accustomed to the isolation of a cruise. Most importantly, it creates the right atmosphere for the passengers."

"What atmosphere? The idea of the fun and excitement of a vacation so you can mask the fact that we are alone and separated from our kind? It's not fair that you removed us from our lives, segregated us, and then placed us in this cage, even if it is a gilded cage. Or are we just some play toys for you and your kind?" Charlie asked.

"It's not a cage, and we would never remove you from your natural-born lives. We don't interfere in the lives of sentient creatures," Jawara said. "We all agree that wouldn't be fair to you."

"What do you call it, then? It's not a real life, and you know we make lousy pets," Charlie said.

"A happy ending? A gift?" Jawara said.

"Literally, huh? A small joke? We're never returning to our normal lives, are we?" she asked.

"No, and you were never returning to your normal lives even before this cruise."

"Why did you lie to us?" Charlie asked.

"We don't lie."

The dispassionate way Jawara made the comments irked her to no end. Charlie gave him a curious look and said, "If you didn't remove us from our lives, that could only mean … what? That you don't want to return us?"

"I am not sure I can honestly answer that now. Since Unioeros with Steve I have found myself questioning the Greeting and your repatriation process, in the spirit of the Quanteme. Frankly, Steve's instincts have taken hold and I now have concerns about whether or not you are being returned to your individual timelines."

"But you told us we would be returned," she said. "You said you don't lie."

"After you woke me from my sleep I had some additional visions," he said. "You should have a seat as we discuss this."

"No, I'm fine standing. So you would return us if you could?"

"Yes, but now I know we can't," Jawara said.

"So you say you won't interfere in our lives, but you can't return us, so that means what exactly? What you are saying makes no sense."

Silence from Jawara.

"Shit, had our lives ended?" she asked.

"Correct."

"This is the *more* you experienced in your dreams that you wouldn't talk about?"

"Yes," Jawara admitted.

Charlie mulled over Jawara's words for a few moments and then asked, "Dear God, why us? Why so many? Why almost all predominately Americans?"

"Americans suffer almost forty thousand deaths in automobile crashes, another forty thousand in suicides, and…." Jawara paused.

"And?"

"And over ten thousand gun murders a year. Your country gives us many suitable candidates for our cruise. So many young and middle-aged adults to choose from, particularly those with no other close family ties."

"What?" she asked.

"You were all dead or soon to be dead, dying within your allotted timelines. We can create minute temporal distortions and rescue you from your imminent fate," Jawara said.

"All of us?"

"All two thousand and nine people aboard this cruise."

"Really? Doesn't make sense," Charlie said as she reviewed all of the passengers she knew. "I'm not going to see Elvis aboard this cruise ship, am I?"

"No, you were all selected from about the same time period, and we avoided celebrities; they'd cause far too much trouble."

"I have to ask, what of Reverend Bannan and his flock? How could they all die at the same time?"

"I believe your newspapers referred to their demise as a suicide cult. They died together after taking cyanide. Reverend Bannan said the Heaven's Gate cult was their inspiration. Whatever message the Heaven's Gate cult received from the Quanteme was wrong in terms of the timing; we never made it in time to recruit them for the Greeting. His flock had a much different— perhaps some would even consider it a more successful—result."

"They took their lives to join with you? That's some leap of faith," Charlie said, amazed.

"We believe that was their goal," Jawara said.

"This Quanteme…. You told me that it's the oneness of the Universe, right?"

"Yes, it's the collective quantum minds, or, if you like, souls of the universe. Some people like Reverend Bannan receive direct messages from the darker elements of the Quanteme."

"Wow, but that's so crazy that so many people died together like that," Charlie said.

Jawara made a point of turning around and staring down on the diminutive Charlie as if to put her on the spot.

"Curious; you purposely didn't ask about your own fate, knowing that most of the people on the cruise died together. I decided to investigate for you. You should know that you and Bradley died together as well," Jawara told her.

"I don't want to hear this," Charlie said.

"Sorry, you must hear this."

Charlie appeared upset and said, "No, that's not what happened to me and Bradley. I was healthy; so was Bradley. This must be wrong. We were fine," she said, hesitating. "Was there an accident?"

Jawara shook his head no and said, "What was your last memory before the cruise?"

"It's very vague, almost like a childhood memory. We were home in our apartment. I was suspicious of him so I went online right before going to work to check the balance in our savings account. I remember feeling very upset and listening to Bradley saying he would make it up to me. There was the smell of that godawful tree … then the next moment, I found myself on a deck chair aboard a cruise ship feeling very tranquil. So how did I die then?" Charlie asked.

"You did check the savings account balance and found that the balance was zero. Your husband wagered and gambled all of your money and lost. You confronted him that morning and you were about to leave him but he wouldn't let you. I believe your people call it murder-suicide."

"Bradley killed me? Or did I…?" she asked.

"You said in your last words that you were leaving him, and in a fit of despair and anger he shot you twice with a handgun as you were about to leave the apartment. One of the bullets struck your heart and you died instantly," Jawara said.

Charlotte grabbed a chair and sat down, trying to comprehend all he'd told her.

"He killed me?" she asked.

"I am sorry, but yes," he said in his monotone voice. "He then committed suicide with the same gun."

"Shit, am I dead?"

"No, you are very much alive. You were between life and death when we rescued you as an active observer in your timeline, much in the same manner we did after your plunge into the water."

"So I'm condemned to spend my remaining life on this godforsaken ship? I can't go home?" she asked as she teared up.

"I cannot help you. We have one basic rule regarding our interaction with another species: We were told that thou shall not change a sentient creature's timeline on their home planet!" Jawara said.

"I don't get it. Keeping us alive is okay after our fated demise?" she asked.

"Consider it a small mercy after your respective brutal endings."

"You call this mercy? It's wrong! You're manipulating us, not allowing us to live our lives fully, reducing us to mere toys to be played with as you see fit. Having a choice, having free will is important to our species, even if the perception of that free will is an illusion. That and our memories comprise our existence."

"I know; as you said, humans make for lousy pets. There is nothing I can do for you."

"So what was Stage 2?" Charlie asked.

"I'm not sure; perhaps an elaborate lie," Jawara said. Charlie seemed sad and he asked, "Would you rather be dead or still have a chance at life?"

She walked away and said, "I just want my shitty old life back. That bastard really did kill me?"

"Yes, I am sorry to say he did."

"Dammit, I want my shitty life back, but without that abusive prick," she said while walking away.

Long after the participants of the orgy had dispersed Bradley remained trapped within the bubble. He watched the horizon and alternated between yelling and hitting the walls of the orbis. Nobody from the ship noticed his imprisonment and he felt claustrophobic and fearful in that tight space. The panic rose in him and in fear he wet himself. As urine dribbled from his pants, he watched the liquid fall from the sphere as a yellow rain upon the ship below.

He continued to punch at the walls of the invisible sphere. Curiously, it wasn't like he was striking anything; his fist just moved through the air and then ceased to move any further. There was no wall containing him, just an end to the personal space he could occupy. The orbis randomly bounced up and down along the deck of the ship, sometimes getting to within five feet of the deck and then rising a hundred feet above the enormous boat. It didn't matter if he sat or stood; the orbis just did its own erratic dance along the deck of the ship.

As dawn approached the orbis gently descended once again. This time, as the sphere touched the deck, it vaporized altogether. Bradley's feet touched the deck. He touched his pants that reeked of urine. Then he wandered back to Charlie's cabin to confront her.

Charlie was undressing when she heard the banging on the cabin door. She moved to the door and was startled to see Bradley standing in the room and staring at her. He looked his wife over, shaking his head at her bald scalp. He barely recognized her without her signature red hair. Even her eyebrows were missing and her pale skin had a discernible blue tinge.

"How did you get in here? You gave me your key," Charlie said.

"It's pretty easy to get an extra key when your name is assigned to a room. What the fuck, Charlie? What was that last night? Please tell me they forced you to do that," Bradley said.

Liar, cheat, adulterer, and now she had to add murderer to her labels for Bradley. Charlie wanted out of the room. She started to back away but Bradley blocked the door.

"So you want the truth?" she asked.

"Yeah, I want to know," he said.

"I wasn't forced, more like compelled last night."

"Compelled, huh, slut? So what was that last night, slut? You were compelled to get back at me by fucking those creatures? Those things had me trapped in some bubble for hours last night while I watched you fuck the lot of them. Think that is fair?"

Charlie turned away from him, searching for an escape, and said, "You're disgusting. You smell like piss."

"Thanks to your boyfriend, you stupid whore. Where do you think you're going?"

Charlie stared at him, puzzled by his anger. It wasn't like Bradley wanted her anymore. Must be the fear of losing one of his possessions.

"What are you, an alien groupie or their old lady now?" Bradley said as he grabbed her by the wrist. "Shit, look at that blue skin. You like being fucked by those stalks? You shaved your hair for them?" he yelled as he rudely rubbed her bald head.

"It's none of your business what I do. You made it clear during this cruise that you want nothing more to do with me. I want out and I want a divorce from you," she said.

"You're still my wife and I'm not letting you debase yourself by screwing those freaks," he said. He grabbed her breast to give it squeeze and tossed her on the bed. He climbed on top of her, pinning her against the mattress.

"You're going to give me a little of the loving you showed the freaks," he said as he groped her body.

Charlie started to tear up, not from shame but anger. She struggled to escape him while her anger intensified. She was no longer fearful; she was angry, knowing he was responsible for her presence on this ship.

"You're with that thing, your skin and your shaved head, all of it for the benefit of those freaks. I should have killed him when I had the opportunity," Bradley said.

"Leave him alone," Charlie yelled and as she willed herself from the bed, a blue orbis materialized and engulfed Bradley. Charlie extended her hand as if to will the sphere forward. The sphere pushed Bradley across the room and hurled him against the wall with considerable force. A split second later his head awkwardly hit the floor with an audible thud.

He rubbed his head and said, "What the fuck?" He was confused as to how she'd managed to toss him so easily.

"Leave me and Jawara alone, asshole," Charlie said and she ran out of the cabin.

"This isn't over; I'll make those freaks bleed yet," he yelled.

Unhappy Herd

Handlers of herd animals know they have to be careful with their physical treatment of the masses. Herds can be more sensitive than a single individual, especially to subtle changes in the environment. Many times, a cumulative vibe lingers over the collective, infecting one individual and then spreading to another. Happy, well-fed animals will play and mate freely while working out their social order without the assistance of their handlers. But once the malaise sets in with a few animals, the feeling quickly spreads among the remaining members of the herd.

The happy, well-fed animals aboard the cruise ship felt dissatisfied as an overall sickness seemed to grip the entire herd. Like a drove of cattle destined for the slaughter house there was unease, nervousness, restlessness, and agitation. Even their collective bowels were loosening as a result of the fear. They retained control but found themselves in the bathroom more often, dealing with their sudden colitis.

On Earth, mental health experts became aware of this syndrome and wanted to create a designation in the DSM for suicide behavior disorder; basically, a deadly depression that spreads from individual to individual. Handlers of animals knew full well the syndrome. Unfortunately, the Epicoids were unaware of it, having forgone the slaughter of livestock many eons ago. They lacked even the most basic instincts of a primitive herdsmen and never recognized they'd lost control of the herd.

After escaping from her cabin Charlotte aimlessly walked the top deck attired only in her underwear. She couldn't find Steve or Jawara and wandered about topside debating what to do next. As she turned, she was startled by a loud thump that originated from behind her and she felt a mist hitting her bare legs. Something heavy had fallen just a few steps away from her. She turned around and saw the blood splatter on the deck but she avoided looking at the broken, twitching body. She glanced above and saw that the body, or should she say person, had climbed up and fell from the top of one of the three large smokestacks that stood a hundred feet tall. On her legs were droplets of blood. She shuddered at the carnage and quickly decided to risk returning to her cabin.

Ahmed's touch spread throughout the humans, precipitating a rash of suicides. The Sentinels eagerly encouraged Ahmed to use his evil touch to unleash an orgy of death. Unlike the Sentinels, the healing Ahmed could approach the humans. The touch of the Sentinels caused madness, but no sane human would willingly let those vile-looking creatures near them. Ahmed's touch was more subtle but equally disturbing. It was Jim, one of the young teen boys, who had climbed the smokestack and jumped to his death. Jawara had saved Charlie and Steve, but he couldn't save all of the passengers.

Other people were far less dramatic in their deaths, choosing a secretive, quiet end by throwing themselves off the stern into the vast ocean. Those surviving the plunge found themselves paddling aimlessly as the ship steamed toward the horizon. Dead bodies began appearing in all manner of weird locations. One was found floating in the kiddy pool and another in a ventilation shaft, his legs dangling in the air.

Inside one of the luxury cabins there was more horror to be discovered. An older matron decided to slip away by taking an overdose of sleeping pills. Others opened veins in their bathtubs, some successfully, others not. Slowly the passengers watched as life began to dissipate from their temporary human community.

The mounting body count caused considerable consternation among the clerics and the older men. The herd immediately blamed the Epicoids when many of the deaths could be directly attributed to Ahmed and his horrific touch. However, there was more at play: a sense that this cruise was a sham and was soon to end. There was a malady at work, a feeling that more than just the cruise was about to be over; perhaps life itself was nearing the finish line.

The thud of Jim's body hitting the deck behind Charlie sounded the start of the revolt. Horrified humans gathered around the mangled body, staring at the spreading pool of blood on the deck. The back of Jim's head had hit first, cracking and partially spilling the contents of his skull. Women gasped and men cursed at the sight of the youth's twisted and broken body. It was a cruel reminder that the cruise perhaps wasn't necessarily a benign trip to nowhere.

Two Epicoids had also witnessed the plunge and they moved towards the body. Unable to save the dead youth, the Epicoids shed their clothes and began their bizarre tasting ritual of the youth's still twitching body before the stunned humans. Confused by the Bitter Tasting and convinced that they were watching cannibalism, the men attacked the two naked Epicoids. The two giants were beaten and driven from the body, but cooler heads among the people suggested they take the pair as prisoners.

When the word spread, many of the passengers felt compelled to take action and go into full revolt. Sensing an opportunity to lead once again, the clerics were the vanguard in the revolt against the Epicoids.

The clerics hastily organized a meeting at the theater. Before starting, and covered in blood, the captive Epicoids were paraded before the humans. People began yelling and cursing at the Epicoids. Bradley joined in and began agitating by yelling, "Like your women being used by these things?"

The number of blue-tinged humans increased at an alarming rate, and some were actually present in the crowd. None would come to the defense of the Epicoids—not with that fervent crowd.

Steve arrived late to the meeting and gave Bradley a stare that backed him down for a moment.

"Godless creatures, taking our women. Were they sent by Satan himself?"

Pastor Jones asked. The pastor was still peeved by the Epicoids' slight and their apparent favoritism of the reverend.

"So how do we stop them? Any weapons we can use?" one man asked.

"The crew must have some guns," someone said. The Italian crewmembers shook their heads no.

"I'm sure their overlords don't allow for that. No, we have to improvise," another man said.

Bradley stood up and said, "I've been thinking about this. The gym—we can use the hand weights as clubs. Grab any long rods, anything we can strike them with. Despite their size, they're not so tough. I knocked one on its ass with one punch."

"We have to seize the bridge and the engines; that's what you need to do to control a ship. Control both and we control this ship," Pastor Jones said.

Steve didn't want to engage the incoherent mob but he stood up and said, "Pastor, can I say something?"

"Sure, Steve."

Steve paused for a moment to allow the crowd to settle down and said, "If we were on Earth, your plan makes sense—actually, damn good sense. But we're not. We are not sailing this ship to a safe port. There is no safe port. Frankly, I don't believe we are on Earth."

"Why do you say that?" Pastor Jones asked.

"Come on, people, use a little reason. Did you take a look at the fricking stars and notice how different they appear? Have you seen the moon? No. Has anyone seen a single ship or plane the entire time we have been at sea? No. A fool can see this entire ship is a prop. There's no crew to take hostage, there's no bridge to take control of, and I'm almost positive there are no engines. We exist in a shell, a phantom ship," he said.

"Where are we, then?" the reverend asked.

"Not on Earth, that's for sure. Better yet, when are we?" Steve asked.

"What do you mean?" Pastor Jones asked.

"Humor me with a small survey. How many people here think the year is 2012?" There was a smattering of hands and some grumbling.

"2013?" More hands and murmuring.

"2014?" Even more hands and chatter.

"You see my point, people," Steve said.

The show of hands upset many of the passengers. It was one thing not to know where you were; that wasn't exactly an unknown fate to humans. But not knowing when … well, that was particularly disturbing and normally associated with the truly demented. Stranger yet, no one had bothered to ask.

An angry man yelled, "Why are we just finding out about this now?"

"Because up to this point we have all been managed very well by the Epicoids," Steve said. "My point is that we need to exercise some caution before acting rashly. We're up against something we can't even begin to understand."

"Screw this shit. We can't just do nothing and watch each other die," Bradley said while glaring at Steve.

"Yes, let's do this. Break up into two teams: one aft, the other stern. Let's take the bridge along with the engines," Pastor Jones said.

And with that remark by the pastor, Steve knew he had lost control of the mob. Action was always preferable to inaction when dealing with a mob mentality. With the teams' departures, the dreadful Muzak began playing once again over the ship's PA system. A saccharine instrumental cover of "Afternoon Delight" blasted at full volume for all to hear.

"Take those damn speakers out as we go," someone yelled. One of the men smashed the speaker but the music kept playing.

The two teams ran through the enormous ship, wandering around and getting lost. During their search some of the passengers spotted Jawara. They captured the passive giant, taking him prisoner with little resistance and securing him with several belts. Steve watched, waiting for his opportunity to intercede. Timing was everything and without weapons it would be difficult for him to manage the angry mob.

Once secured, some saw their opportunity and started beating Jawara. Steve had to act and began pulling the men away from Jawara while yelling, "Don't kill this son of a bitch; a dead Epicoid is of no use to us. We need live hostages to negotiate with."

Steve was talking common sense and the men pulled away from the fallen giant.

"I'll take him back," Steve said.

One of the passengers said, "You're friends with that freak!"

Another man who saw Steve's anger the other day with Jawara said, "I can assure you that the young man is no friend of the alien."

Steve knew that he and Jawara were in a bad spot. He turned and punched Jawara in the stomach, causing the giant to double over.

"Like I said, I'll take him back," Steve said. The anger in the black man's eyes was enough to convince the white passengers.

As they walked away, Jawara whispered, "Thanks, Steve."

"No problem; had to get you out of there before they did some real damage to you."

"You pulled your punch?" Jawara asked.

"Really? A little. Maybe I'm losing my touch," he said.

"Or maybe I'm getting used to being hit by irate humans. You know that what they are doing is futile, right?"

"Shit, yes. I tried to tell them, big guy, but I'm just the lone black dude trying to talk sense to a lot of angry white guys. We all know how that's going to turn out. Okay, you get lost and I'm heading back to the fools and see if I can change their minds."

"Get lost?" Jawara repeated.

"Just hide, will you? Otherwise they'll be lynching me next."

The other team moved forward toward the bridge and found their way blocked.

"They locked the doors. Quick, someone find an axe," one of the passengers yelled.

There were no axes to be found. The men broke the door to the bridge with fire extinguishers and oars they retrieved from the lifeboats. The door ripped open and the men tumbled onto the bridge. As they searched, they found a large, empty white room with no equipment, no coms, and no personnel. The only thing present was a large panoramic window overlooking the ocean and some overhead lighting.

"What the heck? Is this thing just for show? Did they move it?" Pastor Jones asked.

"How the hell do they navigate this thing?" another person asked.

Sensing they were being played, the team raced to the back of the ship, upsetting the other passengers along the way. They quickly secured the engine room. The room was a vast, cavernous area with three massive engines. Each of the engines was larger than a locomotive, but not a single engineer or mechanic was present to operate the equipment.

Steve finally caught up with them and quickly surveyed the twenty rampaging men. Bradley was among them. *Shit*, Steve said under his breath.

"Hey, asshole, I told you they had to have massive engines to move this rig," Bradley said.

"Doesn't make sense," Steve said as he scanned the equipment and put his hands on the surface.

"Why?" Pastor Jones asked.

"No dirt, no oil, way too clean. Hell, you could eat off this equipment. Nothing is warm, never mind hot; no heat is being generated. Also, I hear the rumbling of the engines but I feel no vibrations on the actual equipment. Something's wrong here."

The men put their hands on the equipment in the room; they couldn't feel any vibrations, either.

"Are you kidding me?" Steve asked.

"You're right. I feel nothing," Pastor Jones said.

"That's fucked up. I don't care how advanced these engines are. Not to feel some vibration is impossible," Steve said.

He grabbed a hammer and lightly tapped at a metal housing. The tapping made a strange hollow sound.

"That doesn't sound right," he said.

Steve started wailing at the engine with the hammer while someone yelled at him to stop. "What are you doing?" Pastor Jones yelled.

Steve continued to hammer at the engine wall and it cracked like plaster board.

"This is an engine? What the heck is coming out of the smokestacks?" another man asked.

Steve continued smashing away until he saw a light. "Come on, give me a hand." The others joined in and, when done, they uncovered a glowing blue sphere twenty feet across inside.

"Whatever that is, it's not being controlled by the bridge, my friends," Steve said.

Pastor Jones looked confused and said, "All right, all right, we can work this out. I was hoping to avoid this, but time to go to Plan B. Let's kill one of the captive Epicoids to show them we mean business. That will force them to return us to Earth."

"That's it? That's the plan? More bloodshed? You're a holy man and you want to kill?" Steve asked.

"They're killing our people and they're not human. We have a right to defend ourselves," he said.

"Our people are killing themselves, if you haven't noticed. The Epicoids are watching us right now and they'll be ready for us. Don't you see that this has been one long, elaborate experiment and we're the lab rats?" Steve asked.

"What are you talking about?"

"I know you really feel this, but you're wrong. You're not paying attention to the facts. The Epicoids are not trying to hurt us," Steve said.

"Yeah, but I wouldn't put it past those walking horror shows to be behind this," Pastor Jones said.

"The Sentinels? Yeah, I wouldn't put anything past those freaks," Steve said. "Nevertheless, attacking the Epicoids will do no good. They may be our only allies, and they may be protecting us from those horrors."

The men ignored Steve and left the engine room in search of weapons and more Epicoids to take hostage. Bradley led one party of men and they methodically began a search. "Remember, grab anything sharp that you can strike with," he ordered.

As the rebellion spilled to the top deck, Bradley's party grabbed several Epicoids who were unaware of their intentions. They began to strike and beat the taller creatures, who fell to ground, and pelted them with a series of kicks. Steve stood between the mob and the Epicoids.

"I can't let you do this," Steve said.

Bradley pushed Steve, trying to force him aside.

Steve turned to face Bradley and said, "So, asshole, do you really want to tangle with me again?"

"Yeah, I do, Kanye."

Bradley sized Steve up and swung. His wild punch missed and Steve threw a counter-punch that landed flush on Bradley's temple. The other men swarmed Steve and knocked him to the ground. They moved forward to continue striking and beating the two fallen Epicoids.

Their attack was interrupted with the arrival of two Sentinels. The ugly creatures stopped the men in their tracks and they released the captive Epicoids. Several men, along with Bradley, crept away, not willing to tangle with the vile creatures.

The Sentinels moved quickly against the remaining men and didn't even have to strike the humans with much force. A simple touch of their clawed hands was enough to infect the stricken humans with the pain all Sentinels had to endure during their gruesome transformation. Upon their touch the human victims stopped for a moment and within seconds were transformed into crazed masses of self-destructing flesh. The touch of the Sentinels ignited every nerve ending in the human body, turning their existence into a sheer hell. Lit by invisible flames and sliced a thousand times on their skin, the men threw their bodies about in a haphazard manner, trying to extinguish their tortured lives. Their hellish screams filled the air as they hurled themselves into walls and one another, grabbing each other and trying to rip the flesh from their bones. One of the Sentinels moved toward Steve and he avoided its touch by hurling a deck chair between himself and the creature.

Steve ran among a half-dozen victims in that tortured state, causing a panic among the remaining mob. He had to avoid the anguished humans as they attacked anything that moved, including themselves. Several jumped off the deck into the ocean. One infected human was crazed enough to attack the Sentinel, and the Sentinel knocked him aside with a single blow of its hand.

As the Sentinels moved forward to attack other humans, they were intercepted by an Epicoid party. Ten Epicoids stood before the Sentinels to stop their rampage.

"Killing our subjects is not the purpose of the Greeting. The Council would not approve of your behavior. We must insist that you stop," Janet said.

The Sentinels hesitated. Before turning away, they released a series of the red spheres.

The remaining humans quickly dispersed; however, they couldn't elude the spheres. The spheres would randomly appear in a haphazard manner as if anticipating the fleeing humans' paths. Soon the rebellion ceased and the human aggressors were captured within their respective red prisons.

After the failed rebellion, an eerie calm settled among the humans. The leaders were imprisoned and for many, thee memory of the rebellion was seemingly erased.

Steve was shaken by the violence he'd witnessed, yet he had managed to avoid the red spheres. He sought to hide but the screams of the tortured men continued to haunt him. He went in search of Charlie. When he couldn't find her, he instead found solace in drink and smoking a joint. Drunk and stoned, he returned to his room, wondering where the hell she was.

Day 10 – The Line

"Will all passengers of Tour Group M please gather your belongings and remain in your room until called. When called, please assemble at Staging Point B. Your tour group is moving to the next stage of your voyage. Thank you," said a soothing female voice over the announcement system.

The horrible Muzak began playing again and Charlie buried her head under her pillow. Within minutes she heard a bustle outside her door as her fellow passengers began their departure. Departure to where?

Charlie got up, dressed in her bathing suit, draped a wrap around her shoulders, and went out to investigate. Unable to find either Steve or Jawara, she went in search of Rachel, needing to talk to a familiar face. She knocked on Rachel's cabin door and an Indian woman answered.

"Is Rachel here?"

"There's no Rachel here, just me and my husband. You must have the wrong cabin."

"No, this is the right cabin. When did you arrive on the ship?" Charlie asked.

"This morning," the woman answered.

"This is wrong. Are you sure they didn't move Rachel and Hank to another cabin?" Charlie asked.

"I don't know; like I said, we just arrived. Do you know who is in charge here?"

Charlie shook her head and left. She decided to confront Jawara regarding Rachel. She found him on the top deck appearing a little battered.

"What the heck happened to you?" she asked.

"More human spontaneity. You seem upset," he said.

"I am. Where is she—my friend Rachel?"

"My understanding is that they've gone to the next stage of interaction."

"With more of your kind?" she asked.

"Yes, that is what we were told."

"You know this how? Because someone told you?" she asked.

"Yes."

"Have you seen this so called interaction?" she asked.

"No, I haven't."

"You're a very trusting soul. I wish I shared your faith in others," Charlie said as she walked away.

"Where are you going?" Jawara asked.

"To open your eyes."

Charlie trusted Jawara; however, that trust only went so far. She particularly feared the influence of the Sentinels. She needed to confirm her suspicions and made her way to Jawara's space at Deck D, Hall E.

"How am I going to get through that wall?" she said as she hit it with the palm of her hand. Her hand went through.

"Shit, I'm in!" she said in surprise.

She moved about the seemingly endless dark space and saw the floating orbises representing the many interfaces to Jawara's technology. As she examined them, she realized that for some reason she actually understood the technology they represented. Thousands of the spheres danced in the room, gently riding up and down in the still air, seemingly eager for her interaction.

As she examined one orbis, she saw it teeming with thousands of small creatures. She glanced inside and found herself in the middle of the squealing swarm. As she searched, a rat jumped onto her shoulder. She was horrified to find thousands of rats scurrying about with a number of them climbing on top of her. Distraught, she quickly abandoned the orbis and continued her search.

So many spheres danced and vied for her attention. While searching among the shiny orbs she heard a lone voice in the space, an older woman seemingly talking to herself about her younger lover.

"He is so fit and handsome and he wants me so badly. Can I keep this from my husband?"

Charlie could taste the woman's desire and called out, "Who's there?"

She looked around but the space was an empty void. No response. Moments later the lone voice was followed by more voices—some joyful, others filled with fears and trepidations about the cruise and the presence of the aliens. They weren't actually voices; they were more the thoughts of the passengers aboard the ship. Only, Charlie wasn't hearing them; it was more vibrational. She could taste their thoughts and emotions, a stream becoming a river and then a waterfall that roared with its intensity. Soon there was a cacophony of thoughts filling the space that threatened to overwhelm Charlie. The passengers' fears and emotions hung in the air like frozen crystal artifacts for her to review and examine, but she found so many painful to her taste.

A lone man expressed his bitterness about his wife in a single thought: "She can't even push out a baby. I want that needy, sick red-headed bitch out of my life forever." It was Bradley emoting his hate for Charlie, his animus nearly doubling her over in sickening waves of repulsion.

When Charlie could take no more, she tried to step away from the voices. She found in their stead an airy layer of tranquil thought and well-being that dampened and softened the darker and confused crystal thoughts of the humans. It was the soothing reflections of the Epicoids repeating several simple mantras: "They seem very nice and very polite," and "We are all one." Yes, she was right. Their soft reassurances were like an alien Xanax to the human soul. They tasted delightful and their pleasant, sweet vibrations resonated deep within her loins.

Apart and in the distance there was the discernible presence of hate and revulsion that filled the enormous room with bloodlust. Those voices were a horrific Greek Chorus of doom, sadism, and pain. They exuded equal portions of hate, fear, and anger in a loathsome mix that combined with the blaring Muzak to reverberate deep into her bowels.

Farther away, a sympathetic voice was telling sweet lies about the afterlife, saying, "Kill yourselves and be one with the Quanteme. End your wretched existence on Earth and join me in heaven." This deceitful voice was speaking directly to the reverend and the GodNauts.

Shaken, Charlie wanted out of the room and hastened her pace in search of the spheres, doing anything not to taste the thoughts of the other humans or of the Sentinels. Her hand touched one sphere and disappeared below its surface. "Ah, I want you, little one," she said as she entered the orbis and wondered how it actually worked. She thought about going into the corridor and the orbis began moving and navigating the ship, undetected by the Epicoids and the humans.

She headed to the meeting area and observed a thin line of humanity that stretched on for hundreds of yards through the corridor. She moved along the queuing humans undetected in her orbis. People were in line with their luggage, moving to their next destination just like any vacationer, always a strange non-reality even on Earth. Knowing their time was up on their vacation put them into a strange netherworld as they stood in line with their few meager belongings.

Charlie noticed the horrible Muzak playing again. She observed the lines of people queuing in strict numerical order. There was much laughing and kidding among the people on the line. A group of young girls sold Girl Scout cookies to the people waiting in line as they walked by. Everybody seemed to be in good spirits, almost eager to move to the next phase of the cruise.

As Charlie watched she noticed a small flash of orange light at the end of the line. She moved the orbis toward the end of the line to find the source of the light. She watched a family of four—a mother, father, daughter and son—rigidly facing forward at the front of the line.

"Dears, this will be fun, don't be worried," the mother said as she grabbed the boy with her free hand.

"Stay in single file," a voice commanded.

As she spoke, the daughter disappeared, followed by the son. A flash of orange light and a wisp of a cloud was all that remained. The mother and father held hands and were gone seconds later, accompanied by the same light and smoke. Some turned to see their partners disappear, only to vanish themselves a millisecond later. Entire families went in order and within seconds half of the line had vaporized into nothingness. The crackle of static electricity in the air and their luggage were the sole reminders of their prior existence. A peculiar haze obscured one end of the line from the other.

Charlie left the orbis and ran back to warn the others in the line. She saw Rachel in line with her husband and yelled, "Run! Get off this line! They're killing everyone!" but she couldn't be heard above the blasting Muzak. Rachel appeared to notice Charlie, but in a moment Rachel and her husband were gone.

The peculiar sweet smell of ozone lingered in the air. Nobody was left; even the two Girl Scouts had vanished, replaced by a hazy vapor that hung in the air.

Charlie was badly shaken by the disappearance of everyone and raced back to Deck D, Hall E to return the orbis. She had to warn Steve about the horrors of the line. Jawara saw her anguished face but Charlie wanted to evade him. Jawara moved faster and he easily blocked her way.

"You lied to me," she said.

"I don't lie. You have to be more explicit about what is upsetting you."

"You're wasting my time. I have to warn Steve," she said. She walked away from him but he aggressively grabbed her by the wrist.

"What happened to you?" he asked.

"I took your cloaking orbis and went to the staging area for Tour Group M. They're all gone; the passengers have all disappeared. Everyone, including whole families. My friend Rachel and her husband are gone."

Jawara was confused. "It wasn't yours to take."

"To hell with what is mine to take. This ship, what you told me, is all a lie. I felt the emotions of the other passengers bubbling to the surface. You're suppressing their feelings, aren't you? That's why we never panicked, right?"

"Think of our presence like your medications. We just take the edge off, nothing more. We neither change nor implant thoughts."

"Bullshit; we get to choose to take our meds. What about the people disappearing? Don't try to shrug that off."

"That's probably how they move them to the next stage," Jawara said.

"Don't you know?" Charlie asked.

"No. What exactly did you see?"

"They were in line and then one by one they disappeared in a flash of light, as if they were caught in a human bug zapper. Tell me that's how they move them?"

"This is important: What color was the light?"

"I guess it was reddish. No, it was more orange."

"Not blue?" Jawara said. His faced was etched in worry.

"No, definitely not blue, orange. Why do you look like that?" she asked.

Jawara staggered and slumped against the wall.

"They lied to us," Jawara said. "The Council lied to us."

"What?"

"The Council and the Sentinels lied to us. I didn't know they could lie. That orange light is the calcium in your bones and the iron in red blood cells vaporizing as the time wormhole collapses. I must confront them about this lie," Jawara said.

"I don't understand. Did they say how much time we are to spend in Stage 1?"

"Roughly ten of your days."

Charlie made a small, guttural sound and said, "Jawara, this is my tenth day; I made sure to keep track." With tears running down her cheeks she asked, "Am I next?"

Jawara motioned into the air as an orbis appeared. He peered into the sphere. "You have an hour left."

"I don't want to die," Charlie cried with tears streaming down her face. "You weren't going to tell me?"

"I was hoping to go with you to the next stage. I put a request in with the Omni."

"They're killing us? How can you let this happen? You lied to me!"

"No, the flash of light is an indicator that the temporal distortion used to continue your existence is inherently unstable. They lied to us about the efficacy of this technology. I can't believe they lied. They can only keep you here for so long. So many of my kind have grown attached to you as a people. This is cruel; we can all agree to that."

"Screw them, I just won't go on the line," Charlie said.

"Won't matter; my guess is that the line was just a means to hide your inevitable demise from your fellow humans so as not to create a panic. Continuing their interactions with you appears to be their priority. Your end will follow you wherever you go, aboard this ship or elsewhere."

"So I am doomed?" Charlie asked fearfully.

"Yes, it would appear so. You were only given ten days of added life. I'm sorry."

Charlie began hitting Jawara, yelling, "You stupid bastards, you gave us all false hope. It's not fair! I want my life, a full life. I want a husband, I want children. Who are you to play God?"

Jawara looked down at her, expressionless, confused by her fury.

"Say something, you big jerk!" she yelled.

She collapsed to the floor, a hysterical mass of tears and sobs. Jawara just watched, not sure what to make of the distraught woman.

"You are right, who are we to play God?" Jawara said. "I will address this with my people. I will be your advocate before the Council," he said. Jawara helped Charlie up and held her in hopes of calming her.

"We don't have much time. They will realize very soon that I am no longer among them. They will assume I am hurt and in trouble and begin a systematic search of the ship. This is not easy for me. My engineering skills are somewhat rudimentary," he said. "I can use the cloak to go undetected but you must make it past them to Deck 57 on your own. The cloak only moves one entity at a time."

"Just how large is this ship? Can I really evade them on my own?" she asked.

"I can help you. Come over here," Jawara said. Charlie stood before him and, with an orbis, he began spraying her liberally with a smelly vapor.

"Ugh, that stuff is hideous. What in the world is this crap, some type of alien bug spray?" Charlie asked. "Smells almost like an aftershave."

"Don't worry, it will protect you. The Sentinels can't see but they can smell or taste; this will allow you to walk right past them. Just don't talk to anyone."

"Where are you going?"

"I have to talk to the Council and end this madness. Go to Area 51 and wait for my return."

"I need to bring another with me; otherwise I stay," she said.

"Just one more," Jawara said. "That's all we can accommodate. Find Steve and hurry."

"How did you know I would take Steve?" Charlie asked.

Jawara quizzically smiled at her and said, "There was another choice? Go!"

The Omni – Collective

From lightness Jawara was plunged into an unfamiliar darkness. Alone and afraid, he was reborn from the collective to a solitary soul. Similar to a human birth, he had no loving, warm mother to greet him with his arrival to this new state. He was suddenly afraid for the first time and he now understood a very basic human condition of existence. Fearful he was facing the cold universe alone, he reached to his sole remaining connection with Charlie for solace.

Fearing that the Council had now turned against the Greeting, he decided to press forward and intervene on the part of the humans before the Omni, the supreme ruling body. The Omni was a collective, consisting not of individual Epicoids but rather a projection of the whole, a separate entity fed by the collective quantum minds of Epicoids. The Omni was, in essence, the spokesperson for the collective. As Jawara's orbis entered the other realm his small sphere appeared before the Omni, a much larger sphere populated by trillions of orbises similar in size to his own.

The lights of the Omni were synchronized in both their modulation and blinking. The hues changed and a vibrational noise could be felt by Jawara.

"Omni, may I join council with you? In the spirit of the Quanteme," Jawara asked. It was very unusual for an individual Epicoid to interact alone with the Omni. He knew the conditions of such a unique meeting required that he communicate as a Solitary with the Council so as not to share with the other Epicoids the proceedings of the meeting. Everything was controlled and filtered so the Epicoids could be governed as one.

"Have you completed and accepted the terms of the Solitary?" they asked.

"Yes, in the spirit of the Quanteme," he said with more than a little trepidation. He did so knowing that in a Solitary state he was apart from the collective and if left alone in that state would live at most for a year, a very hellish year, as life ebbed slowly from his physical body. Would they allow him to return to the collective after he confronted them about the Greeting? He couldn't be sure.

"Please control yourself and regain your composure before addressing the Council," said the Omni.

Prior to the meeting Jawara had collapsed into a small ball of misery as he struggled to gain control over his fears. He had no choice but to force himself up and move forward with his requested meeting.

"Your request is very bold. We understand you have questions and concerns about the Greeting?" the Omni asked.

"Yes."

"Good, we have many questions for you. Begin."

"Why not tell us of the true nature of interaction with humans? There appear to have been some important omissions," Jawara said.

"Yes, you could accuse us of lying to you. When you agreed to the

Greeting you gave away certain rights to protect the collective; you knew that. The collective agreed to the clause providing incomplete disclosure for the protection of the collective."

"I never knew the truth was a right to be given away to the collective."

"Not the truth; rather, access to certain information, and done so in the protection of the collective. For example, we needed contingency plans in case one of our own fell into *harmony* with one of the test subjects, a fear that wasn't necessarily unfounded. You have feelings for the one called Charlotte, I believe."

"Yes, it's true. I have grown very fond of her."

"Do you not see how this could be potentially threatening to the harmony of the collective?"

The colors of the Omni changed, turning redder and brighter from the previous calm blue state.

"I do not see the threat. I have learned much about the humans and they have much potential," Jawara replied.

"And therein lies the problem. What do you see in her? They appear so inherently emotional and violent."

"Perhaps, but in many ways they are beautiful sentient creatures," Jawara said.

"Sentient perhaps; however, they only see the individual and have but a cursory interest in the collective. They are aggressive, selfish creatures constantly at war among themselves. We're sensing another within you exerting some influence. The one the humans called Steve."

Jawara was confused and said nothing. Steve's feelings for Charlie bubbled over him but he wasn't entirely sure why. Bonding to two humans had been a unique experience for Jawara with little precedent for him.

"We ask again. What did you see in her?" the Omni asked.

He hesitated for a moment. He noticed the past tense. Was he to be separated from Charlie? He had other motivations that he didn't want to divulge to the Council.

"For the first time in my life someone actually saw me, saw me alone. It is incredibly liberating."

The Omni raised its voice and said, "Liberating from what? The collective?"

He didn't answer at first but then said, "Yes."

"The temporal distortion is only good for a small amount of time. We felt that was best for the experimenters and the subjects, in case we had to address unforeseen complications."

"Would those complications be love or harmony?" Jawara asked.

"Yes, attraction was always a risk with empathic sentient creatures; this interaction is to be closed. Save for some outliers, we have also learned that the humans interfacing with this so-called higher species is not factually based."

"Yes, they call it faith," Jawara replied.

"Faith? No, it's just more of their self-delusion and lies. Their prayers go nowhere. We have already lost Freyr to disease spread by the humans."

Surprised, Jawara said, "We didn't observe that. The cause was unknown, perhaps foul play."

"The cause was unknown to you but not to us. The risk is too great; our studies are now done and so is the need for this given study group."

"And Charlotte?" Jawara asked.

"The Sentinels will see to it that she joins the line like the others of her kind when her time comes. This concludes your council with the Omni, Jawara."

"Can we please make an exception for the human called Charlotte, in the spirit of the Quanteme?" Jawara pleaded.

"NOOOOO!" came the thunderous reply from the Omni.

It was a deep, booming rejection that viscerally shook all of the Epicoids in the galaxy.

"In the spirit of the Quanteme, you are not to have any further contact with Charlotte or any of the other humans. You will report back to the origination point for review. We need to understand your interactions with the humans and how they managed to manipulate your thinking. Go now to your designated quarantine."

Jawara turned away and left. Somehow, and he wasn't sure why, he knew the Council had been turned against the humans. He had his suspicions. Just to think those thoughts was heresy; however, being a solitary freed him from the societal constraints of the collective.

Upon returning to the orbis Jawara felt different. Having stepped out from the collective to address the Omni he found that he could not readily return. He tried; however, for some reason they weren't reaching out to him. Instead, Jawara was filled with images of killing the Sentinels by some of the most horrific means.

Defeated, Jawara made his way to his orbis. As the sphere made its journey, Jawara quickly realized he wasn't heading back to the origination point as ordered but instead back to the *Mandjet*. How was that possible? Jawara was acting in direct defiance of the Council, yet not of his own accord. Had the Council changed its collective mind? As he drew closer to the *Mandjet* he suddenly felt weaker, having experienced prolonged loneliness for the first time in his life.

1 Hour to Nexus – Daphne Pursued

The passengers were lined up against the wall of a corridor, terrified as the Sentinels reviewed them. At the Sentinels' side was a horrible guard dog called a magnos that resembled an ulcerated hairless hyena. The quadruped animal's large head sported canines that caused the upper lip to curl, and its hind legs ended in dagger-like hooves designed to rip open the belly of its prey. Charlie walked along the lines undetected until she came upon the magnos. A series of strange grunts and clicks exchanged between the magnos and Sentinels filled the air.

A large serpent-like tongue protruded from the magnos' jaws, smelling and tasting the air. As the magnos sniffed, it began to whimper and cry while moving away from Charlie. The Sentinel, not sensing her, was perturbed at the creature's cowardly behavior and kicked the beast in its side.

"Where is Jawara and the scarlet-colored human called Charlotte?" they asked the humans. No one came forward.

Charlie ran through the corridors, eluding the Sentinels while looking to save one man: Steve. She ran to his cabin hoping to find him. She furiously banged on his cabin door only to find it open.

She went in and found him sprawled across his bed. She went to his side and started shaking him while yelling, "Steve, come with me. We have to reach Jawara's cabin!"

He woke up and asked, "Uncle George?"

"Steve, it's me. We have to move, and now. Shit, why are you so wasted?"

"Why? They're just going to slaughter us all," he said as the smell of alcohol and pot lingered in the cabin air.

"Why do you think I'm here, idiot? Didn't you hear that crazy announcement about Tour Group M?"

"I dunno, might have passed out a while. My head is killing me."

"Drinking and smoking pot will do that to you, stupid," Charlie said, growing frustrated with the boys in her life.

"No, I had this pain before the drink and pot. What is that awful smell, Charlie?"

"I don't have time for fifty questions, just snap the hell out of it. I know we're doomed. I found out that we only have ten days to live aboard this ship. Jawara is trying to rescue me. Come with me."

"What?" he asked.

"He'll save both of us. That is, if you can get your damn black ass moving."

That caught Steve's attention and he angrily asked, "What the fuck, Charlie?"

"It's so easy to push your buttons. You heard me. Jawara can get us off the ship."

"Both of us? You came back for me?"

"Yes, as in you and me, love. Let's get the hell off this ghost ship," she said as she gently touched his hand.

"I gotta shake the cobwebs. Give me a slap when—" he said just as she slapped him hard across the face. The blow sent his head backwards.

"Shit, when I say go, Charlie," he said as he rubbed his face. "Damn girl, you are crazy. Where did you learn to hit so hard?"

Before Charlie could reply they heard a meek rapping on Steve's cabin door. She opened the door and saw a stooped and weakened Jawara.

"What's wrong?" she asked.

"Can I come in?" Jawara asked and he staggered in.

"Steve, help me!" Charlie said.

Each grabbed one of the giant's arms and led him to the bed.

"What's wrong?" she asked.

"So alone, how do you do it?" he asked. He was shaking in the bed, holding himself in his own arms as he began rocking back and forth. He appeared to be having a full-blown panic attack. Charlie almost wanted to find a Valium for him.

"Jawara, you have to pull yourself together. We need you to help us escape," she said.

Jawara held his hand up and waved the two away. She watched him become still in the bed, eyes closed and arms at his side. He resembled a corpse in a coffin. He was frozen in place for a good ten minutes.

Steve sat in a chair, quiet and holding his head. He then said, "When is this shit with Jawara going to be over? We don't have all day, Charlie. This is like waiting for your execution."

Charlie grew concerned and debated what to do. It wasn't like she was experienced in comforting distraught aliens. She meekly moved to her friend's side and touched his arm. Nothing. She began to gently tug on the arm and said, "Jawara?"

"ARRRGHHHH!" he yelled as he bolted straight up and repeatedly wailed like some great wounded beast.

Charlie jumped backwards from the screaming alien. Steve leaped from his chair, unsure what was wrong. Jawara shook his head, composed himself, and appeared to be Jawara once again.

"Better?" she asked.

"Yes," he said in a monotone.

"What did you do?"

"I channeled another to help me survive," Jawara said as he glanced at the pair. His eyes moved about the room and then fixated on Steve.

Charlie hoped he was channeling an action hero, considering her next request.

"There's something going on with passengers. They're continuing to disappear, my friends, one by one. What was in that spray you gave me that allowed me to watch this horror show?" Charlie asked.

"Hai Karate; we thought it was a cologne you would like."

"I really have some serious doubts about the mental health of the intern you have doing the research on us as a species. What the heck is Hai Karate?" she asked.

"I think it was a cheesy men's cologne from the seventies," Steve said. "My uncle used to wear that stank juice."

"We observed that the companions of the Sentinels can't tolerate the odor for some reason," Jawara said.

"For some reason? Jeez, I smell like a seventies porn star," Charlie said.

"Glad your sense of humor remains intact; you will need it. I confirmed my suspicions with the Council. Your kind on this ship was designed for ten days of existence. It was the limit of our technology and a fail-safe in case...."

"In case of what?"

"In case we became too attached to our new subjects," Jawara said as he opened a metallic orbis. "They have real concerns about possible lingering effects from the Greeting."

"Charlie, can I have a moment with you alone?" Steve asked as he pointed to the bathroom.

They stepped in together and a clearly frustrated Steve whispered, "Are you buying that nonsense?"

"What do you mean?"

He paused as if to clear his head and said, "You know, this entire experiment makes no sense. It wasn't very methodical, with little to no separation between the observer and the observed. Just think about a human social anthropologist studying a primitive tribe who does so by sleeping with his subjects. With so many missteps, this was more a clusterfuck by the Epicoids than a controlled experiment. Think about it. Can we really trust them?"

Having lived a lie for most of her adult life with Bradley, she trusted her instincts and said, "You know, I don't think Jawara is lying, but you're not wrong either."

Flustered, he said, "Charlie, you can't have it both ways."

She stared him down and said, "No, Jawara isn't lying, but that doesn't mean he hasn't been lied to. We've been looking at the Greeting all wrong right from the start, and that includes the Epicoids. Steve, did you ever run a double-blind experiment on your fish?"

"No need with fish. What's this got to do with Jawara?"

"Maybe the Epicoids are blinded, like in the double-blind experiments I participated in during my college psychology class."

She walked back into the room and said, "Jawara, you need to hear this.

The Greeting, this so-called experiment, was never about the humans; it was about studying the Epicoids and how you would react to your first contact with another species. They were observing you and your kind, not the humans. The Sentinels were the observers, doing the watching all along, setting the environment and parameters, while pulling all the strings during the Greeting. And my sense is that now they didn't like what they were seeing on this cruise ship and they feel threatened."

Steve nodded his head while Jawara reflected on Charlie's words.

"Steve, you know what this means?" she asked.

"If you're right, that ten-day technology limit maybe a line of bullshit they gave to Jawara and the other Epicoids. Sounds more like a fail-safe to me. I wonder how much other bullshit they've fed the Epicoids. Holy shit, Charlie, that's a pretty sharp observation. I'm surprised I didn't see that."

"Surprised how? That a redheaded ditz thought of this first?" she asked. "Maybe if you weren't wrecked half of the time…."

"I didn't mean it like that," Steve said.

She held her hand up and said, "Really, does it matter what you or I think at this point? The ten days means they're flushing the specimens they no longer need down the toilet, just like your fish. The experiment is over and the Sentinels have made up their minds. We're disposable—always were, since we were already dead within our own timelines."

"What do you mean, already dead in our timelines?" Steve asked.

"This is a ghost ship. They rescued all of us—or should I say gathered us—when we died on Earth. In my case, Bradley committed a murder-suicide. Steve, that bastard shot me twice. My guess is that you died in some accident," she said.

"We all died?" he asked.

"The entire ship of humans," Jawara said, nodding.

Steve grew quiet and mumbled, "That's not right. I never flushed specimens down the toilet—at least not alive." He paused for a moment and asked, "Shit, really. Jawara, does what Charlie said make any sense to you?"

"Knowing that the Council kept information from us, or should I say lied to us, then yes. And the distrust of the Sentinels towards the Epicoids is well known. Epicoids are not very good at detecting or coping with lies. And yes, you all died within your original timelines," Jawara said. "They suddenly gave me access to that information."

"Wait, how did…? No, I don't want to know," Steve said.

"You drowned during a dive," Jawara said without hesitation.

Steve became quiet and then said, "Shit, I drowned? I thought humans were masters of deception, but this Greeting is just fucking wicked."

Jawara turned to Charlie and said, "What you are proposing is possible, but there are any number of happenings that don't make sense to me. I was ordered back to the origination point but somehow I was returned to the

Mandjet. This was in direct defiance of the Council. Why? Once they find out I haven't reported back to my station we will all be in great peril."

Charlie turned to Steve and her eyes lit up, acknowledging the obvious. She nodded toward him and said, "Go ahead, tell him."

He appeared to be still mulling over his own demise when she yelled, "Steve, snap out of it. Tell him why they let him go."

"Right. Sorry to break it to you this way, big guy, but somebody is setting you up to be the fall guy," Steve said.

Jawara didn't seem to understand. "Fall guy? I'm not sure who is falling."

"You're a dupe, a scapegoat, being played for a sucker, whatever you want to call it. They want to blame you for the failings of the Greeting, and you not returning to your base is clearly the action of a traitor. You were set up to fail."

"But I had nothing to do with the Greeting failing. Clearly they must know this?"

"That's the funny thing about a lie: the bigger the lie, the more the truth doesn't matter," Charlie said. "Somebody, most likely the Sentinels, is pushing their own agenda at any cost, including the truth. It would seem that you, my friend, are also disposable."

Jawara appeared confused and then blurted out, "Charlie, you and Steve have less than an hour before it's your turn in the line. And what of my dreams?"

Charlie stared at Jawara and realized there was more than just her own life at stake. The expression on her face was one of horror and resignation that she wouldn't be the only one to draw her last breath.

"Steve, there's more," Charlie said.

"Shit, what now? I need some aspirin." He went in search for some.

"Jawara had a premonition about the Sentinels," she said.

"Really," he said as he swallowed the pills. "So go ahead."

"The Sentinels want to destroy Earth and kill us all," she said.

"Technically, they just want to kill all the humans, not the planet," Jawara said.

Steve was about to comment when there was a loud knocking at the door. The knocking soon became a pounding.

"This shit just gets better and better," Steve said.

"Let me in, Charlie, I know you're in there," Bradley yelled in desperation.

"Shit, how did he find us? We'd better let that fool in before he alerts everyone on the ship," Steve said.

She opened the door and Bradley ran in. He stopped and glanced at Jawara before hugging Charlie while saying, "Charlie, we gotta get out of here. People are just disappearing. Get your friend to take us away from this ship."

"I can't do that," she said.

"I beg of you, for the love of God, take me with you," he said.

She shook her head, her eyes welling up. "I can't, Bradley, I just can't."

"I'm your husband," he said. "I see your tears. I must mean something to you, right?"

"You're mistaken; those tears are not for you, but for us. You killed us, you condemned both of us to this hell, not me. And given half a chance, I'm not repeating this mistake with you again," she said.

"But you can go with this—"

Steve yelled, "Charlie, forget this asshole, let's go."

"Fuck you," Bradley said as he threw a punch and started brawling with Steve. Steve threw him back but as Bradley tried to throw a second punch a strange halo surrounded his body. Steve stepped away from him, watching Bradley's transformation.

"What's happening to me?" Bradley asked as he faced Charlie.

"Bradley?"

Bradley vaporized before Charlie and Steve. Charlie watched in horror and let out a small sob.

"Jesus, is he dead?" she asked.

Jawara calmly said, "As good as dead."

"Come on, Charlie, let's go before we join him in hell," Steve said.

"I need to get you and Steve out of here now." Jawara pointed at the globe and gently touched its surface. A projection emerged of a large machine. "That's it. There's one portal that I know supports a larger and longer temporal distortion. It may save the two of you but it requires us to leave the ship. First, we must assemble at Area 51."

"Area 51?" Steve asked.

"That's his personal room," Charlie said.

"Whatever. Okay, so let's go, people," Steve said.

"We can't just walk to his room—" Charlie said as she was interrupted.

The phone rang in Steve's room. The three stared at the vintage phone, frozen by the sudden intrusion.

Ring! Ring! Ring!

The lone phone was joined by the ringing of all of the other phones in the nearby corridor. They rang in unison for a couple of minutes, as the three turned to one another, unsure what to do.

Jawara started to pick up the receiver but Charlie yelled, "Jesus Christ, don't answer it!"

Jawara backed away from the phone and Steve said, "That's pretty pathetic. Why are they calling, Jawara? Why not use one of those spheres to find us?"

Jawara was troubled and said, "That's not good. The orbis or sensors belong to the Epicoids. We wouldn't allow the Sentinels to use our technology during the Greeting unless there was a conflict. That was one of the ground rules. This means it's the Sentinels and not the Epicoids that are coming after us."

Jawara suddenly appeared sad and lost again.

"What?" Charlie asked.

"I fear I won't be allowed to return. I am alone in the universe," Jawara said.

"No you're not. You have me, remember?" She touched the giant's arm.

"I appreciate your sincerity but I'm not sure that will be enough to survive. Still, your survival is worth the personal risk. We must get to my room. Steve, we need to spray you. Take your shirt off."

"No freaking way," Steve said. "Why?"

"Just do it, Steve," Charlie said.

He reluctantly removed his shirt and Jawara sprayed his chest and back liberally. He began rubbing the spray into Steve's skin. Steve felt that tingling and forcibly grabbed Jawara's hand. "We're not getting kinky again, are we, Jawara? Can't we let Charlie do this?"

"Touching you is helping me cope," he said.

"You're shitting me," Steve replied.

"This spray will work. The Sentinels cannot use their advanced technology during the Greeting or on Earth without incurring a violation from the Council. They are technically blind," Jawara said.

"This is a joke, right?" Steve asked.

She leaned over and whispered into Steve's ear. "If our alien friend—who, by the way, is risking his own life to help us—gets some comfort by rubbing some stank cologne into your skin, then I suggest you better damn well oblige him." She crooked her head at him to make sure Steve got the message and said, "Unless, of course, you have your own plan for escape out of this fricking fish bowl?"

Steve gave her a disgusted look and said, "Shit, knock your socks off, Jawara. Gawd, this crap reminds me of my uncle—and believe me, he wasn't a favorite."

Jawara continued rubbing the spray into Steve's skin. Charlie then sprayed herself again.

As they readied to leave, Steve asked, "So, are we finally good now?"

Charlie nodded as Jawara vanished in the cloaking orbis, leaving Steve and Charlie to run the gauntlet of Sentinels on their own with just the cologne as a defense.

As they walked, Steve asked, "This shit actually works?"

"Yep, I walked right by them earlier. It seems that the gargoyles are as blind as bats, including their horrendous doglike companions. One even sniffed me, but remember, you can't talk so please just shut the fuck up," she said in hushed tones.

She turned a corner and saw the Sentinels were out in force in front of Jawara's room waiting for their arrival.

"Ah shit," Steve said upon viewing the Sentinels' magnos companions.

"Quiet, just keep your shit together and follow me," she said as she held his hand.

Following Charlie's lead they walked slowly and deliberately right by a dozen Sentinels with magnos. The snarling, vile beasts were nervous and clearly agitated. Steve sweated profusely, fearful he would give the pair away. Charlie turned around and saw the beads of sweat on Steve's face. She grabbed his hand and held it tenderly while looking into his eyes, assuaging his fears and calming his body.

The Sentinels sensed something was amiss and they voraciously sniffed the air but they couldn't sense the pair. One of the magnos took a sniff of Steve and gave a slow whimper.

The pair continued to walk past the Sentinels undetected and slowly made their way to Jawara's room.

As they walked, Ahmed arrived with several other Sentinels, including Pessimus. Ahmed stopped and stared at Charlie and Steve. He couldn't believe the couple were brazenly standing right next to the Sentinels and had gone undetected.

The Sentinels noticed Ahmed staring at the wall. They pointed to him and Ahmed yelled, "You morons, they are right next to you!"

One of the Sentinels noticed them as well, but not before smashing Ahmed in the head for his insolent comment. Ahmed fell to floor but he quickly got up to charge the pair.

"Ah shit, we got company," Steve said.

The Sentinels alerted, they joined Ahmed in rushing Steve and Charlie.

Steve turned and faced the three. "Go, Charlie, I got this! Leave!"

"We're not leaving without you," Charlie said.

"Don't worry, I have no intentions of staying with these assholes!" Steve said. "Go find Jawara to help us."

Charlie ran to Jawara's area while Steve turned to engage the trio of pursuers. Ahmed took aim at him with a pistol, but before he could pull the trigger a Sentinel knocked the gun out of his hand. Ahmed glared at the Sentinel but the creature stared him down.

"What?" Ahmed asked.

"No guns. We want the girl alive for our studies. We have to halt this disease among the Epicoids. Remember, alive, Ahmed!"

The Sentinels released one of the bewildered Sentinel guard dogs. Steve grabbed a fire extinguisher from the wall and the snarling beast lunged at him. He smashed it squarely on the head with the extinguisher. Stunned, the beast shook the hit off and attacked again, but Steve sprayed the beast with foam from the fire extinguisher. The beast turned away and he sprayed the others. His antics infuriated the Sentinels and Ahmed, but the extinguisher finally ran dry.

A fog from the extinguisher filled the air, clouding Steve's vision. He strained to see through the haze when a large charging beast emerged from the mist. It was Ahmed!

Ahmed was continuing his transformation and was now halfway between human and a Sentinel. His limbs had entirely grown back and his body was massive, like a body builder's. However, his head was also transforming and the strange Medusa growths sprouted from his skull. The clothes he wore barely contained his enlarged body.

Tackling Steve, Ahmed threw him backwards as if he'd been hit by a charging linebacker. Ahmed wrapped his arms around Steve's mid-section and pinned him against the wall. With Ahmed's head down, Steve pounded him in the back of the neck with his forearm; Ahmed staggered from the blow and released him.

"Why are you helping these ugly fucks?" Steve asked, hoping to buy some time for Jawara and Charlie. Charlie was feverishly searching the wall for the entrance to Area 51 but she was unable to pass through.

"Simple: I have no use for humans anymore. Your kind is already extinct," Ahmed said.

Steve backed away from the larger Ahmed, appearing to almost cower. Ahmed recklessly advanced forward, assured he was stronger than Steve.

"Fuck extinction," Steve yelled while smashing Ahmed in the head with the fire extinguisher. The blow was enough to crush a normal man's head but Ahmed was only stunned for a moment. Steve looked for other weapons and noticed the old-school fluorescent light fixtures. He jumped up and pulled the fixture from the ceiling, ripping one of the tubes out. He smashed the tube and held an end with jagged glass. Ahmed regrouped and approached, only for Steve to stab him in the abdomen with the broken glass.

Ahmed staggered backward but then calmly removed the broken glass from his tough, leathery skin. He laughed and said, "You have no clue how pointless your efforts are, do you?"

"Keep talking, asshole," Steve said as he ripped a handrail from the wall. He retreated back to Charlie as she continued her hectic search for Jawara's room.

"Listen to me. This Greeting has been going for centuries; it's an ongoing experiment generations of Epicoids have participated in, but they don't fully understand. They keep thinking that at some point the door will magically open and they will introduce themselves to the humans, when in fact it's just a continuous set of observational events. There will never be a joining of the Epicoids with the humans. The Sentinels will see to that."

"Why would you tell us this?" Steve asked.

"Because you and that stupid bitch are doomed," Ahmed said.

"Charlie, find that goddamn door, will you?" Steve said as he hit Ahmed with the handrail, but Ahmed barely flinched. He knocked the handrail aside and moved towards Steve. Steve punched Ahmed in the head but Ahmed just shrugged him off. Steve tried to take a step back, but slipped on the foam. The half-human monster grabbed Steve around the throat and Steve knew he was doomed—if not from the stranglehold, then by the creature's touch. Ahmed threw Steve into a cabin door, causing the door to break. The two fell together into the room as they continued to grapple.

Steve struggled to free himself and he was about to gouge Ahmed's eyes. However, Ahmed's massive hands didn't tighten around Steve's neck. Instead, he drew Steve closer and in a whisper said, "Go with your woman, my friend; escape with her to the Khajuraho Temples in India."

Steve stared incredulously at Ahmed and said, "What the fuck? I don't understand."

"I can't do these sins they ask of me. Do you know what they do with their ictus? Do you know what they have planned for all of us? No human is that perverted. Now hit me and make good your escape with her. I will make amends and join you later."

The two stumbled out of the room back into the presence of the Sentinels. Steve surged forward and gave Ahmed a headbutt, causing the creature to stagger and release him.

Steve ran to Charlie and took her hand. Before taking another step, a halo enveloped his body and his head began to pound with pain. Within moments he began to fade and disappear. Steve instinctively released Charlie's hand and seemed puzzled by his transformation. He turned to Charlie and smiled at her while mouthing some words.

Ahmed and the Sentinels stopped to watch Steve's transformation. With the Sentinels within earshot Ahmed said, "Goodbye, asshole."

In moments there wasn't a trace of Steve except for a strange ozone odor that lingered in the air of the corridor.

From the darkness Steve emerged, floating in a blue-green netherworld. He existed, but without knowledge of who, what, or where he was. He felt only a strange ambiguity about his existence, knowing only that he existed.

Steve regained consciousness to find himself underwater again. He was perfectly comfortable in his aqueous world and quickly realized he was using a respirator. No panic, just a strange sense of familiarity and calmness about him. He heard the release of air bubbles into the water.

As his vision returned he realized he was back at the coral reef off the waters of Australia. Emerging from the haze, he knew he had blacked out. Charlie, the Epicoids, and the Sentinels—all had been just a bizarre hallucinogenic dream. The entire adventure aboard the cruise ship could be written off as the result of oxygen deprivation. He tried to move his hand to check his oxygen level, but it was wedged between two rocks. He was stuck, with little air left in his tank. He started to panic. Planting his feet against the rock, he pushed up with his legs, still unable to free his hand.

How the hell had he wedged his hand in there? He looked up and spotted a clean break in the coral and realized a massive chunk had broken off from the main ledge. For several minutes he desperately pulled on his trapped lower arm but he couldn't budge it.

He removed his diving knife—the large, nasty one he carried to ward off nosy sharks. He had no choice but to severe his hand. He knew to start cutting the topside of his arm first, knowing the underside contained the soft veins and arteries. Severing them would cause him to bleed out before he could saw through the bone. While gathering his wits about him, something large struck him on the head from behind. Startled, he dropped the knife. It fell away from him before he could reach it. A shadow loomed above him while several small sharks swam close by, no doubt checking on the wounded prey.

Steve gazed upward towards the surface and light. No more oxygen; he was drowning and just mere minutes from his death. The realization that his end was near left him empty and defeated. Accepting that his life was over, he stopped struggling and tried to feel at peace. Within moments he felt a hand lifting him from the pain and horror of his present existence. His final thought was that he was not alone in his wretched demise.

Taking the Bull by the Stones

Ahmed and the two Sentinels moved towards Charlie. Instead of feeling fear, her rage rose over losing Steve. She picked up the handrail and threw it in their direction while yelling, "You fucking bastards!"

Surprisingly, Ahmed and the Sentinels stepped backwards and began running away from her. From behind her a loud crashing noise could be heard as the walls and ceiling began to explode and collapse around everyone. She was at first pushed to the side and then felt herself drawn into a void. A twenty-foot orbis appeared out of Jawara's room, knocking the attackers over and taking Charlie aboard. Before the Sentinels and Ahmed could regroup, the orbis shrunk in size and disappeared before them.

Distraught beyond words, she collapsed within Jawara's room. Her hysterics were upsetting the normally stoic Jawara. Between her body-shaking sobs and strange guttural cries, he tried to comfort her with his touch. She glanced up and realized his entire space comprised the orbis.

She sat up and tried to compose herself. Between gentle sobs she asked, "What happened to Steve and all the people in the line? Are they all dead?"

"He was returned to his original timeline like the others, in the spirit of the Quanteme."

"Dear God, if his timeline was like mine, he's dead, right?"

"Yes, odds are he has already joined the Quanteme," he said. As Jawara completed the words his body began to violently shudder.

"What?" Charlie said between tears.

He struggled for a few minutes and seemingly regained control once again. He said, "It's nothing; this will pass."

"You don't feel anything?" she asked.

"Quite the opposite; I feel more than you can possibly imagine," he said as he returned to navigating the orbis.

"I don't understand. Steve arrived at the same time as me, so why is he gone and I'm not? We were both in Group M."

Jawara didn't reply; his eyes were now focused below the orb.

Charlie also looked down, prompting her to say, "Oh no, what is that?"

As the orbis slowly ascended above the cruise ship a strange glow began to emanate within the hull of vessel. Numerous spheres could be seen leaving as the ship's structure started to glow and rupture. Hundreds of smaller orange flashes could be observed going on and off throughout the ship like flashes from a camera. Within seconds the cruise ship began to buckle and Decks A through J collapsed into the core of the vessel.

The massive radar tower above the control room slowly sunk into the bridge and toppled forward into the decks beneath. Below, the cabin decks started to collapse upon one another, pancaking the structure as they folded inward. The smokestacks crumpled and collapsed into the interior, releasing massive clouds of smoke. The ship shuddered and turned on its side, making a horrendous roaring noise as it was swallowed into a massive whirlpool of its own making.

Within the collapsed shell, a small, dark hole emerged from the ruins of the ship. The hole swallowed and ingested the walls and hull of the ship. Once the ship disappeared, the surrounding ocean water began to pour into the black hole. A loud howling noise caused Jawara's orbis to vibrate and resonate. The surrounding ocean poured in as a massive circular waterfall formed and flowed into the voracious vortex. When the ocean disappeared, the greenish-orange miasma was finally sucked into the hole. Within minutes nothing remained but the black hole that drifted aimlessly above the faded scarlet surface of a dusty, dead planet. Strangely, she immediately recognized the alien landscape.

"So it's true, we were never on Earth but on Mars?" she asked.

"Correct; after your demise, you were all sent here," Jawara said.

"But Steve said the night sky seemed different."

"The sky patterns of the past are different. The stars continue to move and change position over time."

"The rebellion, the fight to escape, it was all futile?" Charlie asked.

"To use your own words, you had no more chance of escaping than one of Steve's fish making it from a fish tank back to the ocean. Possible, but certainly not very probable. Yet here you are, making your escape."

"Oh my God, those poor people. Those vindictive bastards killed them all?"

"I'm afraid that they are all dead now. They were all returned to their original timelines."

Charlie became quiet, feeling lost and alone. She wanted to shrink and disappear like she used to as a little girl when her father was on a rampage. She tried walking off into the distance only to find herself returning to Jawara. There was no hiding in his space.

"It would appear the Council decided to end the Greeting based on the Sentinels' recommendation. My guess is they assessed the cultural contamination was too great a risk," Jawara said. "The Sentinels were more than happy to supply a violent ending to the Greeting. And you're right, they are vindictive bastards taking glee in their work."

Charlie remained silent, hoping the universe would leave her alone with her dark thoughts.

"Charlie? Are you okay?"

"Did they kill everyone because of my escape?" she asked in a timid whisper.

"No, my visit to the Omni may be as much to blame for their reaction. They must have felt threatened by the entirety of the human and Epicoid interaction aboard the cruise ship," Jawara said.

"There's something Ahmed said that I think I should share with you. Ahmed told Steve the Greeting has been going on for hundreds of years and that the Sentinels are basically stringing the Epicoids along."

"Stringing?" Jawara asked.

"Playing your people, deceiving you. They have no intentions of introducing your people to my kind."

"I don't know if that's true, but that's not their decision to make," Jawara said.

He began shuddering again. **Jawara didn't know why, but he felt a strange surge with Steve's disappearance.**

"What is wrong with you?" Charlie asked.

"I keep changing and these violent thoughts and dreams are filling my consciousness," Jawara said.

"Funny, with all these changes you're almost like an alien to me now," she said.

"But I am an alien to you," the Epicoid said between shudders.

"A play on words, but I'm finding these changes troubling. I can't predict your behavior."

"I remind you that your own species replaces cells on a regular basis, including a new liver every six weeks. We happen to do it much faster and with some significant genetic modifications along the way," Jawara said.

"Really, Jawara, who gives a shit?"

"But I will agree these recent modifications have been a bit bumpy. Unioeros with Steve has had some unexpected alterations for me. He's a very strong personality. Add to the equation the Unity orb with you and the results have been unpredictable."

There was no reaction from Charlie, who sat with her knees drawn to her chin.

Jawara stopped shuddering and said, "So many unexplained happenings. For example, how did you obtain the cloaking orbis?"

"I just walked into your room and borrowed it. Sorry for not asking."

"How is that even possible? There were safeguards in place to keep humans from utilizing our technology. How did you even know how to use an orbis?" Jawara asked.

"Actually, your stuff is pretty easy to use," Charlie admitted.

He just stared at her.

"What?" she asked.

"Stop touching my stuff," he said in his usual monotone, but he suddenly appeared distracted.

"A little late for that, Dad."

He blankly stared ahead and commented, "We're being followed. I have to return us to Earth."

"And I can go home?" an excited Charlie asked.

"No, we need access to a portal, and you must be returned to your timeline at the precise time; otherwise, you will share the same fate as Steve and the other passengers aboard the cruise ship."

The orbis moved towards Earth and Charlie felt her spirits soar with the sight of the familiar blue-and-white world. Charlie watched as they descended towards New York City.

"Anything to get out of this damn bubble, but why New York City?" she asked, emerging from her depression.

"We have to make our way to the portal, and it's located downtown."

"Where downtown?"

"In a not-so-convenient location."

"What the heck? Why not in the middle of a desert where nobody would see you?" she asked.

"Hiding in plain sight?"

"Your people are just bizarre," Charlie said.

The orbis descended to Earth and they made their way down a quiet side street. A sleeping homeless man awoke and watched the sphere descend with Charlie's and Jawara's reflections on the surface. Upon touching the ground, they emerged from the vanishing orbis and began walking away. The man stared at the tall alien and the bald girl in the swimsuit. Jawara smiled at him and said, "Hello." He smiled backed at the couple and returned to his sleep.

Jawara produced a silver orb before him and he handed it to Charlie. "Here, take this and use it when I tell you."

"You know, I don't exactly have pockets to hold this. What does it do?" she asked as she stuffed the orbis in her bikini top.

"It can push objects away with great force at a range of about twenty feet."

"Can't you just give me a ray gun like in every other science-fiction novel?" she asked.

"We don't have a ray gun. Epicoids don't have weapons in general, so we must learn to improvise."

"Where to now?" she asked. "Looks like we are about Midtown."

"Our coordinates were a bit off. We need to be south of here. Are you familiar with the city?"

'Yeah, I spent a summer here as a college intern. Where are we headed?"

"Financial District. Can we walk there?" Jawara asked.

"No, let's take a downtown subway to save time. Follow me. By the way, should I be welcoming you to Earth? This is your first visit, right?"

"It is."

"So what do you think?" she asked.

"Different; it seems very hard and grounded."

"Oh," she replied.

"It's also somewhat dirtier than I thought it would be," Jawara added.

"Funny, you're probably not the first alien to say that about New York," Charlie commented.

Jawara turned to her when a blur moved by them.

"Shit, what was that?" Charlie asked.

"We'll have to forgo the welcome. A Sentinel followed us," he said. "I don't understand. They are forbidden to visit this planet. That's why we set up the Greeting in the first place."

"I guess all bets are off now. Since when do they move that fast?" she asked.

"They can do many things if so inclined. This is not going to be pretty," he said as the two picked up their pace.

"Why are they such assholes?"

"They are Epicoids that don't want to be Epicoid. They reject our genetics and culture. Only one in a thousand Epicoids is insane enough to become a Sentinel. They are apart from us, but they were once used by us to provide protection during our civil war. Now I wonder who is using who."

"Let's go into that department store before they attack us," she said. "Maybe they'll hesitate to attack in front of a group of people."

"Doubtful, but we could hope they will show a little discretion," Jawara agreed.

They entered a revolving door with the crowd of people and a Sentinel followed right after the two. People seeing the Sentinel started to scatter from the vile creature.

Jawara clumsily stepped out of the counter-clockwise revolving door. Charlie was about to follow when she was abruptly grabbed by her shoulder. A Sentinel was in the wing behind her and held her shoulder, still covered by the wrap. She screamed and ducked, not wanting the creature to touch her bare skin, but she was unable to free herself.

Jawara glanced back and immediately jammed his foot in the revolving door to keep it from moving further. Trapping the Sentinel's arm, Charlie escaped. The Sentinel, still clutching the wrap, began pounding the glass into Jawara's leg, but he held fast.

The Sentinel tried to force its way into the store head-first. Jawara pushed his entire body against the revolving door, breaking the rotation mechanism and forcing the door to rotate in the clockwise direction. He had the Sentinel's head firmly wedged between the door and frame. The creature gave a horrible screeching noise when it realized it was trapped. Jawara tried battering its head with the door but he couldn't crush it. Still alive but firmly trapped between the door and the frame, the Sentinel struggled to find a means of escape and lowered its head down to the floor to gain leverage. A mob of people watched the battle in horror, looking for escape.

Jawara pinned the creature's head to the floor with his foot as he yelled, "Terrorist! He planted a bomb. There's a bomb in the store!"

He stomped the fallen Sentinel's head one more time and stepped away from the door just as the escaping crowd surged through the large revolving doors. The door pushed forward from the panicked shoppers, crushing the pinned head of the trapped Sentinel with a series of bone-crunching sounds. Within seconds the glass panes shattered and a wave of humanity poured through the broken door.

The two watched in horror and fascination while Charlie asked, "Jesus Christ, Jawara, where did you learn to do that?"

The giant was confused by his own actions and could only shrug. "From TV?"

"Julie never did sick shit like that on the *Love Boat*. In any case, we've got to leave here and take the subway. Come on," she said.

Hesitating a moment, Charlie bent down. "Give me my damn wrap, asshole!" She pulled the wrap from the dead Sentinel's hand. When they exited to the street, she saw the 1 line subway stop nearby and they descended the stairs. They looked about, fearing the Sentinels were still in pursuit.

"Wait, we don't have a subway card. Follow me," she said. They saw the turnstiles and Charlie deftly hopped over one. Jawara's lumbering stature didn't allow him to follow and he seemed confused by the obstacle.

"Forget the turnstile and follow me to the exit door," Charlie said as she moved to an 'exit only' door. She held the door open for Jarawa.

"Good thing there wasn't a transit cop nearby," she said.

Just then an MTA cop yelled at the pair to stop and she added, "Spoke too soon!"

While they were standing on the platform, something moved quickly past them.

"This is going to get worse. They're here," Jawara said as he spotted more Sentinels.

A pair of Sentinels followed the pair but the strange creatures were intercepted by the MTA cop. The cop studied the large, evil creatures that towered over him and froze in his tracks with his hand firmly locked on his gun. One of the Sentinels gave the cop a look and then touched him. The officer's face became anguished and his body started to contort. Within seconds he was convulsing and began running in a haphazard manner on the platform, screaming in agony.

A subway train arrived at the station and while waiting for the train to stop, Charlie saw movement in the gap between the train car and the platform. Behind them the tortured cop started shooting his gun.

Charlie yelled, "Get on!"

She led Jawara onto the train and the giant hit his head against the low ceiling of the car. With the train leaving the station, they watched as the officer shot himself in the head to end his anguish. The pair slowly moved between the cars, hoping to escape their pursuers. They were on the platform between the front and second car when Jawara said, "Stop! There's nowhere left to hide. It's time to train-surf. We can climb on top of the train to evade them. Just keep low."

"Are you crazy? People get killed all the time doing crazy stunts like that," Charlie said. "I kind of like keeping my head attached to the rest of my body."

"We can't fight two of these things, so we need to move and hide."

Jawara gave Charlie a boost to help her up. Almost on top of the car, she spotted an approaching beam and ducked her head. She felt the wind on her scalp. She immediately headed down and said, "No freaking way. You're not fitting up here, Jawara. I'm coming down."

Charlie jumped down, covered in dirt. "Any more great ideas?"

"Let's try a variation on this. Let's do some skylarking. Give me your sandal."

"What the hell for?"

"Just do it."

"What is skylarking?" she asked while handing him the sandal. "Where are you getting this from?"

"The Internet," the Epicoid said.

A couple of minutes later the Sentinels followed and saw a sandal dangling from the top of the train. The Sentinels eagerly climbed up on top of the subway car in pursuit. They tried to stay as low as possible, struggling to follow their elusive prey.

Jawara and Charlie hung precariously on to the side of the train. His large arm shielded her, forcing her up against the train. Occasionally an abutment grazed his large body, causing it to shudder with the impact. Charlie practically hyperventilated with fear.

"For God's sake, let's get back on the train," she yelled above the roar of the subway.

Jawara held up his hand, signaling to her to wait. She heard a thud and watched a Sentinel head with its tentacles twitching fall onto the platform between the subway cars.

She screamed, "We're going to die here. Let's go!"

"Wait for it," he said.

"What? Wait for what?" she asked incredulously.

A second head hit with a thud and cloud of red mist. It flew backwards onto the platform, settling next to the first head.

"Who the hell are you?" she asked Jawara, realizing that this wasn't the action of the gentle giant she had come to know. He moved from the side of the subway car to the platform while guiding her. She grabbed her sandal while gingerly stepping around the severed Sentinel heads.

They entered the first subway car and sat down towards the end. A few people stared at the giant and the dirty girl in the bikini, but they were otherwise left alone. The lights and fans of the older subway car kept intermittently cutting on and off, creating a bizarre strobe effect. Charlie straightened herself up as she noticed a crowd of fearful passengers making their escape from the far end of the car.

"Jawara, something is wrong." Before they could take a step, a Sentinel emerged from the conductor's booth behind them with the decapitated body of the conductor. It dropped the body and charged the pair.

"Get behind me, Charlie," Jawara said.

He stooped his head to fit in the car as he moved forward to take on the large creature. They locked their arms and began a fierce hand-to-hand combat battle that prevented Jawara from using an orbis.

The Sentinel tore at Jawara with his long claws, drawing blood. Charlie grabbed a passenger's abandoned equipment case and smashed the Sentinel across the head. It looked up and took a swipe at her. Its razor-like nails tore the case apart by the hinges.

With the Sentinel distracted, Jawara was free for a moment and yelled, "Toss the orbis I gave you at the door!"

Charlie threw the orbis just as the train neared Rector Street station. The flung orbis stopped in mid-air and floated to the door; the Sentinel saw it and watched for a moment. The doors opened and Jawara hurled the Sentinel towards the doors. Taken by surprise, the Sentinel fell through the open door. Falling, he used his claws to dig deep into Jawara's arm, dragging the Epicoid with him. Charlie grabbed Jawara and desperately held on to him. Without a conductor, the train sped past the platform without stopping, smashing the falling Sentinel into an abutment. The broken Sentinel dropped to the tracks in a shower of sparks as his body made contact with the electrified third rail. Just behind the Sentinel, Jawara and Charlie fell to the tracks, with Jawara shielding Charlie from impact.

In the darkness below the platform, Charlie lay dazed and shaken. She glanced up, surprised to see she was still alive, with just a few scratches. She was about to put her hand on a metal rail when she realized her head was mere inches from the third rail.

Jawara was next to her but not moving. She then noticed the pungent odor of burnt flesh that filled the air. Charlie carefully sat up while watching the roasting Sentinel body smolder a few feet away. Intermittently the creature's roasted flesh would sizzle and make a peculiar popping noise. Next to her Jawara opened his eyes and smiled.

"Any chance you saw my sandals on the way down?" she asked with a trace of a smile.

Jawara could only shake his head. Charlie got up in a hurry when she spotted a rat running across the tracks and stopping by Jawara.

"Stupid vermin," she said as she shooed it away and helped Jawara sit up. Above the platform she saw the Rector Street sign. Funny; that was their stop.

Shocked passengers jumped down to the tracks to assist the pair and helped them up onto the safety of the platform. Charlie saw Jawara was battered but still alive. He was too stunned to move and the curious onlookers stared at the fallen pale giant.

"Oh my God, he's hurt real bad. Please, we need help," Charlie tearfully yelled out to the crowd. More people surged forward to help and a crowd of twenty people milled about the fallen giant.

She leaned over and whispered into his ear, "You're okay, Jawara. Sorry, but it's my time to return to my people. I owe you everything for my second chance."

Scared, Charlie realized it was her opportunity to escape. She walked away from the crowd and, despite being barefoot, she began running. She exited the subway station by the stairs, desperate to separate herself from Jawara and her alien encounter. Charlie kept pace with the city crowd, wanting to blend in with the rest of humanity.

As she walked among the crowd she tightened the wrap about her shoulders and felt a welcome sense of relief. It was such a simple pleasure to be walking among complete strangers. She smiled to herself and for a few minutes she actually felt good being among her own kind.

While walking, Charlie noticed several people quickly running away from her. Before she could turn, a large hand forcibly grabbed her by the shoulder. She stared at the large gnarled finger, realizing it wasn't Jawara's.

She turned around to hear a strange hissing sound. A Sentinel held her and looked her over.

The Sentinel started to pull her towards it but a burst of blue energy emanating from Charlie's body hurled the huge creature backwards. The creature landed on its back some ten feet away from her. The shocked Sentinel was surprised to be thrown that easily by the small human and stood up to charge her. His ictus emerged from the folds, resembling a large warped stinger rather than an Epicoid organ of love. He ran towards her, trying to impale her with the organ.

Before Charlie could react, the Sentinel's head exploded in the air before her. Bits of gore sprayed over her bare skin. A piece of its flesh splashed across her left cheek, stinging and burning her flesh.

Jawara stood behind the fallen Sentinel holding a gun and said, "That wasn't very bright. You stay here, you die. You can't escape this timeline or the Sentinels. I have to place you back at the right time to save you."

"You're going to save me? You didn't save Steve," Charlie shot out.

"You must learn to trust me," Jawara said.

"Where did you get a gun?" she asked.

"Officer lent it to me," he said. The people around them scattered, seeing the carnage.

Charlie stopped and sat down on the sidewalk while looking straight ahead. She sat for several minutes not moving.

"Come on, Charlie, let's go," Jawara said. There was no acknowledgment from her, just a vacant stare. Police sirens wailed in the surrounding cityscape.

"Charlie, enough, we've got to go," Jawara said as he tried to pull her up on her feet.

She began hitting him, her face flushed with anger while she yelled, "Leave me alone! Just get away from me."

She stormed away as he grabbed her arm. "Don't touch me!" she yelled. "I wish I never met you horrid creatures."

Jawara grabbed her arm a second time but she violently shook him off while she continued walking away.

"You ruined my life," she said.

Jawara followed her. "Your life was ruined long before you met us. It's time you took responsibility and stopped blaming others," he said.

"Go to hell! You're not my fucking therapist," she said. "I can't do this anymore! I'm so tired of this bullshit, Jawara." Tears flowed down her cheeks. She reached up and wiped the Sentinel gore from her face. "Bradley is dead and I finally meet a man I trust, and he gets taken away from me, and then these horrid creatures are pursuing me," she said. "I don't deserve this nightmare. What did I do wrong?"

She stopped walking and sat back down on the curb as she started bawling like a young child. "I just want a normal life," she said as tears streamed down her face. "What the fuck is wrong with this world?"

Jawara pulled her up and said, "I think the normalcy train left a long time ago, and remember, this is much bigger than you now. I hesitated to share this with you, but some say the toughest steel is forged in the hottest fire."

With one hand Jawara began dragging the dead Sentinel to a side street while ushering Charlie along. Unceremoniously, Jawara deposited the Sentinel's body into a small dumpster. He peered into her eyes and said, "I'm going to share with you what I saw of the Greeting for your planet. Close your eyes." He held both of her hands.

Charlie found herself with Jawara in an orbis circling the Earth, observing the unfolding of the Greeting together. A number of large spheres the size of small moons appeared, orbiting the planet. In the beginning, a few people gathered outside to watch the translucent spheres. As word spread more people stepped outside to watch the celestial event. Five larger spheres joined the other ten spheres circling the Earth. Soon tens of millions were outside watching the show as the Greeting was officially underway.

A dazzling light show began, clearly visible to all of the inhabitants on Earth. Strangely, there were no communications—television, radio, or otherwise. Within an hour hundreds of millions were outside watching the strange events unfold; a sky show resembling a massive aurora borealis shrouded the Earth. There was still no panic, just curiosity as to what was happening. And there was no obvious message to the humans watching the show.

From the orbis, a massive electromagnetic pulse emerged, knocking out most of the electrical devices on the planet. Fuses, transformers, and all computer circuitry failed simultaneously on all of the electrical grids. Everything came to a halt. Cars, lights, computers, and planes all had their circuitry fail from the pulse. Jets tumbled out of the sky and crashed to the ground. In the wake of the destruction a strange orange miasma covered the entire globe, visible in day or night.

Jawara realized the Sentinels had orchestrated the attack without restraint from the Epicoids. In fact, no Epicoids, save himself, were present to observe the atrocity.

With no technology and only rudimentary weapons left operational, the Sentinels began the wholesale slaughter of the humans unopposed. A strange force moved across the landscape in the guise of a barely visible wall that passed through solid objects, but upon contact with a human body seemingly vaporized the person into thin air. Hundreds of millions of people—young, old, rich, poor, men, women, and children—literally dissipated into the air only to find themselves deposited naked on a barren, rocky planet. The lack of air on the planet and the extreme cold caused the frightened, hyperventilating humans to pass out within fifteen seconds. Those that tried to hold their breath had their lungs ruptured. Many were deposited into the same pile of humanity and they crushed the people below them. Within three minutes of their arrival on the planet they were all dead.

Naked human bodies covered vast swaths of the surface of the planet, some still twitching together in a vast orgy of death that stretched into the visible horizon. Their bodies eventually froze as hard as the rocks of the barren planet. Many Sentinels gathered above the planet to watch in amusement the deathscape covering the planet's surface.

Some of the remaining humans on Earth became cleverer and, through trial and deadly error, learned how to escape the transport wall. Billions were dead but millions remained on the planet, hiding in fear for their lives. The Sentinels, with their magnos, resorted to hunting down the remaining humans in an arduous manual hunt that they relished partaking in, a true bloodsport.

"Is that vision real?" Charlie asked quietly.

"I believe that is what the Sentinels have planned for Earth. Now do you understand why you have to go on?" Jawara asked.

"But why? Why kill us?"

"The Sentinels have deemed humans a threat to the status quo. Like I said, we Epicoids like your kind better than these beasts."

"So why the hell me?"

"Because sometimes the fight picks you," Jawara said.

"This fight is picking a weakling. Let's be honest, I'm not bringing much to any fight," Charlie said.

"We have escaped from the ship and taken out four Sentinels so far; that's a good start. Just stay alive and warn the others for now; keep hope alive, as they say. Right now your world is betting on you and me to stop this massacre."

"Then they're betting on the wrong horse. I couldn't even save myself from a bad marriage."

"Perhaps, but you are a survivor. Just remember, in the real world heroes get chosen. Nobody in their right mind volunteers for this bullshit."

She noticed that it really didn't sound like Jawara talking and replied, "I'm it, then? I got chosen to play the hero?"

"Yes, but then again, some get chosen and fail miserably," Jawara said.

"Oh," she replied. Now that sounded like Jawara.

"Yes, I remember one spirited Epicoid rebellion against the Sentinels that was particularly inspiring to us all. A thousand of our best soldiers rebelled against their Sentinel overlords."

"Did they succeed?"

"No," Jawara said.

"What happened to them?"

"They were easily defeated by the Sentinels and all one thousand of the rebelling Epicoids were either killed or eventually captured."

"So some were imprisoned?"

"No, the Sentinels are not big on long prison sentences. They were all tortured and then skinned alive by the Sentinels, but the campaign was very inspiring. Foolish, pointless perhaps, but very inspiring nevertheless."

"Jawara, you really suck at pep talks," Charlie said.

"The moral to this story is, don't get captured by the Sentinels. Now follow me and try to blend in," Jawara said harshly.

Charlie seemed despondent as she walked.

"Not to worry, snowflake, stop thinking you're alone in this journey. I've got your back," Jawara said.

Now she knew this wasn't just Jawara talking. "That's not you. Is Steve somehow in there with you?" she asked.

"I'm keeping his memories alive with me after my tasting. I think we both could use his help," Jawara said, and he gave her a big body hug that lifted her from the ground.

Charlie felt better with the hug and Jawara placed her back down. They continued walking, when a Hispanic man handed the giant a flyer for a gentlemen's club.

"What's a lap dance?" he asked.

Charlie grabbed the flyer and threw it to the ground. She said, "I'll tell you what, if we somehow survive this ordeal I'll give you one later. Trying to distract me?"

"I figure if you are talking, you will have less time to be scared."

"When I'm scared, I actually talk more, but on to more important matters. Why aren't there more Sentinels chasing us, and why aren't they using their weapons?" Charlie asked.

"The Council no doubt gave them strict instructions on what technology they could use on Earth; otherwise, this chase is going to become the Greeting. If they use their weapons here, the Council will be the first to know. It seems like they want to be somewhat discreet. Besides, they rather enjoy getting their claws dirty on what they deem to be two relatively soft targets: an effeminate Epicoid and a weak human female."

Charlie saw their reflection in a window. She was still only clad in her bikini and one sandal while walking with the strange, seven-foot-tall giant. Both were dirty, Charlie a disheveled wreck while Jawara was bruised, bleeding, and limping, with rips in his blue uniform.

"Shit, we're not exactly inconspicuous. We look like two refugees from the world's worst cruise ship," Charlie said.

"We are two refugees from a cruise ship, but is anybody paying attention to us?" Jawara asked.

She surveyed the crowded street, noticing that everyone was going about their own business. "Not really," she said.

"It's New York City; they've seen stranger," Jawara said.

"Now I know that's not you talking," she said as he stared at her.

"What now?" she asked.

He grabbed her by the head with his large hand and noticed that, after two days, her head had a fine orange fuzz.

"Hey, hands off. What are you staring at?" she asked.

"Oh no, we need to shave your head," Jawara said.

"I need to groom now? It's not that hair phobia nonsense again?" she asked.

"Now. We need to obtain a razor for you," he said sternly.

"Don't you have an orb or something for that?" Charlie asked.

"No, we don't have an orbis for your personal grooming needs," Jawara said peevishly.

The two soon approached a pharmacy. Peering inside, Charlie asked, "You got money?"

"Can't we just take one?" Jawara asked.

"Yeah, right. Did you ever try to buy a razor? Sheesh, get real, will you?" Charlie said as they walked to the personal grooming aisle. She pointed to the padlocked cage. Jawara tried to open the sliding door but it was locked.

"I don't understand. Why so much protection for a thin piece of metal and plastic?" Jawara asked.

She just shrugged and said, "Don't get me started."

Jawara tried to open the display. Failing, he turned to Charlie.

"Feel free to wail on it," she said. "As for me, I'm personally going to enjoy watching this."

He picked up the unit and smashed it against the floor. She was impressed with his show of brute strength as he started to break up the display. Several store employees rushed over to stop the rampaging giant.

"We have company," she said as he continued to break up the display.

She turned to the two men. "Please, he's having a bad day and is off his meds. Anti-psychotic meds, actually."

The two men approached but hesitated when the giant stood tall. A third man showed up with a bat in hand and he wasn't as afraid.

"Hey asshole, I'm going to bust you up!" the man yelled.

The other two men grabbed the giant but Jawara easily threw the pair. The man hit him with the bat across the chest but Jawara just smiled at him. A red orb rose from his body and moved wildly from man to man, stunning and subduing them. A customer looked on at the fight and Charlie smiled as she pointed to the store camera and said, "A YouTube prank. Smile for the camera!"

The customer quickly exited the store. Among the debris Charlie picked up a razor and grabbed a can of shaving cream. She lathered up her head and began shaving.

"So why are we in New York City?" she asked as she shaved her head.

"That's why," Jawara said as he pointed out the window to a sculpture standing in the middle of a traffic median. It was the bronze Charging Bull sculpture of Wall Street.

"I don't understand," she said.

"The emergency transport is located there, somewhere inside the bull. Let's go," Jawara said,

"You people are just weird," Charlie said.

"Strange sense of humor," he said.

"I don't have to shave anything else?"

"No, your head will suffice for our meeting."

"Batch of freaks," she said as she took off down the store aisle.

"What are you doing?"

She grabbed a towel and wiped her head. She pointed to a display of sandals and said, "Size 6, please!" as she grabbed a pair to put them on. She went to grab a clean wrap and shorts, too. Jawara stared at her and she said, "What? I'm tired of giving everyone in New York a free show."

Jawara rudely pulled her away with her purloined goods and said, "We have no time for your petty larceny."

The pair walked out of the store to the cobblestone median where the sixteen-foot-long bronze bull stood. Jawara began crossing the street without looking. She pulled him back as a taxi zipped by while yelling, "Watch for the cars, dammit. Don't need to lose you to an errant Uber driver!"

She stared at the Charging Bull overrun with tourists. "You've got to be shitting me."

When they got to the bull Jawara said, "Give me your hand so I can give you the sensor. Just run your hands along the surface of the bull and this will change color if you find the activator."

She studied the strange purple color of her hand.

"Remember, check everywhere," he said.

They mingled among the crowd; many of them were Chinese tourists taking selfies with the bull.

"Time for you to grab the bull by the balls," Jawara said.

"What?"

"You heard me."

"Why do I get the back of the bull?"

"I think you groping the genitals of the bull is a little less conspicuous than me," Jawara said.

"Shit, just a little," she said.

"Rest assured, you won't be the only one. Besides, I don't think I could bend that low."

Charlie made her way to the rear of the bull to observe the spectacle. The Chinese tourists were all over the bull's rear, taking photos of themselves rubbing the statue's large testicles. Charlie couldn't wait her turn so she dropped the wrap and shorts. She blatantly photobombed their shots as she rudely began inspecting the rear of the bull. She turned to Jawara for some assistance but one of the Chinese tourists asked Jawara to take a group photo.

"Fricking unbelievable," she said. Charlie, realizing the strange sense of humor the Epicoids possessed, began aggressively stroking the brass balls of the massive bull. An older Chinese man, seeing how skimpily attired Charlie was in the bikini, just assumed the pretty bald girl was looking for tips for taking her photo.

The grey-haired man took her picture stroking the bull's balls and thanked her while saying in flawless English, "An inch of time is an inch of gold, but an inch of time cannot be purchased for an inch of gold. This is the exception: throw this bill into the mouth of the dragon and this will buy you much-needed time."

Smiling, he gave her a twenty-dollar bill as a tip. Charlie stared at him, confused.

He followed in broken English, "It's good luck!"

"Yeah, sure," she said and was about to say the tip was too much, but the color of her hand changed to red as she stroked the bronze balls.

"I guess you're right," she said to him and smiled. "Got it, Jawara!"

Jawara returned the camera to the tourists and shuffled to Charlie's side. He grabbed her hand while touching the testicles. Their combined touch caused two ten-foot spheres to emerge from the butt of the bull, to the surprise and delight of the tourists.

Each transparent orbis floated and levitated with Charlie and Jawara's reflections on the surface of the spheres. The orbises rose into the air and combined into one large sphere while gently floating in the breeze. The crowd watched in awe as the orbis vanished into the low-hanging clouds, with dozens of smartphones recording the event.

The orbis passed slowly through the sky and left Earth as they headed into space. Charlie wasn't sure if she was standing or sitting but she was transfixed by the view. Soon the sphere gathered speed and they were heading away from the sun.

"How come there are no seats in this damn thing? What if I have to pee?"

"It's not a ship, per se. We're not moving in a ship; rather, the universe is moving about our bodies. If you must sit, just assume a sitting position and the orbis will accommodate you. As to peeing, you're on your own."

"The universe is moving about us? What does that even mean? How does this orbis actually work?" Charlie asked, confused.

"Something about what you call quantum wormholes," Jawara said. "I just use the technology, like you do. Know how your cellphone works?"

She shook her head. *Fair enough,* she thought.

"You know, you've been kind of snotty to me lately. What's happened to nice and polite?" she asked. "Is that you, or are you channeling Steve?"

Jawara ignored her comment.

She saw her strange bubble moving among the stars and planets. She was scared as she stroked the twenty-dollar bill.

"What are you doing with that? There are no tolls out here," Jawara said.

Charlie scrutinized the twenty-dollar bill in her hand. "Jeez, this is a 1922 twenty-dollar gold certificate. You know how rare these are? I'm keeping this for good luck. The old man said something about an inch of time is like an inch of gold. Time cannot be bought for an inch of gold, but this is the exception. Any clue as to what he meant?"

"Not sure; I suggest you look it up in a fortune cookie the next time you are on Earth," Jawara said as he worked the orbis.

"Your condescending attitude aside, I love how your technology is so awesome yet has such a tiny footprint," she said.

Behind the orbis a massive structure several miles across trailed, propelling the unaware occupants of the orbis. The sphere shook as Charlie turned around to look. Two large dark spheres that bristled with tentacles were in pursuit. Looking closer, Charlie realized the tentacles were in fact weapons. The Sentinels, with their very militaristic black spheres, were firing some strange light at their craft. One of the beams missed them and in the distance struck an asteroid, obliterating the rock into a thousand pieces.

"How come they get real ships with weapons and all we have is this damn bubble? Doesn't seem fair that we don't have a better ride," Charlie said.

"Because they are allowed to shoot at us; that's why they *get* the ships they *get*. And it's not a damn bubble."

Ahead of the orbis in another plane, a massive machine several miles wide rendered a hole in space-time for the sphere. Their machine shuddered and spewed debris from the constant Sentinel attacks. Bits of wreckage exploded in space before them.

The massive structure suddenly appeared before the two in the orbis.

"Jawara, what was that?" Charlie asked.

He peered into his interface and said, "Not sure." He gazed at some instruments and then yelled, "That's our engine! The Sentinels have damaged it considerably."

She studied his face. "Christ, you didn't know that was our engine? Even I know where the fricking engine is in my car. Now what?"

His demeanor changed. "This won't be pretty. Hang on!"

"Hang on to what?" she screamed as they rolled about the sphere.

He turned the orbis into a local star to lose the Sentinels.

"What are you doing, crashing into that star?" Charlie shrieked.

"This may hurt quite a bit!" Jawara yelled.

The Land of No

"Close your eyes; this will be very uncomfortable!" Jawara yelled. Charlie wanted to hide but there was nowhere to disappear.

"Where are the Sentinels?" she asked.

"They broke off the attack; even they aren't crazy enough to go so close to a red star."

Outside the orbis a giant red star passed by, its roiling surface sending blasts of hot plasma into space. The light was blinding and Charlie huddled alone in the sphere.

Before disappearing into the sun, Jawara saw the hyper-jump, a large ring of plasma just above the surface of the star. It was directly powered by the red star.

"There!" he said.

He pointed the sphere into the hyper-jump and they disappeared into the plasma.

The orbis passed a yellow-white sun and stopped to orbit a small green planet. Jawara studiously scanned its surface.

"We're home. This is my planet that was designed for the Greeting," Jawara said.

"You created this planet and a people just to greet us? How many are there like you?"

"Yes, we are approaching a billion in number. We breathe the same atmosphere and share much of the same physicality as you do."

"So you really don't know what your people originally look like?"

"Strangely, I do not know; we are probably something horrid. The Epicoids, as you see me and the others, are all I know."

"How many are there of the other Epicoids?"

"I can't feel all of them. Someone said a trillion, but I'm not sure that number is accurate."

"Where are the Sentinels?" she asked, hoping that the chaotic chase was over.

"Their cruisers are not allowed in this system; it's part of the agreement they made with us. We're safe on my home planet until we leave. But you're right. They'll be waiting for us to make our move, and we need a better ride, as you say, to pull this off. Do you believe in taking risks?" Jawara asked.

"I have an understandable aversion to gambling, but do we have any other options?" she retorted.

"No, this is our only option. Doesn't really even qualify as a long shot, what we are doing."

"Play the cards you are dealt, Jawara. So, where to?" she asked.

"Into the lion's den, literally: a hatchery for new Sentinels on our planet. We need a Marauder. It's a much faster, more robust vessel than the damn bubble, as you called it."

"So get one," she said.

"They are exclusively the province of the Sentinels on my home planet. We may have to use force to take one."

"Great. I would really prefer to avoid those bastards, but do we have a choice?"

"No, unfortunately. Our spinal columns are up against a vertical buttress, as they say."

"What the fuck, Jawara?" she asked. She thought for a moment and then said, "You mean our backs are against the wall?"

"Yes."

She smiled and teased, "You said that on purpose, didn't you?"

"Yes, I like seeing you smile," he said with a quirky grin.

"Holy shit, Jawara, humor and now you smiled again," she said. "Really, what's going on with you?"

"Changes," he said. "We're nearing my home planet."

Looking outward, Charlie viewed a planet with a familiar blue-and-white coloring and said, "Looks like Earth. What do you call your world?"

"Cossaea."

"Am I the first?" she asked.

Jawara thought for a moment and said, "I think you are the first human to see our world."

The orbis slowly descended below a layer of low-lying clouds and the surface became clearly visible. Charlie looked over the lush green landscape, which had been terraformed and melded into the living fauna and Epicoid architecture of the planet. Above the landscape millions of spheres floated in the air, reflecting the sunlight and shimmering in the sky. Fat green trees filled the land with incredibly tiny branches. Strange umbrella-shaped trees stood a hundred feet tall, providing shade. Below, their root-like structures moved the massive plants painfully slowly over the landscape. Among the creatures were giant sequoias transplanted from Earth, standing majestically against the blue-green skies of the alien world.

A series of small, puffy white clouds scattered across the horizon, releasing gentle showers during their peaceful journey. Amid the clouds floated mystical shimmering lights. They were translucent, changing in hue and varying in intensity from moment to moment.

Among the flora strange adobe-like buildings were interspersed, some a single story, others soaring a hundred stories into the air. A froth-like layer of larger spheres encircled the cities, swaying up and down in the air while reflecting the yellow sun. Some buildings were floating in massive spheres held to the ground by a single, seemingly delicate tendril. Others floated freely and rose above and within the clouds while proudly displaying their disdain for gravity.

Jawara turned to Charlie but she was uncharacteristically quiet for several minutes while watching the alien landscape unfold before her. Several tears trickled down her cheeks as she gazed upon the serene extraterrestrial world before her. She seemed overwhelmed by the sights but eventually broke her silence by saying, "Jeez, your people aren't much for obeying the laws of gravity, huh?"

"We find gravity, how do you say, fucking boring. So what do you think?"

"It's a lot cleaner than I thought it would be," she said with a smirk.

Jawara just smiled at her. "That's it?"

"No, it's all amazingly beautiful, Jawara. It's almost overwhelming. I just wish Steve was here to share this moment with me; he would have loved this. But if I'm going out, at least I'm going out on a high note," she said.

"You're not done. Not yet, if I have any say in the matter," he replied while giving her a touch. She felt her anxiety level off.

Closer to the surface, they passed an aqueous sphere containing a large throng of naked Epicoids some fifty deep, writhing together in unison. Their bodies were intertwined within their water world and Charlie felt the sexual vibrations even from within the orbis.

"That isn't...?" she asked.

"Yes, a massive group Sacour Feast. It's a very popular event on my planet."

"Shocker, discovering that you Epicoids are a horny lot. No transportation system?"

"Unnecessary with our orbs."

She looked Jawara over and noticed that he looked different. The Epicoid's normal blue uniform had transformed into a shiny gold-silver color.

"You changed?"

"Yes, this is a traditional warrior uniform for my people. I think it's now appropriate considering what we will be facing," Jawara said.

The orbis descended to the surface and disappeared, and the two found themselves walking towards a tall, pale, female-looking Epicoid. Charlie stuffed the twenty-dollar bill in her swimsuit top for safekeeping. Her hands immediately went to her head to adjust her hair, but then she remembered that she had none.

The approaching Epicoid was more feminine-looking than Jawara, with a pronounced womanly figure. The two Epicoids embraced and began exchanging communication but Jawara said, "Mentor, out loud in English so my human friend can hear."

"You appear somewhat different, Jawara. Is this from Unioeros with the humans?"

"Yes, in part."

"And so this is one of the humans the Council is talking about?" the Mentor asked as ze eyed Charlie. The Epicoid's voice wasn't discernibly male or female.

"The very same," Jawara said.

"From your reports and meeting this delightful creature, they don't seem such a threat. What is all the fuss that the Sentinels keep warning us about?"

Charlie extended her hand up to the tall Epicoid to shake.

The Epicoid was confused by the gesture. Jawara gave the Mentor a small nod to encourage ze to shake Charlie's small hand.

The Epicoid took Charlie's hand. Charlie felt the tingling cascade through her body, deep to her nether regions. Charlie quickly withdrew her hand.

Jawara's friend said, "She is very tasty, this one."

"Please, don't say that around humans," Jawara said.

"Why?"

"There is some confusion and they have this peculiar fear that we are carnivorous."

The Epicoid didn't understand.

"That we want to devour their flesh for nutrition," Jawara said.

The other Epicoid's body shook. Charlie was afraid ze was ill but she soon realized the Epicoid was filled with laughter.

"You laugh?" Charlie asked.

"Yes, it's another trait we are acquiring from humans. It's all the rage on our planet. Rest assured we do not consume the flesh of others," the Epicoid said. Ze turned to Jawara. "They are a bit primitive, but maybe that's the attraction to them."

"You have heard what happened to us?" Jawara asked.

"No, not a word. I was surprised when you appeared," the Mentor replied.

"Really? There's more to this story. The Council and the Sentinels are hiding something from us. I need to protect Charlie. To do so I need to borrow a Marauder."

The Epicoid's face contorted and said, "You're killing me with your humor; this must be something you picked up from your time with the humans. Borrow a Marauder. Sure, maybe you could ask a Sentinel to chauffer the Marauder for you while you are at it."

Jawara's face was expressionless and he gestured towards Charlie.

Charlie looked at the Mentor and said, "Please help us!" Tears began to well up in her eyes and she felt little need to show emotional restraint.

Looking at Charlie, the Mentor was confused and asked, "What is wrong with her eyes?"

"She's crying; she has lost many of her friends today. We need your help before we lose everything," Jawara said.

The demeanor of the Mentor changed as ze turned to Jawara and asked, "What? You're sincere about this. No, if you get caught with this human you will put us all in mortal danger. They will pull from your bodies all the information they need to implicate the rest of us. You know what they did to the thousand, don't you?"

The Mentor turned to face Charlie and noticed several tiny red hairs on the side of her head that she had missed shaving in her haste. Ze quickly began walking away from the pair.

Jawara grabbed the Mentor's arm and twisted it back toward him. The Mentor glared at him and said, "We didn't teach you to behave like that. There is another exerting their influence over you. This is very curious, the effect the humans are having on you. Maybe the Sentinels have a point about the Greeting."

"We asked for your help. Don't turn your back on us because it's personally inconvenient," Jawara said sternly.

"I need to speak with you alone," the Mentor said. Charlie nodded and left the two. As she scanned the sky she noticed the other Epicoids in the nearby vicinity staring intently at her.

"You should be aware that I saw her red hair. You know of the Vedas?" the Mentor asked.

"I have heard of them," Jawara said, showing concern.

"There is a passage in the proverb titled Unioeros, where they speak of one not of our kind," the Epicoid said.

"I would assume they mean 'after its kind,' as in the human Old Testament."

"What else?"

"In our proverbs, a kind is a functional equivalent to an evolutionary species," Jawara said, but he then hesitated. The Mentor's eyes lit up.

"You know of the passage, don't you?" the Mentor said. Jawara nodded. Ze continued, "The legacies speak of a scarlet avatar, not of our kind, uniting all of the different kinds into one kind through Unioeros. You think this human Charlotte may be the Red Avatar that was prophesized, don't you?"

"I find her arrival more than coincidental, but that doesn't matter. Most importantly, she is a good friend that I have promised to help," Jawara said. The intensity was obvious on his face.

"The human has no understanding of her role in this?" the Mentor asked.

"As of now she is blissfully ignorant of our myths."

"Doesn't matter; neither ignorance nor innocence will afford her protection from the likes of the Sentinels. I now understand why you are going through this folly, but are you really willing to resurrect the Cult of the Red Avatar knowing full well what that internecine war nearly did to our species?"

"I do so knowing we need to end the tyranny of the Sentinels, yes."

"Sorry, but I don't share your enthusiasm in this foolish endeavor."

"Too bad, because if I don't succeed you will be the first Epicoid I give up," Jawara said.

"I should expose your plan to the Sentinels myself," the Mentor threatened.

"All that will guarantee is our failure and … your torture alongside me for having been my Mentor. But I'm sure with your erudite ways you could explain your role away to the Sentinels; that is, as they take turns joyfully shredding your flesh into tiny sinews with their ictuses."

"I will tell you the location of the Marauders, but after that you are on your own. This is beyond reckless if you consider the odds of succeeding. To go undetected, both of you will need to wear the robes of a pledge; otherwise, they will sense you in minutes."

"Good, do you have these robes for us?" Jawara asked.

"No, you will have to steal the robes or take them by force. Many of the Sentinel pledges come to the market for one last glimpse at their old life. Those are the less committed, of course. I suggest you find two weaker pledges and forcibly take their robes."

"Where to?" Jawara asked.

"No, I can't help you anymore. We set you up for this mission to gather more information about the humans, not to intervene on their behalf."

"So why do I have all of this engineering and weapons information? You must have shared this knowledge with me," Jawara said.

"No, it wasn't from me," the Mentor said.

"Doesn't matter. How do I return Charlie to her timeline?"

"Take your friend to the Quanteme event horizon. You do know how to reach the event horizon?"

Jawara thought a bit and said, "Yes. Strangely, I do."

"Only I don't. The event horizon information wasn't seeded from me," ze said.

"I don't understand."

"I don't have access to this information. That means someone else is feeding you this information. There is more to this saga than you and your human friend realize. To quote the vernacular of the humans, you are simply a pawn in someone else's game and you don't even have the wits to realize it."

"This is troubling, but I appear to have my role to play," Jawara said. He walked away and began strangely pacing like a troubled human being.

"You are even walking like them," ze pointed out. "I would be very careful about your next moves; whoever gave you this information is an insider at the highest levels of the Council. This is not going to end well for you or your human companion, just like the others that came before you. Worse, I hear there are things at the event horizon—things that jealously guard the portal."

"Others?" Jawara asked.

"Such arrogance. You really think you are the first?"

"I will deal with it. Thanks, we have already taken too much of your time. Charlie, we are leaving," Jawara said.

They walked away from the Mentor. Ze called out, "Jawara, you'd better find out who the chess master is; otherwise, you and the Red Avatar will always be their pawn, even if you do manage to escape from the Sentinels."

They continued walking and Charlie asked, "What is this Red Avatar she mentioned?"

"An old Epicoid superstition that I thought had little basis in fact. With recent events I find myself wondering if there is some semblance of truth in the fables, but it is not your concern. What is our concern is that the Sentinels do want to stop all contact with humans at any cost, and perhaps...," Jawara said, hesitating.

"What?"

"Reprise my nightmare and end your species as a threat altogether."

"And the chess master?"

"This other party assisting us is troubling. I don't know what their objectives could be in this mess," Jawara admitted.

"Your people, the Epicoids.... They would defend us, wouldn't they?"

"We would strenuously argue on your behalf and lodge a protest against the Sentinels' actions."

"So in other words, your people would do nothing?" Charlie asked.

"We are not warriors. We would not go to war for you. We're incapable of violence—what you call on Earth pacifists."

"Then you have to give us the weapons to defend ourselves," Charlie said.

"As pacifists we cannot assist in the violence of others."

"So you would stand idly by on principle and watch us get slaughtered?" Charlie asked.

"I'm fighting for you; that's a start. My goal is to make sure it doesn't reach that point, and if need be, you and I will convince them otherwise."

As Jawara and Charlie walked, they observed all manner of strange creatures that appeared in close proximity to them. Charlie went to touch a chimerical bird-like creature but her hand passed through it.

"What the heck?" she blurted, confused.

"Different dimension. This is just an observational portal. The specimens are in their natural environment, unaware we are observing them."

"What is this?" Charlie asked.

"A petting zoo of sorts," Jawara replied.

Charlie watched as animals of all breeds lived and ate. In one instance, two large wormlike creatures mated.

While walking, Charlie saw two naked humans—a younger man and a more mature blond woman—on display. She recognized them as the couple she had spied on having sex in the Tranquility Area. She watched as they fucked in their cabin room. She noticed several welts on the blond woman's buttocks, no doubt from the GodNauts' chastisement. Charlie walked into their cabin and stood next to the intertwined couple. She could smell their sex filling the room.

Charlie touched the young man and she could feel his skin. He jumped up from his lover and stared at Charlie.

"You're that girl in the chair next to us," he said.

He looked Charlie over; she appeared a little dirty and disheveled in her bikini, but that made her even hotter to him.

"Your hair?" he asked.

Charlie said nothing.

"Want to join us?" he asked. The older blond woman just smiled at her.

Jawara pulled her from the room.

She glared at Jawara and yelled, "Why are they in captivity, as sex toys for your people? What is this, an intergalactic brothel?"

"That's wrong; that is against the orders of the Council," Jawara said.

"Well if not for sex, why then?"

"Curiosity? Mating? Observation, maybe?" Jawara said.

"You don't know? Seems more like zoophilia to me. Is it the Sentinels or the Epicoids doing this?"

"No, this has to be the Council, but it's wrong in any case. We don't have time for them right now. You're the one in peril. Follow me and keep your voice down. You need to shut up," Jawara said bluntly.

That was kind of curt, coming from Jawara. They walked through the marketplace and spotted two pledges in long, dark robes. Jawara glanced at Charlie and gave her a small nod. They followed the pair near a dark alley and Jawara smashed one of their heads against the wall. The other tried to turn around but Jawara wrapped his arm around its neck and quickly choked out the second pledge.

Charlie stared at him and Jawara said, "What? These idiots want to become Sentinels. They deserve this and worse."

"No, it's just that you suddenly have some crazy skills. You seem a lot stronger lately, almost brutish. Whatever happened to that Quanteme business?" she asked.

"I'm channeling Steve's training. As to the Quanteme, I am no longer part of it."

"Just what was his training?"

"He was in the Marines," Jawara said.

"Yeah, he shared that with me, but that only partly explains some of the attitude and training."

"He quit and signed up with the Navy to become a SEAL."

"Shit, that's some kind of hardcore military. So you're a badass now?" Charlie asked.

"Consider this foreplay; the rest of our journey will be hardcore."

Jawara stripped the pledges of their robes and they put them on. Charlie's robe was oversized, literally dragging on the floor.

"These are more like a monk's hair suit," Charlie said. She peered down and noticed the robe trailing considerably along the ground. "I'm a bit vertically challenged for an Epicoid, don't you think?"

"Yes, that won't do. We'll just have to make you taller," Jawara said. Charlie felt herself lift off the ground until she was as tall as Jawara.

"How do I walk?" she asked.

"Just walk normally. I'll keep you suspended; just be prepared if I should be interrupted."

"Be prepared for what?" she asked.

"To fall, of course."

"I have a feeling that will be the least of my troubles."

They came to the end of the market and a large mirror-like wall stood in their way. As they drew nearer, the other side appeared to be shrouded in darkness. Charlie felt a sense of doom emanating from the other side. Jawara took her hand and led her through the reflection.

"You ready for the Land of No?" he asked.

"Yes, ready as I am ever going to be," Charlie answered.

"Be quiet and don't talk," Jawara said. They saw other Epicoids wearing the dark robes of a pledge, covered head to toe and appearing very gloomy and somber. Everything was in shadows and the dim orange light cast a grey mood over all the denizens. No spheres danced in the sky; instead, only dark, dreary buildings with no lighting littered the desolate landscape.

"I forgot to spray you," Jawara suddenly said.

"You're not spraying me with that shit again. Just where do you keep all of this stuff?" she asked. In the darkened alley they heard the screams of the tortured. She shuddered.

"No talking; keep your head down."

"What is that horrid wailing?" Charlie asked.

"Quiet, they can hear you. The Sentinels kill many of their own—or should I say, they kill each other during their purification process."

"They torture one another?" she asked incredulously.

"Yes. For most, sexual torture is the only way they can separate the true believers from the weaker recruits. It separates the true sadists from what you call a wannabe."

The screams intensified and a frisson overtook Charlie's being. As she looked toward the end of the alley she observed other Epicoids who were metamorphing into Sentinels. They walked with an erect culmus that bristled with hard, sharpened edges.

"What's wrong with their culmus?" she asked, the fear showing in her eyes.

"It's not just their bodies; their culmuses also metamorphose. Imagine my culmus serrated with sharp, razor-like edges. They actually transform themselves to obtain this organ by touching the orb of the Creator Sentinel. Imagine two such organs stroking and thrusting at each other. The pain transforms a normal Epicoid into the hideous creatures we call Sentinels. They have transformed lovemaking and contact with one another into a form of sexual torture, forever ending their desire for normal contact and sealing their fate as Sentinels. They call it the Purification."

A series of shrieks reverberated throughout the square.

"What? These horrors fornicate?" she asked in horror.

"Sentinels ravage each other with their culmus, removing entire chunks of their flesh. Sometimes they will tear out each other's culmus, resulting in both having to be put down to end their shared agony."

"Dear God, that is so fucking sick," Charlie said.

"Their mangled culmus hardens and is sharpened into what is called an ictus. It actually gives them great pleasure to use their ictus to rip apart their victims. I told you this is the Land of No. Pain and pleasure, it all gets twisted up within their sick minds; that's the way of the Sentinels. Those who can take their pain to the edge are their sadistic leaders. That's why we get along better with your species than we do with them. You have self-flagellates on your planet, don't you?"

"Yes, we do, but they're not ripping out each other's genitals. Go ahead, spray, give me a bath if necessary," Charlie said as she heard the screams intensify. Before Jawara could spray her a group of Sentinels passed by and scrutinized the pair. A small breeze showed Charlie's bare leg, catching the attention of a Sentinel as it sniffed the air.

"Shit, they are on to us," Jawara said. "Quick, back to the marketplace. We have to lose them."

A team of Sentinels gathered together as one pointed toward Jawara and Charlie.

"You have to run on your own," Jawara yelled.

Charlie stumbled to the ground and hitched her robe up so she could run. The Sentinels pursued them, but Jawara was much faster. They reached the marketplace but the Sentinels continued their pursuit into the Epicoids' territory.

"That shouldn't be; they have no jurisdiction here," he said.

"Jawara, I don't think I can run anymore!" Charlie yelled.

"Shit, time for something totally futile and desperate," he said.

Jawara released a large orb that moved from pen to pen in the petting zoo, opening them all as it journeyed from one to the next, releasing the animals, including the two humans, into the marketplace. The animals ran amok among the Epicoids and the Sentinels, disrupting the pursuit. The enraged Sentinels began slaughtering the released animals that stood in their way.

The two naked humans turned to Charlie, stunned and unsure what to do with themselves.

"We can't just leave them here, Jawara. Please!" she pleaded.

He seemed disinterested at their plight.

"What's your name?" she asked.

"Jan, and this is Peter. Where the hell are we?" Jan asked. "Where's the ship?"

"No time to explain. Jawara, we have to take them," Charlie said.

"Taking them is a mistake."

"Please!" Charlie yelled.

Jawara sighed and said, "Just keep close to me."

"So why aren't the Sentinels using their weapons?" Charlie asked.

"They were either told to take us alive or they just wanted to get their hands wet. Remember, you don't want to be their prisoner. The way the Epicoids find pleasure, the Sentinels can find pain. No surrender! Understood?"

Jawara and Charlie ran up to a large, dark grey thatched hut, followed by the pair of lovers. Charlie began searching for a door and asked, "Are we hiding in here?"

"Get away from there. It's sleeping," Jawara said.

"It?" Charlie asked. She stepped aside, realizing the hut was a creature as it released a massive pile of vile-smelling dung.

Jawara woke the creature with a sharp kick to its side. The large beast lifted up and Charlie saw it was a massive quadruped animal. Jawara struggled to corral and manage a large obine, a massive creature with five-foot-long horns, and a broad back with tufts of hair. The creature's body hair was over four feet long with a circumference similar to one-inch rope. Four massive legs, each with a circumference of four feet, supported a body that stood over fifteen feet tall. Jawara jumped on its back and yelled, "Get aboard!" to the humans. The massive beast stomped and made loud bellowing noises.

"This thing isn't exactly a horse, Jawara," Charlie said. "Give me a hand."

Jawara extended a hand and helped her on top. Charlie helped the pair of lovers clamber aboard the smelly animal.

"Did you have to take the smelliest animal in your petting zoo?" she said.

"The obine's odor is second only to their hatred of Sentinels. Enjoy the ride," Jawara said.

The animal excreted a foul-smelling mist behind them as it lumbered along.

Jawara was bathed in sweat as he struggled to guide the creature by grabbing its horns and directing the animal's great head directly at the Sentinels. The Sentinels, knowing the creature's nasty reputation, scattered from the rampaging beast.

Jawara headed back to the Land of No. More Sentinels formed a line to stop the beast but they were overwhelmed by the large creature. Several tried to hold their ground and were stomped to death by the behemoth. Others surrounded the creature and the large beast lowered its head and gored one of the Sentinels with a massive horn.

The Sentinels attacked by slashing at the creature's tree-trunk legs and slowed the beast's advance. A Sentinel grabbed the screaming Peter off the beast, dangled the thrashing human in the air, and ripped his leg off. Another Sentinel grabbed Jan and yanked at the screaming woman as Charlie tried to grab her hand. The woman fell to the ground and stumbled, trying to get away. A pack of magnoses descended upon the nude woman, tearing at her limbs. From a distance all Charlie could hear were her screams as a red mist filled the air.

A lone remaining Sentinel clutched Charlie by the robe, trying to pull her off the trotting beast. She kicked at the monster and in return it roared at her while revealing its tusks. The roar alerted Jawara, who grabbed a broken Sentinel stanchion flag from a building and hit the monster across the head. Despite having part of its skull crushed, the Sentinel refused to release Charlie, so Jawara speared the creature with the jagged end. Wedged on the stanchion, Jawara flung the Sentinel to the ground.

Surrounded by the Sentinels, the obine started to rear up. Jawara yelled, "Hang on the best you can!"

The animal rose up on its massive hind legs, practically standing when it leaped forward and over the Sentinels. Upon its landing, the ground shook from the impact. The animal began a furious gallop as Jawara and Charlie barely hung on to its rope-like hair. As she clutched the hair, hundreds of small bugs crawled up from the skin of the obine onto her hands.

One of the attacking Sentinels managed to hang on to the beast and climbed up from the side to attack Jawara. Through the gloom Charlie saw the creature and screamed, startling the Sentinel. It smiled and watched as she tried to crawl away from it. It boldly approached the defenseless woman and raised its gnarled hand to strike her. But before it could move any more, the Sentinel's gnarled legs got caught up in the thick hair of the Obine. While it was struggling to free itself, Charlie kicked up at the Sentinel with surprising force, knocking it in front of the obine. The obine's front leg kicked the Sentinel squarely in the head, crushing the creature's skull.

Jawara turned to Charlie and, giving her a thumbs-up, he said, "Adios, motherfucker. Good to see you finally joining the fight," Jawara said.

"Did I have a choice?" she said disgustedly.

"Embrace the suck, Charlie. It's not going to get any easier for you or me."

Charlie smiled at the comment and she felt a little more confident knowing Steve was with them, if only in spirit. They rode and maneuvered the mammoth creature to a large open space, but there was no craft in sight.

"Now what?" Charlie asked. The obine bellowed below them.

"It's here somewhere. Give me a moment," Jawara said as they climbed off the obine. "Where are the other two humans?" he asked.

Charlie shook her head, but there was little time for remorse. She looked down to find that the obine was surrounded by a hundred Sentinels.

"Jawara, we don't have a moment; they're here," she said as she hopped off the smelly beast.

The obine, free of the riders, continued to attack the Sentinels. Dozens of the Sentinels swarmed and lunged at the agitated beast.

Charlie was alone as a Sentinel advanced towards her. Jawara was nowhere to be found. But before the Sentinel could close the distance, Jawara reappeared. He waved his arm and a large orb of different colors materialized before them. It drew Charlie inside.

She suddenly found herself in a room with no dimensions, just a general darkness and a sense of impending gloom. The air was fetid and she could smell the rancid odor of a rotting carcass nearby.

"Jawara, what is this awful place?" she plaintively asked.

"Sorry, I didn't have an opportunity to activate my own space within this craft," he apologized.

Seconds later the sphere resembled Jawara's open space.

"Where to?" she asked as she took off the disgusting pledge robe.

"Anywhere for the moment," he said as the orb left the Land of No. "The universe is not as large as one would think if you have tunnels. That's why we're taking the Marauder; it is a high-energy tunneler."

From the robe, a number of bugs from the obine came scurrying out. "Ugh, these creatures are beyond disgusting. You know, Jawara, you're picking up some crazy skills and now you're cursing? Really? 'Adios, motherfucker'? What is wrong with you? You used to be so nice and sweet."

"Nice guys finish dead," Jawara said.

"Got it, still got your game face on," Charlie replied.

"You should too, but it's more than just attitude. Steve's and my own embedded training is kicking in. Clearly someone besides the Mentor has planted me here; probably an Epicoid within the Council who is also concerned with the Sentinel influence. They seem to be willing to take bigger chances with assisting us. Let's hope it's enough to help us through this cluster fornication. This is a cluster fornication, right?"

"Let's call it for what it is: the very textbook definition of a clusterfuck," she replied.

The white rooms disappeared and they headed into the darkness of space. Their surroundings shook violently and Charlie felt high-energy strikes enveloping the sphere.

"They're firing at us!" she screamed.

"Those aren't weapons; it's an energy field to slow us down," Jawara explained.

Another explosion shook the pair, even stronger this time. She stared at Jawara as if to question him and he said, "Yes, that's a weapon."

"Shoot back, dammit!"

He reviewed a series of smaller orbises and commented, "It appears this is a training vessel; the weaponry is disabled on this ship."

"Just our fricking luck."

Jawara touched Charlie and felt a fringe growing about her body.

"What are you doing?" she asked.

"We're running out of time in this shitshow. We have to do this the hard way and do a jump. Hang on," Jawara said.

"You keep saying that like there is something to hang onto in this damn bubble."

Jawara gestured and suddenly the pair became two-dimensional, a film on the surface of the orb holding them.

"I can't move, Jawara," Charlie said.

The Cave You Fear

Jawara couldn't speak but his thoughts were with Charlie. "This is how we must make this journey. We will be suspended for the duration of this jump; talk to you in a few moments."

Charlie stopped; her existence stopped. It was like anesthesia: one moment, consciousness, and then nothing—no sense of time, just a strobe-light effect, white lights then colors swirling and switching to black. The orb moved from large to small in size, vanishing altogether. Across the multiverse she saw innumerable timelines as they moved through time and space.

Their craft stopped moving. The interior of the orb was replaced by a field of chimerical lights that surrounded them on all sides. Charlie peered down at the floor and realized there was no floor.

"Did we lose them?" she asked.

"No, they let us go."

"How come they didn't fire at us on the obine?"

"They want to take you alive for some reason," Jawara said.

"So what in the world is this twilight?" Charlie asked, struggling to understand the space she was in. The air was heavy and damp, with the peculiar odor of feces combined with the sweet smell of freshly spilled blood. It reeked of collective fear; it was a slaughter yard.

"Not your world, not anybody's world. The end of our universe—an event horizon, if you must, or what we call the Quanteme. There is no time or space here, but a hologram of the entire multiverse and a perfect re-entry point to send you back home to your original timeline."

Charlie took a step, and deep in her bowels she felt a low-resonance rumble that shook her entire body. She scanned her surroundings, not understanding what was causing the tremors. Frightened, she stopped moving.

A horrible roar sounded from the darkness. She went to her swimsuit top and withdrew the bill. She clenched the twenty-dollar bill for good luck, crumpling it in her hand out of fear.

"Jesus Christ, that odor and noise—what is that?" she asked.

She saw the look of fear on Jawara's face.

"The Sentinels must have prepared for this. Not good. I feared this nightmare the most," he said.

"What does that mean?" she asked.

"This thing is a Hydrus, placed here by the Sentinels. It's basically a massive eating machine. They are so sick to be cultivating this creature. "

"Run?" she asked.

"Where to?" he said in a panicked tone. "We're inside the belly of the beast!"

Charlie glanced down and watched a horrific hydra-like monster emerge, seemingly bubbling up from the emptiness, the tentacles grabbing the two of them. The meat-red flesh released a wretched rotting odor that was far stronger than any low tide she had ever experienced. She went to move but saw several massive protuberances that towered over them. Each contained massive jaws with long teeth for eating, grasping, and cutting to shear flesh. A large tentacle grabbed Jawara, hurling him into the air. A tentacle with teeth grabbed him by the waist, accompanied with a spray of blood from his wounds.

Charlie recoiled in horror when a tentacle grabbed her. She began screaming and struggling to no avail. The ooze came from below, the slime stinging her skin, an acid slowly dissolving her swimsuit and flesh. Other, more delicate tentacles began stripping her of her tattered clothes, ripping her bikini top and bottom from her body.

"Jawara, help. What is this freak doing to me? My skin is burning!" she yelled.

"Preparing their meal. The Hydrus are rampant killers but they are also known for being notoriously fussy eaters," Jawara said. "Trust me, the Epicoids are a treat for them. I will be first."

"That just means I'm the entrée. What do we do?" she screamed. "I thought they wanted me alive?"

"I guess failing taking us alive, they have this hideous thing as their failsafe," he yelled.

"Don't you have any weapons on you?" she shrieked.

"All disabled before entering this horror."

The Hydrus turned its attention to a more savory delight: Jawara. It struggled with him, pulling his uniform away with the tentacles. Naked, his arms and legs were pinned against his body by the tentacles.

He lunged from the creature and, while leaning forward, grabbed her hand. Looking into her eyes he said, "It's not over!"

The creature recaptured him but not before Jawara's touch helped the panicky Charlie calm down. Totally naked, she was trapped in the tentacles and struggled to break free. She looked down as she tried to free her arms. She noticed Andrew Jackson's head glowing on the twenty-dollar bill she clenched so tightly.

The voracious heads moved towards her and one of them, with its jaws gaping wide, moved in for the kill. Charlie was no longer screaming but watched as the creature seemingly morphed into the form of a massive dragon.

"Throw this bill into the mouth of the dragon and this will buy you much-needed time."

She made one last desperate push with her arm and managed to free herself from the slimy tentacle for the briefest of moments.

Out of futility, she threw the twenty-dollar bill into the creature's huge, gaping mouth and yelled, "Eat shit, asshole!"

The creature swallowed the bill, stopping for a moment as if to savor its tiny treat. It twitched and the twitches became spasms. From the mouth of the dragon a deep, dark bile-like fluid began to ooze. The slow ooze soon became a torrent of vomit. The creature stopped moving and started to glow while it retched up the remains of meals previously ingested. Charlie cringed at the explosion of black bile that contained the bones and skulls of its prior victims.

A low rumble began and the Hydrus's glowing body started to swell in size. Its grip slackened on both Charlie and Jawara, the body growing larger until it ballooned to the breaking point. The two cowered and Jawara tried to shield Charlie from the exploding creature. With a tremendous roar the creature ruptured, sending pieces of flesh and tentacles of slime into the dark space, freeing Jawara and Charlie.

Jawara looked at Charlie, who was covered in the mucousy flesh. She removed pieces of the slime from her naked body, yelling, "Truly disgusting! I thought you said the Epicoids were a treat?"

"We are, but this one must have wanted to try something new on the menu. Why did you throw the money into its mouth?"

"Desperation. I had nothing else, and I noticed the creature's head resembled a dragon. I remembered the old Chinese man's words. Why in the world did that work?"

"I'm surmising that the bill actually contained a small space-time portal that, once ingested, poured poison into the creature's body. It would appear that some of the Chinese tourists are working on our side. You know what this means?"

"Was it our chess master friend? All I know is that I need a towel."

"Perhaps, but it also means we're not alone in this struggle, Charlie. We have allies in this fight!" Jawara said excitedly.

Naked and shaken, Charlie went in search of her swimsuit, her hands moving among the smelly organic slime littering the space. As she turned over a pile of mucousy glop a partially digested head rose to the surface. As her eyes adjusted to the dark, she saw it was the skull of a decapitated woman with sunken eyes and thick patches of long red hair still clinging to the bone. Charlie began hyperventilating, not able to say a word. Catching her breath, she screamed and jumped back from the remains of the earlier meal. She awkwardly fell back into the slime and landed on her butt.

"What?" Jawara said.

"Over there … a human skull with red hair!" she cried.

"Prior victims, no doubt."

"This is so fricking nasty. Why red hair? More Red Avatars?"

"More unchosen heroes, but there's no time for clothes. Quick, go to the lights," Jawara said.

"No clothes?" she said, but then Charlie saw that Jawara's arm appeared to be broken. "You're hurt; let me help you," she said.

"No, you must go now. Look," he said as he pointed to her hand. Charlie stared at her hand, seeing a strange glow emanating from her fingertips. She was about to be returned to her timeline.

"Go now; there's no time," he said.

"What happens if they catch you? Will they kill you?" she asked.

"Worse, they will shun me," Jawara said.

"Isolate you, but you'll still be alive, right?"

"Unless I can join with those of my kind, I will be dead within a year without Unioeros. I will suffer a slow, tortuous death. Hopefully I got the timing right for your arrival on Earth," Jawara said as he studied his orb. Minutes passed.

"For fuck's sake!" he yelled.

"What now?"

"They've blocked humans from using this technology so I can't deviate from your original timeline. I can't simply send you back in time to the right moment to avoid the murder-suicide."

"Are you saying all of this is vain?" Charlie asked.

Jawara was still scanning some unseen instrumentation and replied, "There's another way. I was seeded with an alternative technology, but it's very risky. We have no choice. Do nothing, and you will die in that apartment with Bradley."

"Just do it, Jawara."

With a wave of his hand Jawara released a large red orbis twenty feet tall and said, "The sphere will make you one with the Quanteme, the persistence of the quantum mind within the cosmos for all living creatures. Survive, and you will fulfill your destiny as the Red Avatar," he said while pushing her forward into the red sphere.

"Survive?"

Charlie started to disappear within the sphere. As she moved forward, the sphere separated into a series of round lights that danced gently before her. They grew and twisted in many different ways, entwining with one another. They felt organic, pulsating with their own existence. A single blue glow stood out among all the lights.

"Is it alive?" she asked.

"Yes, it is all sentient life contained within the multiverse with every thread imaginable being in play. There are ten dimensions, but you must simply focus on following the blue glow."

"It's not that easy, is it?" Charlie said with a sudden sense of dread.

"I cannot lie to you. The journey you are undertaking is called the cave. Few have made this journey and even fewer have returned from it sane. This is a transformative journey for you, yours alone to make—much like life, but many times more intense. It is the exquisite horror and beauty of all possible realities of the universe compacted into a single existence. You will experience everything."

"Jesus Christ, why me?" Charlie asked.

"Destiny, bad luck, karma? Does it matter? For whatever reasons, you were chosen as the Red Avatar. I will be there to guide you. Remember, we are connected until our dying days."

"Please come with me?" she asked. "I'm completely alone now."

"I cannot. I must escape this event horizon and convince the Council about the Sentinel threat. I am afraid of what they will do to your people. You have to rally your own people against this menace. Go now, or else this is all in vain," Jawara said.

"Will I see you again?"

Jawara just looked at her.

"Just lie to me, you big idiot!"

"No lie necessary. I will never leave you; you are not alone. I promise."

She disappeared into the chimerical lights while crying. Propelled into the glaring glow of a thousand suns, Charlie experienced the Quanteme and the multiple timelines of the multiverse. She felt people and the Epicoids, not as three-dimensional creatures but as long four-dimensional beings moving through space in their timelines among the universe and their individual worlds. They appeared as strange caterpillar-like creatures ingesting nutrition and growing from the soil and sun, living their lives, getting older, dying, and returning to the very same soil they had risen from.

She heard Jawara guiding her. *Stay with the blue glowing energy, Charlie. That is the true thread back to your former life on Earth.*

No longer bound by her earthly body and the confines of four dimensions, Charlie could sense the other dimensions, including the paradoxical quantum world of the fifth dimension with its simultaneous multiple states and myriad choices. Beyond, the sixth dimension bubbled about her with the promise and pain of the full multiverse with all of its threads. Among the many worlds there was always the blue glowing energy leading and guiding her to the new timeline Jawara had preordained for her.

She closed her eyes but she still felt each of the lives, the twists and turns, the horrors, the loves of the myriad threads.

Stay with the blue energy; that is your thread in this timeline. The others are alternative threads that you cannot take now.

She heard a baby's cry and turned to see Bradley for the very first time, her heart soaring with love. Such a handsome, charming young man. Moments later, Bradley yelled, fought, screamed at her, little more than a brutal thug. The baby cried again. She wanted to reach out to the baby; she felt this was her baby.

No, Charlie, there's only one thread.

Brokenhearted, she moved ahead. She felt the screaming of millions and darkness among many of the threads. Somehow she could sense millions dying based on her choices and decisions as she moved forward. It was not just her baby dying in the threads, but millions of other sentient creatures.

Keep moving, Charlie; you can only save them if you follow the blue energy.

Over the ages an endless procession of red avatars with their Epicoid companions fought and died by the hundreds at the hands of the Sentinels. A sea of blood being shed in a hopeless struggle against a vastly superior enemy.

Charlie's eyes opened for the first time since taking her journey through the cave. She left the cave and moved toward a beam of sunlight. She was now alone. There was no Jawara to guide her or console her, just the awful emptiness of her lonely existence in a vast, cold, indifferent universe.

As she moved into the light she found herself walking on the surface of a cold and desolate moon.

Where am I?

In the distance she saw a blue shimmering sea lit by a distant sun.

Water?

She trudged forward towards a sea of blue crystalline objects that sprouted from the barren lunar dust. Upon closer inspection she witnessed a macabre landscape of twisted and frozen human appendages rising above the surface of the moon by the millions. All were a frozen blue crystalline color and their faces appeared to be grimacing and tortured.

For miles around all she could see were the twisted, dead, crystalline bodies of humans piled at least ten deep. Young and old alike were naked, their clothes removed during the transport process as a final insult by the Sentinels, as if to say the humans were stupid animals undressed for the slaughter.

Carefully Charlie walked among the frozen dead, hearing ice cracking with each timid step. Strange; there was no air. How could she hear? Separated from the rest of the tangled corpses she observed a mother futilely sheltering her child from the cold. There was a tortured, anguished look on the young mother's face as she stared at her dead baby. The baby in her arms appeared as if it was still sleeping.

As she drew closer and tried to touch the lifeless baby, she came to the horrible realization that the frozen Madonna resembled her. It was her and her baby! She panicked, slipping and falling into the crystalline figures, causing the mother and child to shatter into thousands of frozen pieces. Charlie collapsed in tears with the understanding that every human was put to death by the Sentinels, including her and her child. She experienced the extinction event of her species.

"This makes no sense. I'm fighting for my life, nothing more," she said.

No, she was fighting for so much more—she knew it. It was a horrific feeling, overwhelming her being. There was the tedium of existence, the constant dullness of waiting for someone or something to break the stillness.

When the tedium was broken she was overwhelmed by emotion. So many lovers, so much violence, so many babies, so much illness and death. Always death, stalking her and her loved one at every turn. The pain, sorrow, and pleasure of a million lives tore at her soul. No sentient creature should experience all of that at the same time, the ultimate cycle of aimless existence and misery.

Jawara rejoined her on the journey and was there to reassure her, console her tortured soul, and keep her on her singular mission toward the blue energy. By the end of her journey, all that remained of Charlie was a gentle broken sob that seemed to hang in the miasma before the Chinvat Bridge.

Murder-Suicide

Charlie opened her eyes and looked about her Atlanta apartment. She could smell the repulsive odor of a Bradford pear tree blooming nearby through the open window. Directly ahead, Bradley stood defiantly in her way.

"Okay, you made your point, woman, now sit down," Bradley said.

"I will not. Out of my way Bradley, I'm done. I'm not enabling you anymore."

How many times had he heard her tired routine? "Where do think you're going?"

"Does it matter? I've asked you for years to get some help. Instead, you refused, and now we have nothing. I can have nothing on my own," she said as she grabbed her pocketbook.

"Come on, babe, don't be like that," he said as he tried to hold her.

She pushed away from him and said, "Don't touch me."

"We have each other," he said.

"You mean we had each other. You killed the 'we' in our relationship a long time ago," she said.

Bradley grabbed Charlie by her shoulders. She turned her head away and he said, "Look at me. I promise I'll make it up to you."

"You're always promising to make it up to me."

"This time will be different, I promise," he said as he peered deep into her eyes.

Determined, Charlie pulled away and kept walking towards the door. Bradley ran over to her, smiling as he waved in the air an old .45 pistol he used to protect himself from John and his debt collectors. *Damn,* she thought; he must have retrieved it when she gathered her belongings.

"Like I said, you're going nowhere," he said.

"Bradley, it's Charlie. You won't use that gun. Please let me go. Please realize it's over, that we're done," she asked, her eyes filling with tears.

"You can't leave. You're all I have left," he said.

"You lost me a long time ago," she said. She kept walking to the door.

"Charlie? You know how this ends if you take another step."

"I don't care; better a fast bullet than this lingering death," she said as she walked faster, terrorized at what he might do.

He coldly stared at her and said, "Really, you're going to bluff me when you've got no cards to play? Don't be stupid. You have no money, no real job. You're not leaving me, you're staying with me forever," he said.

She turned to face him, tears streaming down her cheeks, and said, "Please don't. You're not that cruel, Bradley. Let me go."

"Nah, I can't. You're wrong; you still mean everything to me. You're mine—forever," he said as he stared her in the eye.

"Please...."

"I'm calling your bluff," he said as he took aim.

POP! POP!

Shot twice in the chest with one bullet directly to the heart, Charlie fell backwards and collapsed to the floor dead with her eyes open. Her body sprawled behind the couch near the front door. Bradley didn't react; he just watched as the blood poured from the wounds on her body.

"Stupid bitch, why did you test me like that?" he yelled.

The blood covered the floor in a small pool that advanced slowly across the red oak. As his anger dissipated, he dropped the gun.

"God, no, why did you make me do this?" he said as he walked over to her. He prodded her body with his foot; there was no movement. He collapsed to the floor and held her lifeless body. The blood flowed and Bradley was soon bathed in it.

"No, no, what did I do, what did I do?" he said as he studied his bloody hands.

He stood up, his foot slipping on Charlie's blood, and retrieved the gun. He walked back to the bedroom. In his despair Bradley put the gun to his head and closed his eyes. Panicky, sweat poured off his head. He blanked out for a moment and then he opened his eyes hoping to emerge from a nightmare. The domestic horror was still sprawled out before him on the floor.

With his finger on the trigger, a small blue translucent orbis became visible, appearing from the air near the front door. The sphere danced and floated in the air before making its way to Charlie's body. He watched as the tiny sphere lowered to the floor and disappeared near her body.

Bradley slowly squeezed the trigger and held it at the release point as if to mull his fate, a perfect quantum state between existence ψ non-existence. He turned towards the front door and from behind the couch an apparition rose. A totally naked and bald Charlotte stood before him, alive and seemingly unharmed.

"Charlotte?" he asked, in shock at seeing her alive.

Charlie returned his confused stare with a calm, serene expression. She watched as an orange orbis glowed within Bradley's chest. When the glow subsided he stared back, angry and confused, with his finger still on the gun's trigger. With full knowledge of what Bradley had just done to her, she looked him in the eyes and waved goodbye. She said the two most appropriate farewell words she could fathom for such an abusive love:

"Adios, motherfucker!"

Stunned by her words, Bradley gave her a bemused smile. His bloody finger slipped ever so slightly on the trigger, squeezing just beyond the trigger break.

POP!

A shot rang out and a red spray erupted across the room, decorating the wall in a gory crimson flower. She heard the splatter of his blood on the wall. A second later he fell to the ground before her with an audible thud.

Frozen, Charlie stared at Bradley's lifeless body and the pool of blood that pumped and flowed from the gaping wound to his head. She felt a touch of moisture on her cheek and with her finger wiped away a small droplet of his blood.

She slowly walked over to him and nudged his fallen body with her bare foot, taking care not to step in the blood. There was no response. Yes, this time was very different.

She knew enough not to touch anything else, let the authorities draw their own conclusions about Bradley's suicide.

Charlie held her head in her hands, rubbing her eyes, realizing she had been returned at the precise time to save her own life but not Bradley's. More importantly, she had her memories of the cruise, including Steve and her companion Jawara. She realized that Jawara had disobeyed the directives of his kind by allowing her to return to this moment to fulfill a very different destiny. She mused about his sacrifice. She could still feel him, but where was he?

Charlie peered into the kitchen, noticing that the calendar displayed April 2015. She sat down on the couch and pondered her new future, one without Bradley and Jawara. She could hear the neighbors talking loudly next door, no doubt reacting to the multiple gunshots. She knew she had to call 911 and that, upon doing so, they would be at the apartment in minutes. Clothes would be a good idea, but while passing a mirror, she realized that she also had to explain her shaved head. Her blond wig would forestall many of those questions. And then there was the question of her blue-tinted skin. More clothes and makeup would conceal her condition from the authorities as well, but she had no time to spare. The next few hours would be hellish, but at least she was packed and ready to go.

She faced the crimson-colored wall, noticing the bits of gore slowly sliding towards the floor. Gravity held an entire galaxy together, and gravity was doing its damnedest to return bits of Bradley to the earth that he had risen from.

She wondered what to say about Bradley. That he was totally despondent and desperate about his continuous gambling losses and her threats to leave him? That was as close to the truth as she dared share with the authorities.

She huddled on the couch as she glanced down to the floor, shuddering at the sight. She didn't know what was worse: the thought of cleaning the bloodstain from the carpet or having to feign tears for that fallen bastard. She decided to forgo the cleaning altogether and just take the hit on her security deposit. She wasn't staying anyway. That apartment was no longer a home to her anymore; perhaps it never was. As for her tears, she was determined to save them for those she actually deemed worthy of them.

From a Butterfly to a Hurricane

A cool, late spring day in Atlanta was a rare treat before the arrival of the summer's heat. Charlie walked to the park and sat down on a bench, watching the obliviousness and separateness of the human parade before her. Charlie's red hair had started to grow back and her short pixyish cut was at least superficially making her appear as if she belonged with the other humans inhabiting the park.

Strangely, she'd never felt more disconnected from other people. The calendar was nearing the end of May 2015 and she was driving alone to Miami tomorrow to begin the next chapter in her life. She was making good use of her time, even planning to take scuba lessons in preparation for late 2016. In the interim, she would take a side trip to Vegas to make a substantial bet, or should she say investment? Needing some serious money, she was hoping to place a wager on what she knew to be a sure thing. Ironically, it would be with one of Bradley's old bookie acquaintances, one who was familiar with taking long-odds bets on non-sporting events.

It was a curious world that she had returned to with a normalcy that belied the urgency of her mission. No Epicoids, no Sentinels, no news stories about strange encounters in New York City. Nothing, a complete whitewash. Somehow her misadventures had gone unnoticed or were concealed from the rest of humanity.

She mused about her future, wondering what was next, wondering what happened to Jawara. She had seen the galaxy and met a new people, seemingly the only human alive who'd been privileged with such an experience, but she felt so very alone on her own planet. She missed Jawara and Steve, the two beings who could understand the quest she'd been chosen to undertake.

She felt someone's prying eyes upon her. From across the park a handsome young man with dark hair intently watched her. He would actually be a good addition to her growing coterie of followers; perhaps later, she thought. With the hungry leer he was giving her she knew he wasn't leaving her anytime soon. There was still ample time for a simple touch and then a quick encounter to seal the deal with that rutting young man. She just had to remember not to be so aggressive during this rendezvous; it was so much better for his frail male ego to let him think he was the hunter and not the prey.

Almost instinctively her finger touched the small scar on her cheek, a reminder that she was no longer the brittle, frivolous, subservient girl who worried incessantly about her father or her failing marriage. No, that horrific journey through the cave had put an end to such childish sentiments for her in this lifetime. To say she wasn't the same person didn't begin to describe her rebirth. Hell, even a fool could see that the old Charlie had died that dreary rainy day in her Atlanta apartment. She hated the stranger she was becoming and blamed this commanding creature for the loss of her former innocence.

Several soap bubbles floated by her in the light breeze. Unlike the spheres that floated so effortlessly in the breeze, the enormity of her challenges weighed heavily on her fragile being. Watching her, nobody would have thought this small, insignificant woman had been chosen to protect a world; moreover, that she would do so no matter the personal cost to herself or to those that she held most dear. Only a madwoman would willingly shoulder the burden alone and, upon reflection, perhaps she was insane.

Charlie turned away from the young man's gaze and a shimmering reddish sphere suddenly floated before her, gently dancing and drifting in air. Seconds later three other bluish spheres no more than a couple of inches across floated by and joined their companion in front of her. As she watched, the four spheres aligned in the air, changing color, and then they began a strange minuet before her. She felt a lightness with their presence; almost a connection with another. Yes, Jawara was still with her, breaking her intolerable solitude. On their surface the reversed reflection of a spire from Saint Mark's was clearly visible, and on the surface of another sphere, she saw her own face. She broke into a beatific smile at their small dance and implicit promise.

She put her finger to one, gently nudging and toying with the bubble in the still air. A small boy who was furiously creating the bubbles with a bubble wand stopped to watch her toy with his dancing bubbles. She playfully stuck her tongue out at the boy while her right hand waved through the air, simultaneously evaporating the four shimmering bubbles. The boy responded in kind to her with his tongue and then returned to his play, choosing to ignore the antics of the curious redheaded woman. Charlie turned away from the boy, not wanting to share with him her lonely tears.

There will be a sequel to Charlie's journey featuring the founding of her church. We also invite you to visit CuriousEve.com and the Sentientist Church at www.SentientistChurch.com